THE
TRAVELING
CHARBONNEAUS

Bernie Schallehn

Highbridge Press

The Traveling Charbonneaus

Published by
Highbridge Press
www.highbridgepress.com

ISBN: 0-9708220–9-X

Library of Congress Card Number: 2002106796

Cover design by Karen Sealy
Printed in the U.S.A.

ACKNOWLEDGMENTS

Special thanks to: Michael J. Rutigliano, my manager, who knew the story was a winner right out of the gate; my cousin Jack, for his expert legal advice, all performed pro bono; Dr. John Thomas, for lunch and treatment regimens; Crystal Wood, my Texas amiga, for writing a most inspirational rejection letter; the Sealy sisters, for their belief in me and the Charbonneaus, and, as always, my ladies of the Ridge, Alta, Nikki, and Karla, for their support, tolerance, and unconditional love.

DEDICATION

For Irene P. Schallehn
&
Gene D. Schallehn
(You're always with me, old pal)

CHAPTER 1

Wendell Charbonneau took another cinch in the quarter inch rope that ran alongside his scrotum and up into the crack of his ass, flush against the cluster of hemorrhoids that hung like ripe concords on the vine. Tying it off at his right hip, he hauled up his size 40-42 jockey shorts and eased himself down into the cool summer waters of the Vly creek, a stream that ran behind his house.

It was an old French-Canadian remedy, the hemp and the water promising to soothe and shrink the inflamed tissues, a treatment brought down to the States when his ancestors moved from the Province of Quebec to the border town of Chazy, N.Y. in the late 1800s.

As painful as his piles could become, he looked forward to his sitting time in the Vly. It gave him a chance to reflect, on things both large and small, on events and happenings over the course of his fifty nine years, while the hemp and the water did their work. Sitting time, what the doctors, lawyers, and accountants who lived in Chesterfield Village, the brown and grey townhouses erected a few years ago just outside of Chazy, might call meditation.

His first meditation found him thinking about his only son, Robert, a good boy, a skinny kid of seventeen who would always have the mind of a child. To Wendell, who was especially proud that his son had inherited his curly hair and cleft chin, his youngest had seemed normal enough at birth – wiggling like a worm, wailing like a banshee, but then soon satisfied, suckling at his Momma's breast like a hungry little piglet. Nothing had given Wendell or his wife June the slightest indication that Robert would be in anyway limited, his mental capabilities not equal to, or sharper than his older sisters, Patrice and Chantelle.

But the boy's kindergarten teacher had called June Charbonneau soon after the beginning of school to say that she had some concerns about Robert. Later, after the school psychologist had run her tests, she called a conference where she sat Wen and June down and announced that Robert was what they called "educable mentally retarded."

The kids on the bus preferred to shorten it, simply calling him "retard."

Older sister Patrice, who rode the same bus as Robert, bore the pain of seeing her brother being made fun of, even fighting a few of his battles, more than once having her nose bloodied or her mouth punched, resulting in a lower lip that would swell to the size of a nightcrawler.

With each morning a frustrating exercise in attempting to ready an unwilling child for school, his parents decided that at the tender age of 12 Robert would stay home for good. After a number of phone calls from the school, with June offering various excuses for his absence, and failed attempts at home tutoring due to the student slipping down to hide among the trees that lined the Vly creek whenever teacher would arrive, the greater school district of Chazy stopped trying.

Wendell shifted a bit in the stream. Differences...his mind fixated on the concept. Differences among his children.

Patrice, his middle child, had always slept through the night, ate what was fed to her, and was able to occupy herself in the playpen when he had needed some time with June between cool linen sheets on a hot summer Sunday afternoon.

And it was Chantelle, his oldest, who had always been the spoiler, never sleeping through the night, notorious for flinging her plastic bowl of strained whatever against the kitchen wallpaper if it was not to her liking. And once, having been sent outside to play, defiantly crawling through a downstairs window at the point when Wendell was hitting a muffled high C at the conclusion of a Sunday afternoon interlude with June.

"Daddy all right?" she had asked, bursting into the room.

"Just practicing a bit of a new song," her mother had replied, her face as red and dewy as the tomatoes she grew in her garden.

"Not ready for the bandstand, yet," Chantelle had cracked, parroting a phrase her father would often use at rehearsals.

A smartass. A real pain in the butt, he thought. But Wendell never dreamed, never imagined, she would grow into a young woman who would bareface betray him, nonchalantly touching a match to his Technicolor dreams of The Charbonneau Family Band making it big.

As his eyes came to rest on the stream, the water looking like cut glass as the sun danced and played on the surface, his mind began to play the complete version of his tragic Nashville drama of 1995.

It started with the purchase and conversion of an old bus once used by the Clinton Correctional Facility in nearby Dannemora to transport prisoners. Wendell had bought it at auction, having told June that he wanted to convert it into a recreational vehicle for the purposes of camping trips.

Convert it he did, building bunks and installing a small kitchenette, shower, and toilet. All the conveniences of home, in miniature, but never really intended for the purposes of transporting the family to any forest, lake or ocean camp site.

No, the bus, once ready, would be Nashville bound.

He broached the issue with June one November's eve over coffee at his kitchen table.

"We don't know anybody in Nashville," she had said. "We just gonna pull up to the curb and play for quarters on the street?"

"Got a plan, got a club, got it all worked out, Junie-bug," Wendell had countered, a bit of a pout to his lower lip, confidence inspired by a second cup of coffee.

He had explained to her how he had found the name of *The Crystal Palace*, a night club in Nashville that featured an open mic night to newcomers, in one of his country music magazines. Purportedly, the club was frequented by agents and record company scouts seeking new talent.

"And that's us, June...new talent," Wendell had said, looking her straight in the eye.

June had agreed, right there, that night, but with two conditions to be met before they left.

First, that Chantelle have her chipped front tooth fixed, the dental damage having been done some years prior during horseplay with her sister.

Secondly, that Wendell spring for the family to have matching country-western outfits.

Both conditions were being put down, June had explained, so that the family wouldn't look like "a bunch of ragamuffins draggin' into the big city."

"Agreed," Wendell had announced, closing the deal with a broad smile.

Six weeks later, with new outfits packed and a new porcelain cap installed, the Charbonneaus were headed for Tennessee.

Before leaving, Patrice and Chantelle had wanted to paint flowers on the sides of the bus, maybe a rainbow or two, but their father would have none of it, insisting that when they roll into Music City they needed to look "all bi'ness."

The homemade RV remained a prison gray, save for two strips of black where Wendell had allowed Robert to spray paint over the original owner's name.

As this was the bus's (or "tour bus" as Wendell liked to call it) maiden voyage, Wendell knew that there would be a few bugs and kinks that would evidence themselves, some to be resolved, most to become accustomed to, as the journey progressed. The bunks proved to be hard, the mattresses lumpy as Wendell had purchased five used ones from the Comfort Inn in Plattsburgh when maintenance was in the process of replacing worn bedding. The water pressure in the shower was weak, and the stove pilot light kept going out, sparking June's fears that they would all be killed in a exploding fireball that once served as their motor home.

But the toilet, as was to be expected, worked like a charm.

Wendell knew waste, being the sole proprietor of "Countryman Septic Service", his day job and the primary source of income for the Charbonneau clan.

They found a motor home park on the outskirts of Nashville, a place where the store-bought RVs all docked for varying lengths of stay. Chantelle had been the only one to verbalize any reservations, complaining that their bus looked cheesy parked next to a large beige and brown Winnebago. She was sure their next door neighbors had comfortable beds, a shower that didn't let go of its water in dribbles, and a stove that allowed the matriarch of the family to sleep peacefully at night.

"Our bus got us here, safe and sound, and we got a place to stay, a whole lot cheaper than what we'd have to pay if I put us all up in a motel. What matters when we're down here is that we get seen by the right people and get discovered," her father had told her.

"That's right," June had said, echoing her husband's sentiments, but adding, "Dear, when you get a chance can you look at that stove again?"

For their Nashville debut the girls wore white blouses and skirts, red vests with white fringe, and white cowboy boots with imitation silver medallions sunk into the sides. The boys wore white pants, white shirts with a red bolo tie at the neck, red vests with fringe and black cowboy boots. All members topped off their ensembles with a white ten gallon hat.

Wendell had called them a stretch limo to take them to *The Crystal Palace*. While awaiting its arrival, Patrice caught Chantelle rolling the waistband of her skirt so as to shorten the hemline.

"I got nice legs, why not show 'em," Chantelle had defended.

Patrice had only nodded her agreement and left her skirt at the length selected by her mother.

None of the Charbonneaus had ever ridden in a stretch before, and suffice to say they were awestruck with the luxuriousness of the interior, everything looking so new, nothing cobbled, everything about it saying it came right from the factory, direct. The limo had always been a limo, never having served in another capacity in a previous life.

For the Charbonneaus, the change of a prisoner transport bus to a motor home was more or less a variation on a theme. Their present home had for many years served as a barn...their barn.

Never used to shelter animals, it had been a storage barn, housing tools, tillers, mowers, blowers and various pieces of septic service equipment.

That all changed when Wendell tangled with the IRS.

For the better part of fifteen years, Wendell had played fast and loose with his taxes. When judgment day came, the government was willing to take his house in lieu of the back monies owed. They agreed to leave him the barn and a small shed which Patrice later converted into a workshop.

The family spent the better part of a summer and into the fall converting the barn into a home. By winter they had transformed the structure into quarters that were livable.

During the construction, Wendell kept the family spirits up by erecting a high stockade fence between the barn and the house they'd once owned, purchasing home remodeling magazines that featured at least one article and picture lay-out of a barn restoration, and constructing a huge fieldstone fireplace that would warm body and soul during the brutal winter months to be endured in northern New York.

Just before the limo, which had always been a limo, pulled up in front of *The Crystal Palace*, Chantelle grabbed a red bandanna from her purse, folded it several times lengthwise and began to tie it around her left boot.

"What's that for?" her mother had asked.

"Just adding a little color, a little personalized color," Chantelle had replied, cinching the knot.

"Take it off...you got plenty of color," ordered her father. "The point of matching outfits is to match. Besides, that makes you look trashy."

Chantelle had glared at him, but obeyed, slowly untying the red cloth and stuffing it back into her purse.

Maybe it was there, right there, thought Wendell, as the water washed over his floating hands and a silvery minnow nibbled at his toe. Maybe it was there that Chantelle was showing her difference and getting ready to defect from her family.

Wendell and Robert had hoisted the guitars from the limo's trunk along with a tambourine, an electronic guitar tuner, and a small red cloth bag that held extra guitar strings and an old silver pitch pipe, just in case the batteries in the electronic tuner decided to crap out. The two Charbonneau men shouldered the guitars, two acoustic and one electric, while Chantelle and June carried the smaller items.

Only Patrice carried her own instrument – a cherry red Fender electric bass.

The self-appointed electronics technician of the band, Patrice tried to keep anything that required an electric outlet to function in good working repair. It was sometimes a losing battle, as amplifiers lugged from roadhouse to roadhouse were always prone to a careless drop onto a stage when setting up or a rough shove into the back of her father's station wagon when fatigue of body and mind had set in at the end of a long night.

For tonight's engagement, the Charbonneau Family Band had been told in advance that they would use the house microphones and amplifiers, so no need to bring their own.

The family, all smiles and nervous giggles, shuffled up to the stage door where a bearded, pony-tailed staffer stood with clipboard and wireless head-set microphone. As the young man checked them in, Patrice drew a bead on the high tech head-set and was just opening her mouth to ask him a question when her mother pulled her through the door.

At the same time, Chantelle was pulling off her ten gallon cowboy hat.

"Keep it on," her father had commanded through clenched teeth.

"No, it gives me hat-head and hides my face," she'd argued.

Difference number two, thought Wendell as he plucked a smooth pink and black pebble from the bottom of the river and rolled it between his thumb and forefinger. Difference number two. Everyone else in the band had been willing to wear the hat, but not her.

Backstage the Charbonneau family band had to suffer through seven acts before it would be their turn to take to the stage. The first three were not-even-close Elvis imitators, the next three were solo singers, two strumming guitars, one playing a zither, and the last performer was a short, smiley little man with a harmonica the size of a gherkin who played several polkas double time before taking his last bow.

As the harmonica man was basking in the last few claps of his applause, it was then that Robert made evident his anticipatory anxiety.

"Dad, I gotta pee."

"No time for that now son, hold it."

The curtain was then drawn closed and another head-setted staff member ushered them onto a dimly lit stage.

Chantelle, the group's lead singer, still hatless, took center stage. Behind her in a horizontal line stood Patrice on bass, Wendell and June, side by side, electric and acoustic guitars, respectively, slung over their shoulders, and on the end was Robert, holding his tambourine in one hand, clutching his penis with the other.

Just by luck, Wendell looked over to see his son holding himself with all his might.

"Robert, get your–"

The curtain was suddenly pulled back, revealing the Charbonneaus to the patrons of *The Crystal Palace.*

An emcee bounded up to Chantelle's microphone and read from a clipboard.

"Ladies and Gents let's have a warm welcome for the Charbonneaus from Chazy, New York!"

They kicked their three song set off with a bareknuckled *Two More Bottles of Wine*, Chantelle singing lead, followed with a sultry version of *Angel From Montgomery* and ended, Wendell taking over lead vocal duties from Chantelle, with a standard rendition of *Six Days On The Road.*

A murderous sidelong glance from Wendell to Robert during the chorus of their first song had convinced the boy to release the grip on himself.

Their reception had been favorable, the family band receiving a healthy round of applause, mostly after the first two songs.

Later, at a table, while his family enjoyed soft drinks, popcorn and the occasional compliment from a passing patron, Wendell had sat with his hand wrapped around a mug of lukewarm beer.

"That peckerhead," he'd grumbled.

"Who?" June had asked.

"The emcee, stupid southern cracker son of a bitch. All those jokes about us being Northerners. Dumb bastard couldn't even say our names or our town right," complained Wendell, remembering that the announcer had given both Charbonneau and Chazy the "Chuh" sound.

Patrice, in an effort to distract her father from his disgruntlement, floated a request.

"Daddy, while we're down here can we visit Graceland?"

Chantelle had just lighted a cigarette and after a long, slow exhalation had asked her sister, "Now why would you want to see the home of some dead dope addict?" Chantelle had then turned and was caught unaware by the middle-aged stranger who was standing next to their table.

Wendell picked a sharp stone out of the stream bed that was digging into his thigh and splashed water on a dragonfly that persisted in buzzing near him. If only Conroy had been put off, he thought, insulted by Chantelle's remarks about that beloved son of the South, maybe he would have just walked away.

But Jack Conroy, senior agent with Music City Management had simply smiled, looked into Chantelle's eyes and said, "Oh he had his demons, darlin', but when he was on stage...he *was* The King."

More than the gold rings, the tan, the perfect hair, and the buttons on his suit coat cuff that actually went through the tailored holes could tell, Wendell just knew that this man had a place, a presence, a position in the world of country music.

Conroy was a gatekeeper to the big time.

Wendell had felt the electricity course through his body as he heard Conroy compliment their sound and propose that they meet in his office the following day to discuss possibilities.

And at the time he hadn't thought it strange that Conroy requested that he meet only with Chantelle and himself. Made sense, the lead singer and the leader of the band. Conroy had phrased it as "for convenience sake." Negotiations would go smoother, easier if the number of attendees was reduced, figured Wendell. Besides, he could put his full attention into the perusal of a contract, if one was to be offered, rather than worrying about any antics that might be forthcoming from Robert.

That night in Nashville Wendell had fallen asleep rubbing the gold embossed business card that Conroy had given him.

"To Jack, with thanks and admiration, Buck Owens" read the inscription on the framed 8X10 black and white glossy, one of many, that hung in Conroy's office.

Wendell and Chantelle had been led into Conroy's office by his secretary with an explanation that Mr. Conroy was running a few minutes late, but would soon join them.

Wendell had been staring into the picture for about a minute when Conroy entered his office.

"You a fan of Buck's?" Conroy had asked.

"Probably his biggest. You handle him?"

"Let's just say Ol' Buck's the war-horse in my stable of stars," Conroy had boasted, and asked the father and daughter to take a seat. They obliged, easing down into two wingbacks that faced Conroy's massive desk. Conroy took his place behind the desk in a black leather chair as Wendell made a request.

"You suppose you could get me an autographed picture of Buck? And make sure that he signs a little slash over the dell in my name because it's pronounced Wen-*dell*."

"I'm sure that can be arranged," Conroy had answered in a tone that sounded pat and insincere.

For the next few minutes Conroy had cruised along, in no particular hurry, speaking in generalities – about talent, about the competitiveness of the music business, about diamonds in the rough that will never shine until they're polished.

As a twig of driftwood floated by him in the Vly, Wendell remembered that at this point he was starting to feel a bit itchy and hoped that Mr. Jack Conroy, Senior Agent with Music City Management, would soon shift up to a higher gear.

Wendell had decided to move things along by tromping down hard on the accelerator, interrupting Conroy's blather with a bullseye question that brought a decided snap of Chantelle's head at the sound of his words.

"What can you do for us, Mr. Conroy?"

Conroy's eyes shifted away from Wendell and onto the face of Chantelle.

"I'd like to offer you representation. I'd start you off as a warm-up, an opening act for a name performer. But with time, and some grooming..."

"We accept," Wendell had blurted out. "Mr. Conroy, this is the break the Charbonneau Family Band has been waiting for."

Conroy had then let go of a long sigh and cast his gaze out over the tops of the Charbonneaus' heads. When he looked back again, he lasered a stare into Wendell's eyes.

It was then that Wendell noticed that Conroy's eyes had grown as hard as the steel at Clinton Correctional Facility.

"Wendell. Wen-*dell*. I'm only offering representation for Chantelle. She's the one with the talent, the promise, the marketability."

Wendell began to bluster on about loyalty, marketing the family as a package, his many years as a performer, Patrice's talent.

Conroy repeated his offer.

"She's the one that I want."

Wendell's skin tone had then shot from a healthy pink to a blood red.

"Then the deal's off. We stick together. It's the Charbonneau Family Band. Now, we certainly appreciate..."

The next three words spoken in that room would forever change the Charbonneau family.

"Hold on, Dad."

A little sunbeam coming through the trees that lined the Vly was warming the vortex of Wendell's head, the spot on his scalp that was beginning to thin. Wendell seemed to remember that she had also thrust out her arm in front of him, as if to physically hold him back.

"Who would be providing my back-up, Mr. Conroy?" asked Chantelle, the twenty-three-year-old beginning her own negotiations.

Conroy's mouth betrayed the slightest trace of a smile.

"I'd assemble the best road-tested musicians money could buy, a crack team of country music professionals."

"And I could do all my own originals?" she continued.

"Yes, after I've heard and approved them. A few covers thrown in, but it's your sound we want to develop, Chantelle."

Wendell's older daughter had then lowered her head and asked, "Mr. Conroy, could you give my Dad and me a few minutes...alone?"

A bird in a branch of a maple on the banks of the Vly came forth with a song, its voice confident, practiced, and sure...the same way, Wendell thought, that Chantelle had sounded when she had told him she was abandoning the family band.

"I'm gonna take this offer, Dad. Whether you like it or not, I'm gonna take it."

"Look, I know you're angry with me because I wouldn't let you wear that neckerchief around your leg. I'm sorry, I was a little jittery, worryin' about Robert and things. Next time we play out, you can wear it, no problem."

"Dad, it's not about that. This isn't about any get-back. This is about an opportunity...and I am gonna take it."

Wendell's facial color, which had drained to a pasty white upon hearing his daughter's decision, quickly spiked back to red.

"You're burnin' it down. You're burnin' it down right here, right in front of my eyes."

"Burning what down, Dad?"

"Our dream of the Charbonneau Family Band travelin' around the country, makin' records, making the big time...together."

Chantelle had then looked up into her father's eyes.

"Your dream, not mine. I'm sorry if it's not working out that way."

Wendell, about to burst, had then leaped from his chair.

"You're sorry? Sorry? You're cuttin' us loose, turnin' your back, betrayin' your own blood and all you can say is 'I'm sorry'? You are one selfish little bitch."

It was then Chantelle's turn to rocket out of her seat.

"You're calling *me* selfish? How dare you. Have you ever once asked any of us what *we* wanted?"

Although anger had started to place a strangle hold on his voice, Wendell had managed to squeeze out a mandate.

"You take Conroy's offer, don't you never, ever come back home."

And in the last three years she hadn't.

Just a daughter gone bad, Wendell told himself as he stood and began untying the knot at his waist, drawing his combination hemorrhoid therapy and meditation session to a close. Just a daughter gone bad, happens in the best of families.

He heard the sound of twigs snapping, someone coming through the woods, a stand of trees that separated his house from the stream. Soon Robert appeared at the river bank, munching on an apple.

"Mom says lunch is ready."

"Be right there, Son," replied Wendell as he waded out of the river, "be right there."

CHAPTER 2

Wendell's rusting light brown '89 Chevy station wagon barreled down county road 319 en route to an afternoon gig. Held to the roof with metal strapping stood a hand-lettered plywood sign that dared, "*Ask Me How Western Auto Ruined My Motor*" along with a crushed blue and white oil filter.

Wendell was at the wheel, Patrice in the front seat, and Robert, preferring to have room to stretch out, was in the back.

June, having determined herself "tired" after the Charbonneau's return from Nashville, no longer played guitar nor sang with the band.

It was a pleasant, mid-July afternoon and the car's windows were all down, a dusty wind blowing through the vehicle. Balanced on the transmission hump was a carton of beer; Wendell took sips from an open bottle and then replaced it back down into the six pack.

Ordinarily, Patrice would have been bitching at him for his time honored habit of having one or two before they arrived at the job – to lubricate his throat and loosen his fingers, he would always defend. But today she was thinking about Missouri...

Branson, Missouri, the image on the last picture postcard she had received from her sister Chantelle. In the small white section allotted, Chantelle had written about meeting Dolly Parton and Kenny Rogers, squabbles with Jack about repertoire and stage apparel, and how much she missed her Mom, Patrice, and Robert.

Kept secret from Wendell, the postcards arrived with an intermittent frequency, having begun about six months after her break with the family. Occasionally, during the day when Wendell was at work, Chantelle would place a long distance call, the three Charbonneaus at home all getting on extension phones to hear the voice of the one who was no longer a part of their daily lives.

June and Patrice had impressed upon Robert that he was not to speak to Wendell about the cards or the calls, but both mother and daughter knew that Robert was a high security risk and resigned themselves to the fact that the clandestine communiqués could be found out at any time.

Patrice was wondering if, up close, Dolly Parton's wig looked real or fake when her father brought her mind back into the front seat of the car.

"What are you scowling about? Got a headache?"

"No, I was just wondering…where this job was…what this job was?" asked Patrice.

"One of them Bar Misfits"

"You booked us at a Bar Mitzvah?" she asked, her eyes wide. "A country band at a Bar Mitzvah?"

"Why not?" Wendell defended. "Job's a job, and…

"I know Daddy. You never know who might have a connection in the business."

"Right! It's all a question of exposure."

Patrice wondered, feared that any exposure to be had on this particular afternoon would be in the misplaced trio's inability to come across with an appropriate song repertoire.

"Did you make up a set list?" she asked.

"Didn't have to. The lady, Mrs. Levine, phoned in a lot of the songs she wants us to play."

"And we know all these songs?"

Wendell put his beer back down into the carton and craned his neck around.

"Robert, there's a sheet of paper stuck in the back of my amplifier. Hand it up here, will you, Son?"

Robert, whose head had been drooping in a half-doze, took several seconds to process the request, then pulled the paper from the amp and gave it to his father.

Wendell passed it to Patrice and instructed, "Read."

" 'Color My World,' yeah we can do that, 'Feelings,' I suppose. Daddy your handwriting is atrocious. What is this 'Have a Gran-*ee*-la?'"

Wendell stuck his second beer between his legs and cranked off the cap.

"Not exactly sure," he answered. "I think it might be one of them little cookies or pastries that them people eat."

Patrice studied her father's writing.

"Could it be Havah Nagilah?"

"Yeah, that's it," he said.

"Dad, that's a traditional Jewish folk song. We don't know that."

"Ahh, don't worry 'Treece, we'll throw something together."

Patrice was readying herself for a second round of protest when an urgent appeal came from the back seat.

"Dad, gotta pee."

"Almost there son, I'm sure you can hold it."

"K."

With that, Wendell took a long pull on his beer, checked his watch, and applied a steady pressure down onto the accelerator.

Patrice chose not to continue the conversation with her father, but simply leaned her head out the window, feeling the air blow through her hair and believing that although her sister was not yet at the top, she was a lot closer than what remained of the Charbonneau Family Band.

*   *   *   *

"What seems to be the problem?" asked Wendell as he swung himself down from the cab of his tanker truck.

Elliot Ackerman, 35, CPA, husband, father of two, and new owner of a townhouse in Chesterfield Village had placed a frantic call to the Charbonneau household that Saturday morning.

"Like I told your wife, all the drains are gurgling, the toilets are running real slow. The downstairs one almost overflowed last night," answered Elliot.

"Well, sometimes June leaves out the details, all she said was that you needed help. But let's talk a bit before we start digging up your back yard."

Elliot blanched.

"Are you sure that's what we need to do, these houses are new, I don't understand. . ."

"Just kiddin'," said Wendell with a smile. "The only digging we'll have to do is to get to the stack, the top of the tank, so I can get my hose and snake in. Have you done that yet, sir?"

"Done what?"

"Dug down to the stack."

"No."

"I can do it for you. . .an additional ten dollar charge of course."

"Not a problem," assured Ackerman.

"Next question is what kind of toilet paper do you use?"

"Just kidding again or is that really a consideration here?" asked Ackerman.

"No joke, yes it is a consideration."

"I-I don't know, I'll go see."

Elliot ran inside and soon returned carrying a four pack of toilet paper whose wrapper boasted "soft as cotton." Wendell tore the plastic wrap, extracted one roll, pulled off several sheets, and rubbed them between his fingers.

"This could be your problem right there."

"How so?"

"Paper is soft, but too thick. Works fine in city sewers, but you're out here in the country. This stuff tends not to break down in a septic tank. You need the single ply...it breaks down a lot sooner."

"I'll talk to Marcia, my wife, about getting the right kind."

Wendell rolled the sheets of paper in his hand into a loose ball.

"I *have* talked to my wife about getting *this* type of paper. Easier on the 'roids... some of the cheaper single plies are like fine grit sandpaper. But June is forgetful. See if I needed to, I could suck my tank once a week. Advantage of having your own rig."

"Yes, I suppose," said Elliot. "Now are there any more questions?"

"Nope, just show me where you think your tank is buried."

Wendell knew exactly where the tank was buried. He'd hung around Chesterfield, during breaks and slow times during his own business day when a large developer from Albany had built the houses.

Wendell speculated he could hit Elliot for a few extra labor dollars if he spent some time appearing to search for the elusive septic tank stack.

"Gee, I would assume the tank is somewhere near the back of the house," answered Elliot, wearing a weak smile and raised eyebrows.

"Well I got a general idea, but I may have to poke around a bit before I find it. Course, I'm on the clock when I'm digging."

"Not a problem," assured Elliot Ackerman for the second time.

Wendell drove his tanker into the homeowner's back yard, set the emergency brake, grabbed a round nose shovel off the back, and went to work.

Sticking his shovel into the ground for the first of three false tries, Wendell wondered what it would feel like when, he too, would be at the point where money would not be a problem. That time in the future when he could get up on a Saturday morning and put on a pair of khakis with a razor sharp crease, pull on a polo shirt with one of them little animals sewed on, and slip on a pair of those loafers with the tassels attached.

As he tossed dirt from hole number two, he glanced over at Elliot's shoes.

Well, maybe not the loafers.

It would happen, all a question of just hangin' in. The band was sounding better than ever, only a matter of time before they found their neon rainbow with a pot of country gold at the end.

Clink, Clink.

In the fourth and true hole, Wendell's shovel tip found the metal cover of the stack on the second stab. He lifted a few shovelfuls of earth exposing the entire cover, lay the shovel aside, and pried the cover off with his fingers.

"Gawd, that smell," gasped Elliot.

"Ya get used to it. The solids aren't at the top yet. I don't think that's your main problem, but while I'm here you still want me to suck the tank?"

"Please."

Wendell then went to his truck and tugged on the rubber gloves that went over his elbows and ended at mid-bicep. He attached one end of thick hose to his tanker and dragged the other end over to the stack and shoved it in. Returning to the truck, he threw a switch and the tanker, with a gurgling noise, began to pull the contents from Ackerman's tank.

Ackerman's children then appeared at the back door.

"Can I come out, Dad?" asked the boy through the screen.

"Me too?" asked his younger sister.

"Yes, but don't touch anything," answered their father.

The two kids, who Wendell guessed to be about six or seven, came bounding out the back door. Wendell smiled at them but they simply returned an inquisitive stare – at Wendell, his truck, and his gyrating hose.

Kids, especially boys, are always attracted to machinery and trucks, thought Wendell. He smiled again.

"Daddy that smells!" exclaimed the girl, over the din of the gurgling.

"Yes honey, that it does," agreed her father.

"What's he doing, Dad?" asked the boy.

"Well, he's...he's cleaning out the poopies."

Covering their mouths with their hands, the children exploded into giggles. After receiving a stern look from their father, they quieted.

The boy looked up at Wendell.

"What's your name?" he asked.

"Wen-*dell*. What's yours?"

"Justin."

"That's a nice name, a real strong name," complimented Wendell. "After I'm done here maybe you'd like to sit behind the wheel in my truck. I know you young fellers. . ."

"You're the poopie-man," the boy suddenly blurted out.

Both children again began laughing.

"That's enough," chided their father.

Wendell lowered his head and tapped on the side of his hose.

"Just about empty. Need to backwash, hit it with a hose and then I'll snake the pipe that comes from your house. My guess is that's where we'll hit pay dirt."

"All right," said Elliot, with a nod.

Ten minutes later as Wendell was unhooking the metal snake from the side of his truck, the little boy wandered over to him.

"Why do you wear those big gloves?" he asked Wendell.

Wendell, out of ear shot of Elliot, furrowed his brow.

"Now why do you think?"

"To keep your hands clean?" replied the boy.

Wendell didn't answer but then pulled the snake off the truck with one violent tug.

The boy scampered back to where his father was standing.

Wendell returned to the septic tank, knelt down, pulled out the hose, and started feeding the tensile, flat metal snake, which had a wooden ball attached to the end approximately the size of a golf ball, into the pipe that came out from the house and fed into the tank. Once he felt it hit the elbow of the pipe inside the house, he began a back and forth drawing motion.

"Looks like he's playing tug of war, doesn't it kids?" asked Elliot.

His children smiled and nodded.

"Sometimes it feels that way," wheezed Wendell.

And then suddenly he stopped.

"Got somethin'," he announced.

"One of the kid's toys, accidentally flushed down the toilet?" speculated Elliot, turning and scowling at his children.

"Nope, too soft for that."

Ever so slowly, like reeling in a fish that's in imminent danger of throwing the hook, Wendell began pulling the snake out of the pipe. When the ball end was almost out, Wendell captured whatever it had caught and held it tightly between his gloved hands, hidden from the others.

With a great air of mystery, Wendell looked straight at Elliot and asked, "Your wife got long hair?"

"Yes, yes she does," answered Elliot, extracting his hands from his pants pockets and then crossing his arms over his chest.

"Brunette?"

"Deep mahogany, copper highlights."

With great ceremony, as a major leaguer winds up a pitch, Wendell drew the object up over his head and hurled it to the ground.

A huge mahogany brown, copper highlighted hair ball.

"Yuuck!" cried both kids in unison.

"There's the culprit that clogged your pipe," declared Wendell, beaming with accomplishment.

Thoroughly repulsed, and having shooed the children into the house now that the disgusting little sideshow was over, the best Elliot could muster was a terse, "Thank you for sharing that with us."

As Wendell was preparing to leave, he hoisted his hose up off the ground with a slight swinging motion. Several droplets that clung to the lip of the hose escaped and flew straight onto the immaculate khakis worn by Elliot Ackerman.

"Careful, please," came the brittle chastisement.

"Sorry," apologized Wendell. "I'm used to that happening to me. Occupational hazard, ya know?"

"Mmmm," murmured Elliot through clenched mouth, wiping in vain with his white handkerchief at the brown spots that had peppered his pants.

*   *   *   *

It was his habit, his tradition, maybe even a bit of a superstitious ritual, that if he and the band had an engagement for Saturday night, usually at a bar, a roadhouse, a nightclub, the hours of play being 9 or 10pm to 1 or 2am, Wendell would begin his evening by settling back in his living room and watching a 7pm rerun of his favorite television program, *Hee Haw* – that cornball country music show that had long since been dropped from network programming, but was still very much alive in cable syndication.

Nestled in an upright recliner, a bowl of spaghetti resting against his boulder-like belly, a cloth dishrag tied around his neck for a bib, Wendell alternated between gobbling forkfuls of pasta and laughing out loud at the antics on his TV screen. There was a rhythm, a cadence to it – gobble and laugh, gobble and laugh, gobble and laugh.

Behind him, occasionally looking up to watch, usually when the pretty, short-skirted blondes came on the screen, sat Robert at a card table working on one of his paint-by-numbers.

Robert, who loved paint-by-numbers, had more or less mastered the matching of number and paint color, had covered his walls with his creations, and always gave them as gifts at Christmas and for birthdays. Robert's paintings were unique, always animals and always wearing a painted on, not-by-the-numbers toothy smile, added on as sort of his signature to the piece.

"June? Junie-bug? You got anymore of this?" called out Wendell from the confines of his chair.

From the kitchen came her reply.

"A whole potful, Wen."

"Could'ja bring me some, Hon?"

"No, come get it yourself."

Wendell turned in his chair, caught Robert's eye and said, "Women's lib."

Robert smiled and kept painting.

Wendell shoveled in the last two forkfuls, let out with a sigh, and rocked himself out of his seat. Empty bowl in hand, he began his walk to the kitchen. On the way he stopped to observe Robert's newest creation.

A German shepherd – wearing a very friendly grin.

"Nice job," complimented Wendell, "but how about one of these times you paint somethin' other than an animal…a landscape, a lighthouse. I've seen those in the store."

"No," replied Robert, "I like animals, just animals."

Wendell tousled the hair on his boy's head…his boy who would never grow to be a man. He felt the familiar ache in his heart that usually visited him just before he dropped off to sleep on the nights when thoughts of his son held the last flickerings of awareness in his consciousness.

"Well then you just keep paintin' those animals, 'cause you're damn good at it. You want some pasketti, Robert? Some real good I-tie food?"

"Naah, wanna paint."

"You? The boy with the appetite of a lumberjack. You don't want to eat?"

"Nope, maybe later, wanna paint right now."

"Ok, old buddy, old pal, just means more for me."

Wendell sauntered off, not realizing that when he reached the kitchen, it would hold more than just second helpings for him.

"You shouldn't be using that expression with Robert," admonished June. "He's liable to repeat it when he's out."

"What?" asked Wendell, "what expression?"

"I-tie, I-tie food."

"Yeah, that's right," defended Wendell. "That's what we called them in the service."

"I'm just afraid that if he uses that expression out in public, somebody will take offense."

Wendell could feel his jaw start to tighten. He made his way over to the stove and began filling his bowl from the pot.

"That's the problem with this country, June. Everybody's just so goddamn sensitive."

June sat at the kitchen table, working on a large mug of coffee. He turned and made eye contact with her once again.

"You want some of this?"

"No thanks."

Wendell resumed filling his bowl.

"No wonder I'm so friggin' fat, nobody around here eats anymore."

His bowl brimming, Wendell took a seat at the kitchen table. At the precise moment he sat, June rose.

"What? What now? You mad at me?" asked Wendell, his eyes as

wide as a young child's.

"No, just gonna dump this coffee. You want something to drink?"

"Water's fine"

June splashed the remains of her coffee into the sink, opened the tap, and chased the black liquid down the drain with fresh water. Wendell took the opportunity to look long and hard at his wife from behind.

Her once nicely rounded rump now hung slack and flat in her jeans; her hair, once full of color from Clairol, streamed loosely down her back, black and grey, against a yellowing cotton blouse.

All this since returning from Nashville.

"You lost more weight, June?" asked Wendell, his voice a little reedy.

"No," she replied, whirling to face him. She tugged at the seat of her jeans. "These pants have just gotten a little baggy with age."

"That's funny, you always tell me dungarees get smaller with time."

"Stop staring at me," she ordered. "Now I wanted to ask you something...um...oh yeah, where did you work today?"

June remained standing at the sink as Wendell plunged fork into pasta and began twirling.

"Chesterfield Village. Land of the rich-o-leos. You took the call this morning."

"Oh yeah, forgot. They pay you?"

"In cash. Why?"

Wendell lifted his fork and placed a spiral of spaghetti strands into his mouth.

"I took 'Treece to the doctor today. She had another one of her stomachaches."

"What did the sawbones say?"

"Either stress or a virus."

Wendell wiped his mouth on his dishrag napkin and cleared his throat.

"That's what they always say when they don't know."

"In any event, I-I didn't have enough to pay the bill," said June.

While his right hand kept feeding himself, Wendell's left slipped into his front pocket, pulled out several crumpled bills and dropped them onto the table.

"If we had health insurance," she ventured.

"Don't want to hear it, June. Way too expensive. Plus when the doctors know you got it, they run this test, that test. We're all pretty healthy, hope to stay that way."

"But even these office visits cut into our finances," she argued.

"Finances will be fine once the band is discovered. Now if I remember right, I did order a glass of water."

Wendell dropped his head and resumed eating. June stood there a moment, considering him. She then opened a cupboard, took down a glass and proceeded to fill it.

"Where is 'Treece?" asked Wendell.

"Out in her shop," answered June, delivering the water to the table.

With several large gulps Wendell drained the tumbler and then brought the empty glass down onto the table with thump.

"Another round, barkeep. And if I start gettin' obnoxious after this round you can cut me off."

June picked up his glass, cocked a bony hip, and rested her free hand on top of it.

"Start?"

Hunched over her workbench, under the light of a long fluorescent shop lamp, using a small Phillips head screwdriver, Patrice, 22, pretty and petite with hazel eyes and short jet-black hair, poked and prodded at the innards of the band's drum machine, which went by the trade name of Rhythm Ace.

Those who had yet to experience the band in performance, but were told that the drummer's name was Rhythm Ace, usually expected to see a flesh and bones percussionist who had been bestowed a name befitting his ability to keep the beat.

What greeted them was a scratched, aging plastic box replete with an assortment of dials and knobs used to call up a desired tempo and meter.

Wendell had decided on Rhythm Ace after determining that if a box could keep steady time and not take a cut of the evening's pay, then the machine was the ideal replacement for a string of drummers who over the years had both helped and hindered the Charbonneau sound.

Rhythm Ace did exactly what you asked him to do, never talked back, never questioned a song selection, never played too loud or lay too heavy on the cymbals, never got into barroom fights, never got drunk, hell, never touched a drop.

For Wendell, band members like Rhythm Ace didn't come any better.

Problem was, Rhythm Ace was growing old, and as of late his reliability was coming into question.

Some weeks back, at the Bar Mitzvah, midway through a easy shuffle, Ace accelerated, zero to sixty, punching the beat up to a hard-driving boogie, resulting in a complete standstill of guests on the dance floor and loud foolish laughter from Robert. After a quick pull of the machine's plug, Patrice managed to restore order by increasing her amp volume, plucking her bass strings at a slower tempo, and nodding at the guests as a cue to resume their dancing.

Tonight, Patrice was trying to figure out the workings of the tempo speed mechanism in the old box.

She heard the shop's door open, she turned, and saw her father enter. In his right hand he held a huge wedge of apple pie, his jaws working on the first bite.

"Tummy feelin' better?'

"A little," she answered. "Please close the door."

She turned back to her work.

"I've asked you not to eat in my shop."

Wendell nibbled a second bite, bits of crust falling on the plywood floor.

"And that would be because..."

"Because food attracts mice. I *hate* mice."

Wendell took another step forward, making sure that the sole of his cowboy boot covered his droppings.

"What'cha working on?"

"Trying to figure out this board that controls the speed," she answered.

"Right, if I wanted someone to run away with our songs I'd go back to using live drummers," he snickered.

Patrice then set the dial to a rumba and touched the play button. The machine came forth with the desired beat at a moderate tempo.

She turned, raised her eyebrows, and grinned at her father.

A few seconds later, the box let go a sound like a phonograph needle jumping a record groove, and promptly pumped the rumba to warp-speed.

Patrice snorted angrily, yanked the machine's plug from a wall socket, and tossed her screwdriver onto the workbench.

"I give up."

She turned back to her father who was polishing off the last of his pie.

"Daddy, we need a new one."

Wendell finished chewing and wiped his mouth with the back of his hand.

"Need to get a few bucks ahead. We can get by without it tonight. Just crank up your bass a bit."

"I don't like to."

"Either that," he said, "or we take our chances with the road runner here," pointing a finger at the malfunctioning machine.

"Okay," she agreed, "but let me set my own volume."

"All right."

There was a stillness in the shop and Patrice's eyes fell upon the pile of crumbs that lay at Wendell's feet.

Wendell cleared his throat

"Where's your broom?" he asked.

"Corner."

With four long steady strokes, Wendell swept any attraction for a passing rodent out the shop door.

"Where we playing tonight?" Patrice asked, returning her screwdriver to its designated spot on the peg board.

"*Whiskey River*," came her father's reply.

*   *   *   *

Rapant's *Whiskey River*, where more draft beer than liquor ever flowed, was located in West Chazy, about a fifteen minute ride from the Charbonneau homestead.

After he took an early retirement from the railroad, Joseph Rapant, Sr. had purchased the bar, a spacious nightclub with seating for about two hundred, changed the name from *Dell's*, blacktopped the dirt driveway, refurbished a room upstairs into an office, and started bringing in country music bands for entertainment.

Joe and his wife Martha had one child, Joseph Jr., who was given the nickname of Sonny, a moniker that had stuck with him into adulthood. At 34, Sonny was handsome in a brutish way, with muscles hardened from hours spent alone with dumbbells and a nose made flat from the fists of other men during a stint at boxing while in the Marines. Years after his honorable discharge, Sonny still retained his military brush cut.

Joe and Martha offered light meals for their customers – a sandwich menu, soups, and if Joe was in the mood to cook, an occasional bowl of chili.

Sonny, who worked for his parents, rarely spent time in the kitchen, preferring to alternate his time checking proof at the door, bouncing, and bartending. . .and deriving distinct payoffs from each duty served.

Working the door allowed him the opportunity to flirt (although married with a young son) and make contact with the young ladies so inclined to visit his father's establishment. Often an encounter at the door could result in a hot backseat tryst in the parking lot later on in the evening.

As bouncer, he enjoyed the challenge of ejecting the patron who had grown a set of beer muscles, usually a Plattsburgh State College student who had heard that he might get lucky with one of the locals at *Whiskey River*.

If a protest on the part of the soon-to-leave patron ensued, Sonny relished the possibility of a fight, and would invite the youth to test his pugilistic skills with a simple "try me". His brain wet with alcohol, and not wanting to back down in front of friends or the inevitable crowd that always formed when blood was soon to be spilled, the boy would throw the first punch, and Sonny would counter... in self-defense, of course, as he would explain to the State Police who might later investigate the incident.

Sonny always threw straight to the mouth, hoping that knuckles and a chunky gold signet ring he wore on his right hand would crack loose at least one of his opponent's front teeth – teeth that would be recovered from the barroom floor and added to a zip-loc plastic bag that dangled from the rear-view in Sonny's pick-up.

Standing behind the bar, he liked to give the impression he was the owner, barking orders to the waitresses, setting up the occasional free drink or two, and, if he was in a particularly chatty mood, and the patron was new to the club, boasting about some of the improvements he'd soon be making to the building, the sandwich board, and the caliber and types of bands to be brought in.

But on this particular evening Sonny's mood was one of mean-spirited mischief.

Some old faceless gomer, probably from the trailer park not far from *Whiskey River*, had been downing fifty cent drafts during the afternoon happy hour as fast as Sonny could serve them. Sonny had listened to the man's ramblings, none of them making any sense or holding even the slightest thread of a story as the two hour reduced drink price period had dragged on. And now the old boy was face down, asleep at the bar, a belly-full of beer.

Sonny and his best friend Mike Gonyea, a local welder who worked off and on, and whose arms held tattoos from shoulder to wrist, stood behind the bar, adding tap water to a plastic bucket chock-full with ice, trying hard to stifle snorts and giggles.

When the bucket was full, Sonny looked up and made a quick scan of the club. He saw a few loyal regulars, scattered at some outlying tables, munching on sandwiches, and sipping beers. None, Sonny determined, would raise a fuss about the act he was soon to commit.

"Only fair you ask the gentleman nicely first," said Mike, his mouth fighting a smile.

"You're right."

Sonny leaned over the bar and whispered into the sleeping man's ear.

"Kind sir, happy hour is now over..."

The man responded with a loud snore.

"...and has been for the last half hour, you fuckin' lowlife."

Sonny, pokerfaced, turned to a wide-eyed Mike.

"The customer does not appear to be responding," said Sonny. "We must resort to other methods to awaken him."

"Maybe he's like Sleeping Beauty...just needs a little peck on the lips," offered Mike.

"Fuck you, Gonyea," said Sonny, as he raised the bucket of ice water up over the sleeping man's head.

"Time to rise and shine, Pops!"

With that, he up-ended the bucket, water and ice crashing down on the old man's head, the shock bringing an immediate response.

"Oooooooh!" cried the hapless old man, his arms flailing wildly, as Sonny and Mike broke into peals of laughter.

The old man's cries brought an anxious Joe Rapant, Sr., still in apron and clutching a bread knife, rushing from the kitchen.

"What the fuck's goin' on, Sonny?"

"This stinkin' old bum sucked down a bunch a beers, fell asleep. I don't want him at my bar when more of the regulars start coming in."

"*Your* bar? It ain't your bar yet, boy," said Rapant, Sr. "I still got breath in me."

Sonny could see the fire in his father's eyes, the same blaze that had preceded a punch or a back hand when Sonny was a kid.

Sonny lowered his head and his voice.

"You know, Dad, somebody passed out at the bar is bad for business."

"Then you shoulda' stopped serving him."

Joe Rapant stepped closer to the old man.

"Dry him off and get him out of here," commanded Rapant Sr.

Sonny and Mike waltzed around from behind the bar, small bar towels in hand. Sonny gave his to the old man, while Mike ran the other over the drunk's dripping hair.

"Wha' happened to me?" asked the old man, dabbing at the right side of his face with the towel.

"A little swim, Pops. A nice dip in the pool," answered Sonny, lifting the man off the barstool, he and Gonyea then walking him a few yards away from the bar.

Sonny then turned to Mike.

"You drive him home?"

"Yeah, sure, no problem."

Sonny watched as Mike escorted the still drunk and disoriented old gent towards the front door. When the two crossed the threshold, he turned back towards the bar, noticed his father was gone, but saw his mother standing there, mop in hand.

"Clean it up, wise guy," she ordered.

He made his way to the bar, looked into her angry face but once, took the mop from her, and began passing it through the puddle that sat at the base of the bar stool as she retreated back into the kitchen.

His father, emerging from a back storeroom, floodlight and small piece of plywood in hand, was far from done with him.

"I swear Sonny, sometimes your head's so far up your ass."

"Aw, c'mon Dad, we were just having a little fun," Sonny defended.

"Yeah, would have been a lot of fun if you gave the old bastard a heart attack and he'd croaked in here."

Sonny said nothing, kept his head down, and just kept mopping.

After a few more swipes, the floor almost dry, Sonny stopped and looked up at his father.

"Sorry."

Joe Rapant was beginning to cool. He exhaled a ragged breath, letting go the tension that had harbored itself in his shoulders and chest.

"I just want you to think, Sonny, think before you act, that's all."

"I will," promised Sonny.

Sonny took the mop into the kitchen, found a wringer bucket, and squeezed out what remained of the old man's shower. While in the kitchen his mother did not acknowledge his presence, choosing to busy herself at the meat slicer.

When Sonny exited the kitchen, he found his father up on the stage, balancing on a chair, replacing a red flood bulb, one of four that served as overhead stage lighting.

"While you're up there, you gonna sing for your supper?" asked Sonny, hoping to lighten things a bit.

His question brought a chuckle from a couple conversing with their waitress at a nearby table.

His task completed, Joe Rapant stepped off the chair, and then swung it down onto the dance floor, the impact echoing through the club.

Still on the stage, he looked straight at his son.

"No."

Joe then made his way down the stage stairs, just three steps, and began walking, chip of plywood in hand, towards a table that needed to be shimmed.

Sonny approached him.

"Would this be a good time to talk to you about some ideas I had for changes in music?"

Joe had dropped to his knees and was slipping the plywood under the base of a wobbly table.

"No."

"Well, who you got comin' in tonight?"

Joe stood and wiggled the table, secure now with a wooden shim.

"Charbonneaus."

Sonny snorted and his lips curled into a sneer.

"The shitman, his piece of ass daughter, and the idiot son?"

Joe smiled, nodded his head.

"Yeah."

CHAPTER 3

She'd been petrified, peeking out through the wings at the four thousand plus crowd that had come primarily to see headliner Hal Ketchum. Sure, she'd played the theaters in Branson, but to smaller crowds, and usually opening for performers whose country music star had long since begun to dim. Ketchum had a hit on the charts and a record about to go gold. Hal himself, a gentleman and quite the looker, had come over to her about twenty minutes before she'd gone on, sensed her stage fright, winked, and whispered a few words of encouragement.

That had helped, along with a shooter of Jack Daniels slipped to her on the sly by her drummer just moments before the performance.

But now, clad in a rhinestone encrusted denim jacket over a sleek black unitard, she stood center stage at the *Palais Royale* in downtown Tulsa, her nervousness having been replaced by a fierce determination to capture the crowd. Chantelle Charbonneau gave everything she had, prowling that platform, hammering out rhythms on her six string, punching out the country rockers, but then shifting gears effortlessly, singing soft as spun cotton on her ballads, her hand gently caressing the face of her guitar.

Jack Conroy, her manager, watched from the wings, a wide grin on his face.

After her second number, when the whistles and hoots refused to die, he was convinced that his newest client was indeed starting to lose her rough edges and the amateurish stage presence that had been with her up until now.

Almost there, he thought, but not quite.

He took a closer look at her.

Something was definitely missing.

The brand new straw cowboy hat he'd spent a half hour forming into shape before he'd sent her out on stage.

Unbeknownst to him, after one of her fast numbers, she'd looked over, saw him talking with one of the technicians, and quickly whipped the hat off her head and spun it into the crowd, Frisbee-style.

At the end of her last song she closed her 25 minute set by matching her drummer, beat for beat, with a sassy triplet pounded out with the heels of her Tony Lamas, her long black hair dancing in time to the rhythm.

Although she could have easily taken an encore, the crowd being on their feet and roaring for more, she followed proper opening act etiquette by bowing, blowing a kiss, and waving, before running off stage...and into the arms of Jack Conroy.

"Hot as a pistol, Chantelle. Hot as a pistol," exclaimed Conroy, patting her back.

"Thanks Jack. Hot enough to start headlining?"

Conroy pushed back away from her and drilled in a stare.

"The name of the game is artist and repertoire development, Chantelle. Understand?"

Out of the corner of her eye she saw her lead guitarist passing by.

"Eric," she called out, held up her right hand, and twiddled the index and middle fingers.

Eric shook loose a cigarette from his pack, stuck it between her fingers and spun the wheel on his lighter.

"Thanks," she said, exhaling a long vapor of smoke.

Eric headed on his way, Chantelle licked her lips and turned her attention back to Conroy.

"Yeah, I understand. It's just that I've given up so much for this chance."

Conroy's face crowded into a scowl.

"What makes you so special, Princess? We've all made tradeoffs and sacrifices for this business."

Chantelle lowered her head but Conroy reached over and lifted her chin.

"You don't headline without a record deal. But trust me, kid, when it happens for you, and it will, it's gonna be sweet."

"I hope so," she replied, a haunted cast to her face.

"Nice job out there, lady."

She turned and caught the winking eye of Hal Ketchum, guitar slung over his shoulder, ready to go on.

"But I'm gonna start looking over my shoulder," he added, a smile on his face, "'cause I think you're gainin' on me."

She smiled, blushed, and lowered her head. Ketchum turned and said something to a technician about feedback in his left monitor during the soundcheck. The technician's face took on a defensive look and the two men began walking towards the stage.

"Good luck," she called out to him, but her words were swallowed up by the beginning applause of the crowd as Ketchum took his first few strides onto the stage.

Reaching his mic, Ketchum greeted his crowd, waited until they quieted, and then launched into his first number.

Chantelle watched with rapt attention, hoping to pick up a few pearls from the master.

Conroy leaned in closer and whispered in Chantelle's ear.

"You owe me," he said.

"Huh?"

"For a goddamn brand new hat that you somehow got rid of."

"Hate hats, Jack," she said with a smile. "Stop trying to make me wear them."

*   *   *   *

Wendell, Patrice, and Robert rolled into *Whiskey River* about 8:30pm. They were scheduled to go on at 9:00 and play until 1:00. A half hour, barring any major equipment problems, would give them plenty of time to set up their PA system, position their amplifiers on stage, tune their guitars, and determine the songs for their first set.

Patrice tuned both her own and her father's guitar, and set the volume controls on both amps. She made a point of always keeping the volume knobs on her father's guitar and amp set relatively low.

He was no guitar player, never had been, and the audience didn't need to know how often he fretted the wrong chord or played in the wrong key.

Wendell used to strum an acoustic guitar, painted red, white and blue, in vertical swaths of color, just like his hero Buck Owens. But as the years wore on, and Wendell's belly grew large, the guitar began to sit on top of his stomach, rather than rest against it.

Chantelle had once remarked that if he got any fatter, and the guitar any higher, he'd soon look like he was playing a Dobro.

Robert, sensing his father's discomfort with the situation, wanted to paint a smile on the face of the instrument, hoping that would make everything okay.

Patrice suggested an electric guitar, as the thinner, solid wood body would rest a little more flush against his midsection.

Although heavier than his acoustic, Wendell eventually opted for an off-white Telecaster. Initially, however, a new problem developed as he was now electrified, the playing that came forth through the amplifier was bigger and bolder – but no better. The music from his acoustic had usually been safely buried in the mix of vocals, and the electric guitars of Chantelle and Patrice.

At one point in his career, when the kids were young, Wendell had set about to improve his skills. As his finger calluses grew thick from practice, but seeing no real gains in technique, he determined that most of the contemporary country music stars who were making it were able to get by on only three chords.   Attempts at self-improvement were abandoned, his Mel Bay instruction books eventually shoved under the bed, never to see the light of day again.

Having endured his electrified playing in private, the rest of the Charbonneaus had held a collective breath the first time Wendell had strapped on his Telecaster in public. They were not to exhale until the end of the last set.

The audience that night was treated to a bombastic onslaught of Wendell's wrong key, wrong chord strummings all thrown from the new powerhouse Peavey amplifier he'd purchased to go with his new guitar. Sidelong glances back and forth between Patrice and Chantelle resulted in discreet lowerings of his amp during the times when Wendell had stepped up to the mic to sing a solo.

At the end of the night, wanting to handle the issue delicately, the two daughters, having plotted during one of the breaks, approached their father with the concern that a third electric guitar heard on stage might give an audience the mistaken impression that the band was into "heavy metal", a brand of music Wendell particularly despised. It was the girls' suggestion that Patrice be assigned the responsibility for all the volume settings of band equipment, both electric and electronic, so as to ensure that the band's sound remain "countrified."

Wendell bought it, and most nights his guitar was barely audible, sparing the ears of the audience and not subtracting quality-wise from the band's overall output.

But these days, even with Wendell's muted guitar, any quality that came from the trio was pretty much an exception to the rule.

Still, Wendell, Patrice, and Robert retained a modest following; fans who had come to admire and enjoy the Charbonneaus, now minus wife and mother June and estranged daughter Chantelle.

And Joe Rapant could always count on a modest crowd when the

Charbonneaus played his club. This mostly middle-aged, well-behaved audience drank his draft in moderate quantities, but shied away from hard liquor and mixed drinks, much to Sonny's contempt. He swore to his friends that someday he'd rid the club of those "piss water kegs" and shit-kicker bands like the Charbonneaus.

At approximately five minutes to nine, all of the Charbonneaus stood on the stage – Patrice fine tuning her bass with the assistance of the electronic tuner, Wendell giving Robert a quiet lecture on practicing self-control should his son have the urge to pick his nose at any point during the performance.

Sonny, wiping his hands on a bar rag, ambled on over.

"Hey *Wen*-dell," he taunted. "When you gonna let her breed?" he asked, nodding at Patrice. "You don't want her to wind up a dried up old maid, do you? I'd give you some fine looking grandkids." Sonny then looked dead-on at Robert. "No retards, either."

Patrice blushed crimson and turned her back to him.

Wendell, his lecture to Robert having been interrupted, beckoned Sonny closer with the wave of an index finger.

Sonny smirked and drew closer.

"Why don't you just take your little pencil-dick, go sit in the corner, and play with yourself," Wendell suggested.

Sonny shot a finger into Wendell's face.

"You watch your mouth, old man. Nothing please me better than to have your bridgework hanging in my pick-up window."

Wendell stood his ground, unflinching.

A scrawny blue-haired fan, her jean legs tucked into two-toned cowboy boots, way past her third beer, marched up to where the two men stood, oblivious to the drama that was playing out between them.

"Wen, could you put a Hank Williams' song in the first set?" she asked in a voice roughened by cigarettes.

Wendell tacked on a smile and looked at the woman.

"We'll open up with one, how's that?"

"Thanks, Hon," she answered, turned, and with a slight tilt in her gait, headed back to her table.

Wendell fixed his eyes back on Sonny.

"Now step away from the stage, boy, and let us do the job your *Daddy* paid us to do."

Wendell waited until Sonny took a full step backwards, then turned and looked first at Robert, then at Patrice.

"Your Cheatin' Heart."

*   *   *   *

Lunchbox and thermos in hand, Wendell stepped down from the driver's seat of his tanker. As he plodded his way towards his front door, carrying the weight of his workday on stooped shoulders, he was thinking of a hot shower and a cold beer. Lifting his leg to climb the first of three wooden steps, shifting about half of his weight into his booted right foot, he felt the step give way underneath him with a loud crack.

"Goddammit!"

Pulling his boot from between the splintered wood, he called up through the front screen door.

"Robert?"

"Yeah Dad?"

"Bring me out my tool chest will you, son?"

"Can't, paintin'."

Wendell lowered his head as he felt a twist of irritation deep in his gut.

"Now, son. Put the paintbrush down and bring me my tool chest *now."*

"K."

In back of his home, the barn, still a work-in-progress, Wendell kept his firewood and a pile of scrap lumber. He seemed to recall that he had a length of 1 by 12 that would work as a replacement step.

He trudged out behind the barn, located the board, brushed off the dust, checked it for cracks and warping and was rounding the corner on the way back to the front steps just as Robert was coming out the front door with the tool chest.

"Careful, son, first step is broken."

Robert's eyes widened as he looked down at the ruined board.

"You do that on purpose, Dad?"

"No," replied his father with a chuckle. "That step was just tired, worn out...like the way your old man feels sometimes."

"Oh."

"Stick around Robert, I need your help."

With a short pry bar, Wendell deftly removed the nails and pulled out what remained of the old step. Then, for the next twenty minutes, father and son measured, sawed, and nailed the new board into place.

Well, actually, Wendell did the measuring, and the sawing, and the nailing. At one point Robert did lift a hammer out of the toolbox, but it was a ball peen. The boy's contribution to the new construction consisted of holding the board a total of three times – first when his father measured it, second when his dad sawed it, and third when the elder Charbonneau secured it into place.

"Done," declared Wendell, bringing the hammer down one last time.

He stood up, perused his work, and mopped his brow with a shirt sleeve. For the final test, he planted both boots onto the step.

It held him.

"Just like New York, Robert."

"What?"

Wendell grinned.

"An old expression my father used to say."

"Oh."

Robert frowned and squinted up into Wendell's eyes.

"Grandpa's dead. He's still dead, right Dad?"

"Yeah, he's still dead, Robert," answered Wendell, as the image of his father's headstone instantly came to mind.

Wendell then plunked himself down and flipped his carpenter's hammer into the top drawer of the tool chest, the mallet landing with a crash as it hit an assortment of chromed open-end wrenches.

"Go get me a beer, will you Robert?"

"Can I have one too?"

"No."

Robert disappeared into the house and soon Wendell heard the closing of the refrigerator door along with the sounds of muffled conversation. When Robert came back outside he returned with a beer, a tall glass of lemonade for himself, and an edict of sorts from June.

"Mom says you should be drinking light beer. She says if you drank light beer you might be able to lose weight."

"Tell your mother if she minded her own business she wouldn't be minding mine."

Robert handed both drinks to his father, turned and pulled the screen door open, dutifully determined on delivering the message to June.

"Robert, you can tell her later," said Wendell, knowing that elapsed time would ensure that his smart-ass remark would never make it to June. "C'mere, sit with me for awhile."

Robert closed the door and plopped down on the steps next to his father. Wendell handed him his lemonade and touched the butt of his beer bottle to the glass.

"A toast to my favorite son, my boy," proclaimed Wendell.

Robert beamed, his father's remark having produced an ear to ear smile. He then in turn swung his glass at Wendell's bottle, the lemonade slopping over the brim of the glass, the resulting impact sending out a deep *clunk* into the air.

"Yeah, toast," Robert blurted.

"Easy, pal" warned his father, and then took several long pulls from his bottle.

"Ahhhh," breathed Wendell, after those first few swallows went down.

In loving imitation, Robert drank three large gulps from his glass.

"Ahhhh," he echoed, looking to his father for approval.

Wendell smiled, mussed his son's light brown hair, and stared off into the distance. A few swigs later Wendell's head was lighter, his mood relaxed, and the bottle now about three quarters empty.

He reached down and began rummaging in the top of his tool box. His fingers soon lifted out a six foot retracting tape measure.

Holding the tape measure with one hand, with the other he pulled out the end and handed it to Robert.

"Walk that out there."

Robert obeyed, setting his glass down, walking backwards towards the driveway, tugging the strip of metal tape as he went.

When Robert had pulled out the entire tape, Wendell held up his hand for him to stop, slid the locking mechanism closed, and held his thumb down onto the 72 inch mark.

"Come here Robert, I want to show you something. You can let go of the tape. I got it snugged."

Robert dropped his end onto the ground and ambled back to the steps.

"72 inches," began Wendell, "that marks the end of the tape, just like 72 years usually marks the end of a man's life span."

While holding steady on the 72 inch mark with his left thumb, he let his right travel on down to the 59th inch.

"Now see," he continued, " I'm 59, so this is just about how much time I've got left on this earth, from here to here," nodding at the two separate inch marks.

Robert stared hard at the 13 inches that constituted the predicted remainder of his father's life, his eyes shifting back and forth between Wendell's parted thumbs.

"That's not very far," he finally offered.

"Maybe so, but I'll take it. Still enough time to get us famous," returned his father, grinning and raising an eyebrow.

Wendell then lifted his thumb off the 59 inch mark.

"Go find the number 17," Wendell instructed. "The one and the seven sittin' close together on the tape."

Robert leaned down, squinted, and headed down the tape in search of the number. Soon, with great flourish, as if he had made the grandest of discoveries, he pointed out the designated inch mark.

"Right, that's your age," confirmed Wendell. "So you got from way down there up to way up here to live," he added, passing his hand over the length of the measuring tape for emphasis. "Son, you got a lifetime left!"

Robert beamed.

"Thanks Dad!"

Then, with one fluid motion Wendell whipped the length of the tape into the air, released the lock mechanism, and snapped the tape back into its case.

Robert began a gleeful laugh.

"Looked like a snake, Dad. Do it again, do it again."

"No, that's enough for now, Robert," said Wendell, tossing the tape measure back into the tool box. "Go get me another beer, would you please?"

Still smiling from his father's assurances of a long life, and laughing from the concluding exhibition of measuring tape retraction skills, Robert headed back into the house.

"And while you're in there, bring me out my mail," Wendell called out after him.

In the kitchen, June stood at the counter, chopping carrots and peppers and tearing lettuce for a dinner salad. Patrice sat at the table, crunching on a carrot while she thumbed through an electronics magazine.

Robert entered the kitchen, headed straight for the refrigerator door, and opened it.

June looked up from her work, but her hands remained busy.

"Lemonade's on the table, Robert. You waste energy with all that openin' and closing of the fridgerator door."

"No, beer. Dad wants another beer."

June began tearing the lettuce with a bit more tenacity.

"Man's always complaining about the size of his stomach but doesn't ever really want to do anything about it."

Robert remained at the open refrigerator, his look duller than usual.

"Get him his beer, Robert," instructed June, "and *please* close that refrigerator door!"

Robert whipped a bottle of Coors from the top shelf and slammed the door shut.

He then stood there, bottle in hand, still and solemn as a wooden Indian, with the exception of his eyelids which blinked at a rapid pace.

"Need something else?" asked June.

Robert remained mute.

"Chips? Pretzels? Side of beef?" asked June, her question raising the head of Patrice, causing her to grin.

"No, no," responded Robert.

"Daddy want a glass…a mug for his beer?" ventured Patrice.

A light went on in Robert's eyes.

"No not a mug, mail! He wants his mail."

"Treece, did you bring it up today?" asked June.

"No, I thought you were going to," answered Patrice, feeling her heart rate quicken.

June's knife had just sliced into the flesh of a large red pepper. Both hands froze in mid cut and she looked directly at her daughter.

"I thought you were going to grab it on your way in from town."

"Didn't bother," said Patrice, her eyes wide. "You were home all day. I assumed you already went to the box."

"No."

As the two remained locked in a gaze of fear, Robert sprinted out of the kitchen and back towards the front door.

Patrice leapt to her feet and followed Robert towards the door, hanging back just far enough to stay out of sight but remaining within earshot.

Handing out his father's beer, Robert announced, "Nobody got the mail today."

Wendell rocked himself to a standing position, accepted the beer from his son, and announced, "No problem. I'll get it. Could use a little walk, startin' to stiffen up from sittin' too long."

Still inside the house, Robert watched as his father took the first few steps of the 100 yard walk to the end of the driveway where a slightly battered, rusted pot-metal mailbox sat atop a 2x6 pressure treated post.

In his right ear he heard, "You better pray to God, Robert, that the mailman only brought bills and junkmail today."

He turned and looked into the scowling red face of his sister.

"What? What'd I do?" he pleaded.

He then felt his mother's arms envelope his shoulders.

"Leave him alone, 'Treece," came the directive from her mother.

On his way to the mailbox, Wendell alternated swigs of beer with the whistling of *"On the Wings of A Dove"*, a tune that, for whatever the reason, had been playing in his mind all day.

Upon reaching the rust and silver receptacle, Wendell slid his bottle into the back pocket of his coveralls, pulled the door open with one hand, and extracted the contents with the other.

He began flipping through the deliveries of the day – a full-color glossy flyer from the newest discount mega-hardware store in Plattsburgh, one of those women's magazines that 'Treece and June shared, some babe in full face paint gracing the cover, the phone bill, a cheap, poorly printed tri-fold advertisement for guitars from a music store in Gainesville, Florida and a postcard. A picture postcard.

He gazed at the photo, some street in Baton Rouge, and turned the card over.

His trip out was a lighthearted stroll, his trip back a murderous charge – nostrils flaring, neck veins at full pop, mouth spewing curses and invectives, legs pumping like pistons, raising thick clouds of dark brown dust in the dirt driveway.

Inside, the three other Charbonneaus heard his fast approaching fury and dared not look out a window lest they catch his glare and promptly be turned to stone.

His newly-installed step did indeed hold him as he pounded up the first of three, yanked open the door with such force as to severely threaten the integrity of the hinges, and flew into the house.

In the kitchen, June's hand shook as she chopped yet another carrot, nerves having caused her to dice the entire bag, so that now she considered making a sort of chunky coleslaw in addition to a tossed salad.

Patrice sat at the table, eyes cast upon her magazine, but unable to discern the meanings of words or pictures.

Robert, who had managed to polish off a full two quart pitcher of lemonade, was just coming back from the bathroom when the cyclone that was his father blew into the kitchen.

Pitching the other postal articles to the table, Wendell held the postcard high in the air.

"How long has this been going on?" he roared. "How long have we been accepting mail from this traitor?"

June lifted her knife from the shaft of a carrot and leveled it at her husband.

"She's still your daughter, Wen."

"The only daughter I have is sittin' over there at that table lookin' like the cat that swallowed the canary," he countered.

He then waved the card in the air.

"I'll ask again, how long?"

Without taking her eyes from the text and pictures that were nothing but a blur, Patrice answered, "She started sending us those a couple of months after we left Nashville."

Wendell brought the card from down over his head and stared deep into the picture side.

"Can we at least see where it's from? See where she last played?" begged Patrice.

"No!" barked Wendell, and slowly tore the card in half.

Patrice emitted a moan as if it were her own skin that had been torn.

"Wen!" yelled June. "You have no right– "

"June," he said, cutting her off. "Would Jesus have accepted a picture postcard from Judas. Now would he? Would he? And if he did, what might he write in return? Hope you're enjoying the thirty bucks, but as for me I can now see daylight through my hands!'"

Wendell then finished the job he'd started.

The card was ripped into fourths, eighths, sixteenths, until eventually he was holding a handful of confetti. With that, he dropped the rippings into the kitchen trash can and stormed out of the room.

"Pig-headed, bully bastard," cursed June under her breath.

Robert then burst into sobs.

"Sorry I made Dad mad."

Patrice, whose own eyes were leaking tears, leaned over and hugged her brother. In doing so, she managed to knock over the glass that held the last few ounces of Robert's lemonade binge. As the liquid streamed its way across the table, a little river heading for the falls, Patrice said softly, "It's okay, Robert. You didn't do anything wrong."

CHAPTER 4

Every August the Plattsburgh Fairgrounds hosted a Country Music Jamboree. Usually held on a Sunday afternoon, the event ran from noon to six and promised "six bands in six hours."

The planners of the event had two distinct reasons for limiting each group to 45 minutes. First, they realized that each band would pack the set with only their best material, no filler. Plus, it reduced the chance that any of the members would succumb to drunkenness or stall for time from fatigue, as was sometimes the case when pressed to play several hours.

Secondly, if a band, be it newcomer or seasoned veteran, was particularly bad that afternoon, the audience would only have to endure less than an hour's worth of music not fit for public consumption.

When that happened, the bleachers would usually clear as patrons made a beeline to the beer stands or bathrooms.

The jamboree was a joint venture produced by fairgrounds management in cooperation with the Northern New York Country Music Association – an organization founded and run by the Wakefields, Tommy and Tammy, who, like the Charbonneaus, were field tested pros who had weathered the years and the adversities inherent with holding a band together.

To look at, the Wakefields, Tommy, 44, and Tammy, 45, were an odd looking couple; he at 6 feet 3 inches, barely tipped the scales at 150, a stringbean, with a slow, deep deliberate drawl, though he'd never been south of Albany; she, five two in heels, weight a well kept secret, built like a beach ball, the kind of overweight woman prone to red blotches and matted hair even on the mildest of summer days, with a mouth that sent words into the air like a Thompson gun.

Strange in appearance as the couple might be, the Wakefields had endured – in a marriage that proved childless and as a working team who not only promoted country music in the north country at large, but who had consistently secured a steady string of musical engagements in their years as performers.

For the Plattsburgh Country Music Jamboree the Wakefields were always the first act to go on, with Tommy and Tammy then sharing the announcer duties for the subsequent acts to follow.

This year, on the third Sunday in August, the Charbonneau Family Band was scheduled as the fourth group of entertainers.

For Wendell, the last month had proved a little lean for bookings, with one of his regular bars begging off on a return engagement, claiming that the DWI laws were killing his business. A second owner had sold out on live music, hiring one of those disc jockeys who could play country by the superstars, just like you hear it on the radio, and not some half-assed rendition by a bunch of bangers. And a third club owner had told him point blank that he would not be re-hiring him in that the group needed a little more "flash."

It was that last remark that kept Wendell up at night, ruminating, and finally realizing and admitting to himself that Chantelle's departure had left a huge hole in the band.

So this year, in addition to looking to earn the standard $125 playing fee at the jamboree, Wendell was looking for something a little greater than the cash that would buy his beer and put a few more groceries in the fridge.

He was looking for a little flash.

Wen and Patrice, Robert having stayed home sick with a summer cold, arrived around 12:45pm, well before their time to play, with the distinct intention of scouting out any musicians from other bands who may not have been completely content with their current situations.

Little did they know that their timing would be perfect.

The Wakefields had just ended their set and were walking off stage to a modest applause when the fireworks began.

At the back of the stage, six rectangular areas were duct-taped off, designating where the various bands could leave their empty drum, guitar and keyboard cases. A uniformed security guard watched over the areas so as to prevent an unscrupulous entertainer from upgrading in equipment.

Having reached the Wakefield rectangle, Tommy, with his basset hound eyes and baritone drawl, turned slowly to their lead guitarist, a long-haired, flannel-shirted kid in his twenties by the name of Spinosa.

"Son, you're fired. That's the last time you'll ruin my wife's solo."

Three duct-taped areas away stood Patrice and Wendell. Hearing Tommy's decree, the two turned their backs and pretended to be fooling with a tuning peg on Wendell's guitar.

"I didn't ruin her solo," Spinosa shot back. "If you knew anything about music you'd understand I was simply providing accompaniment, layering the sound, just fattening up her voice a bit."

"My voice don't need no fattenin'," spat Tammy.

Spinosa then raked his hair back and slowly considered her, letting his eyes walk deliberately from the cowboy hat that sat perched on the crown of her moon head on down to her chubby little feet that were squashed into the confines of cheap vinyl cowgirl boots.

"Well," he said, the trace of a smile tugging at the corner of his mouth, "on second thought, you may be right."

"Get on out of here, boy," boomed Tommy.

"Thas' right, get your punk-ass gone," echoed Tammy.

"Yeah, whatever," came Spinosa's response.

But it was the Wakefields who left, as Spinosa knelt to bed his guitar in its hardshell case.

The Charbonneau's backs were still turned when the Wakefields passed. Wendell then snuck a look at the newly-unemployed guitarist and whispered to Patrice, "Wait here."

Wendell strode over to the still kneeling Spinosa.

"You looking for a gig?" asked Wendell.

"Maybe," answered Spinosa, not looking up, "just as long as it's not another Tommy and Tubby Show."

"No, no, no," insisted Wendell. "This is a professional act, no amateurs, only a matter of time before this band hits big."

Spinosa looked up, flipped the hair out of his face.

"Uh-huh. Well, where do I audition?"

"My house," came Wendell's response. "You familiar with the Chazy area?"

"Somewhat."

Wendell pulled a business card out of his shirt pocket, scribbled directions to his barn-house from the Adirondack Northway, and handed it to Spinosa.

"Phone number's on there. You get lost and we'll direct you in," assured Wendell. "Tomorrow night sound good?"

"Yeah, sure."

Spinosa looked down and read the face of the card aloud.

"The Charbonneau Family Band."

"Yessir. I'm Wendell and over there's my daughter Patrice."

Patrice grinned and gave a little wave. Spinosa nodded and waved back. Then, still from a kneeling position he stuck out his hand. Wendell leaned down and took it.

"I'm Dominic Spinosa."

When Spinosa released his grasp, Wendell's face grew serious.

"When our break comes, Dominic, you would be able to travel, right?"

"Ready, willing, and able."

"Course, that means international, too," Wendell added.

"Not a problem. Single, no ties, no strings. Everything I own is over there in my camper," he said, pointing to a champagne Volkswagon Westfalia parked near the back of the stage.

Wendell slowly eased himself down onto his haunches.

"Now one last thing," said Wendell, looking Dominic dead in the eye.

"What's that?"

"You weren't tappin' little Tammy, now were you son?'

Spinosa looked as though he had bitten into a fresh lemon.

"No way, man!"

"Cause if you were," began a sly-mouthed Wendell, "I'd tell you to strap a board across your ass so you don't get lost in her. Shit, I've known guys who went in the first of July didn't come out 'til the end of January!"

Spinosa cracked a laugh, shook his head. Wendell followed with a wheezy chuckle.

Patrice, knowing her father's distinctive snicker whenever his conversation turned bawdy, chose to call out to him from her square rather than approach him as he squatted next to Spinosa.

"Daddy?"

Wendell let the smirk fall from his face and turned to his daughter.

"What's up, darlin'?"

"I'm gonna take a run to the drug store," she said, a pained expression flooding her face. "I'll be back soon...we got plenty of time."

Wendell stood, his eyes deep with parental concern.

"You okay, babe?"

"Stomach's botherin' me, a little, again."

        *   *   *   *

On this particular Sunday afternoon, as was the case on every

Sunday as soon as the weather began to turn warm, Sonny and Millie Rapant held a barbecue for about fifteen to twenty of their friends and neighbors.

Millie, Sonny's wife of twelve years, usually spent her summer Saturday afternoons vacuuming the pool, sweeping the deck, cleaning the house, and laying in a healthy supply of beer, wine, steaks and hamburger meat. As the guests usually brought the salads, Saturday nights Millie's time was spent stocking their garage refrigerator with beverages and patting the hamburger meat into quarter pound circles.

Sonny had spent his Saturday night patting the ass of a blonde coed from Plattsburgh State while sharing kisses and a bottle of Cuervo Gold in the back of her black Maxima.

But the rebound from the tequila and the sober remembrance that he'd failed to wear a condom left him in a foul mood as he struggled through a game of wiffle ball with his only child, ten-year-old Claude.

Claude, having been beaned twice by a fast-pitched ball from his father, stood in a field not far from the house, his lower lip in full quiver.

"Stop that sniveling," ordered Sonny, "it's only a little plastic ball. Doesn't hurt if it hits you."

"Don't want to play, Dad," pleaded Claude.

"I was the best shortstop Chazy Central ever graduated. You better learn to play and you better be good at it."

With full force, Sonny winged another one at his son. Claude didn't even attempt a swing, but closed his eyes in fear as the ball passed harmlessly to his right.

"You coulda' had that one!" shouted Sonny.

Claude then dropped the bat and began to sprint with all his might towards his house.

"Mommy!"

"Get back here, you little girl, you little sissy-la-la", shouted Sonny, as he began to run after his son.

Mike Gonyea, Sonny's best buddy, was just making his way out into the field carrying a fresh six pack of beer.

"Ah, let him go Sonny. He's just a kid."

Gonyea then broke a can loose from its plastic ring and threw it to Sonny, shouting, "Heads up! Line drive hit to Rapant!"

Sonny caught it, ending pursuit of his fleet-footed son.

"Snagged by Rapant," bragged Sonny.

He then popped the top, foam coming out in a spray, and drained the can in several large swallows.

"Thanks man, I was as dry as a cork."

The two men made their way down to where the ball bat lay in the grass. Gonyea picked it up and took several practice cuts.

"Sorry I didn't make it to the bar last night, got tied up with the old lady. How was business?" asked Gonyea.

"Sucked. I keep telling Dad we got to get rid of that country music crowd. They're nothin' but draft beer drinkers and I'm sick to death of those songs."

Sonny cleared his throat and closed his eyes.

"I love to fuck in ma' pick-up truck," he sang.

Gonyea laughed, took another swing with the bat and asked, "So what happens next?"

"Nothin.' Not a goddamn thing," answered Sonny. "Dad's so friggin' loyal to those shit-kickers. Won't change a thing."

Sonny then stuck out an open hand and said, "Gimme the bat."

Gonyea took one last cut and then flipped it to his buddy, the bat spinning end over end three times before being snatched out of the air by Sonny.

Sonny then stuffed the empty beer can into his back pocket and took several measured swings.

"If I had my way," he began, "I'd turn the place into a rock and roll club. Mix those fancy little girlie drinks and charge top dollar.

Imported beer only, get rid of them piss-water kegs."

Sonny extracted the beer can from his back pocket and held it up with one hand, poised, ready to become a projectile.

"And maybe, just maybe you know what I might start bringin' in?"

"No, what's that?" asked Mike.

"Some of those strippers, them exotic dancers like we seen in Montreal."

With that, Sonny lofted the can into the air and with one, precise, violent swing connected, sending it skyward with a loud clank.

Gonyea reached up and tugged at an earlobe.

"I think there's some town ordinance against topless, Sonny."

"Fuck the ordinance."

Mike walked over, slapped his friend on the shoulder, and grinned.

"Right, fuck the ordinance. Sound like good ideas but for right now, partner, you got to go burn some burgers. That's why your wife sent me out here."

Sonny nodded.

"Yeah, I suppose I am gettin' hungry."

Rapant's pick-up was parked in the field, he and Claude having ridden out to their make-shift ball diamond. Sonny retrieved the wiffle ball from where it lay after his last pitch and then tossed both ball and bat into the bed of his vehicle.

"Take the truck?" asked Gonyea.

"Let's walk," answered Sonny, skinning off his T-shirt.

The two men began their trek back towards the house where a swimming pool, guests, and a hot barbecue grill awaited them.

As they walked, Mike turned to Sonny, and smiled.

"Exotic dancers, eh?"

"Mmmhmm," replied Sonny. "Big bouncin' boobs and bare

asses."

Reaching the deck he'd built onto the back of his house, Sonny went directly to a boombox that sat silent on top of an empty ice chest, sorted through some tapes that were scattered about, and slipped an *AC/DC* cassette into the player, cranking the volume to three-quarters maximum.

Not far from the boombox, Millie, with Claude cowering behind her, stood next to the gas grill.

As soon as the music began to pour out of the speakers, Sonny whirled on her.

"You too lazy to put in another tape? Best way to kill a good party is to let the music die!"

"I was busy, Sonny," Millie shouted over the din of the band's screaming lead singer.

"Some people are busy scratchin' their ass, woman!"

Millie gritted her teeth, lifted a platter of uncooked hamburger patties from the side rack of the grill, and held it out to him.

Sonny's lips curled into an ugly sneer and he leaned in closer to his wife.

"You that helpless you can't put the meat on the grill?"

Millie reddened and her eyes began to blink rapidly.

"I-I thought that you liked– "

"I-I Aye *yi yi yi*, what are you a fuckin' Mexican?"

Sonny then feigned a lunge at Claude, shook his head in disgust, and marched off the deck.

The Rapant's guests were sprinkled about the property, in small groups and pockets, some sitting in Adirondack chairs on the lawn, some standing in the driveway looking under the hood of a new car, and some swimming laps or treading water in the pool.

No one had heard Sonny as he berated his wife, the blasting rock music covering his words of belittlement.

Sonny found Mike and his wife Joan, a large woman who shared her husband's penchant for tattoos, in chairs under a weeping willow. A single can of beer, unopened, sat at Mike's feet.

"Mine," announced Sonny, pointing at the solitary brew.

"Go ahead, buddy."

"Shouldn't you be cooking?" asked Joan.

"I look like I got the word chef written on my forehead?" asked Sonny, snatching the beer off the grass. "Don't you start with me, too."

Joan's eyes narrowed.

"You always gotta be so nasty?" she asked.

"Can't help myself, it's genetical."

Joan pushed herself up out of the chair.

"I think I'd rather spend time in the company of your wife," she announced, and lumbered off.

"Good, and tell her I want my burger medium rare," Sonny called out after her, and promptly plopped down in the chair she'd vacated.

About a minute passed, Sonny sipping his beer, Mike surveying the yard from behind mirrored aviators.

"She's pissed," said Gonyea, not looking at Sonny.

"Yep, that she is."

"She's gonna want an apology."

"She and Millie both," agreed Sonny. "I will...later. But for right now you better check out Luanne before she dives in."

Luanne Morrison, a willowy brunette who had been a friend of Millie's since high school, stood at the end of the diving board, wearing black bikini bottoms and a   bandeau top she had recently purchased at a boutique in Plattsburgh.

Talking with a male friend who was treading water in the deep end of the pool, she held cupped hands to her forehead, shading her eyes from a bright sun.

On tip toes, Sonny made his way across the lawn, sneaked up behind her, putting a finger to his lips when the friend who was treading water saw him approach.

The swimmer smiled and kept talking to Luanne, thinking Sonny was about to push her in.

With one fluid motion Sonny stepped up onto the board and with both hands grabbed onto her bandeau top and yanked it down around her belly.

Instinctively, she quickly crossed her arms over her breasts but not before Sonny had turned back to where Gonyea sat under the willow, let out a warhoop, and shouted, "Never mind the Montreal girls, Mike, we got our own homegrown talent right here!"

"You bastard," she hissed at him.

Sonny only laughed, hopped off the board, and headed back to his chair.

Luanne then looked down at her friend in the water, whose face held a pained expression.

"Why didn't you warn me that asshole was coming, you had to have seen him?" she asked.

"I did, but..."

"Look away," she growled, waited until he did, and deftly pulled her top back up where it belonged.

From the deck, Millie and Joan Gonyea had watched the entire show.

"How do you put up with that?" asked Joan, her voice dripping disgust.

Millie pressed her spatula down onto a hamburger, squeezing out fat and juices that caused the flames to flare.

"Oh, he's harmless," she answered wearily. "Just a big kid who never grew up."

Millie wiped her sweat-beaded brow with the back of her hand.

"You want a hamburg, Joan?"

*   *   *   *

Robert Charbonneau, who earlier that morning had exaggerated his symptoms so as to appear too sick to accompany his father and sister to the jamboree in Plattsburgh, sat at the small table in his living room, filling in colors on the canvasboard of a paint-by-numbers (kittens playing with a ball of yarn). He was feeling much better, having relieved himself of the pressure of a performance, and no longer suffered a runny nose and a slight headache, thanks to a recent dosing of Sudafed and Tylenol respectively.

He was just commencing to paint a smile on the smaller of the two kittens, when his mother entered the room.

Without looking up, he told her, "Gonna be a famous artist someday. Gonna make it big. Only a matter of time before I get uncovered."

The first kitten's smile finished, he moved onto the second's.

"You mean discovered."

"Yeah."

"Robert, you are your father's son," she said with a smile.

Robert stopped painting, screwed up his face, and looked at her as if she were the one who was developmentally delayed.

"Heck," he snorted, "ev'rybody knows *that*."

He then lifted his brush from the canvasboard, blew lightly on the painting, and declared, "Done."

June edged closer to inspect her son's most recent creation.

"Beautiful job...as always."

"Can I get another one? The IGA's open 'til six."

"How are you feeling?'

"Lot better."

"I'll get my purse, but I want you to ride straight to the store and straight back. No side trips, no dawdling. You've still got a cold, I don't want you to get overheated. And when you get back it'll be time for me to give you more medicine."

"Right," he said, with a quick nod. "Straight to the store, straight back."

"Now go get your helmet."

Some years earlier, the Town of Chazy had passed a law requiring all youngsters under the age of sixteen to wear a helmet when riding a bike. Wendell had perused the ones for purchase at the Wal-Mart but deemed them sissyish and overpriced, so he and Robert began a quest through the Saturday morning garage sales in search of adequate head protection.

Wendell always had pretty good luck at finding his desired items at the sales. At twelve, when Robert, having learned on his sister Chantelle's bike, finally mastered the balance required for riding a two-wheeler, Wendell had first checked out the boys bikes at Montgomery Ward in Champlain. Selecting a yellow Huffy 10 speed for his son, Wendell had plunked down five crisp twenties, believing that the bills would cover purchase price and tax on the eighty nine dollar, ninety five cent bicycle.

"You realize sir, there is an assembly charge," the clerk had said nonchalantly, while beginning to ring up the sale.

Wendell's eyes had widened, his hands closed into fists.

"A hunnerd dollar bicycle and it isn't even put together?"

"No sir."

With that, Wendell's right hand had opened, swooped down and scooped up his money.

As he stalked out of the store, the clerk had called out after him, "Sir, I'm not sure but we might have a display model for sale. Sir? Sir?"

The next day, at a garage sale in Rousses Point, Wendell had laid eyes on a gleaming silver spray-painted Stingray, replete with banana seat, twenty inch wheels and apehanger handlebars. Thirty five dollars later, the bike was in the back of Wendell's wagon, en route back home to Robert.

Wendell knew that he had taken a chance, having bought the bike unseen by Robert's eyes, so he stopped at a hardware store before going home.

When Wendell's toe finally pushed the kickstand into place, the bike stood in the Charbonneau driveway, literally dripping with add-ons and accessories – a chrome bell, a black rubber-bulbed horn, red reflectors attached to both the front and back wheel's spokes, twin black leatherette saddle bags, a diamond-cut silver reflector bolted to the rails of the banana seat, and two multicolored plastic streamers, one shoved into each of the handlebar ends.

For Robert, it was love at first sight. And as the years passed, and Robert's legs grew, Wendell was always able to find one more inch in the seat post.

Although Robert had liked the helmets at Wal-Mart, especially the purple one with day-glo stickers, Wendell had told his son that they could do better at a garage sale. Their first find was a World War II German "coal bucket" army helmet offered by a neighbor down the road. Although it fit, it made Robert's head list to the left under the weight of all the steel. That, along with the laughter, salutes, and shouts of "Sig Heil" and "Achtung" from his father and neighbors ruined any possibility of Robert accepting the headgear as a suitable piece of equipment.

Their second stop had been in Mooers, at an elderly woman's front lawn where a sign announced, *Tag Sale* – the phrase favored in Vermont. Sitting on the seat of a cheaply made rowing machine was a white football helmet, twin red stripes running from front to back and sporting a full face mask.

Wendell had spied it first, picked it up slowly, and given it a close inspection. Although it bore no visible cracks or splits, the helmet held streaks of grass stains and an abundance of small black rub marks.

"Seen some action," Wendell had whispered to himself.

Robert, who had been instantly drawn to a card table covered with blown glass animals, was summoned by his father.

After placing it on Robert's head and securing the chin strap, Wendell gave the helmet several whacks with his open hand.

"Stop it!" cried Robert.

"Just testin' it out, Son. Think this one will serve you well. You like it?"

"Yeah."

Wendell had then waved the old woman over and asked her for a price, for although this was a tag sale, Wendell was unable to find any type of tag, label, or sticker affixed to the helmet.

She had quoted him an asking price of three fifty, hoping Wendell would make the purchase and that he and his son would soon leave, as Robert had caused a serious spike in her blood pressure, what with all his touching and holding of her glass animal menagerie.

So the helmet was purchased, Wendell and Robert smiling broadly and the old woman finally exhaling when the two walked to their car, got in, and drove off.

Robert returned from his room several minutes later, the helmet having come to reside there on a hook so that a family member could always ensure he left the house wearing it. He met his mother at the front door, he securing the chin strap, she pulling cash from her wallet.

She held out five one dollar bills, but before he could take them, she pulled her hand back.

"Remember, Honey, ride on the right hand side of the road. The *right* hand side."

"I know!" replied Robert, annoyed.

"Then show me your right hand."

Robert slowly brought his hands up in front of himself and, with thumb and forefinger, fashioned capital Ls with both hands, one forward, one backward.

His mother crept around in back of him. Pointing a finger over his left shoulder, she told him, "Now see how your left hand forms the correct L. L is the first letter of the word left. So if that's your left hand, your other hand must be...?"

Robert quickly closed his hand into a fist and pumped it triumphantly into the air.

"My right!"

June planted a soft little kiss on her son's neck and, once again, held out the five dollars, which Robert promptly snatched and stuffed into his jeans pocket.

"Thank you."

"Be careful."

Outside, Robert swung a leg over his Stingray, pushed off with his right foot, and quickly got his feet on top of the pedals. Bearing down hard with the left leg, then the right, he built up sufficient momentum to stabilize the bike. In no time at all he was at the end of the driveway, looking left, then right for any oncoming traffic, ready to brave the open road.

In order to head in the direction of the IGA grocery store, where at least three or four different paint-by-number sets awaited him, he needed to turn left onto county route 309 and travel about two miles. This would first involve crossing both lanes of traffic, veering left, and then riding on the shoulder of the right lane, as cars and trucks passed alongside him, towards the store.

But rather than proceeding across the road, inexplicably, Robert turned his bike sideways, so it appeared as though he would set out towards the right, taking him away from town, and out towards pastures and farmland.

He brought his hands up in front of his face, formed the capital
Ls, closed his right fist and looked down the road towards town over his
right shoulder.

"Right hand side," he said aloud.

Bringing his front wheel around, he pedaled onto the shoulder of
the left lane, and soon began riding decidedly *against* the flow of
oncoming traffic.

The driver of the third car that rolled past him tooted the horn,
scowled, and pointed to the opposite side of the road. Robert, thinking
him friendly, returned the greeting with a grin and a squeeze on the bulb
of his own horn.

John Millington, a dairy farmer who lived down the road from
the Charbonneaus, was also en route to the IGA on a mission to buy beer
and some snack food, anticipating a well deserved afternoon flopped in
front of the TV, watching a ball game.

Alarmed when he discovered Robert riding against traffic, he
feathered the brakes on his El Camino and slowed almost to a crawl.

From across the road he called out, "Robert, my friend, you're
on the wrong side of the road."

Catching him unaware, Robert being lost in thought as to
whether he'd have enough money for a paint set *and* an ice cream
sandwich, the boy's head jerked up and then over, locating the sound of
the voice.

"What?"

"You should riding over here...on *this* side."

Robert shook his head.

"No, Mom says ride on the right side."

"This *is* the right side."

Robert shook his head again, this time more vigorously.

"No, right side's over here."

He then attempted to form his finger Ls which only resulted in a dangerous wobble of the front wheel of the bike.

Millington, frustrated, shrugged his shoulders and eased his foot down onto the accelerator.

"Well, just be careful."

Robert glared at him.

"I know that."

With Millington gone Robert went back to thinking about the money in his pocket, the new paint set which would make the return trip secure in one of his saddlebags, and the ice cream sandwich, which he hoped, would soon be melting on his tongue.

*   *   *   *

Kelly Cobb, nee Harrington, had celebrated her recent divorce by getting quite drunk early on, soon after she'd arrived at the Rapant's for the Sunday afternoon barbecue.

When the rest of the group was ready to eat, Millie Rapant was unable to rouse her from sleep, Kelly having lain down on her back poolside after having consumed three quick shots of Jagermeister, a one milligram Ativan, and at least four ice cold Heneiken chasers.

Upon seeing his wife's efforts, Sonny quipped, "Let her sleep. She's gonna need to lose a few pounds now that she's a dee-vor-say."

Now, an hour and a half later, still snoring soundly in the sun, the green-eyed red head, clad in cut-offs, sandals, and a pink tank top, was beginning to burn, her face, legs, and arms well on their way to an angry red.

Concerned, Millie and Joan helped Kelly to a standing position, whereupon she doubled over and vomited, spattering the tops of her sunburned feet and covering the headrest of a nearby inflatable pool float.

Next, Kelly came forth with a stream of mumbled apologies,

with Millie and Joan assuring the still-drunk woman that no harm had been done.

"Sonny," called Millie, "can you drive her home?"

Sonny had folded himself back into the chair next to Mike Gonyea after the two had consumed their fill of burgers, beer, and macaroni salad.

"Yeah, I suppose so," replied Sonny, affecting a deliberate tone of disinterest for the task.

As Sonny rose from the chair, Gonyea reached over and grabbed his arm.

"You ain't shittin' nobody, partner."

Sonny twisted his arm loose, raised his eyebrows, and broke into a wide, mischievous grin.

"Best of my knowledge, Kel hasn't dropped her drawers since she threw the husband out. No reason why I shouldn't be the first she gives it up for."

Gonyea snickered and Sonny headed out to the field where his truck was parked.

While Sonny retrieved his pick-up, Joan and Millie managed to back Kelly into a webbed chair next to the pool. Joan then wiped Kelly's mouth with a wet napkin while Millie went inside in search of Solarcaine.

By the time Sonny pulled his truck up alongside the pool, Kelly was on her feet, with the front of her arms, legs, and shoulders wearing a light coating of the topical anesthetic.

"That white shit better not stain," warned Sonny from the driver's seat, as the two women loaded Kelly into the passenger side and buckled her in. "Just had my interior detailed."

"Men and their precious little toys," mocked Joan, as she adjusted the shoulder belt.

"I don't mind bein' the Good Samaritan here, but if this chick pukes in my truck she'll be crawlin' the rest of the way home."

Joan glared at Sonny, gingerly raised the shoulder belt a little higher, turned, and walked off.

Millie gently took hold of Kelly's chin and turned her head towards her own.

"Sonny's gonna take you home, Kel. Get some sleep...you'll be all right."

Kelly, who now appeared to keep her head lowered, her eyes half-open, and her mouth shut due more to remorse than drunkenness simply mumbled yet another, "I'm sorry."

Millie then looked over at her husband, her faced lined with concern.

"I'll get someone to drop her car off later. Now, when you get her into the house, make sure you lay her on her side, that way– "

"Yeah, yeah I know so she doesn't pull a Jimi Hendrix on us," said Sonny, shoving the stick into first gear and easing out the clutch.

Kelly Harrington Cobb lived in a neat little brown and white modular with a 20 year mortgage on county route 309, approximately five miles past the Charbonneau barn house. It would constitute approximately a 25 minute drive from the Rapant's.

Sonny had hoped that the fresh air pouring in through the open windows and vents would have revived the woman, but ten minutes into the ride Kelly was again snoring soundly.

"Cobb?" asked Sonny in a loud, obnoxious voice. "Is that like in 'I cobbed up the job' or is it more like corn on the cob."

No response.

"You probably didn't know this little known fact," he continued, "but people used to wipe their asses with corn cobs. Did you know that, Kel? Used to scrape the old bung hole with a corn cob."

He looked over at the snoring woman whose head bobbed and rolled with the bumps.

Sonny pulled a cigarette from a pack on the dash, and looked over once again, focusing on the expanses of white anesthetic that remained on her thighs.

"Looks like King Kong spooed on you, Kel. Is that what happened, Kel? King Kong spoo on you?"

Kelly continued sleeping.

Sonny scratched his lighter to life and pulled in his first puff.

"Yeah, I think that's what happened, Kel. King Kong spooed on you. Spooed on you!"

Sonny depressed the clutch and eased on his brakes, obeying a stop sign. Foregoing his signal light, he shifted into first and turned right onto route 309.

He took another drag off his cigarette and again looked over at his passenger. The stop had caused her legs to splay and she'd slumped a bit more in her seat, causing her cut-offs to rise towards her crotch.

Sonny was then privy to a section of thigh that had remained untouched by a searing sun. He felt a tingle in his testicles.

He transferred his cigarette from his left hand to his mouth, gripped the wheel with his left, and sent his right out on an exploratory mission.

Ever so lightly, he let the four fingers of his right hand come to rest on the inside of Kelly's left thigh.

She remained asleep.

He inhaled smoke deep into his lungs and exhaled twin jets through his nostrils.

Singling out his middle finger, he slid the digit up between the jeans material and her thigh until he felt the silk of her panties.

His lower lip quivered with desire, losing hold of the cigarette, and allowing it to drop into his own crotch.

Sonny came up out of his seat with start, causing the cigarette to roll back farther on the cushion.

His truck was just coming up over a bend.

Reclaiming his right hand, he began to claw frantically at the seat cushion, his eyes finally locating the errant smoke, his hand brushing it quickly to the floor.

When he looked back up and through the windshield he realized that his left hand had hooked his vehicle onto the shoulder and he was headed straight into the path of bicyclist Robert Charbonneau.

Jerking a hard left on the wheel, Sonny stood on the brake pedal with both feet, throwing the truck sideways, the vehicle finally coming to stop in the middle of the road with series of ugly shudders.

Robert kept on pedaling.

Sonny flew out of his truck, stood in the middle of the road, and began screaming.

"You fucking idiot retard! Could have got yourself killed! Could have killed us all!"

CHAPTER 5

As Spinosa's Westfalia was pulling into the Charbonneau driveway, Patrice was in her room, frosting her lips with just the lightest layer of lipstick, and Robert was at his table, about a third of the way from completion of the paint set purchased late Sunday afternoon at the IGA.

Robert had chosen birds, bright red cardinals, alight in a tree that blossomed with little yellow flowers. He had also chosen not to disclose his encounter with Sonny to anyone in his family, fearing that his Mom or Dad would rescind his riding privileges.

The panic stop Sonny had thrown his truck into had succeeded in awakening Kelly Cobb once and for all. Coming out of her drunken slumber, she expressed a strong feeling of nausea, to which Sonny quickly instructed her to hang her head out the window for the remainder of the trip. Upon reaching her house she mumbled a thank you, let herself out of the truck, and, with head hanging, walked unassisted up to the front door.

Frustrated, no longer interested in a woman prone to puking, and still pissed about his near head-on with Robert, Sonny had spewed forth a stream of curses, thrown the truck in reverse, and burned about six months of rubber off his tires exiting Kelly's driveway.

The Charbonneau practice area was an rambling, unfinished room on the ground floor near the back of the barn. A half dozen raggedy throw rugs lay helter-skelter on a plywood floor and several small space heaters, which proved fairly efficient in the late fall and winter, sat unplugged near the outlets that they shared with guitar amps, the PA system and Rhythm Ace.

In summer, however, the room could become beastly hot. Wanting to make conditions as comfortable as possible for Spinosa, as soon as Wendell arrived home from cleaning septics he'd placed a fan in one of the windows and loaded beers and soft drinks into a large metal wash tub packed with ice and set it in the center of the floor.

Wendell wanted so to impress the young man, portray his family as the consummate professionals, demonstrate that he and his kids had what it would take to make the big time.

But Dominic was already impressed, having left the jamboree for awhile and then returned, finding a seat in the stands and catching the entire Charbonneau act. He found the instrumentation adequate, the two part harmony acceptable, and the twenty-two-year-old daughter absolutely gorgeous.

Wendell met Spinosa at the front door wearing a new brown shirt with a red rose embroidered over each breast pocket, brown relaxed-fit polyester pants June had recently purchased for him at Ames, and his battered brown cowboy boots sporting a fresh coat of Esquire shoe polish. Spinosa wore a gaudy Hawaiian shirt – mocha-colored natives paddling outrigger canoes, hula dancers, bare-breasted, but for the exception of a strategically placed lei, orchids, palm trees, and pineapples all cast upon a pale blue fabric – faded and ripped jeans, and a new pair of Tevas.

The two men shook hands and Wendell took Spinosa's guitar case into the practice room. Spinosa went back to his camper, retrieved his amp, and re-entered the house. When he made his way into the room, Robert was trailing.

Taking one look at his son, Wendell was instantly enraged, fearing that the boy's appearance would make Spinosa think he'd walked into a houseful of hillbillies as Robert was clad in a yellow-at-the-armpits T-shirt, a stained pair of white and blue satin shorts that at one time looked as though they had done duty as the lower half of a regulation gym outfit, and bare feet.

But Wendell's rage melted as his daughter stepped quietly into the room.

The CK one she had dabbed behind her knees and at her wrists quickly filled the stuffy room with a light, citrusy aroma. She wore an immaculate sleeveless cotton print sun dress and Huarache sandals. Her hair was down, and gave off the distinctive odor of almonds.

"Dominic, I don't think you've met my son, Robert," said Wendell.

Dominic placed his amp on the floor, turned and shook hands with Robert.

"And you remember Patrice," he added.

"Of course," returned Dominic, and nodded.

Patrice smiled and nodded back.

Wendell, Patrice, and Dominic all unpacked and, in between small talk and comments about the heat and the humidity, began the necessary ritual of tuning their guitars. Robert took his tambourine out of a small scrap-wood case labeled "Robert Charbonneau" that Wendell had made for him, and out of nerves, began shaking the instrument wildly, ceasing only when his father threatened to send him from the room.

Rhythm Ace had been on his best behavior, Patrice having tinkered with him most of the morning, so he was given the opportunity to practice with the group. For the next forty five minutes, without break, the Charbonneaus, Wendell on guitar, Patrice on bass, Robert on tambourine, and Rhythm Ace the drum machine came forth with a set of their best music.

Spinosa was a quick study, adding tasteful lead guitar to all but one or two of the songs, those being selections with which he was totally unfamiliar.

"You played with Tommy and Tammy for three months and you don't know *Let Your Love Flow* by the Bellamy brothers?" teased Patrice. "I'm sure I've heard them do it."

Dominic lowered his head in mock shame.

"If I did play it, I musta been sleepwalking through it, cause I don't remember a note," he said.

He looked up and saw that she was smiling at him. He held her in a gaze.

"Ya sound good, Dominic, real good," blustered Wendell, breaking their trance. Patrice was the first to look away, then began fiddling with the tone control on her amp.

Dominic continued staring at Patrice but answered, "Thanks Wendell, I like what you folks have, too."

Sensing a break, Robert placed his tambourine back into its case and wandered over towards Spinosa who sat on top of his amplifier. He leaned down over Dominic, taking a closer look at his shirt.

"You like all that Hawaiian stuff on there?" asked Dominic.

"Yeah."

Patrice, bass still slung on her shoulder, strolled on over to where her brother was standing and squinted down hard at the forms and figures on Spinosa's shirt.

"He likes the girls, the girls on your shirt."

"Not wearing any underwear," commented Robert, his eyes wide.

Spinosa pulled a section of the shirt away from his body for closer inspection.

"I suppose you're right. They should have told me this shirt was rated R before I bought it."

Patrice smiled slyly, Robert kept on staring.

"How about another five songs, then we call it a night?" suggested Wendell, whose armpits now wore dark circles from exertion and the heat.

The others agreed, the prescribed five were hammered out, and Dominic's formal audition came to a close.

Although Wendell had drunk several beers during the practice, Spinosa had quenched his thirst with soft drinks. Now that the audition was over, thought Wendell, maybe the boy might like a brew.

"No thanks," answered Spinosa, when Wendell held out a cold one. "The cops see my van, think there are a bunch of old hippies in the back, pull me over and...bang! I got beer on my breath."

"Never a problem for Daddy," quipped Patrice.

"That's enough little girl," chastised Wendell.

Wendell cleared his throat.

"Dominic, I, we'd like to offer you the job."

Spinosa pulled another soft drink from the tub, the ice now reduced to slush, twisted the cap off and looked straight at Patrice. The pinkish glow to her skin and the thin sheen of perspiration she wore from the night's work only heightened his physical attraction for her.

"Well...I accept. I'd very much like to be a part of this."

"Great," said Wendell. "We've got a job this Friday night, so you can leave your amp here if you want. Friday we can all head out together."

"All right," said Dominic.

Wendell's face then drew tight.

"S'cuse me, but I gotta piss like a racehorse," said Wendell.

"Daddy!" said a scowling Patrice.

Dominic smiled and held out his hand.

"I need to take off anyhow. See you Friday."

"Right, lookin' forward to it. When our break comes, my friend, you'll be right there with us."

Physical needs then taking precedence, Wendell shook Dominic's hand quickly and then trotted out of the room on the tips of his boots, his face wearing a decidedly pinched look.

Robert was the next to leave, having cardinals who were in dire need of a smile, and he exited wordlessly, bidding good-bye to Dominic with a grin and a quick wave.

"See ya' Robert."

Dominic looked over at Patrice who stood next to her microphone rolling a can of soda across her forehead. She averted her eyes and with an edge to her voice she offered, "Come on, I'll walk you outside."

Once outdoors, Patrice looked up into a night sky full of stars.

"He doesn't play very well," she said flatly.

"Robert?"

"Well, him too. But I was talking about my father."

"His voice is strong, he's comfortable on stage; we can cover his guitar playing."

Patrice relaxed a bit, and for the first time in a while looked at this brand new band member, this outsider, full in the face, a handsome face that held the soft blue light of the moon.

"We can cover him," he repeated. "Not a problem."

*   *   *   *

The Charbonneau Family Band, with Mr. Dominic Spinosa on lead guitar, had just begun the fourth song of the night, one of Wendell's favorites, *Act Naturally*, with the first line sung being, "They're Gonna Put Me in The Movies...", when a beer bottle crashed onto the dance floor and a belligerent drunk hopped up on stage and grabbed Wendell by the collar.

"And *I'm* gonna put *you* in the hospital if you don't start playing something with some balls in it!"

Everyone stopped playing, except Rhythm Ace, the ancient drum machine continuing to pump out its unwavering moderate tempo shuffle beat.

"Take your seat, pal," said Wendell, his voice trying to control a quaver, "we'll play something you like."

Wendell then turned around to his bandmates.

"Asshole," he whispered.

The bar, named *The Yearlings*, a small roadhouse across from a horse farm, attracted a decidedly biker crowd. In the past, Wendell and company had always been successful at satisfying what could be a very mercurial audience. But tonight, a Saturday in early October, with what would prove to be Dominic's seventh engagement with the Charbonneaus, the band was off to a piss-poor start.

Wendell was scared, and watched his hand shake as he reached for his long-neck Coors. He knew he'd better have just the right selection before he turned back to face that sea of leather jackets and loud mouths.

"You got any ideas?" he asked, directing his question to the rest of the band as a whole.

"How about we go home," suggested Robert, whose eyes were the size of ping-pong balls.

"Can't do that," his father answered.

Rhythm Ace kept on pounding out a shuffle.

"Shut that goddamn thing off, will you 'Treece."

With a quick pass of her hand, the drum machine fell silent.

"Yeah, I got a song," said Dominic, his voice clear and confident.

"Play somethin' or we'll get up there and play it ourselves!" came a threat from the audience.

"Back-up vocals are easy," Dominic began, "and chord-wise you'll have no problem following."

He turned to Patrice.

"Program Rhythm Ace for a basic rock beat, snare hitting on two and four. And give me a loud, splashy, open high-hat sound."

Patrice set about following his directives.

Spinosa then turned to Robert.

"Robert, you bang that tambourine just as hard as you can on the two and four beats."

Robert looked at him blankly. Wendell quickly offered an explanation.

"He's a little shaky on his counting and his numbers sometimes. He usually just follows the sound of the snare."

"Not a problem," assured Dominic. "Robert, you smack that tambourine with all your might when you hear the snare drum, okay?"

"K."

"Other than back-ups, anything you want me and 'Treece to do?" asked Wendell.

Spinosa lowered his head for a split-second, and when he raised it he was smiling.

"Yeah, I want you both to crank your amps to just about max. But Wendell, understand that, for you, this is only for tonight."

"Gotcha'."

As Dominic turned to increase the volume on his own amp, a bottle whizzed past his head and shattered against the wall behind him.

Dominic turned quickly, faced the crowd, and spoke.

"Uh, thanks for your patience. Got a little Bob Seger tune for ya' by the name of 'Ramblin' Gamblin Man'."

Dominic spun his head towards Patrice and shouted, "Now!" Patrice flipped the switch and the drum machine poured a loud, trashy rock and roll beat into the PA speakers.

"That's more like it, junior!" came a voice from the crowd.

On the third bar, Dominic added in some hot guitar licks, and soon the first line of vocals...

"I was born lonely, down by the riverside..."

By the time Dominic reached his guitar solo, many in the crowd were clapping along, Wendell was smiling, Patrice couldn't keep her eyes off Spinosa, and Robert had managed to break three of the jingle disks on his tambourine, raised a welt on the pad of his left hand, and produced a sore spot around mid-thigh of his right leg, having followed Dominic's instructions to the letter.

*   *   *   *

"A hot fudge sundae," pleaded Chantelle Charbonneau to Barry, the driver of her Silver Eagle. "Please, c'mon just find a diner where I can get one."

Barry, a heavy-set black man in his forties, kept his hands on the wheel but turned his head so as to speak to Chantelle, who stood in the aisle, maintaining her balance by holding onto a table, while he navigated the bus through traffic.

"Conroy's gonna be hoppin' mad you start bustin' out of those clothes he wants you to wear on stage."

Chantelle scowled.

"And your wife would be none too pleased to know you've been packin' away the ribs when your doctor told you to start eatin' more rabbit food," she retorted.

Barry let out a low, slow chuckle.

"You got me there."

"C'mon, please Barry. I'm not Elvis, not gonna eat a dozen. I just want one... with whipped cream...and crushed peanuts...and a little maraschino– "

"Come on, Barry," came the voice of Eric her guitarist from his bunk, "The gig sucked, let the kid have a little treat."

"Just like you havin' your little treat, Eric?" taunted Barry, knowing the guitarist was probably on his third or fourth bong hit.

"To each his own, my friend," answered Eric, and coughed once.

"Two against one," said Barry, goodnaturedly. "It appears I'm outnumbered. I seem to recall a greasy spoon not far from here."

"You're a doll," gushed Chantelle, and hugged his neck. "I'm gonna buy you one, too."

Eric was right, the gig had sucked. Chantelle and her band, still openers for Hal Ketchum, had taken the stage in an Austin hall to shouts of "Where's Hal?" and "Hurry on up, Honey." The band's first two songs were lukewarm, with many of the audience members meandering out into the lobby to buy plastic cups of draft beer. Halfway through her fourth song two middle-aged women in straw cowboy hats, glasses, and T-shirts emblazoned with the confederate flag unfurled a home-made banner that read: *This is Ketchum Kountry.*

Stupid old bags, Chantelle had thought to herself. Although Ketchum had paid his dues in the Austin club scene, he was born and raised in Greenwich...New York, a small town about three hours south of Chazy. Ketchum, like her, was a northerner.

Deciding to give the crowd what they wanted, she cut her performance about ten minutes short, thanked them, wished them good night, and walked off to polite, albeit disinterested, applause.

It was about 11:10 p.m. when Barry and Chantelle walked into the *Farmer Boy*, a chrome and plate glass diner just on the outskirts of Austin. It was a Saturday night, most of the tables were full, but the two found open stools at the counter.

As she entered, Chantelle found herself aware of the unkind stares and mean sidelong glances of some of the patrons in the restaurant, age not being a distinguishing factor as she and Barry drew the attention of blue-haired ladies in frilly square dance dresses as well as the young bucks in their carefully curled Stetsons and painted-on Levis. Judgmental looks, she decided as she took her seat, that also were not determined by geography, as she could imagine seeing the same hatred in the eyes of diners in beautiful downtown Chazy.

The thoughts were bringing her down even further, and her intent of stopping at the restaurant was to end the night with something that would bring her at least transitory comfort and happiness.

She snatched the menu from its coiled wire holder, and began flipping through it in search of the dessert section.

Barry, who sat with his hands on the counter, fingers interlaced, looking like a preacher about to say grace, remarked, "You must be hungry, girl."

"Barry, sometimes I think I'm starvin' to death."

Barry began to twiddle his thumbs.

"I know what you're sayin', but you gotta trust in Conroy, he's a good man, knows what he's doin', seen him boost a lot of young hopefuls to the top – The Forrester Sisters, Lee Roy Parnell, Sweethearts of the Rodeo..."

"But for sure you're not going to tell me about the ones you've seen who crashed and burned."

Barry stopped twiddling and looked several feet beyond her.

"I don't think that would be helpful, especially tonight."

"Ready to order, folks?"

Barry and Chantelle looked up to see their waitress, a grinning platinum blonde of about thirty.

Chantelle snapped the plastic-encased menu closed.

"Hot fudge sundaes, two, with the works."

The waitress began scribbling.

"You want soda water with those?"

"No I don't want any soda, I just want my ice cream," answered Chantelle, sounding like a bratty child.

"She doesn't mean like a Pepsi or a Coke. Soda water is like club soda, clear, with bubbles, carbonation, some people like it with ice cream," explained Barry.

"Oh, okay, sure," chirped Chantelle, feeling a little foolish.

Within minutes, two large hot fudge sundaes, two long spoons, and two small glasses of soda water arrived in front of them.

"Take a sip of your soda water first, it sort of clears your tongue, your palate," instructed Barry.

"Barry, you old bon vivant, you!" joked Chantelle, but obeyed his directive.

Palates having been cleansed, the two dug into their confections.

"Heaven," proclaimed Chantelle after she'd placed a spoonful of hot fudge on her tongue.

"Wait until she's finished eating, Honey," spoke a soft male voice from behind the two.

Chantelle stuck her spoon in the mountain of vanilla that remained, wiped her mouth on a napkin, and spun around on her stool.

There stood a little girl, about nine years of age, dressed in a fitted gray suit of western styling, matching gray boots, and a grey cowboy hat with a string snugged tight just under her chin. In her hands she held a paper napkin and a ball point pen. Several yards away stood a man, presumably her father, dressed in identical clothing.

"Excuse me, ah don't want to interrupt your dinner, but ah saw you tonight and ah thought you were rill good," said the little girl.

"The Ketchum Concert," added the father.

"Yes, I seem to remember I was there," replied Chantelle, acidly.

The father smiled weakly, shifted his weight from one leg to the other.

"Could ah have your autograph?" requested the little girl sweetly.

"My pleasure," said Chantelle, taking the napkin and the pen from her hands. "What's your name, Darlin'?"

"Mary Lee."

As Chantelle began to write, Mary Lee told her, "Ma Daddy has a band too, but he took tonight off so we could go to the concert."

Chantelle finished the autograph and handed it, along with the pen, back to Mary Lee.

"Ma Daddy is teaching me the git-tar, and I'm takin' singin' lessons, too. Someday I'm gonna play in his band."

"That's great, honey," said Chantelle.

"What do you say to Miss..." prodded Mary Lee's father.

"Chantelle, Chantelle Charbonneau."

"Thank you, Miss Chantelle," said the little girl, smiling ear-to-ear, clutching the autographed napkin to her breast, and walking back to where her father was standing.

Chantelle noticed that some of the same diners were again staring at her, but differently now, seeing that she had been transformed from a cheap whore with an old black dude to some sort of celebrity in a matter of about two minutes.

Mary Lee's father nodded to Chantelle, put his arm on his little girl's shoulders and walked her back to their table. The peripheral vision that held the other diners faded, and all Chantelle saw was a father and his daughter.

When Chantelle turned back to the sundae, her appetite was gone. She dug into her purse and produced a cigarette, lighted it, and drew in the first few puffs as if pulling in oxygen.

"I'm sorry, Miss," said the platinum-haired waitress, "the counter is part of our non-smoking section, I can get you a table in our smoking– "

"No, that won't be necessary," croaked Chantelle, taking one last drag and then pushing her cigarette deep into her sundae. "We're done."

She stood, grabbed some bills from her purse, dropped them on the counter, turned to a stunned Barry and announced, "I'm tired, let's go."

*   *   *   *

A two car caravan, with Wendell leading in his station wagon and Spinosa following in his Westfalia, pulled into the Charbonneau driveway about 3:00 a.m. The band had made it through four sets of music at the biker bar, collected their pay, packed the equipment, and headed on out into the night.

Although the Charbonneau repertoire was, and always had been, predominantly country, Dominic managed to place a rock song in each one of the sets, reading the tone of the crowd and sending one out when he sensed a general unrest or judged the audience to be tiring of shuffle beats.

By the third set, the crowd had thinned and the bar flies who remained could have cared less about what was coming from the bandstand.

Robert rode with his father, and Patrice had chosen to go in Spinosa's van. When the two vehicles pulled up to the front of the barn, Robert was snoring soundly.

Wendell killed the engine and stepped out into the early morning. The temperature had dropped, probably hovering at just about freezing, and he could see his breath.

Fatigue hung on him like a heavy overcoat. He felt like he was a hundred years old. He looked back at Dominic and his daughter as they were opening their doors.

"Would you kids mind unloading my equipment? I'm all tuckered out."

"Sure," replied Dominic.

"We'll get it, Dad. Go on to bed," said Patrice.

"I will. Gotta get your brother first."

Wendell leaned back into his station wagon and shook his son gently.

"C'mon Robert. C'mon old pal. Time to get up. Time to get into your own bed."

Robert stirred and mumbled, "Not an idiot. Right side of the road."

"No, you're not an idiot," assured Wendell. "You're my son, you're a good boy, and I love you."

Wendell pulled on the boy's arm, Robert awakened, and slid groggily across the bench seat out his father's door and into the night air.

"Cold!" he said with a shiver.

"Yes, it's cold, Robert, now let's get inside."

Dominic handed his keys to Patrice.

"I'll unload your dad's car. You grab the stuff in the back of mine."

Patrice went around to the back of his van, opened the hatch, stuck the key ring in her mouth, and pulled out two microphone stands, a canvas bag containing extra guitar leads and PA wires, and a molded plastic box containing Dominic's microphone. She left his amp and guitar knowing that, unlike her father, he liked to practice on his own in between their group rehearsals.

Dominic had already hauled in her bass amp and her father's amp when she met him in the practice room. She deposited the stands in the center of the room and lay the bag and microphone box off into a corner. Taking the key ring from her mouth she looked down and began to study it.

"What's nahh?" she asked.

"Huh?"

"This medallion on your keyring, what's nahh mean?"

He sat down on her amp, flipped a lock of his hair up out of his eyes, and smiled.

"It's En - a...stands for Narcotics Anonymous. I'm in recovery."

"Oh," she said, shrinking a bit. She walked over to him and held out the keys.

He looked her straight in the eye.

"I'm an addict, a coke addict. You ever known an addict

before?"

"A few kids in my high school used to smoke pot on the weekends."

"I'll take that as a no."

A very long moment passed.

"I got ten months clean," he announced.

"That's really good!" she responded, with a bit too much enthusiasm.

"It's not bad."

Another moment dragged.

"I answered your question, now you answer mine," said Dominic.

"Shoot."

"Outside," he said.

Once the two had walked out into the night, Dominic sidled up next to Wendell's car and pointed up at the sign strapped to his roof that read: *"Ask Me How Western Auto Ruined My Motor."*

Patrice laughed out loud, but then remembering that the rest of the house was sleeping, covered her mouth with her hand.

When she composed herself, she began,

"Daddy claims they sold him a defective oil filter...the one up there on the roof. Says that after he changed his oil, put in the new filter, and started the car, the insides just tore out and got sucked up into the engine."

Dominic reached up onto the roof and ran his fingers over the filter.

"Feels pretty dented in. What did Western Auto say?"

"They said he probably crushed it when he screwed it on," answered Patrice, adding, "Daddy does have an arm like a torque wrench."

"So they wouldn't make good on it?" asked Spinosa.

"Nope. So Daddy stuck the sign up. Figures by now he's kept hundreds of people away from Western Auto."

"What do you think?" asked Dominic.

"Maybe a few…those crazy enough to believe his story."

Patrice again began to laugh, and this time Dominic joined her.

Dominic then cast a glance out towards the road.

"Well, I better– "

"You ever seen my shop?" Patrice interrupted.

"No, can't say that I have."

"C'mon," she said. "I'll show you."

*   *   *   *

Nestled down in his bed, sleep eluding him, Wendell stared at the ceiling. He exhaled loudly, then poked at his wife.

"June, you awake?"

"Am now," she murmured. "What do you want?"

"He saved our asses tonight."

"Who?"

"Dominic."

"Well that's good to know someone who'll save your ass every once in a while," said June. "Now try and get some sleep, Wen."

Wendell turned on his side to face her.

"June?"

"Mmm?"

"He's a keeper, he's gonna stick, he's coming with us to the top."

June opened her eyes, and in the dim bedroom light made contact with her husband's sleepless orbs.

"Don't be so sure. He's got that camper for a reason."

*   *   *   *

As Patrice opened the door to her shop, she was greeted with a damp cold, the temperature feeling even lower than outdoors. Her outfit, a new jean jacket over a simple white blouse matched with a long blue, broomstick skirt was fine for the club, but much too thin for the early morning chill that had settled in. In her arms she held Rhythm Ace, who, although he had performed reliably in the first three sets, had begun to malfunction in the last and was being brought in for a check-up. She reached out a hand and flipped on the single fluorescent overhead.

She went directly to her low workbench, set the drum machine down, bent at the waist, and began fiddling with some of the dials.

"I'm usually too wound up after a job to sleep, so I usually come in here and work on a project or make repairs. But I tell you, I'm getting awfully tired of fooling with this old machine. I keep telling Daddy we need to upgrade. There's a place in town that has a used Roland for sale."

"Uh-huh," said Dominic, only half listening as his eyes swept the cozy 9x12 shop, catching sight of the beginnings of a small plywood practice amp, speakers of various sizes piled neatly in corners, shelves holding a VCR, old radio tuners, a cassette deck, and a pegboard laden with pliers, screwdrivers, soldering irons, and coils of wire. His eyes drifted down off the pegboard, past the circuitboards that lay on the work bench, and came to rest on the tight and rounded rear-end of Patrice.

"This is nice, cute, I like it," said Dominic.

Patrice looked over her left shoulder and caught him in the act. She quickly straightened and turned to face him, her cheeks beginning to flush.

"Do, do you have any, uh, interest in fixing or working on e-electronics?" she stammered.

"No, not really. I just like to plug in and play," he said, a mischievous smile finding its way onto his lips.

A shiver shot through Patrice.

"How about you build us a fire," she suggested, pointing to a tiny woodstove in the corner. " I'm freezing."

"Sure."

Next to the stove was a short stack of newspapers and pile of firewood. As he began selecting several pieces he could use for kindling, a gray field mouse ran from the pile.

"Hey!" he exclaimed, startled.

"What's the matter?" asked Patrice, plugging Rhythm Ace into an outlet.

"Just a little mouse."

"A mouse? Oh my God, there's a mouse in here?"

She turned around and sat herself down on the bench next to the drum machine.

"Please don't let him run up my leg, Dominic, please."

She quickly hiked her long skirt up several inches past her knees.

"I won't. But first I gotta find the little bugger. I think he ran..."

The rodent suddenly streaked across the center of the shed.

"I think he's hiding behind those speakers," said Patrice in high squeal, pointing to a corner.

"I'll get 'im."

Dominic picked up a fire poker from alongside the stove and opened the door of the shed.

"You're not going to kill him, are you?" she asked.

"Nope."

Dominic went to the where the loose speakers sat and began moving them, one by one, away from the wall. The fourth one slipped from his fingers and fell, face-first, on the floor. A ball of gray fur scampered over it and out the door.

"He's gone," said Dominic

"You positive?"

"Positive," he assured, closing the shop door and laying the poker back down next to the stove.

Patrice released a long, labored breath.

"Jesus, I don't know why those things scare me so."

Dominic smiled.

"You were afraid he'd run up your leg?"

"Happened to my grandfather once," said Patrice, "scooted right up his pant leg."

Dominic went to where she sat on the bench, and gently placed a hand on her bare knee.

"It's okay," he whispered.

They gazed deeply into each other's eyes. She pulled him to her, parted her lips, and began to kiss him hard, her breathing fast and shallow. He slid her skirt up to her hips and drew himself into her. To accommodate him, Patrice opened her legs wider, and in doing so bumped the housing on Rhythm Ace with her right knee. Ace responded by coming forth with a warp-speed rumba. Without breaking her embrace with Dominic, with one quick, confident sweep of her hand, Patrice reached out and dashed the machine to the floor, silencing his ridiculous accompaniment to their foreplay.

*   *   *   *

"June, you hear that?" asked Wendell, who was still waiting for sleep.

The crash had awakened June.

"Mmmhmm. Sounded like it came from 'Treece's shop. Go check to see if the light is on."

Wendell rolled out of bed and went to the window.

"Light's on, and Dominic's camper is still here. I didn't think I heard him leave."

"Sounded like something fell, maybe slipped off a shelf," suggested June. "A tool, a piece of equipment. She was probably just showing him a piece of her equipment. I'm sure it's all right. Come back to bed."

Wendell obeyed.

"He's a keeper, June."

"G'night, Wen."

CHAPTER 6

Norman Lipschutz Jr. of Norman's Electronics Sales & Repair, twenty four, blonde, bespectacled in thick Buddy Holly glasses, stood behind the counter of his father's store, gingerly touching the dented and cracked face of Rhythm Ace.

"Jeez-um crow," he asked in his nasally whine, "what happened to him, Patrice?"

"He fell out of..."

"Off of the bench," blurted Dominic, who stood next to her.

The two young lovers looked at each other and giggled. Norman nervously pushed his glasses up a notch higher on his nose.

"First, he fell out of the van when we were unloading and later fell off my workbench," explained Patrice, telling a very convincing half-truth. "I tried to repair him myself, but no luck."

"Looks like he's been through a war," said Norman.

"No, just a very tough night," cracked Dominic, earning himself a poke in the ribs from Patrice.

"Does he work at all?" asked Norman.

"Silent as a statue," answered Patrice.

Norman ran his fingers through his thatch of yellow hair.

"He's an FR-1, built in the early 70s. I can open him up, but if it's more than a crossed wire, I'd have to hunt around, maybe do some research on the Internet to try and find some replacement components."

"Do what you can," said Patrice, "but don't worry about it. If you can fix him, he's just gonna be a back-up anyway."

Norman's eyes grew wide.

"Your dad go back to using a real drummer?"

"Never in a million years," said Patrice, smiling. "You still got that Roland TR-707?"

"Yeah, it's still for sale," said Norman, returning the smile.

"For sale at a fair price, of course," said Dominic snottily. "We can just as easily take a spin up to Montreal."

"But we want to buy it from you," intervened Patrice, shooting Spinosa a dirty look.

Norman Lipschutz Jr. looked at Patrice with a face that held absolute sincerity mixed with just the slightest trace of hurt.

"You know I'm honest, Patrice. I would never cheat anyone," he said soberly.

"That's what we like to hear," said Dominic.

Minutes later, a deal was struck, and as cash and goods changed hands, Norman asked, "Band doing well?"

Patrice looked into her new boyfriend's eyes and said, "We're getting there, Norman."

Outside, as the two walked towards the van, Patrice scowled and turned to Dominic.

"You were kind of mean to him."

"Jeez-um crow, 'Treece what makes you say that?" asked Dominic, mimicking a passable rendition of Norman.

"That's not funny, Dominic."

"Oh come on, Patrice," he defended, "you gotta play a little hardball when you're transacting a deal."

"With anyone but him. I think he is honest…and innocent."

"You say innocent, I say doofus."

Patrice slowed and looked Dominic full in the face.

"It's just that I saw him go through hell in high school, the jocks kicking the crap out of him, the kids making fun of his name, his voice, his glasses."

"I can see why," said Dominic. "Guys like that bring it on themselves."

"That's not true. He can't help who is he is."

"Stop!" said Dominic and the two of them came to a halt in the middle of Corbeau Avenue, the main street in Chazy.

"Stop...please? I don't want to fight about this, it's ridiculous," said Dominic. "Can we call a truce?"

"Truce," agreed Patrice. "But next time, be a little kinder to him, promise?"

"Promise."

After the two had reached their vehicle, climbed in and buckled up, Dominic stuck his key in the ignition but did not turn it. Rather, he held it there, his brow furrowed, his eyes blinking, deep in thought.

"Why did you want to tell Norman that Rhythm Ace fell out of the van?"

"I don't know," came Patrice's response as she rifled through her purse in search of a hairbrush.

"Gotta be a reason."

Patrice pulled a brush from her purse, flipped the visor down, and began brushing in the reflection of the visor mirror.

"It's silly, but I was just afraid if I told the real story, I might slip and tell him what happened after Ace hit the floor."

Dominic raised his eyebrows.

"People don't usually go around telling others that they made love on a workbench in a shed."

"I told you it was silly," she retorted. "Now let's get going, I wanna get home and see how well that Roland performs."

Dominic twisted the key and the engine came to life.

"And later bay-bee," said Dominic, mugging, "I can show you how well *I* perform."

She slapped his arm, he broke into a laugh.

"You're impossible, Spinosa. Just drive."

Roland turned out to be the veritable Cadillac of drum machines, replacing Ace's hisses and pops with true drum sounds and offering a panoply of additional percussion effects.

The downside was that Robert and his lowly tambourine began to feel obsolete.

Robert's feeling second best to a machine first evidenced itself at a practice session, when he banged away angrily while shooting murderous glances at the new kid on the block, but was never so obvious than on a Friday night in November when the Charbonneaus were back at Rapant's *Whiskey River*.

Even before they arrived for the job, Robert had been moping around all evening, refusing to watch TNN with Wendell, procrastinating, waiting until the last minute to brush his teeth, take his shower, get dressed and assist Dominic, his dad, and his sister with the perfunctory task of loading equipment.

About twenty minutes before the start of the first set, on stage Robert's tambourine still lay untouched in its homemade wooden case. Patrice was programming Roland for a night of work and Wendell and Dominic were tuning up. Robert stood idly a few feet from the stage.

Dominic was the first to notice that the youngest Charbonneau had not unpacked his instrument.

"You playing tonight, Robert?" he asked, twisting a tuning peg on his guitar.

"Maybe later," came the reply. "Gonna cruise right now."

"You be a good boy, hear?" mandated his father.

"K."

After Robert had wandered off into a moderate-sized crowd, Wendell turned to Dominic.

"In a way I don't mind. Some nights if he gets behind in the beat he and that drum machine sound like a friggin' Salvation Army convention."

Dominic chuckled and continued tightening his strings into tune.

Eventually, after playing a few video games and watching a

rather talented patron run the pool table, Robert found his way up to the bar. Sonny Rapant was bartending with his buddy Mike Gonyea serving as bar back.

After some errant finger picking by Dominic, the bandstand became momentarily quiet and then launched into their first song.

"May I have a Coca Cola please?" Robert asked Sonny.

"Coming right up, Slick. You taking the night off?"

"Maybe. Cruisin' right now."

"Cruisin', eh?" Sonny repeated and smiled at Gonyea.

As Sonny dug a plastic cup into a sinkful of ice, one of the club's waitresses approached the bar with a drink order.

Cara was twenty-three, about five four, with ivory skin and dyed black hair she wore long with bangs. She had a nose ring, and a small crescent moon tattooed over her left breast. This particular evening she wore a crimson red velour mini-dress, black stockings, and black, zip-up-the-side boots that came to the knee.

As soon as she came into Robert's line of sight, his eyes fell upon her and stayed there.

"Two pitchers of Bud, four glasses, and a Jack and Coke," she requested, holding a round, cork-lined tray in her hands.

Sonny swung around and rang a brass bell that hung over the cash register.

"Sweet Jesus, finally get to crack a bottle of Jack," he proclaimed, referring to the fact that the majority of his country music patrons preferred the taste, and price, of draft beer.

Cara smiled weakly and waited for her drinks. Robert appeared oblivious to the sound of the bell, as his eyes had not moved off Cara and continued to walk slowly from the top of her head to the tip of her black-booted toe.

Robert's ogling did not go unnoticed by Sonny.

"You like her, boy?" he asked.

"Yeah."

Soon, Cara's tray held the requested beverages and glassware and she sashayed on back to an awaiting table.

Sonny and Mike Gonyea focused on Robert as the boy watched Cara walk away.

"I didn't think retards had any sex drive," remarked Gonyea.

"Bull*shit*," said Sonny, "most of them are hornier than a three peckered billy goat."

Robert drained his drink and slid it across the bar.

"Can I have another, please?" he asked.

"Coming right up," answered Sonny.

Robert turned back to watch the crowd, Sonny took his cup, looked over at Gonyea and winked.

The bottle of Jack Daniels still sat on the bar and Sonny quickly dumped about four fingers into Robert's cup. He then followed with a fresh scoop of ice, and filled the cup to the brim with Coke.

"Here ya go, Slick."

Robert turned back to the bar.

"A special drink for my special friend."

Robert smiled and said, "Thank you."

Louise Lowry, a hard fifty, wizened, nearly spent, who, for the past 25 years, had sold various parts of her body to men in the bedroom of her trailer, in the front and back seats of both foreign and domestic cars, on the mattress at an occasional no-tell motel, and in the stalls of many a roadhouse men's room, sat alone at the end of the bar, sipping a beer, and working her way through her second pack of generic cigarettes. She wore a purple silk blouse, a plain black skirt, stockings and heels. On the back of her chair hung a ratty, brown and white rabbit fur jacket.

Sonny ambled on down to where she was sitting.

"Slow night, Louise?" he asked.

"Can't give it away," came her reply. "You want me do you,

Sonny? Freebie. On the house."

Sonny looked into her dull, listless eyes.

"No, not me, but I do have a little job for you."

*   *   *   *

Upstairs over the bar, Joe Rapant Sr. kept a modest office – a steel desk, an oak desk chair on wheels, a large and a small metal filing cabinet, and several mismatched upholstered chairs in various states of disrepair. Tonight, as the Charbonneaus performed downstairs Joe sat at his desk, one hand holding his head, the other punching numbers into an adding machine. His wife Martha sat across from him, holding a cup of tea from which she did not drink, her face deeply lined with concern.

Joe tapped in one final number and exhaled a labored breath.

"We can hold out six months, maybe a year," he announced. "If we can't turn things around, we're going belly-up."

"We can always get by on your railroad pension," offered Martha.

"It's not us I'm worried about, it's Sonny."

Martha set her cup down on the desk, stood, and walked over to her husband. She bent down, took his hands into her own, and looked into his eyes.

"He depends too much on you and this bar," she said. "You've made things too easy for him, handed him anything he's ever wanted."

"I wanted him to have what I never did," said Joe.

"But he's got to realize that there are no guarantees in life and that things change," she continued. "If the bar closes, he'll have to find work somewhere else."

Joe began to nod slowly, Martha narrowed her eyes.

"You got to let him grow up, Joseph."

*   *   *   *

The Charbonneaus had just finished their first set when a patron rushed up to the stage.

"You better come quick, Wendell. They got Robert in the bathroom."

In the middle of the men's room seven laughing males, including Sonny and Gonyea, had formed a circle around two individuals in the center– Louise Lowry and Robert Charbonneau.

Louise had stripped off her skirt and panty hose, unbuttoned her blouse, and attached her hands to the penis of an intoxicated Robert whose pants and underwear were shoved down around his ankles, his eyes swimming, his lower lip hanging.

As Louise stroked the boy's shaft she encouraged him with, "Let's get one on, Hon. C'mon, that's it. Thatta boy, we're gettin' there."

When Wendell, with Dominic right on his heels, burst through the door, Robert was about at half-mast.

It took less than a second for the proceedings to register with Wendell.

"Get the hell away from him," he growled at Louise through gritted teeth.

Louise unceremoniously dropped Robert's penis from her hands, took one step back, and closed the front of her blouse.

She then frowned and turned to Sonny.

"I want another twenty. This took longer than five minutes."

"Shut up, you dried up old bitch," spat Sonny.

Wendell, who stood across from Sonny, approximately ten feet away, fixed him with a blistering glare.

"You set this up, Sonny? You did this to my son? What kind of sick son of a bitch are you? He's got the mind of a child."

"Maybe, but he's got the dick of a donkey!"

Laughter burst from the men.

"And if you hadn't come in here," continued Sonny, "in another five minutes or so he would have been a man. Ain't that right, Slick?"

"Right, gonna be a man," agreed Robert, raising a wobbly fist into the air.

Wendell, his face purple, every part of his being screaming for blood, lunged at Sonny only to be stopped short about three feet from him by the restraining arms and hands of Sonny's compatriots.

"Easy there, old man," taunted Sonny, having raised his hands and dropped into a fighting crouch. "I done told you before, nuthin' please me better than to bust out some of your crockery."

Dominic then added his arms to those that held Wendell back and put his mouth close to Charbonneau's right ear.

"Let it go, Wen. You can't win this one. Let it go."

Wendell blew out a breath and Dominic felt his body relax a bit.

"It's okay, guys," Dominic said to the others, "I got 'im, I got 'im, he's okay, he's all right."

Tentatively, the others loosened their grip and, along with Sonny, who kept Wendell in a tight stare, started edging towards the door. Soon they disappeared, peals of bawdy laughter beginning as they entered the main part of the bar.

That left Dominic, Wendell, Robert....and Louise.

During the stand-off between Wendell and Sonny, she had buttoned her blouse to the neck. Now, with head bowed, she stepped into her skirt, slipped into her shoes, balled and stuffed her pantyhose into her purse, and headed quietly for the door.

"Come back, feels good, do it s'more," Robert called out after her, his eyes barely in focus, pants still down around his ankles.

Louise kept on walking. Wendell, his face having again become purple at the sound of Robert's words, broke free of Dominic's loosened restraint, reached out and slapped his son hard across the face.

Robert fell back against a urinal, caught his grip on the handle, slid down to the floor, and began to cry.

Wendell threw his fist into one of the two bathroom mirrors, shattering it, and cutting the knuckles on his right hand. His head swung back and forth, like a bull in a ring, his eyes searching for something or someone on which to vent the remainder of his rage. He caught his reflection in the second mirror, slammed his left fist into it, snatched several paper towels from the dispenser, and stalked out.

Robert was still weeping and the imprint of his father's right hand on his left cheek was beginning to show.

Dominic went to him.

"Come on, Robert," he soothed, helping the boy to his feet," let's throw a little cold water on your face."

As soon as he had his feet under himself, he sniffed hard twice, ending his flow of tears. Two bleary eyes then looked into Dominic's face.

"Louise coming back?" he asked, his lower lip dribbling spit.

Dominic snorted, grinned, and shook his head.

"No, I don't think so. Not tonight, Robert."

Robert's lower lip quivered, and within seconds the wails and the weeping once again filled the confines of the room.

The following morning, the sounds of Robert's retching rang through the house. In an upstairs bathroom, June held a wet washcloth to his forehead, as Robert, on his knees with his arms encircling the bowl in a death grip, commenced another round of the dry heaves.

Downstairs Dominic and Patrice sat at the kitchen table, silently sipping coffee, peering into their cups as if the liquid might hold an answer. Wendell paced between the kitchen and the living room, occasionally running a finger over one of his scabbed knuckles.

The Charbonneaus had managed to finish out the night at Rapant's, Wendell dabbing at his bleeding hands with a paper towel and shooting murderous looks at Sonny who stood behind the bar, joking and laughing with his friends. Dominic and Patrice had concerned themselves with Robert, watching over him as he sat in a chair a few feet from the stage, his head bobbing drunkenly, from time to time a hand floating up and slowly sweeping the air.

Dominic had told Patrice an abbreviated, but unsanitized version of the story as soon as he'd returned to the stage, Wendell having been too angry and too embarrassed to share any of Sonny's misdeeds with her.

At the end of the night when they were packing gear, Wendell had pulled Dominic aside and asked him, "How would they have done it, you know...the sex?"

"How?" asked Dominic, his eyes wide.

"No, I don't mean how, I know how, I guess I mean where...and how?" corrected Wendell.

"In a stall, with him sitting on her. Or maybe, with that crowd watching she woulda bent over a sink."

"Bastards!" Wendell had cursed. "Dirty rotten pervert bastards."

After the equipment had been loaded, in a move that broke with tradition, it was Dominic, not Wendell, who went to Sonny to collect the band's pay, an action suggested by Patrice in an effort to keep her father out of close proximity to the man who had taken her brother's innocence.

Robert's heaving eventually subsided and was replaced by a soft moaning. Wendell's pacing had him in the kitchen when Dominic spoke.

"Alcohol naïve," said Dominic, "that's probably why he's so sick."

"Meaning?" asked Patrice.

"Meaning his body's not used to the alcohol, hasn't built any tolerance," answered Dominic.

He then looked up at Wendell.

"Do you know how much he had?"

"You mean how much did Sonny feed him? I don't know, but I do know I'm gonna get that son of a bitch."

"Let it go, Daddy," pleaded Patrice.

"Treece is right, Wen," agreed Dominic. "What's done is done. Let it go."

Wendell stood over Dominic and glared down at him.

"He's not your son. It wasn't your boy who was degraded, made to perform like some dumb animal in a carnival sideshow."

Dominic pursed his lips and looked across the table at Patrice.

"You wanna call the Sheriff's Department, Wen? Turn Sonny in for serving a minor?" asked Dominic.

"No I don't. Besides, I'm probably on their shit list anyway," answered Wendell.

Patrice looked up at her father, her mouth opening in disbelief.

"Why, what did you do?" she asked.

"Me? Nothing personally. But one of the deputies, one of them young blond bucks with the skinned head and big-feelin' attitude pulled his cruiser up next to where I was working last week."

"And?" asked Patrice, her eyes widening.

"And he said that he had seen Robert a few weeks back on his bike and he had concerns about Robert's helmet. Said the helmet wasn't regulation."

"What did you tell him?" asked Patrice.

"Told him a helmet's a helmet, and that your head don't know the difference, doesn't really care, as long as something else hits the ground first."

"That's not entirely true..." began Dominic.

"Then I asked him," interrupted Wendell, "to show me some paper, some evidence, some proof from the ordinance that specifically says a football helmet can't be used."

Wendell smirked.

"His skinned head turned as pink as a pig's ass, he mumbled something about just wanting to make sure Robert had adequate protection, wished me good-day, but I don't think he meant it, almost clunked his own noggin getting into his car, and took off."

A moment passed. Dominic blew across the surface of his coffee.

"State Police?" suggested Dominic.

"Any type of cop, Sheriff or State Bull, would question why we let him loose in there," answered Wendell. "He wasn't bangin' his tambourine, wasn't playing with the band, he had no business being up at the bar. I'm sure Sonny could make up a pretty convincing story that Robert got himself shitfaced by drinking out of other people's glasses when they got up to dance or go to the bathroom. Sonny'd lie and his friends would swear to it."

Wendell's face hardened into a fist.

"Don't need any help from the law. I'll get him."

"Get who?" asked June, just having entered the kitchen.

"Robert. I was just saying I could get Robert and take him out and buy him a milkshake at Stewart's. Milk would help settle his stomach and ice cream's always good when you got a hangover," said Wendell, not missing a beat.

"Not that you would ever know, Dad," wisecracked Patrice.

"Not now, he just fell asleep, maybe later," said June, a scowl beginning to wander onto her face. "Wen, I need to talk to you...alone."

Patrice looked across the table at Dominic.

"I could use some air," she said. "C'mon, let's take a walk."

She and Dominic rose, then deposited their coffee cups in the sink. They exited the kitchen, disagreed on the weight of the coat she should wear, and finally left through the front door.

June waited to speak until she presumed they were a distance from the house.

"No more of this, Wendell, no more of this. I'm sick of it," she told her husband wearily.

Wendell had backed himself up against the refrigerator.

"I should have kept a closer watch on him. I'm sorry, it's my fault. Can't let him wander off like that. From now on, he plays in every song, in every set. If he's bored with his tambourine, maybe I'll get him a pair of those Spanish mariachis – those things that look like gourds, got pellets in 'em."

June pressed her lips together, trying to hold back the flood of anger rising in her throat.

"Maracas," she finally said.

"Huh?"

"They're called maracas, not mariachis, and you don't get it, do you?"

Wendell's eyebrows lifted as his shoulders began a slow shrug. June's hands began to tremble.

"Get out of it," she began, her voice rising an octave. " I want you and Treece and Robert to get out of this stupid band business… now…*today*!"

Wendell crossed his arms over his chest. His lower lip slid forward in a stubborn pout.

"Can't do that, June. With this kid Dominic we're closer than ever."

"Closer to what?" the tremor from her hands now having traveled to her throat. "Look at you, almost sixty years old and still chasing this, this pipedream….this poor man's pipedream."

Wendell wet his lips.

"June, Junie… I know you're upset about Robert but– "

"No Wen, it's the whole package. What happened with Robert is only part of it. If it's not Sonny Rapant, it's some other sleazy club owner pullin' cheap tricks, tryin' to cheat you out of your money or drooling over Patrice like she's a piece of meat. I know, Wen, I been there with you. Drunks who want to fight and flatten your tires if they don't like the music you play. You and the kids walking around here the next day like zombies, half-dead, having spent the night in some filthy gin mill. And that smell, that reek of smoke that I can never get out of your clothes or Robert's hair. Can't you understand what I'm saying? It *stinks*, the whole thing...and I want you out of it."

Wendell cleared his throat.

"Sonny's not the owner," he said in a low voice.

"What?"

"Sonny's not the owner; his father Joe is," he clarified.

"That's doesn't matter, Wen, you're missing the point," June pleaded. Her voice was becoming shrill.

Wendell uncrossed his arms and cocked his head to one side.

"Well, maybe we can get out of the bars, try to book more parties, and weddings and such. Exposure is just as good in those places."

June walked over to the kitchen table, sat down and spread both of her hands out, palms down.

"That's the worse part, Wen."

"What?"

"That...*crap* about exposure," she said, trying to control her voice. "Misleading the kids into believing that they're going to be stars...celebrities."

Wendell's nostrils began to widen into a full flare.

"Misleading? Now June, *now* you're startin' to piss me off."

June Charbonneau kept her hands flat on the table and looked deep into her husband's eyes.

"Chantelle will be a star," she began slowly, "not you, not Robert, not Patrice...Chantelle."

Wendell's right hand balled into a fist, and although he had never spoken to June with his hands, and never would, the fist and forearm began to shake.

"Enough!"

He stood there glowering at her. June held his stare.

"Enough," he repeated, with less intensity while forcing his right hand to relax.

"What are you guys fighting about?"

It was Robert, looking pale and pasty in a T-shirt and red flannel pajama bottoms.

"Nothing," said Wendell. "Nothing. Get dressed, I'm gonna take you out for a milkshake."

For the first time in about 12 hours, since his father had interrupted his sordid little liaison with the town whore and slapped him down to the men's room floor, Robert smiled.

"K," he said, beaming.

The sky was the color of the fur on the mouse that Patrice had so intensely feared, but who had been responsible, in part, for her first night of passion with Dominic and the beginning of their love affair. Leaving Wendell and June to battle it out back at the house, the two had decided to walk through the woods and to the banks of the Vly creek. There they found a large rock, sat down, and were in the process of studying the sky through the leafless, late autumn limbs of the trees.

"Days like this make me feel...sad," offered Patrice.

"Classic case of melancholia," said Dominic.

"What's that?"

"An old fashioned name for depression."

"I'm not depressed, just sad. For me there's a difference."

"Explain."

Patrice shifted her weight on the rock.

"For me sad is when I miss something or someone...like my sister Chantelle. When I get depressed I feel hopeless, like there's no way out, or like nothing's gonna change."

"You missing Chantelle today?" asked Dominic.

"Yeah, but I don't feel hopeless about the situation. I believe I'll see her again...someday."

The two fell silent, but the frigid waters of the Vly, swollen by recent rainfall, continued to rush by.

"I like days like this...no distractions," said Dominic.

"Distractions from what?" she asked.

"Distractions from practicing my guitar, writing songs– "

"Being with your girlfriend," she blurted, then giggled.

"Wise ass."

She giggled some more.

"Going to meetings," he continued, "reading my big book, writing in my journal, those sorts of productive, recovery-oriented things. Give me a sunny sky and warm afternoon and I'm outside playing, hanging out, doing anything but work. Days like this–cold, grey, overcast–help me to focus on working towards the things I really want in life."

"Like me!" she chirped.

"You're really pushin' it, Charbonneau," he said, throwing an arm over her shoulders and rocking her towards him.

He hugged her tight and rocked her to and fro.

"So how is today productive?" she asked. "Right now, you're outside, hanging out."

"But I am hanging out with you, so I figure this is time spent working on our relationship," came his answer.

"Clever."

He nuzzled his nose into the nape of her neck.

"Actually, my NA sponsor thinks *you* are a distraction."

"What?" she asked, stiffening, sitting bolt upright, and scowling. "How?"

"He thinks it's too soon in my recovery to have a relationship. That by focusing on you, I'll distract myself away from the things I need to do to stay clean and sober."

Patrice leaned away from him.

"And what do you think?" she asked.

"I think he's got a hidden agenda."

"The agenda being?" she asked, her face holding lines of concern.

"The agenda being that I think he wants you for himself," said Dominic, smiling. "I showed him a picture of you."

"Picture? I didn't give you any picture."

"I borrowed one from your mantle."

Patrice's mouth went slack and she slowly shook her head.

"Not that picture of me in 11th grade with the frizzed perm, the three pounds of pancake make-up, and the Ruby don't-take-your-love-to-town lipstick?"

Dominic raised his eyebrows impishly.

"Uh-huh."

In mock anger she began to muss his hair, all the while accusing, "Thief! Thief! Burglar! Picture Stealer! Criminal!"

Dominic put his hands to his head and protested, 'Stop, cut it out, cut it out."

Finally, he wrested her hands away from his hair and held them tightly in his own. She lowered her head, batted her lashes slowly, and looked seductively into his eyes.

"Am I your favorite distraction?" she asked.

"Without a doubt," came his answer.

She leaned over and gave him a deep, soulful kiss. Pulling back she arranged a part in his hair with her fingers.

"So what's it like?" she asked.

"What's what like?"

"Cocaine."

Dominic blinked twice and swallowed hard, as if Patrice had invoked the name of the devil himself.

"It's like you're totally in control...of everything. You're the master, the center of the universe."

Patrice pursed her lips.

"Sounds like Daddy," she said acridly.

Dominic smiled.

"Ahh, he just seems like sort of a take charge guy to me."

Patrice's expression grew decidedly somber.

"You don't have to live with him. He controls everything. Never once has he asked me what I might want to do with my life. It was always a given that after high school I'd stay home and get ready for the "big break." She paused and shook her head. "That's a hoot."

Dominic looked at her, his expression revealing deep disbelief.

"You don't like playing music, you don't think the band has a shot at something more than local?"

Patrice snorted and her mouth twisted into a sardonic grin.

"Yeah, maybe someday we'll play Albany."

"Hey, don't sell the band short," encouraged Dominic. " A lot of family acts have hit big in country music – Jeannie and Royce Kendall, The Judds, The Osmonds, The Carter Family..."

"The Partridge Family," interjected Patrice, her tongue firmly in cheek.

"They weren't really related," said Dominic earnestly. "They just played a family on– "

Patrice was smiling mischievously.

"You know that," said Dominic scowling. "I'm trying to make a point here and you're goofin' on me."

"Sorry, but if you're trying to convince me that we could ever be in the same league as those, those professionals you just mentioned I'm not buyin' it."

Dominic slid off the rock, picked up a pebble and flung it into the Vly.

"You never know, 'Treece. The music business is incredibly fickle."

Dominic threw a few more stones into the stream before Patrice broke the silence between them.

"You're making the same mistake my father does. He assumes that I want to keep working towards the big time."

Spinosa stopped throwing and turned to face her.

"So what do you think you want?" he asked.

"No, you'll laugh."

"I won't," he promised.

Patrice drew a breath and lifted her chin.

"You already kinda know this, but I like fixing things...electronic things. Taking things apart, trying to figure out what's wrong. Sometimes I can fix them, good as new, sometimes better than new. But I need to learn more, the technology changes so fast. Clinton Community College has a two year program in electronics, but Daddy'd never hear of it."

Dominic nodded, sucked at a tooth, and resumed throwing rocks into the Vly.

"I knew it," he finally said.

"Knew what?"

He turned and tossed a tiny stone at her knee.

"You're an egghead," he said, chuckling.

Feigning contempt, Patrice narrowed her eyes.

"I knew you'd laugh. I knew I couldn't trust you."

For a split second, Patrice caught a look in his eyes that could have been hurt, but Dominic quickly averted his gaze.

He then hopped back up on the rock with her.

"Trust me about this one. You got talent. You got a certain "it" quality. You definitely got a chance at makin' it."

"God!" she exclaimed. "You're starting to sound like my father. Who are you? Wendell junior, the non-retarded son he never had?"

"No," he began, in measured, even tones. "Just telling you straight up what I believe in my heart. The program teaches you to be honest, and I'm being honest with you." He paused, put his arm back on her shoulder. "Course, if you wanted to be some nerd with a soldering gun, you should."

"I could never..."

"Yes, you could. Wouldn't be easy, but you could."

Patrice rested her chin in her hand.

"You need to understand that I see the situation as hopeless."

She forced a smile.

"But that's good news for you because I'm not going anywhere."

He gave her a quick kiss on her forehead and then glanced down at his watch.

"The cold from this rock is startin' to go right through me. Safe to go back to the house?" he asked.

"Yeah, I'm sure Momma has had enough time to tear Daddy a new asshole for letting Robert stray off like that."

Dominic popped his eyes and let his mouth drop.

"You kiss your Momma with that mouth?"

"*And* you," she said, drawing him in and planting a fat wet one on his lips.

*   *   *   *

On that same ashen Saturday morning in November, Sonny Rapant sat in one of the upholstered chairs in his father's office over the bar, squeezing a hard black rubber ball. With each successive pump his face grew a deeper shade of red. His father sat behind his desk, tipped back slightly in his chair, waiting for the verbal response to the news he'd just delivered to his son.

Sonny crushed the ball a few more times before he spoke.

"And if you close the bar, what am I supposed to do?" Sonny finally asked.

"Same thing I did at your age, work for somebody else," his father answered.

Sonny transferred the ball to his other hand and increased the frequency of his compressions.

"Oh that's just fucking great. You expect me to make house, truck, and snowmobile payments on a bartender's salary."

Joe Rapant leaned forward in his chair.

"No one's saying you got to keep bartending, Sonny. There's other jobs out there. I can probably get you on with the railroad."

"No thanks."

Sonny then pushed himself up out of the chair and went to one of the three windows in the office. There he began tapping the ball lightly against the glass.

"You let me bring in rock bands and I can turn this place around," said Sonny.

Joe Rapant bit into his lower lip.

"I been telling you for a long time, those shit-kickin' country bands have ruined our business," continued Sonny. "They don't draw enough of a crowd and the yokels they do attract don't spend nuthin'."

"No, that's not true," argued Joe, "It's the economy and the tougher DWI laws that have been killing a lot of the bar businesses, not just ours. People don't have the money to throw over the bar or piss away on some lawyer to try and beat a drunk driving charge. It's cheaper, and there's certainly no risk involved to sit home with a six pack and a video."

Sonny stopped rapping and turned to his father.

"Unless you can tap into the crowd that's looking for a piece of ass. Blizzards, three feet of snow, roads slicker 'n shit with ice won't stop them if they think we got what they want...what they *need*."

A long moment passed as Rapant Sr. stared off into mid-space.

"Ass," he said, finally breaking the silence.

"Right," confirmed Sonny.

Joe took a pencil from an empty juice can that had been transformed into a pen and pencil holder by his grandson Claude and began doodling on a scratch pad.

"So what do you call this crowd?" asked Joe.

"Young," said Sonny.

Sonny started pumping the ball again, only this time with excitement rather than anger.

"You said we can keep our heads above water for another year," said Sonny, his voice high in his throat.

"Six months, a year tops," confirmed his father.

Sonny began to pump fast and furious.

"Let me take over booking the entertainment. I'll bring in the best, no bullshit hard drivin' rock and roll bands I can find. I'll run happy hours with mixed drinks, have ladies nights. Those young bucks smell pussy, they'll be breaking down the doors to get in."

Joe penciled the number three onto his scratch pad.

"Three months," said the elder Rapant slowly. "I'll give you three months."

"I won't let you down, Dad," said Sonny excitedly. "We'll have a grand re-opening, run a few ads in the paper, put up flyers, it'll be great!" He paused and held the ball tightly in his grip. "And it's gonna work."

Joe ran the tip of his pencil in a zig zag fashion over the three he'd written.

"But go easy, Sonny, don't go too hog wild with this," he warned. "I want things kept on the straight and narrow, understand?"

"I understand," answered Sonny, his eyes now shining brightly, "and thanks, Dad, you won't regret this."

*　　　*　　　*　　　*

When the phone rang at the Charbonneaus the week before Thanksgiving, only June was at home. Wendell was working, pumping several septic tanks around the village before the hard frost set in for the winter. Patrice and Dominic had taken the van into Plattsburgh, intent on doing a little Christmas shopping. Robert had tagged along, bringing money for some paint sets to be purchased at one of the malls, but hoping that Dominic and his sister would pay for his lunch at McDonalds.

After June answered, the caller whispered two words.

"Lake Placid."

"Chantelle?"

"Hi Momma, I miss you so much."

June felt the hot sting of tears.

"Me too, Sweetie," she replied. "How are you?"

"Fine, fine."

June noticed that her daughter's voice had affected just the slightest trace of a southern twang.

"So how are *you*, 'Treece , Robert?"

June mentioned that she had had a little sinus trouble, always happens this time of year, the air being a damp cold, soon to snow, she reminded her daughter. She went on to highlight Patrice's romance with Dominic, deleted Robert's recent men's room performance, offering instead, with a chuckle, that he now probably had enough paint-by-number creations to open his own gallery. And although she hadn't asked, June volunteered that Wendell was quite pleased with the addition of a new guitar player to the band.

"So 'Treece's got a hottie, huh?" Chantelle gushed.

"Appears so," was all her mother said.

There was a millisecond of dead air between the two.

"Lake Placid, you said Lake Placid," repeated June, reminding Chantelle of her opening words.

"Right!"

Chantelle went on to tell her mother that she and Ketchum would be part of a triple bill at the Lake Placid Olympic Arena the Friday night after Thanksgiving, with Mary Chapin Carpenter as the third performer. Ketchum and Carpenter would share the headliner bill, and as usual, Chantelle and back-up band would be the opening act.

Chantelle, Ketchum, and their respective musicians would fly into Albany and then be driven by limo to Lake Placid. All they need bring were their guitars, as they would use Carpenter's PA and band equipment.

"Mary is already doing an east coast tour, and we jumped at the chance when the promoter invited us to make it a triple bill. The place is nearly sold out! I'll only be in New York State probably about 12 hours, tops. After the gig, they transport us back down to Albany where we fly out for a show in Toronto on Saturday night."

"My head's spinnin', Chantelle," exclaimed June. "Your life is a whirlwind!"

Chantelle's voice became almost child-like.

"Momma, I would like to see you...all of you, any of you...except Daddy."

June's mind raced, trying to bring rise to a plan to make that happen.

"First, let me see if our band has an engagement that night," said June.

As June walked herself and the cordless into the kitchen where a calendar with penned-in band dates hung from a magnet on the refrigerator, a pang of sadness rippled through Chantelle's heart, as her mother's words affirmed that Chantelle was indeed separate and distinct from the rest of them.

Our band, she thought, hearing her mother's words echo in her head. Our band, which no longer includes me.

"The Charbonneaus will be playing at the Paradise Lounge in Plattsburgh, some state office party, looks like from 4 to 8pm," read June from the calendar.

"So can you come see me, Momma?"

"Oh Hon, I don't drive that much anymore," she said flatly, "besides your father would have the car for the job."

"Well can't you come after he gets home?" pleaded Chantelle. "I open at 8, play for half an hour, maybe a little more, maybe less. I'll be done by 8:40, 8:45 at the latest. We could watch Hal or Mary, or both, go out for dinner, coffee, whatever you like."

There was a silence at the other end of the line.

"I just couldn't hop in the station wagon and tear off down to Placid. How could I ever explain that to your father?"

"Why do you have to explain anything to him?" asked Chantelle, an edge to her voice.

"This wouldn't work for me, but it might for 'Treece. I'll talk to her as soon as she gets home," was June's response.

"Okay," said Chantelle, knowing that she'd gone as far as she was going to go with her mother. "I've got a cell phone now, keep it with me wherever I go."

She relayed the number to her mother.

"Tell 'Treece not to call until after, let's say... 9:00 to be safe. I wouldn't want it ringing when I was on stage," she instructed, chuckling.

June repeated the number back to Chantelle who confirmed it.

"You understand that we can't include Robert in on this," added

June.

"Do I understand? No. Do I like it? Hate it! Will I accept it? Gonna have to."

"It's the just the way it is, the way your father is, the choices the two of you have made," said June.

"But Momma..."

"We've been down that road before," said June calmly. "Nothing ever comes of it. Now whatever you may think, your father loves you."

Chantelle could feel a lump rising in her throat while the hand not holding the phone balled into a fist.

"Now where will you be having your Thanksgiving dinner?" asked June, abruptly changing the subject.

"On the road, probably in the restaurant at one of the hotels where we stay."

"That's nice," said June, "I'm sure I'll talk with you before Christmas."

"Of course."

"Well, say a little prayer that Patrice and Dominic–"

"Who?"

"Dominic, her boyfriend," reminded June.

"Oh, right."

"I'm sure we can get her down there to meet up with you. You girls have always been quite crafty."

"I'll take that as a compliment, I guess."

"I'd better close out, Hon. I'm sure this call is costing you a fortune."

"I've got an expense account," said Chantelle.

"You never told me where you're calling from," said June.

"It doesn't matter... Bye, Mom, I love you. My love to 'Treece and Robert."

"I love you, too. Take care of yourself, Sweetheart. Good-bye."

*   *   *   *

Wendell, fearing that he'd run short for the winter, had three cords of wood delivered the day before Thanksgiving. The seasoned hardwood, cut in two-foot lengths, but unsplit, sat on the lawn, having been dropped there by a dump truck about 7:30 that morning. After a hearty breakfast of pancakes, link sausages, and fried potatoes, the boys, Wendell, Robert and Dominic, headed out to begin a day's work of splitting.

The night before a short spell of freezing rain had left the ground slippery and all three took turns at alternately losing and recapturing their footing as they made their way out to the huge pile of firewood.

Wendell dragged his splitter, a homemade contraption that utilized a Ford Cortina engine he'd taken in barter for a septic cleaning, out from behind the barn. He told Robert to bring the wheelbarrow that was leaned up against the barn and seeing that Dominic wore no gloves, sent him back in the house with instructions for him to ask June to find him a pair.

Dominic had recently moved in with the Charbonneaus, letting go of a room he'd been renting in Beekmantown, a small village south of Chazy. He'd taken up residency in a corner of the practice room, having set his sleeping bag on an inflatable mattress and using the space heaters to warm the room. Although Dominic offered, Wendell would take no money for rent.

Dominic leaked information about himself to the Charbonneaus in dribs and drabs – originally from Hicksville, Long Island, his father a sax player and a junkie, his mother prone to nervous breakdowns and hospitalizations while he was growing up. Accepted as a student at the Crane School of Music in Potsdam, he'd lasted two semesters before falling under the spell of the "white lady," a relationship he'd keep for several years, and pay homage to by having the image of an angelic figure tattooed onto the outside of his right calf, an ethereal icon he'd later attempt to have removed by a plastic surgeon's laser. The procedure proved to be only partially successful though, as Robert continued to ask Dominic to raise his pant leg so that he might see the outline of what he believed to be a picture of the Virgin Mary.

After leaving college, Spinosa had kicked around the Adirondacks for several years, playing various pick-up jobs, managing, in between coke binges, to scrape together enough money to buy his Westfalia. Finally, he hit his bottom, got into a program in Ogdensburg, and cleaned up his act. He'd been drug-free for six months when he'd landed the job with Tommy and Tammy Wakefield.

June was lukewarm about the young man moving in, as she continued to have doubts about his character. Wendell always defended the boy, stating that no one has the power to pick their parents, and that Dominic appeared to be a survivor, rather than a victim of rough times. June bought some, but not all of Wendell's advocacy, believing that her husband's perceptions of the young man had been strongly colored by the fact that bookings as of late had never been better, undoubtedly due to the sterling guitar work of this long-haired kid from Long Island.

June outfitted Dominic with a pair of shearling-lined dark brown work gloves and sent him back outside. When Dominic came upon father and son, Robert was just finishing up pestering Wendell to let him run the splitter.

"I told you Robert," Wendell then argued, "this can be a dangerous piece of machinery. I've seen guys lose fingers up to the second knuckle. I got a job for you, don't you worry about that."

Robert dug his gloved hands deep into the pockets of his red and black check jacket as his mouth formed into a pout.

"Where do you want me?" asked Dominic.

"You place a log in front of the splitting wedge, I'll throw the lever, then after the wood pops open, you take both halves and throw them in a pile."

Wendell then looked at Robert.

"Son, then you throw the wood into your wheelbarrow, push it on over to our woodpile and start stacking."

"Yeah, I already know that. Do the same thing every time," complained Robert. "It's boring."

"Well, sometimes work is boring. If it was fun, it'd be play. Ain't that right, Dominic?" asked Wendell.

"Guess so," replied Spinosa, distracted, as he had begun to obsess on Wendell's words about losing fingers to the machine.

Wendell fired up the splitter and Spinosa carefully positioned the first log in front of the splitting wedge. Wendell pulled back on the power lever and the wedge, welded to the end of a lengthy piston, began a long, slow travel, eventually making contact with, and then penetrating the cut end of the log. This first chunk of maple, being dry and well-seasoned, popped open easily with a loud crack.

Inside, in a kitchen made toasty warm by a oven pre-heated to 350 degrees, Patrice and June rolled out dough for pumpkin pies as they finalized the details of Patrice's rendezvous with her older sister.

"Now, you sure you got her cellular phone number?" asked June.

"Memorized, but Dominic's got it written on a slip of paper tucked in his wallet if I ever did forget."

"Good."

June flopped her dough into an awaiting pie plate, pressed it into the sides and bottom, and began crimping the edges.

"Now tell me again what you told your father."

Patrice stopped rolling, blinked hard once, wet her lips, and began.

"Told him that after we pack up at the Paradise Lounge, Dominic and I were going to take the van down to Placid to do some more Christmas shopping, look at the holiday lights in town."

"And he said?" asked June.

Patrice dropped her voice an octave, attempting to sound like her dad.

"Thought'cha went shopping in P-burgh?"

"And you said?"

"That's when Dominic chimed in. He said he wanted to buy me a new watch for Christmas and seemed to remember there was a real nice clock shop in the Alpine Mall in Lake Placid."

"And…"

"Dad never questions what Dominic says or does. You know that."

June's lips drew tight, she nodded and took an opener to a can of pumpkin filling.

"You've been checking the newspaper, nothing in there about the concert?" June asked.

"Oh yeah, big ad in yesterday's *Press Republican*," answered Patrice nonchalantly.

June froze. Patrice, satisfied that her dough was now thoroughly rolled, lifted it from the pastry cloth.

"Read something like, 'Olympic Region Development Authority presents Mary Chapin Carpenter and Hal Ketchum with special guest'."

June exhaled.

"Special guest, that's all?" said June, her breathing returning to normal.

"That's all," confirmed Patrice. "Daddy, nor anybody else around Chazy for that matter, knows she's touring with Ketchum."

"Unless someone we know goes to this concert."

Patrice wiped flour from her hands onto her apron.

"I'll take my chances, Momma. I wanna see my sister."

*   *   *   *

"We almost done? I'm hungry," shouted Robert over the din of the splitter, standing with both hands gripping the handles of an overfilled wheelbarrow of split cherry and oak.

"What?" shouted his father.

"Done. We almost done?" repeated Robert.

Wendell looked at Dominic, and yelled, "What did he say?" Dominic shrugged and shook his head. Wendell killed the power on the splitter and looked over at Robert.

"When do we eat?" asked Robert.

Wendell snorted a laugh, tugged up the left sleeve on his jacket, and squinted at his watch.

"'Bout an hour. Think you can you hold out 'til then, Son?"

"Starvin', Dad."

Wendell and Dominic looked at each other and burst into laughter.

"You had stack of pancakes as tall as a silo, half an acre of potatoes, and more sausage links than you got fingers and toes," said Wendell with a snicker.

"Yeah, well, so, 'm still hungry."

Wendell softened.

"We'll break for lunch in about 45 minutes...okay Robert?"

"K," responded Robert, put his back into the first push of the wheelbarrow, and lurched towards the woodpile.

Wendell flashed Dominic a grin and then coaxed the Cortina engine back to life.

As opposed to Robert, who fought and wrestled with the wheelbarrow every unstable step of the way, minutes dragging by like hours, the two older men had established a rhythm, a flow to their work, and for them time passed quickly. A singularity in purpose having been established, what only seemed to matter was the log that was currently undergoing a transformation, the two held in a focus, a trance that remained unbroken until Wendell felt a tap on his shoulder approximately 30 minutes into the 45.

It was Robert and he was pointing a finger at his open mouth.

For the second time that morning, Wendell silenced the splitter, knowing that trying to squeeze a moment more of labor out of Robert would be futile.

It was only when the three walked back to the house that Wendell felt the ache in his back and Dominic recalled fears of the machine, as he wondered how he would fret guitar strings with a shortened digit or two.

Patrice and June waved them away from the cooling pies and served the three canned chili, tumblers of whole milk, and thick slices of marbled rye. The men ate quickly and quietly, hungrily spooning in the chili, chewing off hearty chunks of bread, Wendell or Dominic speaking only to comment on a log that had taxed the power of the splitter or had made an unusual sound when coming apart. Robert complained about the fatigue in his arms, and his father both admonished and offered a solution by instructing him to load fewer sticks of wood into his dump cart.

The meal was consumed in less than 20 minutes and was followed by large mugs of steaming coffee for Wendell and Dominic, hot cocoa with Marshmallow Fluff for Robert. Robert was the last to finish, slurping slow and loud. Wendell was well aware the boy was stalling, his mother taking a wet napkin to his mouth to wipe off the errant stripes of marshmallow before the three rose from the table and headed towards the front door for the second shift. Before they left the house June asked if they'd finish it all today. Wendell quickly responded in the negative, but assured her that they'd make a pretty darn good dent in what had started out as a mountain of cord wood.

Dominic was the last to pass through the kitchen's entryway and as he did he held Patrice in a long, loving gaze, a look that he knew was being witnessed by June.

June had made a third pumpkin pie in a small Corningware dish to be enjoyed with Patrice after the two had washed the dishes and wiped down the counters. Those tasks quickly completed, June sliced the pie in half and set out two plates as Patrice poured their coffee into bone China cups that had been passed down to June by her mother.

Before she brought the cup to her lips or pushed the side of a fork into her pie, June looked down at what would be her lunch and released a contented sigh. Patrice followed with a question.

"You still love Daddy? I mean, after all these years?"

June looked at her daughter with clear, calm eyes.

"Of course."

"As much as you did when you first met him?"

"Like the way you feel now about Dominic?"

Patrice's cheeks flooded red.

"Oh c'mon 'Treece, you think I don't know?"

"No, I'm sure you do."

June traced her finger lightly along the rim of her coffee cup.

"It's the same, but it's different. When you first start out it's all chemicals and hormones," said June.

"Momma!"

"Oh, stop," said June, "you know exactly what I mean. You want to talk about this like two grown women, or not?"

The force of June's tone took Patrice by surprise, causing her head to jerk upward.

"Yes, yes I do. Wouldn't have brought it up if I didn't."

June took a small sip of her coffee, set the cup down gently, the saucer emitting only the slightest of rattles, and began anew.

"Like I said, it's the same but it's different. Over the years it just becomes...quieter."

"Is that why I never see you and Daddy hold hands, cuddle, hug

–that kind of stuff," blurted Patrice.

June smiled.

"I was never much one for public shows of affection, even when we first started dating. But that doesn't mean I don't love that man with all my heart."

Patrice screwed up her face.

"Even though he can be incredibly hard-headed and act so bossy."

June looked deep into her daughter's eyes.

"You take the bad with the good. You and Dominic are just starting out, both of you got your best foot forward." She paused. "But in time, both of you will show a side of yourself that's not so pretty."

A look of worry wandered across Patrice's face as she remembered back to the unkindness Dominic had showed Norman Lipschutz, Jr. when they were negotiating a deal for the new drum machine. June felt compelled to respond to her daughter's distress.

"Dominic is your first love, and that's special. But no one knows, no one can predict where the relationship will be a year, two years from now. Just enjoy what you have now, the moment, and see what happens."

Patrice lowered her head, breaking eye contact with her mother.

"Daddy says Dominic's a keeper," said Patrice, her tone childlike and defensive.

"Daddy wants to *believe* Dominic's a keeper, but that's more in relation to the band," said June.

Patrice sniffed, and cut into her pie.

"You know what you said about enjoying what I have now?" asked Patrice.

"Uh-huh."

"I mean, I can't help that, it comes naturally because Dominic is always like, right here," said Patrice, pressing the tips of three fingers to her forehead.

June drew a deep breath and exhaled it slowly.

"I might not always agree with, or support what your father says and does, and I don't think about him constantly, but he's always with me…in my mind and my heart."

Patrice felt the beginnings of a lump in her throat. Just then, the two heard the front door open and slam. Heavy footfalls advanced towards the kitchen.

"Dad said I can have another cup of hot chocolate," announced Robert, as he stood in the kitchen entryway, his nose in dire need of wiping. "If we got any left."

"Plenty," said June, as she began to rise from the table. "Take me two minutes in the microwave."

"With Fluff?" asked Robert.

"With Fluff."

*   *   *   *

Wendell, who had placed a bagful of post-Thanksgiving turkey sandwiches alongside the traditional six of beer on the transmission hump, looked over at Patrice in the passenger seat.

"You okay?" he asked.

"Fine, why?"

"I dunno, you seem kind of jumpy, nervous. This gig is nothing, buncha state workers. They usually get drunk early, leave early, we get an early quit."

"I know," said Patrice. "Maybe I had a little too much coffee before we left."

Patrice then made a conscious effort to slow her breathing and relax the muscles in her face; anything that would help give the appearance of someone who was cool, calm, and collected.

Inside, her stomach churned and her head spun like a top. She desperately wanted everything to go right, everything to go as planned so she could successfully rendezvous with her sister in Lake Placid.

The last thing she wanted to do was arouse suspicions in her father.

Ordinarily she would have been riding with Dominic, but a rift had arisen between her father and her brother, a tension that was present all of Thanksgiving Day, having begun the day before when Robert had not returned outside to help with the firewood project. After having consumed his cocoa, he'd fallen asleep in the living room in front of a television set tuned to MTV; a station Robert favored, and his father abhorred. When Wendell had come looking for his son, he found him snoring in front of a screen that held several scantily clad black women gyrating provocatively around a gold-necklaced rapper. Wendell had vaporized the picture with one angry click of the remote but allowed his son to keep sleeping, exiting the room only after he'd shaken his head in disgust and passed judgment on the boy, calling him a shirker.

It was a label Wendell continued to use, ignoring Robert's presence, speaking only to other family members about his son in the third person, as in "my son the shirker" or "the shirker who lives here" or "that shirker who won't get a nickel out of me for his next paint set."

When it came time for the band members to leave for the job at the Paradise Lounge in Plattsburgh, Robert, out of habit, slid into the passenger side of his father's station wagon. Wendell, who was loading the last of his equipment, declared loudly, "I don't really like to ride with shirkers." With that, Patrice, who was just opening her door on the Westfalia, exchanged glances with Dominic, went to the wagon where she waved her brother out of the car and pointed in the direction of the other vehicle. He exited without question, but as he passed before Patrice on his way to Dominic's van, he asked in whisper, "What's a shirker?"

"Ask Dominic," came her response.

"Hand me one of them samidges, will you please?" requested Wendell, having polished off his first beer and was in the process of returning the empty to the paper carton.

Patrice dug into the brown paper bag and pulled out a fat turkey on white with mayo. Unwrapping it so the plastic wrap served as a dish on her open palm, she held it out to her father.

"Thanks," he said, and lifted it from her hand.

For the remainder of the trip to Plattsburgh, Wendell ate bites of his sandwich, returning it back down to the Saran wrap covered hand of Patrice while he chewed and intermittently sipped on his second beer. In between the food and drink, he came forth with snatches of speculation about the possibility of an audience member having a contact "in the business" and the expressed hope that none of the state workers would ask for a square dance, an art form that Wendell viewed as "ignorant" and not becoming for a band the caliber of the Charbonneaus.

Patrice, only half listening, having heard both bits of monologue too many times before, said little, responding usually by a verbal affirmation of her father's beliefs when she heard a pause in his discourse, freed her mind to play a movie of her upcoming reunion with her sister in the quaint Olympic village of Lake Placid.

"What's a shirker?" Robert had asked, seconds after closing the van's door behind him.

"A shirker is...," replied Dominic, searching for an explanation Robert could comprehend, " a shirker is somebody who quits, bails out on a job before it's done."

"Oh," said Robert, looking out the window and watching as a powdery snow was beginning to dust the passing landscape.

"Like my sister Chantelle is a shirker," he then offered, as he raised a sleeve to wipe his section of the windshield that had begun to fog over.

Dominic looked over and saw him rubbing vigorously first with his sleeve and then with the back of his hand.

"Don't use your hand," said Dominic, " it leaves streaks. The defroster will clear it in a few minutes."

He hadn't forgotten Robert's take on his explanation, and was well aware that the boy's statement was more of a question that either begged additional clarification or a simple yes or no. But knowing that whatever he'd say would most likely filter back to some other member in the Charbonneau clan, he wanted to choose his words carefully. He wanted to come off as diplomatic, but most of all he didn't want to offend Wendell, having, as of late, started to grow fond of the old guy, and knowing that the wrong words held the possibility that he might be seen as someone who had aligned himself with the other party in this father and daughter feud that continued to drag on endlessly.

The flakes were coming down at a frequency that warranted use of the wipers, so Dominic flipped them on and asked a question.

"How so?" asked Dominic.

"Huh?"

"How is Chantelle a shirker?"

"Well, she quit our band, she bailed out before we had a chance to hit the big time," said Robert.

Dominic pushed the defroster lever up a notch.

"I guess that's one way of looking at it... and in that way she is a shirker."

A big smile broke out on Robert's face.

"But," added Dominic, "in another way I don't think she's quit on herself, she hasn't bailed out on her own dreams of being a solo performer who hits the big time."

Robert's face crowded into a scowl and Dominic wasn't sure whether he was angry or simply confused.

"I'll bet Dad would say she's a shirker," said Robert testily.

"Oh, I'm sure he would," agreed Dominic quickly.

Robert's face took on a smug look.

"But he also thinks you're one too," added Dominic. "And if you want him to stop thinking you're a shirker, I'd tell you to start stacking wood, that pile you left on Wednesday and more that we added to it after you never came back outside, as soon as you wake up tomorrow morning."

The smug look had fallen from Robert's face and had been replaced by a series of twitches and movements around his eyes and mouth that Dominic took to be signs of a thought process.

Looking straight ahead, through a completely defogged windshield, on which fat snowflakes fell and were quickly whisked away, Robert, with a certain decorum, announced, "I'll do it."

For Wendell, the late afternoon, early evening job for the state workers at the Paradise Lounge in Plattsburgh turned out to be a mixed bag. He wound up calling three square dances, playing two polkas, a dance he considered to be even more ignorant than the square dance, and was asked by one inebriated middle-aged woman in a pantsuit to yodel *Una Paloma Blanca* in full Slim Whitman fashion. He flatly turned down the request, adding to the refusal a statement to the bleary-eyed female that he was a musician, not a pig-caller.

On the upside, as he'd predicted, he wrangled an early quitting time with the state supervisor with whom he'd booked the job, as most of the audience had drifted out of the building by about 7:00. By 7:35 the Charbonneaus were broken down, packed, and ready to roll.

The light snow had continued to fall, off and on, for the three hours and fifteen minutes the band had played, accumulating about an inch on the ground. As their cars warmed in the Paradise Lounge's parking lot, Wendell walked over to Dominic's vehicle and made a circular motion with his index finger to indicate he wanted Spinosa to roll his window down.

Dominic obeyed.

"You kids gonna be okay?" asked Wendell, leaning his head into the van. "The snow's stopped for now, but you never know, it might pick up again and get heavy." Wendell then looked over at his own car.

"Either of you two see Robert drawin' a beer from that keg they had in there tonight?" he asked.

Wendell turned back to the open window to see Patrice shaking her head. Dominic responded with, "No, why do you ask?"

"Well he's sittin' in the car with his eyes closed, looks like he's gonna go to sleep, thought he might have been drinking," said Wendell.

"He's probably just trying to avoid contact with you because of that shirker thing," offered Patrice.

Wendell nodded slowly.

"So anyway, why don't you two make the trip south on Monday," said Wendell.

"Oh Daddy, we'll be all right, besides with this snow Lake Placid will look so Christmasy," said Patrice.

"Now I gave you your pay, didn't I?" asked Wendell.

"Yep, all set," said Dominic, patting a wad of folded bills in his shirt pocket. "Just ask your daughter not to burn through all my hard earned cash."

Patrice reached over and punched Dominic in the arm.

"Wiseguy."

Wendell pushed the back of his hand across the stubble that had sprouted on his chin.

"There's something else I wanted to ask you…tell you…just can't remember," said Wendell, his brow knitted.

Patrice felt her next breath come hard.

"It was right on the tip of my tongue…"

"Something about Robert's new maracas?" asked Dominic. "I thought they sounded good on a couple of those songs with the Spanish beat. He's just got to work on controlling the roll of those little pellets inside."

Wendell's eyes searched the ground.

"Nope, nope that wasn't it."

"The band," suggested Patrice. "How the band sounded tonight?"

Wendell looked up, his eyes bright, and snapped his fingers.

"That's it! Mary Chapin Carpenter and her band are playing in Placid tonight. Double header with that guy from around Saratoga. What's his name?"

"Hal Ketchum?" said Patrice, using all her energy to push out his name.

"Yeah, that's him. Saw it advertised in the paper. Maybe you can still get tickets."

Dominic smiled and said, "We'll check it out."

Patrice was having difficulty breathing and she could hear the steady swish of blood coursing through her ears. She was thankful that the dome lamp was off, the only illumination coming from the pale green dash lights.

Wendell tapped the door lightly with his fingers.

"Listen, safe trip, I'll see you kids in the morning."

"Thanks, Wen."

"Bye, Daddy," came the squeak from Patrice.

Wendell walked away, Dominic rolled up his window and shifted into reverse. Turning to look out the rear window, his eyes first grazed across his girlfriend, then came back for a second look.

"Deep breaths," he instructed, "slow, deep breaths."

Dominic pulled his van onto the entrance ramp of the Adirondack Northway at precisely 8:00pm. If the road was good they'd reach Lake Placid in approximately an hour. By then it would be time to call Chantelle's cell phone and arrange for a meeting place.

The right lane of the Northway was clear and dry, the road made bare by the cars and trucks that had traveled before them. The middle and left lanes were dirty-white strips of snow that lay quietly until a passing vehicle, not content to travel at a moderate speed in the right lane, caused the snow to fly high into the air like a fine white dust, a dust that was quickly swept away by the Westfalia's wipers.

"How fast are you going?" asked an anxious Patrice.

"Fifty," said Dominic.

"You could go faster, use the passing lane like some of those other cars are doing," she urged.

"You don't know how the van would handle on that, it's still snow, could be slippery." He looked over at Patrice. "Don't worry, babe, we'll get there in plenty of time."

"I'm just so excited," said Patrice, squeezing her knees tightly together.

In an effort to get Patrice's mind off the journey and onto the destination he decided to focus on their itinerary in the village of Lake Placid.

"When we get into town where do you want to eat?" he asked.

"Mirror Lake Inn is really ritzy, the Black Bear has great burgers. I don't know. I'll have to see what Chantelle might be in the mood for."

She turned her head and looked over at Dominic.

"Didn't you eat anything from the buffet table?" she asked, referring to the food offered back at the Paradise Lounge.

"Some radishes and dip, slice of cheese on a cracker, nothing substantial," answered Dominic.

"I got to be honest with you, Dominic, right now I'm not even thinking about food, I just want to see her."

"And you will," promised Dominic.

Checking his left sideview mirror, Dominic caught the flash of a blinking yellow light. Shifting his eyes up into the rearview, he saw the headlights and front end of a state sander approaching. Routine pass, a precautionary measure, he thought, some of the workers just logging in a little overtime. Or possibly, he thought, as an uneasy feeling rippled through his stomach, is the truck on a mission to clear deeper snow or roughen some slickness on the stretch of road that lay up ahead?

Instinctively, Dominic felt his foot back off on the accelerator bringing the van's speed down to forty five miles per hour.

Patrice noticed immediately.

"Why are you slowing down?"

"There's a sander about to go by."

The truck made a wide pass around the back of the Westfalia, the sanding mechanism on the back peppering the side of Dominic's van as the hulking vehicle moved into the snowy left lane with a show of muscle and authority.

When the sander merged back into the right lane, it momentarily put the Westfalia in the middle of a white-out, its plow and bulk having kicked up a tremendous amount of snow. For several tense moments, Dominic was driving blind and Patrice began to panic.

"I can't see!" said Patrice.

"It'll clear," assured Dominic, straining to see the road through a swirling mass of white.

When some distance grew between the back of the truck and the front of the van, the man-made snowstorm began to subside. Moments later, Dominic regained a clear view of the road and began to relax, bringing the van back up to fifty.

Just as the sander faded from sight, the Westfalia crossed a bridge over a small stream. Approximately 100 feet from the end of bridge, the van hit a patch of black ice, a frozen oval that the sand had missed or was resistant to, and Dominic felt himself losing control of his vehicle.

The van began to skid to the right, and remembering what he'd learned in Driver's Ed many years before, Dominic fought the urge to apply his breaks and steered into the direction of the skid hoping to get the vehicle moving again in a straight line.

But it was too hard a right, and the van, after leaning dangerously to the left, went off the road and down into a gully of icy grass covered with light snow, the wide divider separating the south and north bound lanes of the Northway.

A scream came from Patrice and she reached over and grabbed his arm, an arm that was rock hard as he held the wheel steady in their slide down the hill. His foot then gently feathered the brakes in an effort to bring the van to a stop.

The van slowed and eventually slid to a stop at the bottom of the gully.

Dominic let out a loud sigh through an open mouth. He could hear the beginnings of a whimper from Patrice and he turned to her.

"We could have... we could have been killed," she said softly, her voice and her body in a full tremble.

He pulled her to him and held her tightly, her body quaking in his arms.

"But we weren't, and we're okay. Now let's get back on the road."

He kept the engine running partly for the heat, but primarily because he feared that if he shut it down, for whatever the reason, it might not start again. He rifled through the glove compartment in search of a flashlight, found one, but soon discovered the batteries were dead. Uttering a curse, he threw the worthless light back into the glove box, opened his door and hopped out of the van.

Dominic went to each one of the wheels, gripped the top of the tire with both hands and tugged hard, making sure that nothing had broken or come loose in the skid or the descent down the hill. He found them tight, intact, with no obvious damage that could he could detect manually.

"Van's okay," he said as he hopped back up into the driver's seat. He looked over at Patrice whose shaking had subsided but whose eyes seemed to have widened to the size of dinner plates.

"Are we going to make it to Lake Placid?" she asked, her voice flat.

"Don't see why not. Just got to get us out of this ditch."

But over the next half hour, their best efforts would prove futile, as the freezing rain that had fallen several nights prior had coated the grass in the gully with a thin layer of ice, a film that would not allow the van sufficient traction to climb the hill.

First, they attempted the most obvious route of escape. Dominic in the driver's seat, with the van still at the lowest point in the culvert, maneuvered the vehicle around so it pointed back up towards the road, dropped it into gear and eased his foot down on the gas pedal. This action produced nothing but the sound of spinning tires that refused to grab and an engine turning out high rpms Next, they tried with Patrice at the wheel and Dominic pushing from behind. Zero progress. Abandoning the idea of climbing straight up the hill, Dominic aimed the van at an angle, but succeeded only in sliding sideways and moving only slightly farther down the length the gully. Lastly, they found an old gray woolen blanket, placed it under the drive wheels and attempted to get a running start in this fashion. The tires quickly spit the blanket and returned to spinning unproductively, emitting that annoying high-pitched keening as the two looked at each other with frustration and dwindling hope in their eyes.

Five minutes into their efforts a motorist had stopped and called down to them, asking if they wanted him to call a tow truck. Confident from the inspection he had given the van, sure that the vehicle would soon be back on the road to Placid, Dominic had thanked the man but declined any assistance.

Now, his decision would come back to haunt him.

"Why didn't you let that guy call a tow truck for us?" questioned Patrice, a sharp edge to her voice.

"I thought we could get out of here by ourselves, I'm sorry, I made a mistake."

"Why doesn't anybody else stop?" asked Patrice.

"Afraid. An old mom and pop in their Caddy see the van, figure we're a bunch of druggies so wasted we went off the road. Or think maybe we're psycho-killers on the loose."

"What about some college guys from Plattsburgh State. They wouldn't be afraid to stop," said Patrice.

"Home for Thanksgiving break."

"Oh, that's right," said Patrice, her voice trailing off.

For the next few minutes the two sat in silence, peering out into the night through their respective windows.

"The emergency call boxes. Forgot all about them," said Dominic, his voice bouyant with promise.

He looked up towards the road where passing traffic seemed to have slowed to a trickle, the blackness broken only by the occasional running lights of a tractor trailer hurtling by.

"Can't be one too far from here. I'll go," said Dominic. He switched on the van's flashers and told Patrice to turn on the headlights several times in succession if she saw a car coming from the north.

As he started to exit the van, she grabbed his arm.

"I'm coming with you. Thanks to you, I got that notion of psycho-killers stuck in my head."

On foot, slipping, sliding, occasionally falling, Dominic instructing Patrice to walk sideways like a crab and bear down on the edges of her soles to grab a foothold, the two eventually made their way to the top of the hill.

As they stood side by side on the shoulder of the road, their breath coming hard from the energy spent on the climb, Dominic threw an arm over his girlfriend's shoulders, and felt her shivering against the cold. Neither was dressed adequately for the outdoors; he wore jeans, and a thinly-lined denim ranch coat over his ubiquitous flannel shirt; she was also in jeans, and wore a white acetate Western blouse under a short brown leather jacket.

Dominic blew warmth into hands that needed gloves.

"Left or right?" he asked.

"What?"

"Should we start walking to the left or the right in search of the call box?"

Patrice thought a moment.

"To the right, towards Lake Placid."

"Let's go."

The two, their toes starting to become numb in cowboy boots not designed for extended stints in cold weather, headed south along the shoulder of the Adirondack Northway, from time to time looking over their backs to be aware of any approaching vehicles.

Ten minutes into their trek a car or a truck had yet to pass.

Dominic spied it first, a silhouette of a rectangle on top of a post -- an emergency call box, one of many installed by the state at intervals on the more desolate sections of the Northway.

He ran to it, tugged open the yellow front cover, stuck his hand inside, felt around.

"Shit! Fucking Bastards!" he cursed to the night sky.

Patrice was about 15 feet behind him.

"Not there?" she asked.

"Some drunk-off-his-ass college boy probably liberated it when he stopped here to take a piss. A little souvenir to show his buddies back home."

Dominic hauled off and kicked the heel of his boot hard into the post that supported the call box.

"Goddammit!"

Patrice had both arms wrapped around herself, with her hands stuck under her armpits for warmth.

"Dominic I can't feel my feet. I think I better get back to the van."

The descent down the hill was easy, as the two slid down on their butts for much of the way, and provided a moment or two of comic relief for an otherwise frustrating situation.

After brushing the snow off their clothes, Dominic reclaimed the woolen blanket from the ground as Patrice climbed back into the van, jacked the heater up to high and removed her boots. Dominic, having shaken snow, bits of grass and frozen dirt from the blanket, opened Patrice's door and bundled her in it. He then went over to his door and climbed in.

"Give me your feet," he said.

She said nothing, leaned back and swung her legs up onto his lap. He began rubbing with both hands.

"Well?" she asked.

She felt his fingers knead a little harder into her flesh.

"I was thinking I could go back up to the road, try to flag down a car, and ask them, maybe even pay them, to get off at the next exit and call us a tow truck."

"What about me?" she asked.

"You stay here, get warm, I'll come back down after I get someone to call for help."

"And if you can't...what if nobody stops?" she asked.

Dominic looked down at his gas gauge. It read three-quarters full.

"We spend the night here. Got enough gas to keep warm– "

"Or to get us to Placid if we get out of here in time," she

interrupted.

"Right."

He gave her feet one last squeeze.

"You can lie down in the back if you want."

"No, I prefer to stay here so I can look out the window and keep an eye on you."

He leaned over and kissed her.

"Be back soon."

A young couple with a sleeping baby in a car seat in the back stopped about fifteen minutes after Dominic had reached the top of the hill and began waving a white handkerchief at the handful of cars and trucks that passed. After explaining his predicament and making his request, he pulled his band pay from his shirt pocket and offered them money for their time and trouble. The husband waved off the cash and assured Dominic he'd get off at the next exit, Keeseville, and locate a towing service.

Dominic transferred the wad of cash from his right hand to his left, reached in, shook the husband and the wife's hand, and thanked them profusely. After they drove off, he looked down at the bills in his hand and decided that, as he'd need them for the tow, a safer depository was needed. He dug into his back pocket and extracted his wallet. Just as he opened it, he looked down at the van trying to see Patrice, and a gust of November air blew across the highway, and unbeknownst to him, lifted two small scraps of paper out of the wallet and cast them into the night. He then wedged the bills into the wallet and shoved it back down into his pocket.

*   *   *   *

In a Lake Placid newspaper and magazine shop, Chantelle penned a greeting and an address on a picture postcard of a ski jumper to her mother, making sure to use the box number at the Chazy post office, a box her mother had rented in secret after Wendell's discovery of Chantelle's missives that came directly to the house.

While waiting for the clerk to ring up her other purchases – two packs of cigarettes, a disposable lighter, and three stamps – Chantelle pulled her cell phone from her purse to check that the unit was on and functioning. A glance at the glowing LED lights assured her that it was. While receiving her change her eyes fell upon a wall clock behind the clerk. The time was 9:55.   She and her entourage were scheduled to depart Lake Placid at approximately 11:30pm.

Her first thought, as she walked back outside, was that her father had somehow found out about Patrice's plan to rendezvous and summarily had forbidden his middle child to make the journey under threat of yet another banishment from the family. Chantelle's emotions came rapid-fire, one right after another – contempt for her father and disappointment at the cowardice of her younger sister.

She came to a halt in the middle of Main Street in Lake Placid, shook a cigarette from her pack, lighted it, and took a deep inhalation. She stopped herself from any further criticism of her father and sister in this imaginary scenario, realizing that any one of a number of factors could be responsible for Patrice's absence in Lake Placid, and consciously chose to steer her mind onto the subject of her own situation.

She was just about half-way through her fourth year of estrangement and, as of late, was starting to have grave doubts about her decision to break from the family and begin a solo career. The four song demo she'd cut within the first year of management under Conroy hadn't been able to raise a shred of interest from any of the recording company executives to whom Jack had pitched. Three and a half years under the personal management of Nashville hot-shot Mr. Jack Conroy and he still hadn't been able to get her signed to a major label. Usually opening acts have some label, a small label, an independent label, *any* label when they tour, but she had none. She had begun to feel as though she was stuck, forever destined to remain in "special guest" hell.

She looked over at the twinkling Christmas lights in the lobby of the Best Western Motel. She could see logs burning in a fireplace, a fireplace like her family's fireplace, and people smiling, talking, laughing.

I'm so close to home, she thought. All it would take would be for me to tell Chris the road manager that I was done, quitting the tour, heading home.

Home. The sound of the word brought a welling of tears.

Chantelle dug deep into her purse, pulled out the cell phone, and stared down at it, long and hard. One phone call, she thought. One phone call and an apology and she could go home. That simple.

She imagined her father coming to get her, if he still owned it, in that stupid old station wagon with the sign and car part stuck on the roof. He'd come, middle of the night, didn't matter, he'd come to take his daughter home. She'd cry, throw her arms around him...

"Excuse me."

Chantelle looked up from the cell phone and into the faces of two couples, nicely dressed, who looked to be in their mid-thirties.

"Yes?"

"We saw you at the arena tonight," said one of the females. "Couldn't stay for Mary Chapin Carpenter, babysitter problems, you know? But we thought you and Hal were great!" The other three nodded enthusiastically.

"Thanks, thanks very much."

"We were wondering if we could trouble you for a couple of autographs," asked one of the males.

"Sure, no problem."

Chantelle took one last lingering look at the phone in her hand and then shoved it deep into her purse.

"Now who's got a pen?" she asked, forcing her mouth into a smile.

*   *   *   *

"Nobody's coming," said a forlorn Patrice from her seat in the van.

Dominic looked down at the gas gauge. It had just moved off the three quarter mark and was heading back to the half.

"Still got plenty of gas if we're stuck here for the night."

"Don't want to spend the night here," replied Patrice brattily.

Dominic looked out his window, up at the road, his eyes searching for the belated rescue truck.

"The program teaches you that there are things in life you can't control, so you have to accept..."

"Please, spare me the program," said Patrice, holding her hand up like a traffic cop signaling to stop. "Just spare me the program, okay?"

It had been nearly an hour since Dominic had hailed down the young couple and made his request for help. The heater had kept them comfortably warm but Patrice's tensions about their plight were heating up to the point where things were becoming unbearable.

"What did you tell those people, are you sure they understood you?" questioned Patrice.

"We've been through this, Patrice," said Dominic, his eyes still searching the road.

"Just tell me, I mean the words you used, when you asked— "

"It's here!" shouted Dominic, scrambling out of the van.

"Wait, I'm coming with you," she called after him.

As the two slipped and fell up the hill, Patrice pleaded with Dominic to finish the trip, to complete the journey to Placid. Dominic assured her he would, but suggested she call Chantelle's number as soon as they got to a phone.

When the two reached the tow truck, the driver, a burly, beer-bellied little man who wore a Fu Manchu, the shellacked head of a rattlesnake on a strip of rawhide around his neck, and a name tag that said "Bucky", slowly climbed down out of the cab.

"Where have you been?" asked Patrice, her tone sharply accusatory.

Bucky looked at her with steely eyes.

"You think you're the only one dumb enough to slide off the road tonight, lady?"

Dominic intervened before there was a chance for Bucky and Patrice to tangle.

"Please just get us back on the road."

"Cost ya seventy five bucks," said Bucky.

"No problem," said Dominic reaching for his wallet.

"Do you have a cell phone we could use?" asked Patrice, her voice markedly sweeter.

"Cost ya," replied Bucky, pulling one from a leather holster on his belt.

"I'll pay, I'll pay," said Patrice, greedily taking it from her hand.

Bucky then turned to Dominic.

"Not that I don't trust ya, but I need the money up front. Been stiffed by people who say they got the bucks, but don't."

"Got my wallet right here," said Dominic, pulling out three twenties.

He looked over at Patrice who was staring blankly at the phone in her hand.

"Don't know how to work it?" asked Dominic.

Bucky turned and looked at Patrice who raised her head and stared off into the distance.

"Can't remember the number," she said.

Dominic handed Bucky the three twenties and turned his attention back to his wallet.

"It's okay 'Treece, don't you remember I wrote it down, put it in here as a back-up." His fingers searched through the wallet, seeking in vain for the slip of paper. "Well, I thought, it should..."

He moved over towards the front of the truck to catch the beam from the headlights.

"Hey pal, this is only sixty bucks," complained Bucky.

"I can't remember Chantelle's number," repeated Patrice, her eyes now focused back on the face of the phone.

"You'll get the rest in a minute," said Dominic tersely to Bucky. "I just gotta find this piece of paper."

He pulled out an appointment card from a dentist in Tupper Lake, a Charbonneau Band business card, a claim slip for photo development at a pharmacy, a scrap of paper bearing the name and number of a guy in Malone who did guitar repair and customizations, but no cell number for Chantelle.

Patrice was standing, eyes wide, mouth open, as if she'd been struck dumb, still holding the phone in her hand.

"I'm sorry, Patrice," said Dominic, "I don't have it, I did have it, but I must have lost it."

Patrice walked over and plopped herself down on the truck's running board.

"We can still try to make it to Lake Placid," offered Dominic.

"And what, wander around town trying to find her? Drive through the village calling out her name like she's some lost dog?" She looked down at her soiled white blouse and grass-stained jeans. Tears began to flow. "Try to get backstage at a packed concert? You think anybody would believe I'm her sister. Look at me, I'm a mess."

Dominic did look at her. In addition to her filthy clothes, her hair was matted, errant strands sticking to her forehead and mascara was beginning to streak her cheeks.

She handed the phone back up to Bucky who twirled it once like a six gun and slipped it back into its holster on his belt.

"Just take me home, Dominic," she said, crying freely now. "Please just take me home."

She lowered her face into her dirt encrusted hands as giant sobs wracked her body.

"Hey!" said Bucky, addressing himself to Dominic and pointing in the direction of the Westfalia. "If you want *that* vehicle out of *that* ditch I need another fifteen bucks."

*   *   *   *

As the stretch limo carrying Chantelle and her band traveled southward on the Northway, destination Albany airport, Chantelle looked down at the cell phone in her hand that had remained sadly mute all evening. While her band members slept, either from exhaustion, drugs, or a combination of the two, somewhere just past the South Glens Falls exit, Chantelle fingered the electric window button. When the motor had ground the glass down about five inches, she slipped her hand out the window and flung the phone as far as she could throw.

CHAPTER 7

June Charbonneau awakened on the Saturday after Thanksgiving to the sound of her husband's groaning and something knocking into the side of their house.

She sat up in bed, looked over and found Wendell stretched out on his back on the bedroom floor.

"What's the trouble, Wen?"

"June, I'm so stiff they could cut me up and use me for pricks."

"You got a way with words," she said, shaking her head. "Arthritis?"

"Nah, I think it's because I spent yesterday morning lying on that cold ground tryin' to figure out what's up with my tanker's punkin."

"Punkin?"

"The differential, the gears in the back of my truck," explained Wendell. "Truck's been shakin', rear end's been roarin'. I'm gonna have to call Lanfear's on Monday morning."

The sound of knocking against the side of the house had subsided, but now started up again.

"Now what is that?" asked June.

"I suspect it's Robert stacking the wood he should have three days ago," said Wendell, still prone on the floor. "I think Dominic had a little talk with him."

Wendell rolled over onto his side so he could face June.

"He and Patrice have a good time in Placid?" asked Wendell.

"No."

"No?"

"Never made it. They slid off the road near the Keeseville exit."

Wendell started to scramble to his feet.

"Where are they? They get hurt? They all right?"

June put both of her hands up in front of her, palms open, like she was readying herself to fend off the charge of an angry beast.

"Calm down. They're fine. No damage to them or the van. They were both just a little dirty when they got home. I was up watching TV when they got in, you were asleep."

As June's information registered, she watched as Wen's protuberant belly slowly began to drop – a sign he was starting to relax, that his brain had told his body there was no cause for alarm. Now on his feet, he shook out his hands, then placed them on his hips and began rolling his head in a circle, trying to work out the kinks.

"Wouldn't listen to me," he said, "I told them it would have been wiser, safer to have made the trip next week."

June threw back the covers, swung her legs off the side of the bed, and was working her toes into a pair of pink terrycloth bedroom slippers.

"They're young, Wen, they're going to take risks, make mistakes."

Upon returning home from her aborted jaunt to Lake Placid, Patrice, standing next to an exhausted Dominic, had given her mother a teary, abbreviated version of the story, and headed straight to the shower. Later, clean and clad in a white bathrobe with a towel turbaned around her head, she went to her mother who sat sprawled on the couch in the living room, and snuggled deep into her breast. Over the background music of her dirty clothes agitating in the washer, Patrice relayed details of the story including the part where Dominic had cursed and kicked the emergency box and the bizarre trinket that hung from Bucky the tow truck driver's neck.

As Patrice talked, June patted her youngest daughter's arm and occasionally planted a little kiss on her forehead. Soon, a pause came in Patrice's storytelling and she looked up into her mother's eyes.

"I acted like a baby," said Patrice. "Dominic was doing the best he could, and I was a little brat."

June smiled and hugged her.

"You were scared and disappointed."

"Don't cut me any slack, Momma. I'm almost twenty-three-years old. He deserves an apology."

"So give him one."

That same night when Patrice had slipped into the shower, Dominic had quietly walked into the kitchen, soaped his face and hands at the sink and dried himself with a paper towel. On his way through to his room, he had muttered a tired 'good-night' to June in the living room and asked her to wish the same to Patrice. For a few moments, June heard the sound of his nylon sleeping bag brushing against the inflatable mattress as he tossed and turned, seeking a comfortable position, but shortly thereafter the room fell quiet.

About 10:00 the next morning, Robert opened Dominic's door and strode in.

"Hey Dominic, guess what?"

Dominic opened one eye and identified the intruder as Robert.

"What?"

"I don't think I'm a shirker anymore."

"That's good, Robert. You stack some wood?"

"Yup."

"Good, I'm happy for you."

Dominic closed his eye and buried himself a little deeper into his sleeping bag. Robert stood his ground.

"Got something else to tell ya."

Dominic pried opened both eyes.

"Go ahead."

"Patrice said to come out, 'cause she made you a nice breakfast."

Dominic ran his tongue over the front of his top teeth and grimaced.

"Tell her I'll be out in about ten minutes."

"K."

Patrice had risen early, showered again, used a blow dryer on her hair, applied make-up and perfume, and dressed herself in a short black skirt, a black sweater, and black boots with red tooling. She'd cracked three eggs, chopped a small onion, and shredded some cheese into a bowl which she covered and placed on a shelf in the refrigerator. About 9:30 Wendell had made his way into the kitchen, on the prowl in search of his own breakfast, and had lifted the bowl out of the refrigerator only to have Patrice grab him by the wrist and escort his hand that held the bowl back onto the shelf.

"What, what's the problem?" protested Wendell, his fingers still clamped onto the lip of the concoction.

"For Dominic," insisted Patrice, and held him in a stare until he released his hold on the bowl.

Wendell scratched his belly and sniffed.

"What about me?" he asked.

"You go in the living room, turn on one of your Saturday morning shows– "

"Love to watch them infomercials," he interrupted, smiling and rubbing his hands together. "Those hucksters try to sell you just about anything."

"I'll make you up a nice tray, bring it in to you," she continued. "Momma's already in there, I fixed her a plate."

Wendell put a little spring in his step as he headed into the living room.

"A little date with my mate, plus some food on my plate," he sang. As he passed through the doorway, he stopped and turned back to face her.

"Who was driving?" he asked, his tone suddenly turned serious.

"Dominic."

"Glad you kids are all right."

"Thanks, Daddy, now go get settled in your recliner."

June sat, her eyes glued to the TV, finishing a breakfast of orange slices, a buttered bagel, and tea. She didn't look away from the set when Wendell entered the room.

"Stiffness going away?" she inquired, chewing a small mouthful of bagel.

There was about a three second delay as Wendell considered her question.

"Oh yeah, but I figure it's probably better if I keep moving. Don't want to seize up again."

"No," said June, staring hard at the image of a tanned young man with huge gleaming caps as he made an impassioned pitch for his product, "I don't think I'd have any use for a rusted tin man of a husband."

Wendell looked at her askance, smirked, and plopped into his recliner. June tore her eyes away from the set.

"After Patrice serves you, stay in here awhile. She needs some privacy with Dominic."

Wendell nodded a promise of compliance to her request.

Patrice had just returned from serving her father a refill on his coffee, a second bagel with cream cheese, and the last sausage patty in the freezer, as Dominic, his feet gliding noiselessly in white athletic socks, his head lowered, slunk into the kitchen. He wore a rough stubble, his hair slicked back with water, jeans and an untucked rumpled T.

"Hi," he greeted softly, then quickly averted his eyes.

"Good morning," she answered, her voice barely a whisper.

He took a seat at the kitchen table where she had arranged place settings, side by side, for the two of them. As Patrice approached the table, she caught sight of a small pool of milk on the edge of the table, having missed it the first time when she cleaned up after Robert's ravenous downing of an overfilled bowl of sugared cereal – fuel for his wood stacking. Snatching a dishcloth from a nearby counter she quickly wiped up the spill with one pass.

"How about an omelet, a cheese and onion omelet?" she asked, her voice as sweet as the cereal Robert had devoured earlier that morning.

Dominic sat slumped in his chair, arms hanging loosely in his lap. He reached up and massaged his face with his hands.

"No thanks," he mumbled, "cup of coffee will be fine."

Patrice fought the urge to push the omelet, the struggle manifesting itself physically by her lips clamping tightly together. After a moment, she exhaled and said, "Okay."

She brought the carafe from its hot plate and filled the cup that sat in front of him. Knowing that, with no discernible pattern, he took his coffee different ways, she moved the creamer and sugar bowl towards him.

This morning he took his coffee black.

She took the seat next to him and wrapped her fingers around a large cup of blackberry tea she'd been nursing all morning.

"Some toast?" she asked.

"No...thanks."

She took a sip of her tea.

"You sleep okay?" she asked.

For the first time that morning he made deliberate eye contact.

"No I didn't. Went to sleep fast, but I kept waking up, thinking about you."

Patricia could feel her face becoming warm. She looked away but then forced herself to look back into Dominic's eyes.

"I apologize for last night. I acted like a child, a frightened little baby."

"You think swearing at a dead flashlight is a mature way of

expressing frustration?" he countered.

"No, but– "

"But nuthin, 'Treece." He pursed his lips and looked in the direction of the living room, cognizant that Ma and Pa Charbonneau may be trying to hang on their every word.

He lowered his voice.

"What bothered me, what hurt me, was the fact that you doubted me, didn't trust me."

Patrice's face became quizzical.

"Just before the tow truck showed up," reminded Dominic, "you started questioning me about what I had said to that couple, doubting, not trusting that I explained to them what we needed."

Patrice bit into her lower lip and nodded slowly.

"We don't talk about it that much, Patrice, but I am an addict. When I was active, I lied to my friends, my family, I couldn't be trusted. I conned everybody. So in recovery trust is the hardest thing to try and reclaim." He paused. "You pushed a button, a very painful button."

"I'm sorry, really," said Patrice.

Dominic took a drink of his coffee and then looked back at Patrice. She could see that his eyes were rimmed with red.

"At the risk of sounding like I'm on a roll here...please don't make fun of the program," he pleaded. " I know I fall back on it, maybe a little too heavily, especially when I'm feeling scared or confused, but it's saved my life, Patrice, honest."

Patrice remembered asking Dominic, rudely, to spare her any NA philosophy. She drew a deep breath.

"I want to learn more about this NA program. Are you going to a meeting today?" she asked.

"Yes."

"Can I come?"

"No."

Her lower lip dropped.

"Why, why can't I come with you?"

He gave her a lascivious look.

"And have all the other guys at the meeting trying to 13th step you? Forget it."

Her face crowded into a scowl.

"What's that mean, 13th step me?"

"Hit on you."

Patrice smiled, reached over and stroked his bare arm. He took another mouthful of coffee, his swallow then an audible gulp.

"In fact, some of the guys have actually asked me to bring you to a meeting...after they saw that picture."

Patrice narrowed her eyes, gritted her teeth, and squeezed Dominic's arm until he let out with a yelp.

"It better not be that one from high school with the troweled-on make-up and my hair that looks like a toilet brush," she said menacingly.

Dominic smiled impishly.

"Only one I got. Guess it'd be to your advantage to have a new one taken."

"You bastard," she hissed, and began thrusting her hands into his back pockets.

"Where's your wallet? You keep it in your wallet, don't you? Give it to me, give it to me right now."

"You keep your hands to yourself, young lady," giggled Dominic. He then reached over and began tickling her ribcage. She squirmed wildly.

"Stop, I hate to be tickled. Dominic, I mean it, stop it."

The sounds of their good-natured sparring snared the curiosity of Robert, who had been standing in the entryway to the living room, looking over his parents' shoulders at the TV.

He wandered to the doorway of the kitchen but by the time he arrived, Dominic and Patrice had quieted.

Robert walked purposely back into the living room, like a speaker striding to the podium, and came to a halt directly in front of the TV. He looked first at his father, who sat in the recliner, eyes closed, mouth open, having been lulled into a light doze, and then at his mom, who returned his look with raised eyebrows and a lean of her head.

Robert's shoulders then shot up to his ears and he covered a fast emerging smile with his hand.

"What is it, Robert?" asked his mother.

"They're kissing," came his voice from behind his hand, "in the kitchen."

"You all done stacking that wood?" she asked.

Simultaneously, his hand, smile, and shoulders all dropped.

"No."

"Then I suggest you get back to it."

"K."

*   *   *   *

Sonny Rapant arrived at his parents for Thanksgiving dinner with half a load on, a huge heavy plastic banner that read, *Grand Re-Opening - THE FORGE,* a cardboard box containing newspaper tearsheets, yellow legal pads with marketing notes scrawled in pencil, and a thick stack of freshly printed bumper stickers that boasted: "I Got Hammered at *The Forge.*"

Over a meal that Sonny ran more like a marketing meeting, he explained to his folks that he had set the re-opening of the club for the second Saturday after Thanksgiving, December 4th. The students would be back at Plattsburgh State after their holiday and he was sure they'd be ready, willing, and able to party. So sure, in fact that he'd taken out a full page ad in the campus newspaper announcing what he referred to as the "newest rock and roll club in the north country." Wanting to draw a mix of students and locals, he'd also taken out several days of quarter page advertisements in the *Chazy Courier, The Northcountryman,* and the *Plattsburgh Press Republican* advertising "Two-fer Townie" drink specials, promising two bottled beers or two mixed drinks for the price of one, as long as the patron's license could prove residence anywhere north of Ticonderoga.

During his windy monologue, Sonny's wife Millie and his boy, Claude, sat silently, eating forkfuls of turkey, mashed potatoes, and stuffing, having heard Sonny's plans and strategies ad nauseum. In the meantime, Joe and Martha listened attentively, the information being brand new to their ears.

When Joe decided to let Sonny have a crack at turning the business around, he and Martha took a giant step back away from the bar, lined up an impromptu vacation in Florida, and returned only two days before Thanksgiving. The two wanted to give Sonny a wide swath in his plans to transform the bar and feared their presence might result in their being shocked at some radical changes that Sonny might have in mind.

During dessert, Sonny passed the tearsheets from the various newspapers around the table, along with several of the bumperstickers. Joe read the advertisements carefully. Martha preferred to skim them as she busied herself with pouring coffee for the adults and scooping vanilla ice cream onto the warm apple pie she had served her grandson. Sonny's wife, Millie, having already seen the print ads, held onto one of the bumper stickers and sipped at her mimosa.

Sonny took a slug of his Black Velvet and water, waved off a slab of pecan pie his mother was offering, looked in the direction of his father and asked, "Any questions?"

Joe was impressed with his son's efforts.

"Looks tight, Sonny. Looks like you've done your homework,"

praised the elder Rapant.

"Thanks, Dad."

Millie looked at her father-in-law over the rim of her glass.

"What with workin' at the bar, writing the ads, running around, getting things printed up, I don't think Sonny's slept more than three hours a night in the last couple of weeks," said Millie.

Sonny scowled at her and then smirked.

"I'll sleep when I'm dead," he said.

"What an awful thing to say," chided his mother, handing another napkin to Claude who had ice cream running down his chin.

"Just an expression, Ma."

Joe Rapant lifted his bifocals off his nose, laid them on the table, and looked at his son.

"I *do* have a couple of questions," said Joe.

"Shoot," said Sonny.

"You planning on changing anything about the interior of the bar?"

"No," answered Sonny, "other than making the stage a little bigger, 'cause rock bands usually have more equipment, the inside of the former *Whiskey River* will stay the same."

"Wouldn't you want to put pictures of famous rock and roll musicians on the walls or something?" asked his mother.

Sonny brought two fingers to his temple and massaged lightly.

"I thought about that, Ma, initially. But I figured club patrons will either be looking at each other or watching the band."

"Speaking of the bands, are they more expensive than the country groups?" asked Joe.

"Nah, 'bout the same," lied Sonny, as the rock bands he'd priced out were about a third higher than the country ensembles his father had been bringing in for years. Sonny planned on showing his father the books, which would show the monies spent on band fees, after *The*

Forge started turning a profit.

"What's the name of the first band you've hired," asked his mother.

"Blitzkrieg," answered Sonny.

The elder Rapant's face twisted into a frown.

"Are they Nazis?" asked a very concerned Joe Rapant.

Sonny threw his head back and laughed.

"No, Dad, a lot of heavy metal bands have names like that. Most of the groups I auditioned had names like Mainliner, Mac 10, Hatchets from Hell – names that try to sound tough, ballsy– "

"Angry, violent," interrupted Millie, her head a little light from her champagne and orange juice.

Sonny leveled a glare at her.

"Even listened to an all-girl band," continued Sonny, "called themselves Gangbang."

"Sonny!" snapped his mother, nodding at Claude who was oblivious to his father's words, so immersed in the process of making a mess of his dessert.

"He's all right, Ma," assured Sonny.

"Now speaking of girls," began Joe Rapant, " before your mother and I left for our little vacation I heard your friend Gonyea shootin' his mouth off to some customers about– "

Joe Rapant stopped and looked over at his grandson.

"About you wantin' to bring in those, uh, go-go dancers...you know, those hoochie-coochie girls."

Sonny smiled wide, shook his head, and waved his hand dismissively.

"Ah, that's just Mike blowin' smoke."

"I have a question," said Millie, emboldened by the wine and feeling safeguarded by the presence of her in-laws. She held up the bumpersticker she had palmed. "Get hammered at *The Forge*," she read.

"Don't you think that kind of promotes heavy drinking?"

For a very long moment Sonny said nothing, preferring to look at his wife with a gaze of pure disgust, his mouth twisted into an ugly sneer. Millie nervously took another sip of her drink. Sonny's finger began to tap the table.

"How do you think, my little bride," he began, "that we're going to make any money if people don't drink...and drink a lot?"

"Well I just, I just meant," she stammered, "that maybe you could emphasize, promote something else."

Sonny lowered his head and began nodding.

"You're right, Millie," he said, raising his head. "you're absolutely 100% right." He wiggled the first two fingers of his right hand in a beckoning motion. "Give me that bumpersticker, give it here."

Millie stood, leaned across the table, and handed him the sticker which Sonny immediately began ripping into pieces.

"Easy, Sonny," warned his father, as he watched his offspring's face grow a shade redder than the glow the whiskey had given him.

"It's okay, Dad."

Millie drained the rest of her drink, set the glass on the table and looked wide-eyed at her mother-in-law for some sort of direction. She could see Martha's chest heaving slightly, but the older woman's eyes gave her nothing.

When he had completely shredded the sticker, Sonny formed the rippings into a small pile and looked back over at his wife.

"You're right, we need something else. First thing tomorrow morning I'm gonna have some new stickers printed up."

With the index finger of both hands, Sonny then traced the outline of a rectangle in the air.

"The new ones will say, 'Come see Millie stripped to her skivvies.'"

Sonny let his hands fall to the table with a loud thump as Millie's breath came out of her with a start.

"You, Millie, you can be our first go-go dancer, the club's first hoochie-coochie girl. People will come to the bar to see *you* dancin' in your undies."

Millie sat frozen, welded to her chair as tears instantly welled in her eyes.

"That's just about enough, Sonny," said his mother angrily.

Sonny leapt to his feet and stuck a phony smile on his face.

"Excellent dinner, Ma. Delicious."

He picked up his napkin, gave his mouth a quick, glancing wipe, then turned to his father and Claude.

"Boys? I think the game's on. A little football?"

*   *   *   *

Rapant's *Whiskey River*, soon to become *The Forge*, was a rambling two story clapboard structure built in the late 1930s. When the business and the building came up for sale in 1985, Joe Rapant, looking to retire from the railroad, bought the bar, which at the time was named *Dell's*, with money saved from overtime, the small inheritance left by his parents, and a loan from the bank.

Set back from the road, in a clearing surrounded by woods, the bar boasted a spacious parking lot, which Joe had blacktopped soon after acquiring the property. He also constructed an addition, more floor space for tables and dancing, and started bringing in country music on the week-ends.

Although there were several rooms upstairs, Joe had furnished only one, his office. He had left the others essentially vacant, with the exception of housing a stray chair or table from the bar that had been broken and stored with the promise of one day being mended.

Through the eyepiece of the Redfield scope mounted on his bolt action Winchester model seventy, Wendell Charbonneau could see that Joe Rapant's office on the second floor was dark on this Friday night, December 3rd. He swung the rifle down and to the right. Sonny's truck, tucked close to the side of the building, came into the cross hairs of the scope. As luck would have it, a full moon was shining, bathing everything in a silvery-blue light and as Wendell glanced down at his wristwatch he could make out that that the second hand would soon join the hour hand at the number 12. Two more hours to closing time.

Wendell had taken up his vantage point in a wooded area not far from the club at approximately 11:00 p.m. Now with a couple more hours to go, he made his way back to his truck, which he had piloted into a pull-off alongside the main road, to munch on pretzels and chips, to sip warm soda, and to wait.

He'd spent the day puttering – re-stacking some of the wood that Robert had balanced sloppily against the side of the house, raking the last of the autumn leaves, polishing the body of his guitar, and, in secret, pouring over the ads Sonny Rapant had placed in the various north country newspapers, heralding the grand re-opening of the roadhouse.

Wendell had an appointment booked at Lanfear's Garage in Plattsburgh for Saturday, December 4th. The mechanic had told him that repair or replacement of his truck's supposed ailing differential would be an all day job, and they wanted to start the work around 7:00 a.m.

June had not shown any suspicion when Wendell had booked a room at the Super 8 motel in Plattsburgh for the Friday night prior, stating that it would be easier to just roll out of bed and head to the garage, which was less than a quarter mile down the road from the motel.

Wendell had eaten dinner with his family, watched a little TV, and packed his duffel bag and rifle into his truck, the gun to be used for a little deer hunting on one of the remaining days in the season with his old buddy Henry Wagner, a dairy farmer in Plattsburgh.

Just before leaving, under the cover of darkness, while his family was inside enjoying a sitcom, Wendell popped his truck's hood and quickly pulled a plug wire. When, at about 9:30, he hit the ignition switch, the truck shook like it would tear itself apart, further cementing his story that the vehicle was in bad need of repair.

As the truck idled roughly, Wendell went back inside to say good-bye to his family. Patrice, her head cocked, listening to the sound of the engine, questioned her father's diagnosis of a bad differential.

"If it was your punkin," she said, parroting her father's terminology, "that roughness would only happen when you're moving. Your truck's just sittin' there."

"I'll have 'em give the old girl a complete checkup," assured Wendell, giving his daughter a quick peck on the forehead. "She's gettin' some age on her."

He turned to his wife and flashed her an impish grin.

"Wasn't talking about you, Hon. The truck. I was referrin' to the truck."

"Get goin'," chided June, and gave him a good-natured slap on the arm.

About a mile down the road, he pulled over, opened the hood and pressed the dangling spark plug wire back into service. But although his engine returned to its former state, humming nicely as he navigated the back roads of Chazy, his anxiety about his plans for the night was beginning to build. Seeking relief, when he spied the lights of the Stewart's Convenience Food Shop, his hand automatically drifted over and lifted the turn signal lever.

He had spent a long time perusing all the different beers in the cooler, wondering if he wanted a quart, a six, a twelve, or a twenty four pack. Deciding that he needed his senses sharp and keen for the upcoming event he had planned, he opted rather to calm himself with two boiled hot dogs in rolls with mustard, ketchup, and relish.

As he ate in one of the two plastic booths Stewart's provided for their customers, Wendell made a point of nonchalantly telling the store's shift supervisor his Plattsburgh itinerary – the motel, the garage, the hunting – and keeping the fellow smiling by purchasing three grocery bags full of snack foods and soft drinks upon leaving.

Now, as he sat in his truck, eating, drinking, watching, and waiting for 2:00am to come, in his mind he forced a reverie of the incident that was the impetus for what he knew would be an event greater than any grand opening that son of a bitch Sonny Rapant could ever plan.

As he remembered the sights and the sounds – his drunken son, pants around his ankles, that dirty old whore touching his privates, the bystanders' cruel laughter at Robert's expense, Sonny's grinning, evil mug – he felt a raging fire sweep through his body. He'd sworn revenge, and tonight he was going to take it.

At 1:45am he again took up his post in the woods, leaning against a broad oak with the gun's stock resting flush against the bark of the tree. Through his scope he counted ten cars remaining in the parking lot. Within fifteen minutes the number had thinned to three.

At 2:05am the last patron's car left, leaving only Sonny's truck next to the building. Wendell felt his heartbeat quicken and he drew a deep breath to steady himself.

Ten long minutes elapsed before he saw Sonny's muscular form emerge through the front door. He watched as Sonny looked left, then right, eyes scanning the moonlit night, and then turn back to lock the front door.

As Wendell held the back of Sonny's head in the cross hairs, he felt his finger float over and onto the cold metal trigger. His heart slammed beat after beat in a chest that felt like it would explode as he dragged in rapid, shallow breaths through a wide open mouth.

Seemingly without conscious control, he felt his finger beginning to curl, increasing its pressure on the trigger.

"Bang," he whispered in the darkness.

As Sonny finished up his business at the front door, Wendell straightened his trigger finger, backed it ever so slowly out of the guard, and snaked it onto the gun's wooden grip. As he exhaled in relief, he watched as Sonny strode slowly to his vehicle, yank open the door, and duck inside. Within seconds, Wendell heard the truck's engine come to life with a sharp bark.

Sonny left rubber in the first two gears as he jackrabbited through the empty lot. Instinctively, although there was almost no possibility Sonny could see him hiding in the woods, Wendell brought his rifle up to a vertical position and pressed himself hard against the oak. Sonny was soon out of the lot, up onto the main road and headed home.

Wendell lost no time making his way out of the woods and back to his truck. Without headlights, he piloted his vehicle onto the short stretch of highway and then down into the club's parking lot. Now it was his turn to sidle his truck up close to the building.

A sense of calm and absolute resolve flooded through him as he once again opened his door and stepped out into the night. His filled his lungs with the crisp, early December air, looked up and smiled gratefully at the full moon that been so accommodating by providing a continuous source of illumination for his mission – a mission whose climax was just minutes away.

From having played the club countless times, he knew that the Rapants hadn't installed any sort of alarm system, but a flicker of fear passed through him as he imagined a guard dog, a pit, a pinscher, a new addition for club security thanks to Sonny, roaming through the empty roadhouse.

He pulled his rifle out of the truck, went to a window, and began rapping on the pane, hard enough to make the glass rattle. He waited, listened close for any activity inside. Nothing. He rapped again. Waited.

Still nothing. Then with one fluid motion, he swung the butt of the rifle up and through the window, shattering the pane completely.

Only for an instant, as he thought about Joe Rapant, a decent man who always paid his bands and who had never caused him or his family any trouble, was he seized with a sliver of doubt about what would be his next, and most decisive action. He quickly bought off his doubt by remembering the splashy ads for the grand re-opening, a reasonable indicator to him that the club was now in Sonny's hands, as Joe was no fan of rock and roll.

He grabbed the hose off the side of the truck and began feeding it deep into the hole where a window pane had existed moments before. When he heard the hose flop onto the nightclub's floor, he went to the front of the truck and flipped a switch turning on a vacuum pump, but not before making sure he had reversed the action. He heard a gurgle deep within his tanker, a tanker full of raw sewage that had been marinating since Wednesday, the contents of a very full septic tank of none other than the Chazy mayor, Charlie Senecal. Wendell then went to the window, cocked an ear, and waited to hear the first splash hit the floor.

*   *   *   *

Around 6:00am, having only logged about three and a half hours sleep, Sonny Rapant rose without the aid of an alarm clock, slapped his wife Millie's rump and instructed, "Breakfast, woman! Make me some breakfast!"

"Is Saturday," she murmured, her face pressed into a pillow. "Too early."

"Big day, Mill. A lot to do. Gotta get up, get movin." He put both hands on her buttocks and began shaking. "Up! Up!"

While Sonny shaved and showered, whistling and singing during his respective tasks, Millie, still dressed in her flannel nightgown, prepared him a meal of eggs over easy, bacon, and English muffins. When he strode into the kitchen, clad in boxers, athletic socks, and a black tank top, she couldn't help but notice the brightness to his eyes, the bounce in his step, his overall ebullient glow of enthusiasm.

"We oughta' have a grand re-opening more often," she remarked. "It's good for your disposition."

"That's funny, Mill. But you only get one shot at this." He shook a half empty coffee pot. "This fresh?"

"Reheated," she said.

He scowled at her.

"Sit down, your food's ready. I'll brew some, only take me a minute."

In between shoveled portions of his breakfast, Sonny laid out his schedule for the day, while Millie listened, still half-asleep, one hand supporting her chin, the other bringing a blue mug of coffee to her lips.

"Gonyea and I are gonna get to the club around eight, hang the banner, clean the bathrooms, wash the floor, polish the glassware... really spiff the place up. If we got time, we're gonna practice making some of those mixed drinks we're not so familiar with, try 'em out on each other."

"I'd go easy on that last little...chore," she warned. "This is gonna be a long day and a long night."

"Yeah, but I'm pumped. Feel like I stuck my finger in a wall socket."

He looked down and appraised the food left on his plate – a rasher of bacon, a triangle of egg white, a crust of muffin – and then abruptly pushed the plate away.

"I'm done," he announced, and turned his attention to his wife, leaning his head sideways, giving her a questioning look.

"What?" she asked.

"How come you never wear those frilly little black nighties I buy you every Valentine's day at the mall in Plattsburgh?"

"It's almost winter, Sonny," she retorted. "It's too cold now, I wear them in the summer," she defended.

She could see that his eyes had fallen on an expanse of white just below the hollow of her neck.

He then looked up at her with a wry smile and hooded eyes.

"Food was great, Hon," he complimented, his voice low. "Now how 'bout dessert? Right here." He patted the tops of his thighs.

Millie turned and looked towards the entryway to the kitchen.

"I'm afraid Claude might walk in on us," she whispered.

"He's still sleepin'," assured Sonny, "but if he does, we just tell him Mommy and Daddy are hugging, that's all."

He leaned over and kissed her on the neck.

"Now c'mere, Ole Sonny's gonna give you a nice slow ride."

"A quiet ride," she added, standing and slipping out of her white cotton panties.

Sonny, already half-erect, the fabric of his boxers stretching to contain him, stood and moved his chair away from the table.

"Position it so I can see over your shoulder," instructed Millie, "so I can see Claude if he comes in."

Sonny obliged, slid his boxers to his ankles, sat back down, and stroked himself three times.

"Time to mount up, Lady," he said, holding his fully erect member in his hand.

She straddled him, and he entered her deftly, emitting a grunt in the process. She placed a hand over his mouth.

"Quietly," she whispered into his ear, as he began a steady pattern of thrusts.

In a rare gesture of tenderness, he took her face into his hands, cradled it gently, and looked deep into her eyes.

"I've been waiting for this day for years," he whispered. "I'm gonna make it work."

"I know, Babe," she said, relishing the softness of his touch and beginning to move in rhythm with his pelvis. "I know."

About an hour later, fed and freshly fucked, his tough demeanor snapped firmly back into place, Sonny rummaged through his basement in search of a box that had arrived via UPS.

"Millie! Millie!" he roared from a corner of the basement.

Upstairs, Millie was pouring Captain Crunch into her son Claude's bowl.

"Be right there," she called, splashing milk over the cereal.

Knowing patience would never be her husband's virtue, Millie sprinted to the cellar door and flung it open. Sonny was just beginning his climb.

"What? What is it? What do you need?" she asked.

"Had some promotional materials delivered. UPS guy dropped them off, now I can't find them," said an exasperated Sonny.

"A tall, thin box?" asked Millie

"Yeah, that's it."

"Wedged it between the washer and dryer. I was afraid whatever it was might get broken if it was stepped on. I wanted to keep it upright," explained Millie.

"That was a good move, Mill. Something I'm sure you're not too familiar with," said Sonny, heading back down the stairs.

"Ha, Ha," she responded flatly, closing the basement door.

She heard a truck pull into the driveway and a horn begin to blow.

Gonyea.

Millie went to the front door, opened it, and waved Mike in.

Just as Gonyea and Millie were making their way into the kitchen, Sonny had reached the top step of the cellar stairs, six thin plastic rectangular signs, fifteen by twenty five inches, resting in the crooks of his arms.

"Wait you two, don't come any closer," warned Sonny.

Gonyea stuck his hands high in the air, as if he were being held up by a gunman.

"Wait a minute, mister, I didn't even kiss her," pleaded Gonyea, stealing a line from an old Lynyrd Skynyrd song.

Millie giggled.

"Stop fuckin' around. Just stay where you are. I want you to get the full effect...from a distance."

Sonny separated one sign from the six and held it aloft. On a black background, lettered in yellow it read: "Follow me to *The Forge*–Chazy's newest nightspot." Underneath the larger lettering, smaller copy gave the address, phone number and displayed a logo of a bright red anvil.

"Damn, that's cool," complimented Gonyea.

"Now, I like these signs better than those bumperstickers," said Millie.

"Don't start with me, Mill," warned Sonny, handing the sign to Gonyea.

"See, they're magnetized," said Sonny to Gonyea. "You stick 'em on the side of your car or truck."

"Gimme two," said Gonyea. "One for each side of my truck."

Sonny smiled, handed him another, then turned his attention to Millie.

"We gotta head out, but throw a couple on the doors of your car, too."

"Okay," agreed Millie, taking two signs from him. "What time you want me to come out to the bar?"

"Swing out around 2:00, see what sort of shape the place is in," answered Sonny.

"If you guys are testing cocktails, maybe I better come out to see what sort of shape *you* guys are in," she joked.

Sonny flashed her a tight grin and said, "See you later."

He looked over at his son, who was still at the kitchen table, an empty cereal bowl in front of him, now watching cartoons on a 9" TV that sat on a nearby counter.

"Bye, Claude. Wish me luck."

"G'luck, Dad," said Claude, making no attempt to tear his gaze away from the television.

Sonny and Gonyea sped out to the club. With Gonyea in the lead, Sonny playfully let the front of his truck creep up to tap bumpers at each stoplight, laughing each time he saw his friend's head lurch forward, and returning the middle finger Gonyea flashed soon after feeling the impact. It wasn't until they turned into the club's parking lot did Sonny floor it, blowing past Gonyea, and making a beeline for his usual parking spot alongside the building.

As soon as he exited his truck, he noticed the broken pane and immediately a hot flush of anger began to rise within him. Kids, he thought, a carload of drunken teenagers cruising Chazy on a Friday night, pull into his empty parking lot to piss, one the young punks decides to heave a stone through the window. Big fun in a small town. Little fuckers.

A gust of morning air caught the scent of Wendell's handiwork and delivered it under Sonny's nose. Nostrils flaring, face cringing in revulsion, his first thought was that one of the toilets had overflowed. But...

"Hey," called Gonyea from the front of the building. "You gonna open up this dump up or what? Freezing my bawls off out here."

"Coming," yelled Sonny.

Gonyea stood in the parking lot, hands in his pocket, jumping up and down to keep warm. When Sonny reached the front of the building,

Gonyea could see that his face was drawn with worry.

"Hey whatsa' matter, Son? You're supposed to be happy. This is your big day."

"Something's fucked up, I don't trust it, I don't trust it," replied Sonny, head down, as he hurried to the front door, key in hand.

As he opened the door, the smell was so overwhelmingly putrid, anyone watching would have thought Sonny had been nailed with a roundhouse right. He staggered back, his legs rubbery, and he felt his breakfast come up fast into the back of his throat. Pulling his handkerchief from his back pocket, covering his mouth and nose, he took the first step into his club, the morning sun casting more light on the inside as the door widened. He looked down to see that he'd placed his boot in a standing inch of raw sewage, an inch that covered the majority of floor space in the club.

"It's shit!" he screamed, his body vibrating with rage and revulsion. "The place is covered in shit!"

CHAPTER 8

"Don't ask questions Millie, just *move*," instructed Sonny, as he sat on the hood of his truck, speaking into Gonyea's cell phone. "Just get out here fast and bring garden hoses, buckets, detergent, push brooms, mops, hip boots, duck boots, go to the hardware store if you need to, and call Gonyea's wife. Tell her to get her ass out here, too."

"Okay, okay, whatever it is, it'll be all right" said Millie, trying to calm her husband.

"And don't call my parents and don't say anything to Claude, little kids have big mouths," he added, pushing the end button on the phone without saying good-bye.

While Sonny made his first call, Gonyea, wearing a bandanna over his nose and mouth, a piece of cloth which would soon become the fashion of the day, slogged his way through the club opening every door and window, allowing the cold December air to blow through.

Sonny hopped off the hood of his truck, walked to the front of the building, cupped his hands around his mouth and called into the depths of the club.

"Mike?"

"Yeah?" answered Gonyea who had just opened the ladies room window as wide as he could.

"Should I call the Sheriff or the State Police?"

Gonyea stepped out into the main area of the club.

"Neither," said Gonyea with conviction. "Wait there, I'm coming out."

When Gonyea was outside, he pulled the bandanna from his face and fished a cigarette out of its pack.

"I know this is the work of that old fuck Charbonneau," spat Sonny.

"I know it is, too," agreed Gonyea, " it's get-back for messin' with his retarded kid." He then lighted his cigarette and took a tentative puff. "But you call the cops in here now, they're gonna see this as an environmental spill and you can forget about any grand re-opening for tonight, my friend."

"So, what do we do?" asked Sonny.

Gonyea's second pull on his cigarette was longer, deeper.

"We take a bunch of pictures, good pictures, showing the broken window and the extent of this mess. Call the cops tomorrow," suggested Gonyea.

"And play dumb about the environmental laws," said Sonny, catching on.

"Correct," said Gonyea.

Joan Gonyea arrived about forty five minutes after Sonny had placed the call to Millie. The back of her pick-up bristled with new push brooms and mops, while coils of garden hose lay like long sleeping snakes on the floor of the bed. Millie arrived minutes later, her back seat packed with powder and liquid detergents of all strengths, makes, and sizes.

When Millie exited her car, she caught the tail end of Sonny and Mike offering Joan Gonyea an explanation for the frantic call home.

"Charbonneau's had a hard-on for me ever since I played a little practical joke on his idiot boy," said Sonny.

"Yeah, but that don't give him the right to dump a load of sewage into a man's business," said Gonyea

"He dumped sewage into the bar?" asked Millie, wide-eyed. "How much? A little? A lot?"

"We're swimming in it," said Sonny, "but the four of us are gonna clean it up. We're gonna be ready for tonight." He turned to Mike. "Ain't that right, Bro?"

"Betchure ass we'll be ready," confirmed Gonyea, slapping his friend hard on the shoulder. "But before we start," he added, pulling some bills out of his pocket, "Joan, run to the drug store and buy up a few of those disposable cameras."

Joan took the money and looked at him blankly.

"So we can preserve this scene for all time?" she asked.

Sonny snorted and Mike could see his jaw begin to clench.

"Joan, please just get the cameras," he asked again, this time with a little sugar on his words, "I'll explain later."

After using up five disposable cameras, shooting the scene of the crime from every possible angle, the four began their clean-up by using the push brooms to move the standing sludge out the front, back, and side doors. Every so often, one would choke and the others would laugh nervously, knowing by the end of the job all would eventually take a turn at fighting the gag reflex.

When most of the liquid was off the floor and out the door, the wives rested while Sonny hosed down the inside of the club, and Mike sprayed the sewage that had come out the front door, hoping to disperse it as far away from the building as possible.

Next, the women brewed up sudsy buckets of detergent and set about scrubbing the club's wooden floor with their mops. For a while, the sweet aroma of the soap powders and liquids gave them all a sense of hope that, indeed, the club would be ready for its grand re-opening.

The mopping completed, the men returned with their hoses, rinsing everything down. The remaining push brooms, those that had not already seen duty, were used to coax the rinse water out the doors.

When the floors appeared just about dry, Mike Gonyea, as a test, closed all the windows and doors. The four then sat at the bar and rested, while Sonny turned the thermostat up to 68 degrees.

Joan Gonyea was the first to voice her opinion.

"Still stinks bad."

"This old wood floor was bone dry," said Mike, dragging the toe of his work boot across a plank, "soaked a lot of that sewage right in."

"Could we try painting over it?" suggested Millie.

Sonny had been sitting perched on a bar stool, shoulders stooped, his head lowered, his hands clasped in front of himself.

"No, it wouldn't have enough time to dry," he said quietly, and looked down at his wristwatch. It was 12:30. Opening time for the bar on Saturday was 1pm. He then stood, reached behind the bar and pulled out one of the waitresses' order pads and pencil. The other three sat in silence as Sonny scribbled words onto the paper, ripped off the top sheet, handed it to Millie, and said, "I need you to run for some more supplies."

Millie gazed upon the paper, and blinked twice as her mouth parted.

"You want *how* many of these?" asked Millie, staring at the words Sonny had scrawled.

Sonny's jaw clenched and a vein stood out in his forehead.

"As many as it says. Now don't fuck with me, just get going," he seethed, his head still lowered, shoulders still stooped.

He then turned to Mike.

"On a sheet of that plywood we got out in back, make a sign that says, 'Closed until 9:00pm'. Put your pick-up sideways in the driveway up near the road, like you're blocking it, and lean the sign against the side of your truck." Sonny then spit on the floor and added, "And stay up there, make sure nobody gets down here until we're ready. Even though I got rid of the kegs, some of the old gomers might want to get in for a few last drinks before the change-over tonight."

"No sooner said than done, Boss," said Gonyea

For the first time in a while, Sonny straightened his back, lifted his head and forced eye contact with each of the three.

"We can do this," he said, his voice rich with conviction, "we can pull this off."

*   *   *   *

Wendell had checked into his Super 8 in Plattsburgh in the wee small hours of the morning, set his alarm clock for 6:50am and was at Lanfear's Garage, 12oz complimentary cup of Super 8 coffee firmly in hand, by a little after 7.

His hunting buddy, Henry Wagner, picked him up at the garage around 7:30. Wendell told the mechanic he'd be back to check on the tanker about 2 in the afternoon.

Although they saw no deer, Wendell enjoyed his time with Henry, an old boyhood friend with whom he'd kept contact over the years. The two traversed much of Wagner's land, rifles cradled in their arms, talking about the past, the present, and the future, their successes, their failures, their dreams. When fatigue overtook them, they rested on a stump or a fallen tree, and rejuvenated themselves with steaming black coffee poured from stainless steel thermos bottles.

Back at Lanfear's the mechanic could find nothing wrong with Wendell's differential, as Wendell knew darn well any honest mechanic wouldn't. When Wendell returned to the garage at a little after two, the mechanic shook his head, pronounced the supposed ailing part perfectly sound, not even in need of a slight squirt of gear grease, and charged Wendell only for the labor time it had taken him to diagnosis the truck as healthy. Wendell smiled, and commented that perhaps what he had heard in the rear end of his truck had "somehow worked itself clear." After paying his bill, and exchanging hearty handshakes with Wagner, he set out back home for Chazy, but not before stopping to buy several newspapers, a package of cold cuts, and a loaf of bread at a convenience store.

In the store's parking lot, in between bites of an olive loaf on white bread sandwich he had slapped together, Wendell's fingers flipped through the pages of the three newspapers he had purchased, searching for any article about a break-in or act of vandalism at Rapant's. After two thorough combings of all three papers, Wendell was convinced that nothing, so far, had been reported.

He pondered that fact on his ride home, taking his time, not rushing his speed, not rushing his thoughts. Maybe tomorrow, he thought, the article would appear in the Sunday paper, the reporter, or reporters, assigned to the story having arrived late at the scene and not making a copy deadline for the Saturday edition.

His mind wandered, imagining who had arrived first at the bar. Certainly, he hoped it had been Sonny, opening the door to his new and improved nightclub only to be greeted by a good-luck truckload of Wendell's very special stew. But what if it had been Joe? Wendell held no malice, no ill will towards Joe Rapant, other than the fact that the man had spawned a son who had grown up to become one of the most hateful sons a bitches in Clinton County.

Maybe just a bad seed, thought Wendell, Joe probably having done his best to raise the boy right. Happens in the best of families. Hell, he had his Chantelle, his own flesh and blood, who had grown up to become a female Judas Iscariot, selling him and the whole family out for a few flimsy promises made by some city sharpie. Shit, more than three years into it he'd yet to see her name anywhere near the charts.

Wendell's train of thought shifted onto another track. Who would be there to greet him when he arrived home? The State Bulls? One of those wet-behind-the-ears, peach-fuzz headed deputies from the Sheriff's Department? Or maybe Sonny himself.

Wendell held no delusions, no hopes that he would actually get away with his little act of north country terrorism. He knew he'd have to face a judge, maybe even do some jail time. The ruse about the malfunctioning differential was concocted simply so that he had an alibi for his family. With the exception of Patrice, who had doubted that the differential was at all problematic, June, certainly Robert, and Dominic, who was now considered more or less a member of the Charbonneau clan, had all bought the story of a guy who, for convenience sake, would head out at night and stay in a cheap motel for the purpose of an early morning appointment in another town.

And the time spent with Henry Wagner? Well, just a few hours with an old buddy, tramping around in the great outdoors, to unwind, relax, and to prepare himself for the inevitable consequences of his actions.

June would be furious about his retaliatory deed, no doubt about that. She wouldn't understand that a father has to do what a father has to do. When a member of his family was wronged, it was his responsibility as the father to make it right.

For Wendell, above all, there was nothing more precious, more sacred than the protection and the preservation of his family.

The lack of sleep, and the physical and emotional expenditures over the last 17 hours were starting to take their toll. Although his mind spun, alert with possibilities with what awaited him at home, Wendell's arms and legs felt like lead and he pulled his tanker off the road, to stretch and breath some fresh air. He set the parking brake, the emergency flashers, stepped out of the truck and let a bracing wind wash over him for several moments. He took some deep breaths, looked up at a beautiful clear blue sky, stretched his arms, stamped his feet, and climbed back into his vehicle.

What if Sonny was waiting for him at the house? The questioning voice inside his head came to him as clearly as the single notes Dominic could pull effortlessly from his guitar strings. What if Sonny, teeming with rage, had decided that he would handle things with Wendell and act as judge, jury and executioner.

Wendell took his Winchester from the rack that hung in the back of the cab, inserted a fresh clip, and threw the bolt, locking the first bullet into the chamber.

Now he was ready to continue his journey home.

*   *   *   *

About three hours after her husband had sent her on her mission, having succeeded in buying out most of the stock of Sonny's requested item from auto parts stores from Plattsburgh to Champlain, Millie Rapant returned to the bar where she found Sonny sleeping, his head down at one of the tables, while Joan and Mike Gonyea sat on barstools sipping St. Pauli Girls.

As soon as she entered the club, Millie's hand flew to her nose, pinching her nostrils tight.

"Still smells real bad, doesn't it," whispered Joan.

Millie nodded.

"You get what Sonny wanted?" asked Mike somberly.

"Yep," answered Millie.

"The boys washed the floor a second time...didn't do no good," said Joan, who Millie was starting to suspect was a little tipsy. "And this idea he's got now– "

"Is gonna work," said Sonny roughly, raising his head from the table.

Millie immediately took her fingers from her nose but continued breathing through her mouth.

Sonny swung his head around to face Joan.

"And if it doesn't, Joan, it'll be my ass out there flappin' in the breeze, not yours," Sonny added menacingly.

Joan averted her look from him, pursed her lips, jiggled her head from side to side, and took another swallow of her beer.

Sonny gathered himself, rose from the table and looked straight at Millie.

"You didn't forget thumbtacks, did you?" asked Sonny.

"No."

"Staple guns, staples?" he pressed, as if hoping for an omission.

Millie held up the list.

"Got everything you wanted, Sonny. Everything. It's all out in my trunk."

For the first time since he'd come upon the disaster area that he had hoped would be his salvation, Sonny smiled.

"Good girl," he said, and turned to the Gonyeas. "Break's over. Time to get back to work."

*   *   *   *

Wendell pulled into his yard, saw only his station wagon and Dominic's van, breathed a sigh of relief, and killed the engine. He sat there a moment, half expecting for the law to come running out from around the side of his barn-house, guns drawn, ready to take him into custody. He snorted, smiled and shook his head.

As he opened his door, it was Robert who was the first to greet him, the boy bursting from the house in unlaced K-Mart winter boots, traces of chocolate milk on his upper lip, his arms open wide.

"Daddy, I missed you," gushed Robert, flinging his arms around Wendell's legs, essentially ending any progress of his father's dismount from the truck.

Wendell patted his son's shoulder.

"I missed you too, son. But leggo my legs, I can't move!"

Robert released him and a high-pitched giggle. Wendell stepped out and down onto solid ground.

"What's everybody doing?" asked Wendell.

"Well, I'm painting," announced Robert, with a great deal of self-importance. "Mom's watching TV and Dominic's helping 'Treece write some songs."

"Really," said Wendell, his interest piqued about the last item. "She been singin' them yet?"

"Nah," said Robert, "she says they're not ready for public?...for public?" Robert's eyes glazed over and he stood there, mouth agape, as if welded in place.

"Consumption?" offered Wendell.

"Yeah, that's it...I think," said Robert, instantly unfrozen.

"Well, that's great," lauded Wendell.

"My painting's great too," blurted Robert.

"I'm sure it is, Robert," assured his father. "Let's go inside so I can see it."

Inwardly, Wendell was delighted that Patrice and Dominic were teasing out the songs that he always knew his younger daughter possessed, but he knew that he'd better give his accolades first to yet another paint-by-number creation lest he run the risk of Robert being wounded by attention paid to Patrice, as the boy was exquisitely sensitive to perceived shows of favoritism.

Chantelle was the family member who had demonstrated a God-given talent for songwriting and when she'd left the fold had taken with her the bulk of original compositions performed by the band. Although Wendell had penned a few tunes – June, The Moon, And A Bottle of Boone's; a love song written for his wife, Ode To A Peterbilt; a trucker's song built on top of a hard-driving shuffle beat, and Wounded Heart on Krumkill Hill, a ballad in the traditional country tear-jerker mode – he was acutely aware that, like his guitar picking, his ditties were, at best, mediocre.

Not that his awareness of their mediocrity ever stopped him from sprinkling the trio of tunes in among the covers. Crowd reactions, however, were always consistent from club to club, with bar patrons taking the opportunity to converse or make a trip to bathroom or bar whenever the songs were performed.

So hearing that Patrice was working on chorus and verse was a nice little serendipity. After passing pleasantries and bits of information with his wife, who sat curled on the couch, and heaping large portions of praise on Robert's newest work of art, Wendell headed in the direction of the practice room from where the light strummings of an acoustic guitar and Patrice's tentative warblings could be heard.

"Ready for the bandstand?" asked Wendell, ambling into the room.

Patrice and Dominic sat cross-legged on the floor, facing each other, he holding the guitar, she grasping several sheets of yellow lined paper with both hands.

Patrice startled at the sound of his voice, put a hand to her chest.

"Oh Daddy, you scared me."

"Sorry darlin'."

Dominic ceased playing, looked up, smiled and asked, "Get your truck fixed?"

"Running like a top," answered Wendell. He nodded. "Keep going, it sounds good."

Patrice blushed a bit.

"You think so?" she asked. "They're not polished or anything."

"But they will be," said Wendell confidently. "And this is gonna make us much more attractive to any A&R people who might come to our shows. The more originals you got, the better chance of being signed."

Wendell nodded his head slowly.

"You, Patrice, you're locking in the missing link."

Patrice felt a sudden wave of nausea pass through her gut as she immediately understood the weight of the responsibility he was trying to place on her.

"We'll see how it goes, Dad," said Patrice. She looked over at Dominic. "We're just getting started. No promises just yet, okay?"

Wendell said nothing, but simply smiled, winked, and then left the room.

As soon as he was out of earshot, Patrice, eyes ablaze with anger, leaned over and whispered to Dominic, "See, see how goddamn hard he pushes?"

Dominic pressed his lips together into a tight grin and raised his eyebrows.

"Guy just really wants it bad," he said.

Wendell ate a spaghetti dinner with his family, all the while June noticing that he was drinking more wine than he was eating his food. When the meal was finished, June began clearing the table and saw that her husband had left a small clump of capellini towards the side of his plate.

"You always ask for seconds and you always clean your plate," she remarked, her face quizzical. "You did neither tonight."

"You feeling all right, Daddy?" asked Patrice.

Wendell ran an open palm over his ample stomach.

"I got one of them bellyaches like you get from time to time, 'Treece."

"Then maybe you should have had something light to eat instead...like tea and toast," suggested Patrice.

"And stop slugging down the wine," ordered June, picking up the jug of cheap red and moving it out of his reach.

Robert giggled. June's words and action also succeeded in bringing a faint smile to Dominic's lips.

"Alcohol acts as an irritant to the stomach," offered Dominic. "A lot of the guys in rehab who were drunks had ulcers from all the drinking they'd done."

Wendell brushed a napkin roughly across his mouth and tossed it to the table.

"I can tell you what's givin' me a gut ache – *you* people, tellin' me what to do, buncha' know-it-alls."

He rose from his seat and started out of the room, mumbling, "Goin' for a ride."

"Can I come?" Robert called out after him.

"No." he answered crossly.

The family sat quietly, looking at each other, not speaking as they heard the front door slam and the first few coughs from the station wagon's engine.

"Is Daddy mad at me?" asked a sorrowful Robert, finally breaking the silence, his lower lip starting to quiver.

"No, of course not, Robert," soothed June. "Daddy just seems to have a little trouble on his mind. I'm sure he'll be fine by tomorrow."

It was the anticipation, the anxiety, the not knowing of who or when or *if* they'd come calling for him that was pumping acid non-stop into an already burning stomach. He knew the tank had emptied into the bar, no doubt about that. He'd heard the contents gushing in, caught a whiff of the smell, even rapped on the side of the tank for confirmation when the pump started to suck dry. So why hadn't he been paid a visit by the authorities or the Rapants? Curiosity tugged at him like a insistent pooch pulling on a pant leg. He just had to see for himself what the hell was going on out at the nightclub.

Noticing that the needle in the gas gauge was on E, cursing both June and Patrice, prime suspects in the crime of running the car around on fumes, Wendell pulled up to the Stewart's gas pumps and self-served himself five dollars worth of regular.

Once inside to pay, he scooped up several rolls of Tums and lined them up on the counter.

"How'd you make out?" asked the clerk, the same shift supervisor who had waited on him the night prior.

"Huh?"

"Last night," pressed the clerk. "You told me about your plans."

"I did?" asked Wendell, feeling himself go ice cold.

"Yeah, you get your truck fixed? Bag any deer?"

Those plans, thought Wendell, feeling warmth begin to trickle back into his body.

"Truck's fine, those guys at Lanfear's do a great job," boasted Wendell. "But no deer – saw tracks, droppings, but never fired a shot."

"Well, maybe next time," encouraged the clerk, handing him change for a ten.

"Yeah, next time."

Back on the road, eating Tums like candy, Wendell checked his watch. It read 8:45pm. When he was within a half mile of Rapant's he decided to use the same pull-off and the same vantage point in the woods that he'd used the night before.

After extinguishing his lights and setting the parking brake, Wendell made his way down into the wooded area, leaned against a tree, and cast his eyes in the direction of the club.

What he saw made his breath come out of him with a start.

Cars. Cars and trucks. A whole parking lot full of 'em. Packed. And more coming in off the main road.

*   *   *   *

Sonny Rapant and Mike Gonyea had stationed themselves, arms folded across their chests, outside the front door of the club just under the banner that proudly proclaimed, Grand Re-Opening - *The Forge*. A long line, which had begun to cue up around 8:30, stretched out in front of them.

The evening was mild; most had dispensed with gloves and mittens, and waited with their coats and parkas unzipped.

"Come on, man, let us in!" shouted a girl who wore silver earring studs that crawled from her lobes to the top of her ear.

"Band starts at nine, doors open at nine. When you hear the music, then we let you in!" Sonny shouted back. "And have your IDs ready," he added.

His directive caused a sea of hands to go diving into purses and digging into back pockets. Sonny looked over the tops of their heads and smiled as he watched a procession of vehicles continue to stream into his parking lot.

"What's the name of the band again, Sonny?" asked a young man with a mullet.

"Blitzkrieg!" roared Sonny, pumping a fist into the air. "They're from the city, man, and they *kick ass!*"

Sonny's announcement brought forth a mix of cheers, warhoops, and rebel yells.

Over the din, Gonyea turned to Sonny and asked, "They're from the city?"

"Yeah," snickered Sonny, "city of Schenectady."

The two men shared a laugh as the sound of a guitar riff and a cymbal crash leaked out of the club. There was bit more noodling on the guitar, a thumping of bass strings, and then silence. Moments later, Sonny heard drumsticks clicking out four even beats and the band exploded into their first song.

Opening the front door, Sonny called out, "Ladies and Gents, welcome to The Forge!"

As the patrons filed in, passing ID cards and cover charge to either Sonny or Gonyea, they were immediately hit with a full-frontal attack of perfumed rancidity.

In six neat rows of twenty five, across the ceiling of the club, the Gonyeas and the Rapants had thumb-tacked auto air fresheners, small cardboard cut-outs impregnated with scent in the shape of tiny evergreens. Pine-scented. Not strawberry, nor vanilla, nor peppermint, nor pina colada, though the choices had been there. Pine, only pine, just as Sonny had specified.

Another sixty seven were discretely stapled to the undersides of chairs, tables, and barstools.

And at exactly 8:55, as instructed by Sonny, Joan and Millie had also sprayed the club thoroughly with eight cans of aerosol air deodorizer.

Pine, of course.

Upon entering, some patrons wrinkled their noses, some pinched their nostrils, some simply looked around quizzically, finally catching sight of the mini-tree farm that grew down from the ceiling.

As one nineteen-year-old girl, her short blonde hair pinned tight to her head with tiny pink barrettes, handed Sonny her chalked ID, she asked him, "What *is* that smell?"

"Toilet overflowed, no big deal," he answered nonchalantly, handing back her ID, taking her money, and letting her pass.

After about twenty five minutes had elapsed, the club was almost at capacity and the line at the door was beginning to thin. Sonny turned to Gonyea.

"You handle this by yourself?" he asked. "I wanna go see how Millie is doing."

"Sure, sure, I'm fine," said Gonyea.

Behind the bar, Millie had dumped a bottle of champagne and a quart of orange juice into a pitcher. In between serving customers, she took long sips of the concoction she had poured over crushed ice in a tall tumbler.

In her left hand she held a blue bandanna that she had sprayed with air freshener, bringing it to her nose whenever she had the opportunity.

As Sonny threaded through the crowd, he caught sight of Millie sniffing her handkerchief. Upon reaching the bar, he waited until she had completed an interchange with Cara the waitress before erupting.

"Put that away, will you?" he spat, nodding at the bandanna. "At least try and pretend like it doesn't bother you."

Millie looked at him through watery eyes.

"I can't stop from gagging," she pleaded.

"Oh, it's not that bad," he chided. "You're such a baby. It'll clear up soon."

Sonny turned his back to her and looked out over the crowd.

"Look at this, *look* at this," he lauded to no one in particular. He spread his hands out. "A full fucking house...and just listen to that band."

Behind his back, from underneath the bar Millie brought out a canister of air freshener, spritzed a bit into her bandanna, and lifted the cloth slowly to her nose.

CHAPTER 9

By 10:00 p.m., exactly an hour into the maiden voyage of *The Forge*, most of the customers had departed, save for a few diehards and some of Sonny's drinking buddies.

Nearly full bottles of beer and watery mixed drinks littered the tables, the patrons unable to consume more than a few sips due to the overpowering ripeness of pine and shit.

Only Millie, it seemed, had been able to stomach her cocktail, having consumed her entire pitcher of mimosas.

By 10:30 p.m. Sonny's friends filed out, averting eye contact with him, and patting him supportively on the shoulder as one would to a mourner at a wake. At 11:00 p.m., the bar was empty with the exception of Cara the waitress, the Rapants, the Gonyeas, and the band, who were stalling longer and longer between songs.

Cara approached Sonny, holding her head in both hands.

"Mr. Rapant, can I leave? I've got a migraine and I forgot to bring my medication with me."

"Go," he answered, with a dismissive wave of the hand.

Sonny wandered over to the bar, where Joan Gonyea sat on a stool. Mike and Millie were behind the bar.

Millie, whose eyes were now watery from the drink rather than the aroma, tried to focus on her husband.

"It didn't clear up, but they sure cleared out," she cackled at him.

"Shut the fuck up, Millie, you drunken skanky bitch," he hissed back at her.

Joan jumped to Millie's defense.

"Don't talk that way to her, Sonny."

"It's okay, Joanie," said Millie, her arms flapping like a rag doll's. "I am drunk."

Just then the lead singer of Blitzkrieg, a tall, lanky man in his late twenties, walked up to Sonny. He wore a long shag, reminiscent of the 80s, and a strip of grey duct tape across his nostrils, apropos for the evening.

"You want us to keep playing?" he asked, "'cause like there's nobody here, man."

Sonny eased himself down onto a stool.

"I'm here," Sonny began snottily. "My lovely bride is here. My two loyal friends are here. So it appears that you have an audience." He paused and Joan saw him working the muscles in his jaw as several veins began to rise in his neck. Sonny's right hand rocketed from his lap, his thumb and forefinger forming into a pistol which he trained on the lead singer's duct-taped nose.

"You were hired to play four fucking sets, asshole, and you're going to play four fucking sets."

The singer stared back at Sonny with a deadened look in his eyes.

"Whatever you say, man, you're the boss," he said, turned and headed back towards the bandstand.

Sonny closed his hand into a fist and slammed it hard back against his chest.

"That's right, I'm the boss," he said, beating his chest a second time. "And nobody better never forget that."

The next morning Mike Gonyea and Sonny drove in silence to a one hour photo in Plattsburgh and had the film in their disposable cameras developed. By noontime, Wendell Charbonneau was in handcuffs.

Wendell's family surrounded him in the vestibule of his house as he stood flanked by two grim-faced New York State Troopers.

"Have you gone crazy?" June shouted at him through angry tears.

"Nope, just did what I knew was right," he said, smiling sadly and winking at a sobbing Robert.

Patrice stood hugging herself, her face red, fighting back emotion. Dominic tried to place an arm over her shoulder, but she shrugged it off.

"Keep an eye on things, while I'm gone, will you, Dominic?" Wendell requested.

"I will, I promise," said Dominic earnestly.

Wendell then turned to his daughter.

"Keep workin' on those songs," he instructed in a low voice, at which point Patrice burst into tears.

Wendell then nodded to one of the Troopers and was lead summarily out his front door and placed into the back seat of a cruiser.

The charge was criminal mischief, second degree, a class D felony, which carries a maximum term of two and one third to seven years in state prison. Although Wendell flatly refused to have himself bailed out, he did allow June to hire an attorney, a thin young man in wire frames originally from the Buffalo area, to defend him. Wendell insisted on pleading guilty, telling his lawyer nothing more than that he had sought revenge on the man who had treated his son "improperly," a word Wendell hoped would spare his son from any disclosure of the gritty details of the incident in the men's room.

The local press repeated his word, and soon Sonny was suspected by some to have buggered the boy. A rumor, which when he heard it, only fueled Rapant's hatred for Wendell Charbonneau.

Wendell, a first time offender, was sentenced to 90 days in the county jail. But in an interesting turn of events, Sonny too, wound up standing before a judge.

Certain environmental laws had been broken when the sewage was dumped. But upon hearing that Sonny had waited more than 24 hours to report the crime, Wendell's lawyer argued that Rapant should be held responsible for any fines or charges.

The judge agreed and lectured to a fuming Rapant that he had "selfishly and willfully exposed his customers to a potential health hazard." Rapant's lawyer argued that the spill had been cleaned by Sonny himself, but the judge would hear none of it, fined Sonny five thousand dollars and mandated that a licensed environmental clean-up firm be hired to inspect the bar and surrounding property. And until the firm could get out to perform the inspection, the club would have to shutter its doors.

Two weeks passed before Sonny was able to locate a company in Ogdensburg who would send someone out to peruse both nightclub and grounds. Although *The Forge* passed inspection easily, thanks to time and about six inches of snow that had fallen in mid-December, the opening night fiasco and the fact that the club sat dormant for fourteen days did irreparable damage to the business.

Wendell adjusted to jail life quickly, encountered no trouble from other inmates, many of whom saw him as the grand old man of the Clinton County jail, his crime viewed as a heroic act by some, comedic by others.

He would allow no visitors to the lock-up, which he termed the "crowbar hotel," other than June. During their first visit they spoke of the night before his arrest – his insomnia, his thrashing about in the bed, his trips to the bathroom, which, when June had questioned, Wendell had blamed on a swollen prostate. She was still very close to her anger, the emotion white hot, and upon conclusion of their first meeting Wendell was wounded by what he perceived as an aloofness in her manner.

But in subsequent visits, her anger having begun to cool, she spoke of missing him, and wanting him to return, confirming what she had said to Patrice a while back on the order of disagreeing with the behavior but still loving the man.

Back home there was a dreadful pall that hung in the house, as once again the remaining Charbonneaus coped with a loss of one of their own. June told the family that they probably had enough in a small savings account to get them by for the next couple of months, but that they needed to economize, and for God's sake don't get hurt, as they were still without health insurance.

The furnace was turned down and the fireplace became the primary, rather than the supplemental source of heat. All members of the household took to wearing knit hats and sweaters and all were thankful that a good supply of wood had been laid in for the winter.

The boys, Robert and Dominic, decided that rather than purchase a Christmas tree they would take it upon themselves to cut one down in the woods behind the house. Finding no spruce or balsam, only scrawny scrub pine, they decided on a small cedar, which held the ornaments well and gave off a pleasant aroma, especially when the living room was toasty warm, compliments of a well-stoked fire.

June took on the task of canceling the band engagements that had been booked for the months of December, January, and February, informing the club owners and holiday party planners that Wendell had unexpectedly been called out of town on business. Although most of those whom she telephoned knew the truth, none let on, allowing June to maintain her dignity in the midst of a humiliating situation.

When June canceled she always gave out the phone number of Tommy and Tammy Wakefield, Chazy's own Jack Sprat and wife country duo, hoping they might pick up the jobs the Charbonneaus were not able to honor. The Wakefields, in appreciation, asked Patrice to play with them on New Year's Eve, telling her to leave her bass at home, but that they could use her back-up vocals. Patrice accepted, knowing full well that it was charity, but pocketing the needed seventy five dollars at the end of the evening.

By New Year's Eve, Sonny Rapant's business was little more than a trickle, and he canceled the rock bands he had booked for the upcoming months, opting instead for the services of a toupeed middle-aged disc jockey who worked cheap, but with whom he argued frequently about playlist, as the entertainer was fond of 70s disco.

By the end of January, Sonny, having been financially cut off at the knees by advertising fees, the unexpected court and legal costs, and finally, the lack of revenue, let his kitchen and waitstaff go. He and Gonyea would run the bar, with the wives helping out with the cooking and the waitressing.

Livid about Wendell's attack on his bar, Joe Rapant asked Sonny for a full account of what had motivated the man to do such a thing. Sonny fed him a story about Robert already being intoxicated when he had arrived at the club, the lad then approaching Louise the hooker about a quickie in the bathroom when the band launched into their first set without him. Sonny went on to explain to his father that when Louise agreed to the proposition, he and his buddies had followed the two into the men's room out of mere curiosity, wanting to watch a simpleton get it on with an old whore. When Papa Charbonneau had entered upon the scene he somehow had it in his head that Sonny had orchestrated the whole affair, when in fact, Sonny swore to his dad, he was merely just one of the bystanders.

Sonny detailed how the old man wanted to swing on him. Sonny assured his dad he would never mix it up with a gent of Wendell's age. To Sonny's way of thinking, Wendell, absolutely humiliated by his idiot son's actions, was looking for a target, and for whatever the reason Sonny was wearing the bulls-eye.

Because he was his son, the elder Rapant believed what his only offspring had told him. Only one piece about the whole incident still stuck in his craw.

"Improperly. Papers said Wendell accused you of acting improperly with his boy. What the hell does that mean?" asked Joe.

"I have no idea," came Sonny's reply.

*   *   *   *

Believing that Patrice had simply blown her off for their Lake Placid rendezvous, her sibling having been brainwashed by the father who had disowned his oldest in a swank Nashville office some years before, an angry Chantelle Charbonneau had chosen not to contact her family over the holidays.

Although June had kept a copy of Chantelle's cell phone number, (a source that the traumatized Patrice had never thought to use when she was unable to produce the proper digits by the side of the Northway), whenever she tried repeated dialing, a recorded voice continued to inform her that the party she was trying to reach was unavailable.

Tell me something I don't already know, thought June.

But as Chantelle waited in Jack Conroy's receptionist's office on the fourteenth of February her need for familial contact overrode the anger she'd been harboring.

"Can I use the phone?" she asked Conroy's receptionist, a doughy woman in her fifties who had two ashtrays on her desk – one for ashes, one for butts.

"Sure, Babe," she answered huskily. "Use that one there," she said, pointing to a secondary unit that sat quietly off to her right.

"It's long distance," Chantelle said tentatively.

"Don't worry, Babe," assured the receptionist. "Jack'll pay, he always pays."

During her four minute conversation with her mother, with the receptionist taking and placing calls on the primary phone, Chantelle learned the real reason for her missed connection with Patrice in Lake Placid. Nearing the third minute, the receptionist reached out and touched Chantelle's wrist.

"Jack'll see you now."

Informing her mother that she'd soon have to close out the call, Chantelle then listened to June's breathy, abbreviated account of Wendell's crime and subsequent incarceration. After denouncing her father as a stupid old goat and wishing her mother a Happy Valentine's Day, Chantelle hung up the phone.

Conroy appeared in his doorway, and clasped his hands in delight at the sight of Chantelle. She was dressed in a satin, fire engine red rodeo suit replete with chain stitch embroidery and encrusted with rhinestones.

"My, my, do I get to unwrap you like a big box of chocolates?" he asked.

"Fat chance, Jack," she said curtly. "We need to talk."

Jack ushered her in, rolled his eyes at his receptionist, and closed the door behind them.

"Is that a original Nudie?" asked Jack, as the two took their seats, he behind his desk, she in front of it.

"No."

"A Manuel?" he ventured, his eyes concentrating on the embroidery running down her left sleeve.

"No," she echoed, crossing her legs.

"Katie K's on 17th Avenue South sells a lot of Manuels– "

"It's a Nudie knock-off," she blurted, grabbing the fabric on her cuff, "probably made in Taiwan. Look, Jack I'm not here to talk about clothes."

"Coulda' fooled me, Lady, you're pretty well gussied up," said Jack, trying to sound down-home.

She uncrossed her legs and leaned towards him, her face tight with frustration. "I dressed like this because I wanted to impress you, remind you that I've got what it takes to make it."

"Remind me?" Jack asked. "I haven't forgotten you, Chantelle."

He paused. "But you gotta sell more than good looks in a shiny suit," said Jack.

Chantelle pursed her lips as her hands balled into fists.

"I know that Jack, but goddammit– "

"Chantelle," he said, arresting any words that were poised to spill from her lips. "Maybe this is a good time to evaluate, talk about your progress...or lack thereof."

He leaned back in his chair and took a deep breath.

"Make no mistake about it, Chantelle, I haven't forgotten you. I continue to shop your demo tape around to the labels. To date, there have been a few nibbles, but no bites."

"So what's the problem, what am I doing wrong?" she pleaded.

"Perhaps nothing. Oh, there were a few opinions about your music not having the necessary magic, the songs being a bit derivative... but opinions are like assholes, everybody has one." Conroy paused, waiting for a smirk, a chuckle from her. She gave him nothing. He continued. "Luck and timing play a part in this business, but maybe..."

"But maybe what?" she asked.

"But maybe I have made a mistake with you."

"A mistake," she repeated, as both fear and hope rippled through her mid-section.

"You have no fan base," declared Conroy. "Most performers build up a fan base, proving they have a draw, a following. Maybe by putting you on the road as an opening act I made a mistake."

"But the audiences, most of them, I think, liked me," defended Chantelle.

"They've long since forgotten you."

"But I've signed autographs," she pressed.

"The only autograph that matters, kiddo, is the one you sign on your record company contract," said Jack emphatically.

Chantelle's hand slowly moved up to the side of her head where she began to twist a lock of her hair.

"So how do we fix this?" she asked.

Jack folded his hands on the desk.

"I was thinking that if we sent you back up north, you build a following, I'll boost for a four song CD, new songs, of course. You sell a significant number, then maybe we can convince the record companies you're bankable."

"Up north? How far up north?" she asked warily. "New York City?"

"No, I meant northern New York," answered Jack. "Up around where you call home."

"You're serious?" asked Chantelle, her eyes widening.

"Yes."

"I don't call that area home anymore, let's just say that's where I came from," she corrected.

She swallowed hard and her eyes shifted back and forth.

"And I could bring my musicians with me?" she asked.

"No," said Jack with a scowl and shake of his head, "I don't believe they'd be willing to work for the little money I imagine you'd make playing in…"

"Chazy, Plattsburgh, maybe Lake George and Placid in season," said Chantelle.

"Right."

Jack then scrubbed his face with his hands, as if rousing after a long sleep.

"So, the way I figure it, if you did consent to move back north, without your back-up band," he said, "you'd then have three choices."

"You're a regular Monty Hall, aren't you Jack?" she said.

Conroy blinked, and looked across at a face in which a storm was beginning to brew.

"You want me to stop?" he asked.

"No keep going, you're on a roll."

"Choice number one," he began, his words tiptoeing. "You perform solo, unplugged, just you and an acoustic guitar."

"No good," she shot back. "I think I'd suck at that folk singer-on-a-stool routine. Besides, I'd be competing against my family's band, cutting their throats. Next choice."

Conroy wet his lips.

"You go back home, hire local musicians to back you up."

"Buncha' bangers, Jack, week-end warriors. And again, I wind up taking jobs away from my own family," came her reply.

"Then maybe the last choice is the best," said Conroy, forcing a smile, knowing full well that with his next statement he might be entering a mine field.

"You reconcile with your father, rejoin your family's band, with their understanding, of course, that they are first and foremost your back-up musicians, a vehicle for you."

Chantelle pushed herself out of the chair, put her hands flat on the desk that separated the two of them, and searched deep into Conroy's eyes.

"Jack? Jack?" she implored. "It's the Charbonneau Family Band. Family band, get it? My father would never consent to reducing himself, my sister, my brother to become back-up musicians for me. If I go home it's with my tail between my legs."

"You're sure he'd never agree to it?" asked Conroy.

"Positive. Whipped puppy is what I'd be, and I'm not sure..." She stopped, her breathing a steady pant. "I'm not sure I'm ready to concede defeat...yet."

She raked her fingers through her hair, turned, and in two broad strides was at Conroy's door, her hand on the knob.

Flinging it open, she asked the startled receptionist, "Can I bum a cigarette?"

Without a word, the woman withdrew one from her pack and flipped it to Chantelle, along with a pack of matches.

"Thanks," she said, lighting the smoke and tossing the matches back to their owner.

She then closed the door, walked to her chair, and dropped back into it.

"So when's my next tour?" she asked, as if their interchange had never occurred.

"None scheduled," returned Jack coldly.

Chantelle drew her smoke deep into her lungs, held it for a long time, exhaled and again raked her fingers through her hair.

"I'm so fucking frustrated, Jack."

"I know," said Conroy, nodding. "And right now I'm out of ideas for your career, you shot 'em all down." He paused, lowered his head. "If you were a man..."

"If I was a man, what?" challenged Chantelle. "You'd punch me in the nose?"

"No, if you were a man I'd tell you to go out and get drunk."

"And laid," she added. "Isn't that the complete prescription for what ails you?"

She then lifted her boot, cocked it to the side, and stubbed out her cigarette on the sole.

"You know, Jack, that's the best suggestion you've had all day."

With that, she breezed out of his office, and passing the receptionist's area, dropped her cigarette butt into the correct ashtray.

Looking up at her, the receptionist complimented, "Love your outfit, Babe."

"Thanks," acknowledged Chantelle.

"But I'd add a hat," offered the woman.

Chantelle whirled on her.

"No. No trips back home, no solo acts, no week-end warrior

sidemen, and definitely, positively, no hats."

Two hours later, still wearing her red Nudie knock-off, Chantelle sat perched on a stool at the Broadway Brewhouse and Mojo Grill, smoking and working on her fourth Tequila Sunrise.

"Jed, that's really your name?" she asked, looking into the handsome, weathered face of a man in his late twenties wearing Acmes, jeans, and a new black denim shirt. "Next you're going to tell me you're a 'fer real' cowboy."

"No Ma'am, I'm a roofer," said Jed, as he sat on the stool next to her, having introduced himself moments earlier, the twenty-six-year-old's black hair, slim build and bright red suit having drawn him like a magnet.

"Let's cut the ma'am stuff, Jed. I may look as though I was rode hard and put away wet, but I'm still young enough to qualify as a Miss."

"Sorry, Miss…"

"Charbonneau, Chantelle Charbonneau."

"Can I buy you a drink, Miss Charbonneau?"

"No," she said, looking at his glass which held no liquid, only ice. "But I'll buy you one. You're drinking?"

"Vodka. Vodka on the rocks," he answered.

Chantelle broke into a wide smile and slapped her thigh.

"Two points for you, Jed, " she lauded. "Most people leave out the d when they pronounce vodka. They say, 'voka, voka.' Drives me crazy."

"Are you a speech therapist?" Jed asked in earnest.

Chantelle threw back her head, the tequila having started to grab hold, and let go a laugh.

"No, I'm a singer," she said, poking a finger into her cigarette pack. She stopped and looked at him intently. "An *opera* singer."

"Oh," said Jed, aware she was putting him on. "Then you must perform at the Grand Ole Opry."

All expression dropped from her face and her mood grew instantly sour.

"No, never have, maybe never will," she said, her voice deadened of all emotion.

She turned away from him, extracted a cigarette from the pack, stuck it between her lips, and lighted it.

"Did I say something wrong?" asked Jed.

Chantelle downed the last of her drink and looked back at him.

"No, in fact you seem like the perfect southern gentlemen. You'll do."

"I'll do?" asked Jed.

"Yeah."

Later, as Jed lay dozing in the eighty nine dollar room at the Days Inn, Chantelle, in black bra and panties, sat on the edge of the bed, smoking, sipping water from the plastic cup she found in the bathroom, and wishing she was in possession of a thousand milligrams of Tylenol.

Soon, she heard the rustle of sheets as Jed began to stir behind her.

"If you really are a singer, those cigarettes are gonna ruin your pipes," he mumbled.

"I really am a singer," confirmed Chantelle, "but you're not a doctor, so mind your own business."

Remembering the tenderness he'd displayed in his lovemaking, Chantelle judged her words harsh, and felt a pang of guilt about speaking to him so roughly.

She crushed out her cigarette, rolled over to face him and poked him playfully in the ribs.

She smiled.

"What I meant to say was stick to what you know how to do best."

"Roofing?" he asked with wry smile.

"Wiseguy," she said, and gave his butt a pinch.

"So I was good?" he asked.

"Very good."

She rolled back up to a seated position on the edge of the bed and began kneading the center of her forehead with her fingertips.

"But I should have eaten something at the restaurant. That tequila left me with one helluva headache."

"Come to daddy and I'll make it all better," said Jed seductively.

Chantelle instantly bristled.

"What did you say?"

"I said come to daddy and I'll make it all better," he repeated. "We got time for another."

Her back had grown ramrod straight and she turned only her head to face him. What he saw in her eyes scared the shit out of him.

"What's that supposed to mean?" she hissed.

"We've got the room for the whole night, I just thought maybe we could go another time," said Jed, now wondering if he might have bedded a psychopath. "But we don't have to, if– "

"My daddy's got a lot of faults, but incest with his kids was never one of them. Are you some sort of pervert, did you imagine you were fucking a little girl, a child when you had me?"

"No," said Jed, his breath coming hard. "No, of course not, it's just an expression."

"An expression I suggest you delete from your pillow talk, Jeb. You've insulted the good name of decent fathers with your sick request and you've blown the moment with me. I want you to leave."

Jed was already searching the tousled bed for his underwear.

"It's Jed," he corrected.

"Jed, Jeb, Jethro, I don't care what your name is, I asked you to leave," she demanded, rising to a standing position.

With a certain violence, she pulled the top sheet off the bed and wrapped herself in it, and stood, with her arms crossed, facing the wall, while Jed hurriedly slipped into jeans and tugged on his boots.

Moving towards the door, holding his socks and his shirt, Jed stammered his way through a combination good-bye, apology, and urging for psychological help.

"Well, uh, good luck, and I'm sorry that I said something that made you so, so angry, but I think, think maybe, like they say, you got some issues you need to deal with."

"Out!"

CHAPTER 10

"Robert, get in here, right now!" yelled June from the kitchen.

When Robert arrived moments later, toothpaste foam oozing from his lower lip down his chin, he found his mother standing in front of an open refrigerator door.

"What? Whad I do?" he asked.

"I know your Daddy had a full six pack in here before he left, and now there's three bottles missing. Did you drink them?"

"No, Ma, I didn't, honest" said Robert.

"I don't want you drinking, is that clear?"

"I didn't drink them," said Robert, his voice rising in volume, droplets of foam coming forth from his lips.

June drilled a stare into Robert's eyes. He didn't look away. She pulled a sheet of paper towel from the rack and swiped the toothpaste from Robert's chin.

"Patrice only drinks wine, Dominic and I don't drink at all, and your father's away. So I guess this'll remain one of life's little mysteries."

She handed him the paper towel.

"Go finish brushing."

Outside, she could hear the sound of Dominic's van trying to turn over. It was the end of February, the 29th to be exact, leap year, and a warm spell had settled in, so cold weather couldn't be blamed for the engine's inability to start.

Eleven more days and Wendell would be out of jail. She had planned a welcome home party, just her and the kids, after she'd picked him up at the gates of the Clinton County Jail at 6:00pm on Saturday evening, March 11th.

They were just about there, the at-home Charbonneaus having

survived Wendell's absence. Although the savings were almost gone, June took a certain pride in her management of the paltry sum that had been available. Her family had remained safe, warm, and well-fed throughout the winter months. She even had a few extra dollars to replace the vanished bottles of beer so Wendell could have a full sixer for his celebration.

Patrice, more so Dominic, had grown uncomfortable with the lack of funds, in that the band had been on hiatus coming up on three months. In an effort to remedy her lack of cash flow, and Dominic's despondency, she had spent many an hour in her shed, finally finishing projects that she hoped she could sell for some extra money, money that she planned on sharing with her beloved Spinosa.

She'd also finished four complete songs, music and verse, recorded with Dominic on a small tape recorder in the practice room.

"If I keep pumping the pedal, I'm only gonna flood it even more," Patrice called out of an open driver's side window, as she sat in the seat, disobeying Dominic's directive.

From under the hood, an annoyed Dominic yelled back insistently, "No, it's not getting *enough* gas, that's the problem."

He brought the hood down with a slam.

"Then why can I smell so much gas it's making me nauseous?" asked Patrice, her head hanging out the window.

Dominic didn't respond to her question, choosing rather to make his own diagnostic statement.

"It's a clogged fuel filter, that's why it's not getting any gas," he declared, then looking over at Wendell's station wagon. "We'll have to take your dad's car into town. I'll pick up a new filter at NAPA."

"Just let the van set a few minutes and I'll bet it'll start right up," said Patrice, climbing out of the vehicle.

"Whatever," said Dominic, who'd been hosting a foul mood for most of a week.

Patrice headed to her shop to retrieve a handmade practice amp she had made from junked parts and a VCR a customer had given to her father outright, knowing that Patrice was good with electronics repair. The off-warranty unit was destined for the landfill as it had played nothing but snow for several months.

The VCR became intelligible again with a simple cleaning of the heads and an adjustment to the tracking device which had been thrown way out of whack. As the VCR had been gifted to her, she was free to turn a profit from the now operational machine.

The practice amp, with its three coats of amber varnish and tacked gold grille cloth, had turned out to be a beauty. A part of her wanted to keep the little amplifier for herself, but she hoped the extra cash it might bring could buy dinner and a movie for her and Dominic, with any remaining money to go into his pocket, both efforts aimed at brightening his spirit and attempting to lessen his growing obsession with being flat broke.

From the kitchen window, June watched Patrice and Dominic go their separate ways – she to her shop, he to the front door of the house. Within moments, he entered the kitchen, flashed her a half-hearted grin, opened the refrigerator and extracted a beer.

"*You're* drinking those beers?" she asked, her eyes widening.

"I plan on replacing them…as soon as we start playing again," he answered, his thumb and forefinger cocked on the cap.

"No, I didn't mean that," she said, her face wearing a pained expression. "You're a..an addict."

"Cocaine addict, June," clarified Dominic, as he twisted the cap free. "I'm recovering from cocaine addiction, not alcohol."

"Are you sure? I mean there's no danger in it?"

"If I know anything June, I know my own recovery plan," he said, and took a small drink. "See, it's a beverage, nothing more, I'm fine."

She said nothing but simply looked at him, and soon her eyes made him uncomfortable to the point where he turned away from her to swallow successive sips. He looked out the window and saw Patrice place the amp and VCR next to his van.

"Not gonna start," he whispered.

He watched as Patrice climbed in and adjust herself in the seat. He then heard the tick of the starter, and the sound of the engine roar to life, first time.

Although he wanted to polish the rest of the beer off in two long pulls, he took great pains to take only one additional swallow, recap the bottle, and return it to the fridge.

"I'll drink the rest later," he said, closing the door. "I'd appreciate it, June, if you didn't mention this to 'Treece. If you're concerned, even though you shouldn't be, I know she'll get nervous, too."

"I can't make that promise,' she said, her eyes focused on his.

"Suit yourself," he said with a shrug. "We're going in to town, be back in a while."

"Be careful."

Before leaving the house, he closed himself in the bathroom, silently cursed the giant globs of toothpaste Robert was notorious for letting fall off his brush and into the sink, squeezed a ribbon of Pepsodent onto his brush, and attacked his teeth with a vengeance.

*   *   *   *

"She's gorgeous!" exclaimed Norman Lipschutz, Jr. of Norman's Electronics Sales & Repair, as he ran his fingers admiringly over the practice amplifier Patrice had just hoisted up onto his counter. "Are you sure you want to sell it?"

"I'm sure," said Patrice, an image of a brooding Dominic crystal clear in her mind. "How much will you give me for it?"

Norman pushed his thick glasses a little higher up the bridge of his nose, inspecting the amp carefully.

"Well, as much as this is a beautifully crafted— "

"Brand new speaker in there, Norman," she interjected.

"Yes, yes I can see that," he said, and cleared his throat nervously. "As much as it's a fine piece of work, it is homemade, and people usually buy brand names."

"Uh-huh."

"Now the VCR, that *is* a brandname," he remarked, his voice a bit brighter. "But," he added, his voice starting to sink, "you check out the Sunday newspaper circulars, you can pick up some of the new units for less than a hundred bucks."

"But not all of them have this slow motion / stop action frame feature," countered Patrice, pointing to the push button on the face of the VCR. "Some hockey dad wants to see his kid slap the puck in for the winning goal in slo-mo, this baby's got the means."

"Yes, that's true," agreed Norman, as his eyes then shifted back to the homemade golden amplifier.

An awkward silence hung between the two.

"I can give you sev-, a hundred for the two," came his offer.

"A hundred a piece?"

"No, a hundred, total, for both,"

"Sold," said Patrice in less than a heartbeat, and offered her hand for him to shake on the deal.

He took it, and she noticed it was cold and moist to the touch.

Norman then took the items off the counter and carried them into the back room. When he returned, he went straight to the cash register where he pulled out two crisp fifties and handed them to Patrice.

"Thanks, Norman," she said warmly.

A light flush quickly flooded his face.

"I w-wanted," he stuttered, "to tell you about Rhythm Ace. I haven't forgotten him."

"Oh, don't worry, let it go," said Patrice, with a dismissive wave of her hand. "The Roland is great, gives us more beats and percussion sounds than we could have ever imagined."

"No, no," insisted Norman. "I'm committed to trying to fix him. I found a website actually dedicated to vintage drum machines, they even have photos from what they call the drum machine museum. I 've sent e-mails, and posted messages on bulletin boards looking for parts."

"That's sweet of you, Norman."

"No responses, yet," he added, "but I'm going to keep trying."

Patrice smiled and tried to make eye contact through his thick lenses, but the glass distorted where his gaze was actually focussed.

He turned his attention to rolling the cord of a soldering iron that had been left on the counter.

"Are you on-line?" he asked.

"No," she said with a laugh, "we're lucky we got cable TV, although Daddy threatens to pull that out on a weekly basis, usually after he catches something on there that he thinks is too sexy for Robert."

Norman bit into the flesh of his lower lip.

"How is your Dad?"

"He'll be home soon," was Patrice's response.

"Good, that's good," murmured Norman. "And is that guy still with your band?"

"Oh yeah, Dominic's still with me, *us*." She glanced at her watch. "Which reminds me, I told him I'd meet him at Stewart's for a coffee."

"I was kind of wondering why he didn't come in with you this time?" asked Norman, secretly pleased that Dominic hadn't.

"Restless. He was restless, wanted to take a walk. Well, I gotta go. Thanks again Norman," she said, turning and heading towards the door.

"Stop in again, anytime. It's always nice to see you, talk with you."

"Bye, Norman," she said, as the little entrance/exit bell tacked to the top of the door jingled over her head.

Dominic sat at the molded plastic booth in Stewart's hunched over a small coffee purchased with seventy five cents he'd bummed from Robert. When Patrice entered the convenience store, he looked up from his coffee and managed the weakest of lopsided grins.

"You have a nice walk?" she asked, sliding into the seat across from him.

"Guess so," he answered sullenly.

"You work up an appetite?"

"Not really, why was I supposed to?"

"No," she sighed. She pulled the two fifties out of her purse, and handed him one, adding with a broad smile, "Maybe, Grumpy, this will cheer you up."

He looked at the currency in his hand as if were worthless.

"Why are you giving this to me?"

She gazed deep into his eyes.

"Because I love you, Dominic Spinosa."

He shifted his eyes and focused on the bill she still held in her hand.

"What about that one?" he asked.

Hurt and anger streaked through her.

"If I wanted, it could be just for me, because it was my stuff that I sold, but I wanted to spend it on us, do something fun together," she answered, her face that had borne an expression of love and happiness collapsing fast.

"Oh," said Dominic blankly.

With his response, she instantly trashed any plans of dinner and a movie with him, and tucked her fifty back down into her purse.

"I thought this would make you happy," she said, nodding at the fifty he still held in his fingers.

"I am, it did," he said unconvincingly.

"Fifty bucks is fifty bucks," she added acidly.

"Yeah…" he said, his voice trailing off as he folded the bill and stuffed it into his front pants pocket. "But I was just wondering that if maybe I had gone with you, Norman would have given you more."

Patrice could feel the heat start to rise in her face.

"I trust Norman, I know he gave me a very fair price."

Dominic nodded slowly.

"You're probably right, I was just wondering."

Patrice put her hand to the side of her head and rubbed a temple.

"Are you almost finished with your coffee?" she asked. "Because I'm tired, I want to head home."

A pathetic, childlike look of sadness took hold of his face.

"You said the other fifty was for us," he whined. "Can't we go somewhere, do something this afternoon?"

"I said I was tired, Dominic. Maybe we can go out tonight, I'm not sure. But right now I just wanna go home, take a nap. We'll take it from there."

                         *   *   *   *

"They went somewhere without me," grumbled a very pissed off Robert Charbonneau to his mother.

June who had been looking at TV, turned to see the scowling face of her son as he stood but a few feet away from her in the living room.

"We've had this discussion before, Robert. Patrice and Dominic aren't obligated to take you every place they go."

"But I'm bored," whined Robert.

"It's a beautiful day outside, close to 55, why don't you ride your bike in the driveway," she suggested.

"Naah, wanna paint. Need a new paint set. Wanna paint a special picture for Dad."

"Then ride in to the IGA, but remember..."

"I know," he snapped, "wear my helmet."

June turned back to her TV program, expecting to hear Robert clump up the stairs to retrieve his helmet from his room. But several moments passed and she continued to feel his presence behind her.

She turned back to him. He stood there, eyes blinking slowly, his mouth agape.

"Something the matter, Robert?"

"Not sure if I have enough money, gave some of it to Dominic," he said.

June pushed herself out of the chair quickly and went to her son.

"How much did you give him?" she asked, her voice brittle.

"I think it was three corders," he answered.

"Why did you give him your money?"

"'Cause he asked me," answered Robert innocently.

June folded her arms across her chest which induced in Robert a sudden urge to pee.

"Just like Patrice and Dominic aren't under any obligation to take you with them in the car, you're not obligated to give that guy any money," she said sternly.

Hearing his mother refer to Dominic as "that guy" scared Robert even more and his lower lip began to quiver.

"I do something wrong?" he asked, his voice starting to break.

"No," she said, softening her voice and putting her hand on his shoulder in an effort to ward off his tears. "I just don't want you being taken advantage of."

"K."

A moment passed. Robert's urge to pee subsided, his eyes stayed dry, and the warmth of his mother's hand on his shoulder felt good.

"Can I still buy a paint set?"

Helmeted, straddling his bike, several dollars from his mama's purse now in his pocket, Robert waited at the end of his driveway, watching as an occasional car passed. When there was no traffic for several minutes, he turned his bike to the right, fashioned his thumbs and forefingers into capital Ls, committed the same error in determining the right hand side of the road that he'd been making for years, swung his handlebars onto the left shoulder and headed down the road, riding dangerously against, rather than with, the flow of traffic.

Because much of the winter's snow had melted, he stayed far off onto the shoulder, lessening himself as a hazard. However, about a mile and half into his journey he heard a loud hissing noise and the bike became increasing more difficult to pedal.

Within minutes, his back tire was as flat as a pancake, having picked up an errant roofing nail from the side of the road.

He tried standing up and riding on the rim, but that soon exhausted him and caused the bike to handle in such an erratic fashion that he almost fell off twice. With his toe he then pushed down the kickstand, racking the bike, and dismounted. He then stood, still helmeted, wearing a forlorn expression, watching the cars and trucks pass, hoping to see a familiar or friendly face that might stop and come to his aid.

After about five minutes he watched as an oncoming pick-up truck slowed, passed him, stopped, then backed-up to where he was standing.

The driver leaned across the truck's bench seat and rolled down the passenger side window.

"You're still ridin' on the wrong side of the road, jerk-off."

It was Sonny Rapant.

A shiver rippled through Robert.

"Flat tire, Slick?"

Robert nodded.

"You got a patch?" asked Sonny.

Robert shook his helmeted head.

Sonny looked through his windshield and then out his back window. No vehicles were coming from either direction.

"Then let's throw it into the back and I'll take you to the Mobil station, get it fixed," he said with a smile.

Robert froze in place, while Sonny hopped out of his truck and lifted the bike into the back of his truck. Sonny returned to the cab and climbed back in. Robert remained by the side of the road, his arms by his side, ramrod straight.

"C'mon, Slick, get in," called Sonny through the passenger side window, his eyes checking the rearview.

Robert peered out at him through the face mask on his football helmet.

"Get in," Sonny repeated, this time more insistently. "I'm not gonna hurt you, but I don't have all day to fuck around with this either."

Although he heard the words of assurance for his safety, it was fear that induced Robert to reach up and open door.

Once inside, Robert still helmeted, sat quietly on his side of the bench seat as Sonny pulled a U-turn and headed towards town.

Several minutes passed as the truck gained momentum, neither driver or rider speaking.

"Your daddy still in jail?" Sonny asked, breaking the silence.

Robert nodded.

"Well that's only right, because he's a bad man, and that's where a bad man belongs. Because of your daddy, my daddy and me are probably gonna lose our business."

"He's gettin' out pretty soon," blurted Robert, "Dominic's in charge now."

"Dominic, huh?" said Sonny with a smirk, "that freak who's fuckin' your sister."

Robert said nothing but his eyes searched for something to focus on, finally coming to rest on the zip-loc baggie of teeth, Sonny's trophies from his barroom fights, hanging from the rearview mirror.

"Are you a dentist?" asked Robert.

Sonny turned away from his driving and saw what Robert was staring at.

"No, more like the tooth fairy."

"Oh."

Sonny then pulled off onto a side road, which caused an immediate reaction in Robert.

"Where we goin'?"

"Relax, Slick," assured Sonny. "My daddy's got a hunting camp on this road. I just gotta check things out."

Sonny was speaking the truth. His father did own a small camp with three other men which, from time to time, local teenagers would use for a Saturday night party house.

The road became quite muddy and Sonny stopped once to get out and change the hubs over to four wheel drive. Robert took this opportunity to look out the back window and when he did he saw no sight of the main road.

He did see a large crow in flight being pestered by a little flock of smaller birds, maybe starlings. He wasn't sure, but his dad would know the type of bird that was swooping and taking pecks at the crow's head. His dad would know.

I gotta get home," said Robert, as Sonny slid behind the wheel.

"We're almost there," said Sonny annoyance ringing in his tone. "I just need to check the camp, then we'll go to the gas station, get a patch for your tire, then you'll be on your way."

"Gonna get a paint set at the IGA," announced Robert.

"A paint set, huh? Well I imagine you're probably a regular fucking Rembrandt."

Up ahead, a small tarpaper shack suddenly came into view.

"See, there it is," said Sonny pointing.

He drove a bit further, until the road ended.

"We walk from here," said Sonny.

Sonny exited his truck but Robert stayed in his seat.

"You comin'?" asked Sonny.

Robert shook his still-helmeted head.

"Suit yourself."

For the next few minutes Robert watched as Sonny plodded his way through the mud, the muck making loud sucking noises as it held fast to his boots, eventually making his way to the small open deck on the front of the camp. Robert could see a large set of deer antlers hung over the front door, and several animal skins tacked to the tar paper. He watched as Sonny pulled hard, several times, on the front door, making sure it was secure, and then cupped his hands around his eyes and peered into each one of the camp's windows.

Sonny then turned back to the truck, smiled, and fashioned his fingers into the "OK" sign.

Robert felt a smile tug at the corner of his mouth and he returned the sign.

When Sonny returned to the truck, he went to the back and Robert heard the clink of metal against metal and what sounded like a moving or shifting of items in the pick-up bed.

As Robert waited for Sonny to return to the cab, out of the corner of his left eye he caught a flash of jet black. He turned his head slightly and watched as a large crow, its feathers smooth and iridescent, land not far from the truck, stabilize its footing and strut in a tight half-circle.

Robert grinned and wondered if it might be the same bird he'd seen being tormented by the smaller birds only moments earlier.

Sonny then appeared at Robert's door, opened it, and grabbed him by the face mask, violently yanking him out of the truck and onto the ground. There, as fast and as hard as he could, he began to beat Robert with a plastic wiffle ball bat.

A high keening noise, like a wounded or terrified animal, immediately came forth from Robert's throat, as his body instinctively drew up into a fetal position, vainly trying to protect himself from the non-stop flurry of blows.

"Scream all you want, Slick, nobody gonna hear ya! You gonna pay, you gonna pay for what your daddy did to me!'"

The attack continued until Sonny's chest began to heave with exhaustion, the vicious whacks then beginning to slow in frequency and lessen in impact. Seconds later he drew the bat high up over his head and drove home one final blow into the flesh of Robert's skinny right bicep.

After this last hit, which had produced a solitary anguished yelp, Robert's screams quieted to whimpers.

In between heavily sucked breaths, Sonny warned the boy, "You tell anybody I did this to you and I'll come kill your whole family. I'll kill 'em, kill 'em dead."

Sonny pitched the plastic bat back into the pick-up bed and dug into his back pocket, producing a large metal rasp.

"You tell people you fell off your bike," Sonny instructed, pulling Robert's right arm away from his body and prying open his fingers, exposing his palm.

"And when you fall off your bike, you always get road burn," he said, raking the rasp hard and fast across the soft center of Robert's palm.

CHAPTER 11

Chantelle did reconcile, not with her father, but with her manager of more than three years, Jack Conroy of Nashville's prestigious Music City Management.

At Chantelle's suggestion, the two met for breakfast, and over coffee and Danish, Conroy told her he'd been thinking about her, a lot, since she'd walked out of his office in a snit two weeks prior. He verbalized his want of keeping her, his fear of losing her, and reaffirmed his rock-solid belief in Chantelle's star potential. He also told her that in terms of her method of getting to where she wanted to be, he'd come to believe that changes weren't an option, they were a necessity.

For now, he told her, there was to be no more touring, and her back-up musicians were to be let go to move onto other projects. She would need to relocate, put down some roots, build that solo following, (yes, with just a guitar and a stool), like Jack had talked about in his office. And lastly, she would need to scrap her old material and begin writing some new songs.

After pursing her lips, she had challenged him, asking him if he had changed his mind, now believing what some of her detractors had said, that her original material lacked the necessary magic and was derivative in nature.

Perhaps they had something there, Jack had admitted.

So, she told him, in a voice thick with sarcasm, "I guess we also scrap the 'opinions are like assholes' speech."

He said nothing, busied himself by loading his coffee with sugar.

Where, relocate to where, she had then asked.

Austin.

"Austin?" she had questioned, crinkling her nose as if the name bore with it a bad aroma. Austin, she reminded him, the city where she

had been more or less hustled off the stage to make room for headliner
Hal Ketchum.

"Austin," he had repeated with conviction, "the live music
capital of the world."

Why not stay in Nashville, she had asked, try and build a core of
fans here.

Too crowded, came his retort, a bozo on every corner with a
pocketful of songs and an old six string, all angling for the big brass ring.

Once she had a cache of new songs he promised he'd pull some
strings, get her gigs at honky-tonks like the *Broken Spoke*, clubs like
Hole in the Wall and *Donn's Depot*, and maybe if she worked up a little
bit of blues material, an engagement at *Antone's*.

By her third cup of coffee she had agreed to the move and the
new material, but she was a hold-out when it came to the solo act.

"I'm no folksinger, Jack," she had said, "need at least a bass and
drums backing me up. I'd feel naked without them."

"Go to Austin, get situated, start woodshedding, then we'll talk
about a band," he had said, signaling the waitress to bring him the check.

Two weeks later, after taking her few meager belongings out of
storage, those items that had not traveled with her in the last three years
that she had lived out of a suitcase, Chantelle loaded her clothes and
personal goods onto the back seat and into a cartop carrier of a rental
Ford and made the trek to Austin. After two nights in a motel, she found
a furnished studio apartment and signed a sixth month lease. Within the
week, she had both cable and a phone installed. While punching the
buttons on the remote, discovering what TV channels she received in
Texas, she placed a call to her mother on a new black cordless.

The first words out of June's mouth told the story of Robert's
terrible accident.

*   *   *   *

After he had finished with his attack, Sonny helped the injured Robert back into the passenger seat. There, Robert, still wearing his football helmet, lowered his head and began to weep softly.

Sonny intended to drop Robert off approximately where he had found him. On the way back to that spot on the main road, Sonny carefully coached and rehearsed his victim.

"Tell me again, Slick, how'd you get hurt?" Sonny asked.

"Was going too fast, got a flat, crashed, fell off my bike," answered Robert.

"Good boy!" praised Sonny, then quickly twisting his face into a scowl, "but if you tell anybody I beat you up, what happens?"

"You'll kill my family dead."

"Now whoever said you were a retard?" asked Sonny, plastering a smile on his face. "You're a very smart kid."

Robert said nothing, kept his eyes trained on the Tasmanian Devil caricature tooled into the floor mat of the pick-up.

When Sonny was approximately a mile and a half from the Charbonneau home, he pulled off to the side of the road, set the emergency brake, and turned to Robert.

"I got one more thing to do, Slick, to make this whole thing fly. And when I'm done, you start walking your bike back home. Understand?"

"Yeah," responded Robert.

Staying vigilant for cars and trucks that may have passed, although none did, Sonny reached into the pick-up bed and pulled out Robert's bike. He began defacing the bike, hoping to simulate damage done by a crash by first scuffing up the right white handlebar grip with his rasp and tearing out a few of the multicolored streamers. Next, he took the rasp to the silver paint on the front fork and then laid the bike down and scrubbed it back and forth on the pavement, ruining the smooth black finish on the right leatherette saddle bag and shredding the plastic covering on the side of the banana seat. He uprighted the bike, ran the rasp over the chrome bell, producing a muted tinkling, and finished the job by plucking out two spokes on the front wheel.

From the side of the road, Sonny yelled to Robert in the truck.

"Get out."

Robert obeyed and walked back to his sullied Stingray.

"Now get this straight, Slick," said Sonny. "When the bike went down, it fell on its right side. The right side, got it?"

Gingerly bringing his bruised hands up in front of his face, Robert started to form his capital Ls.

Sonny snorted, shook his head, swept the air with his hand.

"Skip the sign language, Slick, just start walking."

After arriving home – his grand entrance a frightening experience; bursting through the front door, bawling at the top of his lungs, jolting June from her chair and Patrice out of her slumber – just as he had been rehearsed, Robert told a very convincing lie of crashing and falling on his bicycle.

The two women quickly ministered to the boy, right there in the vestibule, gently removing his blue windbreaker, flannel shirt, and helping him out of his jeans. (Striving for authenticity, Sonny had slashed the fabric on Robert's pants near the knees with his pocketknife, stuck his rasp in, and created abrasions on his legs.) Bathed in their soft, soothing words and mantra-like assurances that he was okay, Robert began to compose himself, as he stood, stripped to his boxers and a T-shirt, tears subsiding, but still sniffling, while his mother and his sister applied petroleum jelly to his palms and his knees.

Dominic, still restless, had taken himself for a ride after dropping Patrice off at home for a nap. When he returned, he walked through the front door and smack into the middle of the administration of Robert's first aid.

"What happened?"

"Fell off my bike!" howled Robert, instantly whipping himself up at the sound of the question.

"Shhh, you're okay," intervened June, her words now more of an edict than an assurance. Robert quickly quieted and became immersed in watching his mother smooth the Vaseline onto his knee burns. June, who was bent at the waist, looked up at Dominic.

"Would you get me the roll of gauze from the bathroom, and a pair of scissors. I forgot them when I grabbed the jelly."

"Sure," said Dominic.

The phone rang.

"But I'll get that first," he added.

He answered the phone in the kitchen. The conversation lasted several minutes, and although June, Patrice, and Robert couldn't hear what he was saying, Dominic's voice was light, upbeat, and he broke into a chuckle several times during the course of the call.

"We got us a gig," he announced, coming back to where the others were standing. Patrice noticed that his eyes were shining, a brightness she hadn't seen in at least a week or two.

"Where? When?" asked Patrice, smiling.

Dominic looked down at a slip of paper in his hand.

"Uh, Plattsburgh, a supermarket opening, the *Pic-Kwic Market*, never heard of the chain, Saturday, March 11th, 4 to 6pm."

June rubbed the tips of her fingers together, feeling the stickiness of the Vaseline before looking directly into Dominic's eyes.

"That's the day Wendell gets released…but not *until* 6."

"I know that," countered Dominic, an uneasy smile creeping onto his face. "I thought that we could do the job as a trio." He glanced over at Patrice, his eyes pleading. "Treece, don't you think you, Robert and I could do it?"

Patrice was quick to bail her boyfriend out.

"Yeah, I'm sure we could get through it. It's only two hours," said Patrice confidently.

"I'm not sure I like the idea of you playing without your father," said June.

"It's two hundred bucks. I got two hundred bucks for two hours. I know Wen wouldn't want us to pass on that," said Dominic testily.

"Dominic," said June, in a sonorous voice.

"Yeah?"

"The gauze, the scissors…and a towel for our hands?"

Dominic exhaled.

"Sure, June, comin' right up."

*   *   *   *

The morning of Saturday, March 11th started off as gray, gusty and overcast, but by noontime the clouds had migrated off and a warm sun brought the temperature to up around sixty.

June had been cooking all morning, Wendell having requested a meal of mashed potatoes and pot roast, with chocolate cake for dessert.

Robert had spent the morning in his room, feverishly trying to finish a paint by number June had picked up for him at the IGA and that he planned to give to his dad as a gift. Birds, bright red cardinals, with big, broad smiles.

Patrice had slept late, having felt sluggish and tired in the last week, not rising until ten and forgoing breakfast, choosing only to sip at a cup of tea and watch her mother prepare food for their dinner.

Dominic, by contrast, was up at first light, going over a two set song list, practicing scales on an unamplified electric guitar. He was balanced somewhere between anxiety and excitement about their job at the supermarket in Plattsburgh.

It was after she had served her children and Dominic a lunch of grilled cheese sandwiches, as she was putting the mustard and milk back into the refrigerator that June noticed the remaining three bottles of beer had vanished.

Up until now, she had chosen not to address the issue of Dominic and the six pack with Patrice, but at two in the afternoon, about a half hour before Patrice was scheduled to depart for Plattburgh, June paid her a visit in her room.

"He's drinking," said June, having closed the door behind her and keeping her voice to a whisper. "Dominic's drinking."

"I know," said Patrice, as she lay on her back on the bed, thumbing through an old *Popular Mechanics* she'd borrowed from the library.

"He drank an entire six pack I was saving for your father," June blurted.

"At one sitting?" asked Patrice, cocking an eyebrow.

"Well...no," answered June, shrinking a bit.

Patrice laid the magazine down and pushed herself up to a seated position on the edge of the bed.

"He's gonna replace that six pack."

"I'm not worried about that, Patrice," snapped June. "The point is he's drinking and he shouldn't be."

"Mama," Patrice began with a quick lick of her lips, "Dominic told me he's been drinking those beers, one by one, and he also told me you got all worked up about it. Cocaine was his drug of choice, not alcohol. He even checked it out with his NA sponsor, there's nothing to worry about."

"Drug of choice" mocked June, enunciating each word. "So now you're an expert in these things."

"No, never said I was,' said Patrice, shaking her head slowly, "but I know my Dominic."

Patrice stood and embraced her mother.

"Please stop worrying," she said, holding her mother tight.

"We've all been on edge, what with Daddy being gone, but he'll be back tonight, and everything's gonna be okay, I just know it."

June returned her daughter's hug as she felt tears begin to well in her eyes.

"C'mon guys, we're gonna be late," yelled Dominic from the bottom of the stairs.

"Be right there," called Patrice.

"Comin'," Robert hollered.

Patrice was the first to appear, trit-trotting down the staircase, dressed in her black sweater, black skirt, and black boots with red tooling.

When she reached the bottom, Dominic grabbed her around the waist with both hands.

"You look hot, little Missy," he complimented, swinging his head to the left, then right to see if June was anywhere in sight. Convinced she wasn't, he whispered in Patrice's ear, "Why don't we go into my room for a few minutes."

Patrice pushed him away with the flat of her hand on his stomach, breaking his hold.

"Silly," she admonished, turning her head to the side and giving him a sultry, sidelong glance.

Just then Robert appeared at the top of the stairs.

"I'm ready," he announced.

Dominic was the first to look up, and when he did his face quickly crowded into a frown.

"You're not riding your bike to the gig, you're going in the van," said Dominic with a snort.

Robert peered down at him from the top of the stairs, head safely encased in his football helmet.

"Need my helmet, might fall again," said Robert.

Dominic shot Patrice a glance, looking for help.

"Robert, go take your helmet off and get in the van," Patrice said politely.

"No!"

Dominic began making a meal of his lower lip.

"Okay, Okay, you can wear the helmet to the job, but once we get there you promise to take it off, right?" he asked.

"No, might fall again!" insisted Robert.

June came rushing out of the kitchen, wiping her hands on a dish towel.

"What's the problem?"

Patrice folded her arms across her chest.

"Robert wants to wear his helmet," she explained, then pursed her lips.

June looked up the stairs.

"Honey, is your painting done yet?" she asked.

"No."

"Then go back in your room and finish it," June told him. "Patrice and Dominic can go do this job without you, all right?"

"K," said Robert, and quickly disappeared back into his room.

June waited until she heard his bedroom door close.

"He did this the other day when I asked him to go grocery shopping with me," said June. "He wouldn't leave the house without it, so I let him stay home. I just think he needs more time to recover from his spill."

"How much time?" asked Patrice, glowering at her mother.

"You're not his mother," said June icily. "Your father and I will figure something out when he gets home. Now you two better get going."

June's chastisement had brought a quick flush to Patrice's face. Dominic switched from chewing his lip to biting the inside of his cheek.

"Um, we're playing at a supermarket, do you need us to bring anything home for Dad's little party?" asked Patrice.

"Yes," said June, staring straight at Dominic, "a six pack of beer."

*   *   *   *

The building which now housed the *Pic-Kwic Market* had started life as a *Grand Union*, served a short stint as a roller-skating rink, and had been vacant for the past four years before being purchased by a Plattsburgh butcher hoping to capitalize on a discount meat, fish, and poultry trade.

"I've always thought everything goes a little better with music," said the new owner as he shook Dominic's hand. "Some friends saw your band at an office party this past Christmas, said you guys were great."

"Thanks," returned Dominic, smiling. "So you're not a chain?"

"No, independent," said the owner. He pointed at a large buffet table which held bowls of shrimp and platters of barbecue chicken and teriyaki steak. "Make sure you and the band eat. All fresh, everything prepared by me."

Dominic felt compelled to clarify one point.

"We're a duo," he said.

"What?"

"The band is a duo, two of us," said Dominic.

"I thought I hired a full band," said the owner, his demeanor quickly souring.

"When you called I promised you two hours of music, and you'll get two hours of music," said Dominic, a thin filament of self-doubt starting to vibrate in his gut.

"You're sure you can handle it? I want a full sound."

"It'll be full," said Dominic.

The owner relaxed a bit and tried to return to the friendliness that had existed between him and Dominic only moments earlier.

"Okay, well… just as long as you're not a vegetarian," he joked, tapping Dominic in the stomach.

Dominic recoiled, his response exaggerated in response to the light touch of the man's tap.

"No, no vegetarian here," he answered, an anemic smile playing on his lips.

The owner's comments had succeeded in tipping the scales in favor of anxiety over excitement and when Dominic returned to the van to retrieve Patrice and the equipment he was in a nasty mood.

"Fucking asshole," he cursed as he hopped up into the driver's seat.

"Problem?" she asked.

"No," he grumbled, "let's just get our shit in there and get this thing over with."

"Hokay," she said, forcing a smile. "You're the boss."

"What's that supposed to mean?" he snapped.

"Well, you booked this."

"Yeah, but you agreed to it, said we could do it," he said, his delivery somewhat frantic, his voice shrill.

From the passenger seat, Patrice reached over to where Dominic sat and placed her hand on top of one of his. It was ice cold.

"Honey, what's the matter?" she asked. "What's going on with you?"

"Nothing," he answered, staring out through the windshield.

"I know there's– "

"I'm scared, all right? I'm afraid, I don't want to make a fool of myself."

Patrice's eyes narrowed as she shook her head in disbelief.

"Dominic, you've been playing out for years, you're a vet, a pro."

"But I'm not a front man," he said, turning to look at her. "I don't know all that patter your father knows, how to make small talk, be gracious, all that crap. I'm a guitar player who can sing lead on a few songs, back-ups on most others."

She squeezed his hand tightly.

"I'll help you, I'm gonna sing, we've got instrumentals, I've seen you work with a crowd, an angry one at that." She paused. "We can do this."

Dominic's brow was a washboard of wrinkles.

"So who's the fucking asshole?" she asked.

"The owner. He's pissed that there's only two of us."

"So what!" said Patrice, her eyes widening. "It's not like we're ever gonna have a return engagement here."

Dominic sighed heavily.

"You're right. I don't know why I'm so worked up about this." He looked at his watch. "Let's unload the equipment, set up, do a quick sound check, then I'll take a little ride by myself, open all the windows, settle down a bit."

"That's fine, we're here early, got plenty of time before we go on, whatever's gonna make you more comfortable," she said.

He nodded slowly.

"And Dominic?" she added.

"Yeah?"

"I love you."

"I love you, too," he returned, leaned over and kissed her full on the mouth.

When Dominic returned about a half hour later, there was a spring to his step and a smoothness to his face, the worry lines having departed. He found Patrice at the buffet table, dipping a boiled shrimp into a bowl of cocktail sauce.

"Hi," he greeted.

"Oh Dominic, these shrimp are out of this world. Try one," she said, bringing it up to his lips.

He turned his head to the side.

"Maybe later."

She pulled the shrimp back, popped it into her own mouth.

"Please get me away from this table," she begged between chews. "I'm sure I've already gained 50 pounds."

"It's okay, I'll still love you if you're a chubster," he said with a smile.

She finished chewing and swallowed the last of her seafood.

"You look better. You feel better?" she asked.

"Much."

"Good."

She licked a trace of sauce from the corner of her mouth.

"Come closer," she instructed.

"What?"

"Come closer, I wanna smell your breath."

"Your mother's been talking to you, hasn't she?"

"Uh-huh. Now just give me a little puff."

Dominic leaned closer and blew a gentle stream of air into her face.

"I pass?" he asked, his eyebrows raised.

"With flying colors," she answered, and turned back to the table where she deftly plucked a toothpick from a cut glass holder.

"Treece, you know where the bathrooms are?" he asked.

"Yeah, back of the store, to the left of the frozen fish case," she said, her eyes shifting back and forth between the chunks of chicken and strips of steak.

"I gotta pee. When I get back let's kick this off."

"Okay," she said, still trying to decide on her next morsel. "Hey, the owner's not so bad, seems friendly enough."

"Won't be if you eat all his free food," said Dominic, as he headed towards the bathroom.

"Funny Spinosa," said Patrice, plunging her toothpick into a heavily-sauced cube of chicken. "Ver-r-r-y funny."

After setting up the equipment and performing a sound check, Dominic had hopped into his van and sped over to an old dealer's house in Plattsburgh, where he had given the pony-tailed man the crisp fifty he'd held onto since Patrice had gifted him with it at the booth in the Stewart's shop. The dealer, knowing Dominic always made good on his debt, had fronted the additional fifty needed and laid a gram of coke on him.

Now, as he stood locked in a stall of the bathroom at the *Pic-Kwic,* his hands trembling in sweet anticipation, he carefully chopped and cut his cocaine into narrow lines with a single edge razor blade as it sat on the smooth porcelain top of the toilet's water tank. Fashioning a tight tube out of the slip of scratch paper on which he had written the specifics of the gig and directions to the market, he then inserted the make-shift instrument into his nostril, leaned over, and sucked two lines deep into his nasal cavity.

Bringing his head back and up, feeling the delicious drip of the drug down the back of his throat, he breathed words spoken to a long lost lover having now returned.

"I've missed you. God, I've missed you."

*   *   *   *

His mother having driven to the Clinton County Jail to pick up his father, Robert had been left home, and was now anxiously waiting by the window, watching for headlights to turn into the driveway. June, knowing that the transition home for Wendell might be stressful, didn't want to show up at the jail with a boy who insisted on wearing a football helmet.

To circumvent any protestations from Robert about not being allowed to come with her, June had deliberately structured some fun activities and tasks that she sold to him as essential jobs and chores that needed to be completed before his father walked through the door.

She gave him construction paper, tape, scissors, and crayons with which to make a crown for his dad. She handed him a bag of balloons and instructed him to blow up about four or five and then scotch tape them to the corners of the door frames in the kitchen. She left a can of chocolate fudge frosting next to the cake with a directive to smear on a thick layer with a spatula, adding that he could have a couple spoonfuls of the frosting once the cake was completely covered. And last, June had snipped the top off a tube of pink cake decorating gel telling him to write "Welcome Home" on the cake, leaving him the words in block letters on a sheet of paper to use as a spelling guide.

By the time the station wagon pulled into the driveway, Robert had successfully completed all his duties, although huffing up the balloons had left him a little light headed.

"Daddy!" Robert cried out, tears leaking from his eyes. He ran to his father and flung his arms around his neck, nearly bowling Wendell over in the process.

"Hey Buddy," said Wendell, staggering backwards, fighting to stay upright just inside his front door. "How are ya? How are ya?"

"Good. Stay here."

Unleashing his father, Robert then dashed back into the kitchen, and quickly returned holding a yellow paper crown, which he promptly crammed onto his father's head.

June, who stood behind her husband, had to stifle a smile as the headpiece looked exactly like a length of picket fence wrapped around Wendell's dome.

"A crown!" exclaimed Wendell. "Thanks so much."

"There's more, c'mon," said Robert, latching onto his father's wrist and tugging him in the direction of the kitchen.

Wendell turned to June and the two shared a warm smile.

As the three entered the kitchen they were greeted by the entire bagful of balloons, fifty to be exact, taped to the walls, cupboards, stove, and refrigerator…as well as the entryways.

"Blew 'em up all by myself," boasted Robert.

"Good job, Son," lauded Wendell. "Good job."

"And look over here. A cake!" said Robert pointing to the table.

Wendell stepped over to the kitchen table, looked down at the confection, and read aloud, "Welcome Home…Robert?"

"Yeah," said the boy, looking his father straight in the eye. "I wrote it and I signed it."

"Oh, oh, I get it, I get it," said Wendell, turning and smiling at June.

Just then, and the three heard the distinctive whir of the Volkswagen engine.

"Treece and Dominic," said Robert, then quick-stepped over to the window.

Robert watched as the dome light came on in the Westfalia, illuminating the animated face of his sister and a smiling Dominic. Patrice's eyes were buggy and her mouth, nose, and forehead all looked as though they were made of rubber as they stretched and contorted with each word she spoke. Robert wanted to laugh, but he knew he shouldn't, because although he couldn't hear what Patrice was saying to Dominic, he knew she was furious.

Moments later the two were in the kitchen, Patrice snuggled deep into her father's breast, Dominic behind, impatiently shifting his weight from leg to leg, waiting his turn at welcoming the leader of the band back home.

"It's okay little girl, I'm home, I'm home, home to stay," Wendell soothed, rubbing her back.

After what seemed like a very long time, Patrice hugging her dad with all her might, she finally unlocked her arms and pulled back away from him, glancing into his eyes but once with a look that betrayed absolute agony.

Wendell figured, wrongly, that she was still angry about his antics out at Rapant's. He was just beginning to think about making his version of an apology when Dominic thrust out his hand.

Wendell took it and Dominic began pumping wildly.

"Great to see you, man!"

Wendell looked into Dominic's eyes and nowhere could he find the young man he'd allowed into his band, his home, his family so many months before.

"Great to see you, too, Dominic," returned Wendell, pulling his hand free. "So how was the gig?"

"It was friggin' great," burst forth Dominic. "We were crankin', Wen."

"*You* were cranking," spat Patrice. "The owner had to tell you to turn it down three times!"

Dominic shrugged and smirked.

"Guy wanted a full sound, I freakin' gave him a full sound."

Dominic then dug into his front pants pocket, produced a crumpled blue check, and held it up.

"He paid *us* with a check, I was hoping for cash. I wanna buy some things," he said.

"Like what?" snapped Patrice.

"Like…a new guitar," Dominic lied.

"Your old one is fine," she countered.

"See, that's the thing about me," Dominic began, gesticulating with his hands, his speech rapid and clipped. "I try not to get attached to things. You get attached, you lose it or it gets broken, you get hurt. It's a Zen thing, the impermanence of life, the fleeting nature of existence, that sort of thing."

"The *what* of life?" asked Patrice, annoyance ringing loud in her tone.

Dominic didn't answer her, clawed deeply at his neck, producing long red trails, and turned to Wendell.

"Any chance you can boost me my cut in cash tonight? Hunnerd for me, hunnerd for Patrice."

June answered for her husband.

"I've got eighty dollars upstairs, the last of the savings."

"Close enough for rock and roll, as they say, June." said Dominic, wearing a too-wide smile.

"No," said Patrice, reached into her purse, sat back into a kitchen chair, and pulled out a twenty. "Take it. Then we won't owe you anything."

Dominic took the bill from her fingers and dropped the check onto the table.

"I already endorsed it. You guys shouldn't have any trouble cashing it at the bank on Monday."

"I'll get the rest of your money," said June coldly, and headed for the door.

"Great," said Dominic, who then began an incessant clucking noise with his mouth, while his boots tapped out a steady tattoo on the linoleum floor.

Dominic's state of drug-induced hyperkinesis, paradoxically, produced a profoundly quieting effect on the Charbonneaus who remained in the kitchen. Patrice sat in a chair, still wearing a long denim western duster, hugging herself, her chest rising and falling with the slow deep breaths she was pulling, eyes averted, staring at the floor. Robert stood next to his father, his lower lip hanging, glancing back and forth from his father to his sister, looking for a clue to the drama that was unfolding. Wendell held a tight-lipped grin as he concentrated on his cake, trying to revivify the warm feelings he'd felt only moments earlier when he'd crossed over the front door threshold and re-entered his home and his life.

No one in the room looked directly at Dominic. For Robert it was too frightening, for Patrice and her father, much too painful.

Dominic broke the silence by bringing his hands together in a sharp clap and making an announcement.

"Guys," he said, to those in the kitchen who listened but would not look. "I gotta take a little trip tonight. That guitar I want is in Malone. 'Fraid if I wait until tomorrow it might be gone."

Patrice could stand it no longer and brought her eyes up to meet his.

"What kind of guitar are you going to buy for a hundred bucks, Dominic? Huh? Huh? I know you, Spinosa. You're not gonna buy any piece a junk."

"It's a, it's a Les Paul," he said, licking his lips repeatedly. "Course it needs a lot of work, hundred bucks wouldn't– "

"Shut up, just shut up," she wailed, leaping to her feet. "You're such a liar, you're making me sick to my stomach."

She then fled the room, passing her mother in the entryway. As June handed Dominic seven tens and two fives, they could hear Patrice running up the stairs.

Dominic quickly folded the cash and stuffed it into his front pocket where the twenty from Patrice resided.

"Gotta pack a few things, I might not be back tonight," he said and glided from the room.

June stared straight into her husband's eyes.

"He's high," she whispered.

"I know," said Wendell sadly.

Dominic proceeded to pack everything he owned. After madly shoving and stuffing his belongings into two oversized duffel bags, one dirty white, the other an olive drab, he made he way out to the front door, dragging his luggage behind him across the floor.

Wendell was at the front door, waiting for him.

"Need a hand, partner?" he asked.

"Sure, thanks," said Dominic, giving Wendell the strap on the olive bag.

As Wendell opened the front door, Dominic's eye was caught by something on the floor, resting flush against the baseboard.

It was the replacement six pack of beer, which Patrice had purchased at the *Pic-Kwic* out of the fifty dollars earmarked for dinner and a movie, events, which once mentioned, had never been scheduled for her and Dominic.

In the flurry of excitement surrounding the reunion with the family patriarch, compounded with the shit dished out to him by Patrice for most of the ride home, and further complicated by the effect of the last line he'd snorted before leaving the market, Dominic had absentmindedly laid the beer on the floor upon entering the house.

"Brews!" declared Dominic, picking the carton up. "I had a few of yours when you were gone." He then handed the sixer to Wendell.

"Thanks."

"Uh," said Dominic, training a stare on the beers. "Could I just grab one for a road pop?"

"Go ahead," said Wendell.

Dominic quickly lifted one out of the carton, and the two men, beer and bags in hand, walked out to the Westfalia.

After the duffels were loaded in the back, Dominic took his place in the driver's seat, and began taking short slugs from the longneck. Wendell stood next to the driver's side door, still holding his five beer six pack.

Dominic ticked the ignition switch and the van started, first try.

Wendell leaned a little closer towards Dominic's open window, where Spinosa's elbow rested on the ledge.

"You're not comin' back, are you?"

"I tell you, Wen," said Dominic, staring straight ahead. "I got some things to take care of."

"The band needs you..."

"I got things..."

"I need you," said Wendell, laying his hand on Dominic's forearm.

"I gotta go," said Dominic, shoving the stick into first, popping the clutch causing the van to lurch forward in what would be the beginning of a U-turn that would take him down the driveway and back onto the main road.

Wendell waited until the taillights faded from sight before turning back towards his house. When he did, he looked up at his younger daughter's room, where, in the dim light he saw a stone-faced June cradling a sobbing Patrice in her arms.

Twisting the knob, pulling open his front door, there stood Robert, hands on hips, chest puffed, nostrils in full flare.

"Guess he turned out to be a shirker, eh Dad?"

Wendell snorted a laugh, nodded his head slightly, and smiled a sad grin.

"Yes, Robert my boy, I guess he did."

*   *   *   *

Wearing latex gloves, Sonny Rapant sat on a barstool at *The Forge*, rhythmically opening and closing the top of his Zippo with a practiced snap of his wrist. Finally, after completing about eight cycles, he left the top open, drew a thumb sharply across the wheel and brought a yellow-blue flame up through the windscreen.

It was 4:00am, the early morning of Sunday, March 12th. The bar had hosted no more than four customers all evening, the last staggering out about 1am.

A little more than three months had passed since the disastrous re-opening of the nightclub. The waitstaff was gone, the music was gone, the customers had whittled down to a pitiful few, but the commingled aroma of pine and the innards of Wendell Charbonneau's tanker had remained.

About ten feet away from Sonny stood three new red five gallon tins of gasoline, each container purchased from a different store and each filled to the brim with fuel from a different gas station in the Plattsburgh area; separate purchases and separate fillings so as not to arouse any suspicion from a clerk, an owner, or an onlooker.

Next to Sonny, sipping Old Grand Dad from a shot glass, sat Mike Gonyea, mesmerized by the flame as it danced within the confines of the lighter, knowing that it would soon be freed to feed on the gasoline and hardwood floors of the club.

"Are you sure you know what you're doin', man?" asked Gonyea.

"I know exactly what I'm doin', said Sonny, snapping the lighter closed. "Giving myself some start-up capital for a new business from the insurance money we'll get when I kill this place."

Gonyea shook his head slowly.

"Your old man would have your balls in a sling if he found out it was you."

Sonny turned to his friend and trained a look into his eyes.

"He won't," said Sonny. "If I play this right, Dad and everyone else will think that Old Shitman Charbonneau torched this place. Just continuing the vendetta against us."

"You sure the old bastard's out of the slammer?" asked Gonyea.

Sonny ran his finger across the face of the lighter, tracing the inscription that read, *Semper Fi.*

"Positive," said Sonny. "You remember Frankie Schoonbeck?"

"From high school? Skinny, big hook in his nose?"

"Yeah, played right field. He was in here the other night. He's a corrections officer at the jail. I fed him a few free drinks, he tells me Charbonneau's due for release, March 11th around six in the evening."

Gonyea took another sip of his whiskey.

"You think the kid has spilled it by now?" he asked.

Sonny snorted a laugh.

"I think he spilled it the minute he walked through the front door," said Sonny. "He's a retard! No way is he gonna keep it a secret that I beat the piss out of him with a fuckin' wiffle ball bat," he added, deleting the fact that he'd also ripped the skin on Robert's hands and knees with a rasp.

Gonyea tossed back the last of his drink, and slammed the shot glass down hard onto the bar, exclaiming, "Damn straight I'd burn your bar down if you did that to *my* kid!"

He then stood, stretched himself, and made his way back around behind the bar, intent on pouring himself another jigger of liquor.

In the process of refilling his glass, the spout on the whiskey bottle fell off, dumping several ounces onto the bar.

"Shit," cursed Gonyea, dropped to his knees, and began searching under the bar for a rag. When he stood he was smiling and holding two cans of aerosol air freshener.

He carefully stood both of them on the bar and declared, "Was a good try...a real good try, Sonny."

"Wha..?" said Rapant, twisting around in his seat. When he saw the cans, he cleared them with one angry pass of his forearm, the projectiles hitting the floor with loud metallic clanks.

"Goddamn Millie," he swore. "I told her to get rid of those

things. Using that stuff only made the customers believe that the place still stinks."

Gonyea said nothing for a long moment, then sucked a tooth and proffered his opinion quietly.

"Well, honestly Son…it still does."

Rapant again twisted around in his seat, and shot his friend a murderous glare.

"Time for you to head on out, amigo. I'll take it from here," said Sonny.

"You sure?"

"Yessir," said Sonny, and went back to playing with his lighter.

Mike Gonyea left the spilt whiskey, downed his drink, fixed a serious look onto his face, and came around from behind the bar. He stopped and stood directly in front of Sonny, pointing a finger into his friend's face.

"Be careful," warned Gonyea.

Sonny snapped his lighter shut and looked up slowly.

"Fuck you," he said with a smile.

Gonyea reached out, slapped his friend on the shoulder, holding it in a tight squeeze for a moment. With that, he turned on his heel, and strode out of the bar.

After the front door closed behind Gonyea, Sonny exhaled a long, tired sigh and looked slowly around his club. A heavy sadness settled in his chest as he thought about the all hopes and dreams he'd harbored for *The Forge*, a club that should have been the north country's finest rock and roll establishment. He thought of the money, the music, and the access to an almost unlimited source of young poontang, all gone. But a hot streak of rage quickly replaced his sadness as an image of that son of a bitch Charbonneau formed like a developing Polaroid print in his mind.

He pocketed his lighter and stood, walked around the back of the bar, and using the same shot glass Gonyea had, poured and drank three quick shots of tequila, holding the last one up in salute to the impending demise of his bar before tossing it back.

Sonny began a final walk through the roadhouse, turning off lights in the main area of the building, over the dance floor, and in the bathrooms. The club was now almost completely dark, save for the green neon that burned in the Heineken sign behind the bar.

A copy of the Plattsburgh *Press Republican* lay on the bar. Sonny peeled off two sheets of the newspaper and rolled them into a tight tube. He then went to the gas cans and, one by one, unscrewed their tops and tipped them over with a quick tap of his foot. The cans came forth with a muffled metallic thud as they hit the floor, with the contents making a loud glugging noise as it poured forth from the containers.

In the dim light he could see the gas running, the liquid appearing black, the pungent vapors quickly rising and filling his nostrils. He dug deep into his jeans pocket for his lighter, the latex glove offering resistance against the material.

Gloves? he questioned as he extracted the Zippo from his pants. He'd skinned on the gloves with the thought that he'd leave no fingerprints that could trace him to the arson. But if all went as planned, the fire would burn so hot, so intensely, the gasoline cans would probably melt down to lumps of metal with no possibility of any fire inspector pulling a print.

Stupid, he thought. Stupid to have worn them. But as he wanted to waste no time he left them on, and with a latexed thumb scratched up a flame in the lighter.

He touched the flame to the newspaper tube, a slight delay as it caught, then a nice little fire coming from the end. He then tossed the torch onto the gas-soaked planks, the floor coming instantly alive with an undulating fire. He backed away quickly.

Maybe if he hadn't have had the three farewell tequilas, just maybe he could have held onto his balance as he stepped onto one of the aerosol air deodorizer cans he had dashed to the floor only a little while earlier.

Rapant went down hard, a loud snap coming from his left knee, his head bouncing off the floor, disorienting him, nearly knocking him out. Fighting through the daze, he reached down with both hands, clutching, sheathing his knee which felt like something had been torn loose deep inside. Battling black-out, soaked in sweat from fear and the searing pain, Sonny tried to regain his footing but the leg would support no weight and he collapsed back onto the floor.

As he began crawling towards the exit, the thick black smoke which was rapidly collecting in the club filled his lungs, choking him. In between wracking coughs, he dragged himself across the floor, calling out, "Help! Please help! Help me!" And then, as he looked down past his boots, seeing the fire drawing closer, its roar edging its way to a deafening pitch, his calls became screams.

"Help me! Please Daddy, Help me! Dad! Daddy!"

*   *   *   *

At around 4:45am, Wendell and June, just having made love after a three month hiatus, heard the town's fire siren begin to wail. Wendell peeled down the covers, rolled out of bed, went to the window, and peered out.

Earlier in the evening, after Dominic's stimulant-inspired performance and subsequent grand exit from the entire Charbonneau experience, June had stayed upstairs with Patrice, cuddling her, stroking her head, whispering soothing words into the poor girl's ear until she finally cried herself to sleep. June, exhausted, soon fell asleep next to her.

Downstairs, Robert and Wendell had feasted on the pot roast, potatoes, and chocolate cake. Rather, Robert feasted while Wendell only picked, favoring the mashed potatoes over the other choices, explaining to Robert that since having spent time in jail, potatoes had become his favorite starch, replacing spaghetti, the I-tie food.

It was when Robert was cutting himself a second piece of cake that Wendell had noticed the abrasion on the palm of his son's hand and decided to broach the issue of the bike crash, June having told him the story on the way home in the car, sans the piece about Robert insisting on wearing the helmet now whenever he ventured out of the house.

Robert had stiffened at the mention of the crash by his father, and told the story in clipped speech and incomplete sentences. Going too fast, got a flat, fell.

Unknowingly, Wendell succeeded in further cementing Robert's affinity for his helmet by commenting that the headgear had probably saved him from any serious injuries.

After dinner the two Charbonneau men had plunked themselves in front of the TV, argued a bit about whether to watch MTV or TNN, and finally decided on an animal show where the host bravely waded through muddy waters in search of alligators. Later, after Robert was snoring soundly on the floor, wrapped in an afghan, Wendell enjoyed a broadcast of Buck Owens in concert, still his country music favorite of all time.

Around eleven, Wendell had roused Robert and the two had headed upstairs to bed.

Sleep had eluded Wendell, his mind a screen of past events, both recent and remote, along with plans, for the most part sketchy, ill-formed, speculative at best, for the future direction of the band. He'd made a mental note to ask Patrice, after she had composed herself, of course, about the status of the songs she'd been working on before he'd been incarcerated.

June had wandered into her own bedroom around one. Wendell

had asked her if she would make love with him; she had said yes, but only after a few more hours of sleep. Wendell's desire and his insomnia remained constant. He clock-watched and stared at the ceiling until about 4:35, at which time he stroked June's rump lightly, she rolled over, mumbled something about being quiet, and then gave herself to him.

"Can't see anything," said Wendell from the window, the fire alarm continuing to sound into the night.

"Then come back to bed," said June, "it'll be on the news tomorrow."

A passing motorist, a newspaper carrier beginning his delivery run, had seen the Rapant fire lighting up the sky and had called the fire department from his cellular phone.

The dry, old clapboard structure had gone up quickly, and by the time the Chazy volunteer firefighters had arrived the building was fully involved, with no chance of saving any part of it.

The fire chief had thought it suspect that Sonny's pick-up was parked close to the club and soon after the company's hoses had extinguished the flames, several firemen carefully made their way into the ruins to search for any victims.

They found Sonny's body a few feet from the door.

Mike Gonyea had been too wired to sleep, lying in bed, thinking about, worrying about his best friend. He, too, had also heard the fire siren, and at around 7:30am heard his phone ring.

Presuming it was Sonny, he answered it with, "Everything come off okay?"

"Sonny's dead," came Millie Rapant's monotone through the receiver. "The club caught on fire and he was inside."

"Oh Jesus, Oh God," breathed Gonyea into the phone, his voice breaking.

"I think he set the fire," said Millie, her voice still devoid of emotion. "Mike, did he?" she then asked.

With the news of Sonny's death, Gonyea had started to shake. Now the hand that held the phone trembled so badly he could hardly maintain his grip.

"Mike, did he?" she repeated. "Please Mike, tell me the truth."

Gonyea drew a ragged breath and placed his other hand on the phone to steady his hold.

"Yeah," he admitted. "Yeah, he did."

In the days that followed, Sonny's identity was positively confirmed through dental records, his corpse having been charred so severely. Mike Gonyea was asked to report to the State Trooper's barracks where he gave a full account of Sonny's planning for the arson, right down his intentions for blaming Wendell Charbonneau for the crime.

Upon learning of the demise of the club, and Sonny, Wendell felt a certain detached sense of sympathy for Joe Rapant...but for the loss of his business only.

At the funeral, Millie Rapant maintained her stoic demeanor, other mourners commenting on how strong she appeared, how well she seemed to be holding up. Inwardly, however, Millie had yet to connect with any real feeling of loss, having only felt a strange sense of lightness, a relief that this man, around whom she'd walked on eggshells for years, was actually gone.

Ten-year-old Claude, Sonny's only child, struggled with the concept of death, shedding tears primarily when he saw his grandmother and grandfather Rapant cry, or when a mourner would dab an eye with a tissue. He felt sadness, but a sadness triggered largely by living in the atmosphere of sorrow that is a palpable presence in the days following a family member's death.

For the most part Claude spent his time wondering, wondering where his father had gone.

At the cemetery, as he watched the priest saying prayers over the coffin, an ornate mahogany casket, the very best Joe Rapant could buy for his son, Claude tugged at his mother's sleeve. She leaned down to his level.

"Do you think Daddy is in heaven?" he whispered into his mother's ear.

"Yes," she responded with a nod. "Yes, I do," she said, lying benevolently and ever so convincingly to her child.

CHAPTER 12

While Wendell had been incarcerated, calls requesting septic service had come into the Charbonneau household. June and Patrice had fielded the requests, easing the phone out of Robert's hand on the occasions when he had answered, and carefully recorded the information given them by callers onto 3 by 5 index cards.

For a septic tank cleaner in the north country, the winter months are the best time to be locked up, if you have to be locked up. Access to tanks is usually prohibited due to a covering of snow and the ground being held in a hard frost. When a caller reported that his toilet was running slow, or his drains were gurgling, or both, the best Wendell could tell him was to hold on until the spring, and advise him to try to nurse the overloaded tank along by limiting flushes, going easy on the volume of toilet paper the family used, and keeping shower times and wash water that went down the sink and tub drains to a minimum. In his absence, his wife and daughter had passed this information onto to the homeowners, some of whom had sounded quite frantic.

On the day following his release, a Sunday, Wendell began returning the calls and setting up jobs for the next couple of weeks – a task which involved quoting fees, arranging service times, and getting addresses and sometimes directions to new clients or those repeat customers whose exact location had simply slipped his memory.

Wendell was anxious to pay off a few overdue bills and build up the small reserve of savings that had been exhausted while he was away. As such, he lined up as many jobs as he could that first week, much to the delight of some of the more desperate homeowners.

At this point in his career, Wendell could pretty much suck a septic tank on automatic pilot. Once the hose was in the stack, he could allow his mind to wander, or as was the case his first week out of jail, steer it purposefully onto some hard thought about the future direction of his beloved family band.

On Wednesday morning, while the truck's pump chugged along, happily pulling sludge from a tank that hadn't been cleaned for quite some time, Wendell, leaning against the side of his vehicle, caught a glimpse of himself in the tanker's rearview mirror that was mounted on the driver's side door.

I'm fading, he thought, feeling his heart sink, believing that his hair was now more white than grey, his face thinner and possessed of a pasty white color, the classic jailhouse tan.

His mind focused immediately onto images of Buck Owens, and his Hee-Haw sidekick, Roy Clark, and how, over the years, their hair had managed to retain its color, maybe not original, as Wendell seemed to remember variances in hue, but color nonetheless.

Not that he suspected that he had ever been a victim of ageism, the band's stardom being forfeited because someone, perhaps an anonymous industry bigshot in the crowd, had held a prejudice against the appearance of a grey-haired Poppa. But perhaps a brightening of his appearance was in order. Something to fill in the color that had been stripped out. Just a little spiffing up, he thought, his head nodding unconsciously in agreement with his conscious thought. Certainly couldn't hurt.

On Thursday, his truck parked in the backyard of an old Dutch Colonial, waiting patiently for his hose to do its work, he was thinking about songs, originals, his own tired three compositions, but more so the tunes he hoped Patrice had finished while he was serving his time in the Clinton County Jail. Even if she only had three, hell, two, that would be enough to go into a studio and cut a nice little demo tape. He seemed to recall a recording studio in Plattsburgh, *Adirondack Sound*, or something of that sort, that Tommy Wakefield had raved about a year back or so, when he and his chubby wife Tammy put some of their originals on tape.

A smile came to Wendell's lips as he remembered the distinct image of Tammy's fat ass jiggling in time to the music whenever she was required to belt out a particularly fast or strenuous number.

On Friday, having been unable to book any cleaning jobs, Wendell left the house early, made a stop at an Eckerd's Pharmacy, and then made a run up to Canada. There, in a Montreal phone booth, after having spent about ten minutes flipping pages in the booth's resident phone book, he liberated several sheets from the yellow pages and discreetly folded and slid them into his jacket pocket. On the way home he stopped at an office supply store where he made fifty Xeroxes at the self-serve copier of an old photo of the Charbonneau Family Band, purchased several yellow legal size writing tablets, five blister packs of blue ballpoint pens, a one hundred count box of nine by twelve brown envelopes, and the same number of off-white two inch by four self-adhering mailing labels.

Late that afternoon, June and Patrice returned from an appointment to find an auburn-haired, orange-faced Wendell, ear glued to the phone, talking loudly, as he sat at the kitchen table, the top of which was strewn with pads, pens, loose pieces of paper on which he'd scribbled names and addresses, crumpled pages from the Montreal phone directory, along with the Xeroxes of the band picture peeking out of the tops of about a dozen or so of the nine by twelve brown envelopes.

"Ma'am, do you have anyone in your office who speaks English?" bellowed Wendell, speaking in a voice that was not only loud, but obnoxious and treated the other person on the line as if she were hearing impaired, rather than lacking in bilingual skills.

Wendell glanced up quickly, flashed his girls a tight grin, and began jotting something down on one of his pads. He didn't notice that June's face held a dour expression and Patrice's eyes were rimmed in red.

June collapsed into one of the kitchen chairs and pulled a Xerox print completely out its envelope. She scowled and whispered up to Patrice, who stood with her hands shoved deep into her raincoat's pockets.

"This is an old picture, you kids are little," said June, holding the picture up to Patrice for her inspection.

Patrice said nothing, simply nodded and dug her hands even deeper into her pockets.

"Yes, I will call Mr. Calmat...Mr. Calmat, yes I understand, later...or tomorrow!" shouted Wendell. "Merci, Merci," he added, and returned the phone to its cradle while letting go a long exhalation through puckered lips.

He then straightened his back, lifted his head, and broke into a wide, full tooth smile that revealed two rows of dazzling white choppers.

"So," he asked "what do you think?"

"What's the look you're going for, Wen?" asked June flatly.

"Brighter."

"It's definitely that," said June.

"What did you put on your teeth, Daddy?" asked Patrice softly.

"Well, why don't I just tell you about the whole package," suggested Wendell. "For my hair, a little L'Oreal, for my face, some self-tanning lotion, and the stuff for my teeth comes in a little container, looks like white-out without the smell. You paint it on with a small brush."

"So what's the plan?" asked June. "You're gearing up for something."

"Right," said Wendell, so caught up in his new look and venture that he remained oblivious to the dismal expressions that the women had brought with them into the kitchen. "Are you ready for this? It was so obvious, but I never saw it. Are you ready for this?"

"Lay it on us, Wen," said June.

He cleared his throat and wet his lips.

"You'll never be a star... in your own backyard," he proclaimed.

"Nothing new about that, Wen," said June drolly. "We already been out of our backyard. Went to Nashville."

"Yes, but we've never been out of the backyard of our own U. S. of A." countered Wendell.

The two women looked at each other.

"*Canada*, ladies!" burst forth Wendell with his new painted-tooth smile. "Our neighbors to the north."

He then began singing the first line of the Canadian national anthem.

"Hold it, hold it," said June, waving her hand.

He stopped abruptly.

"Don't you need work permits, or visas, or something like that?" she asked.

"We'll get'em, no problem," he answered, his lower lip jutted, a gesture that usually occurred when he was feeling particularly confident. "I've been talking all afternoon to booking agents in Montreal. They claim the Province of Quebec loves American bands, especially country acts."

"Uh-huh," said June, having heard a least a zillion earlier versions of Wendell's patented steps to country music success.

"One agent I spoke with," began Wendell.

"I assume he spoke English?" asked June.

"Of course. Anyway, he says that if we do well in Montreal, then maybe we move onto Toronto, Vancouver and then - *Ta Da* - a tour of the British Isles."

Patrice slumped down into a kitchen chair next to her mother.

"So when do you think this whole...thing would start?" asked June.

"I wanna get into a studio first, put a demo tape together, maybe even a CD we could sell. So I figure it'll be, maybe, mid-summer before we'd start performing up there."

Patrice turned to her mother.

"I'll be pretty big by then," she said.

June nodded in agreement.

"What?" asked Wendell, his jaundiced face crowding into a scowl as a panicky sensation snatched hold of his midsection. Was Patrice getting ready to break from the band? he asked himself. Start her own solo career, become big in the world of country music on her own, without the rest of them?

Never in a million years would he have dreamed that Patrice would ever betray him, follow in the path of her older sister, abandon the family for the sake of her own selfish need to be a star...a star that would shine alone.

"You think your songs are that good?" he asked her angrily.

She looked at him quizzically.

"My songs?" she asked.

"You think you're gonna be big?" he continued, his face now a dark shade of orange. "Just where do you think you're gonna be big?"

Patrice placed both hands on her abdomen.

"Here, Daddy, right here. I'm pregnant."

If madman Sonny Rapant had ever thrown and connected with a punch to Wendell's face the night Robert was getting his pecker pulled in the men's room, that would have been the expression that Wendell wore now.

He averted his eyes from his daughter.

"Dominic?" he asked.

"Who else?" she answered quietly.

"Her little Walk-Away Joe left something behind," said June bitterly.

"Momma, please don't start again," begged Patrice.

Wendell started shuffling through the papers in front of him.

"What uh, what are you going to do?" he asked, still not looking directly at her.

"I'm gonna have this baby," she answered, calmly, clearly, and without the slightest hesitation.

Wendell then gathered several scribbled-on papers, tapped them into a tidy rectangle, unearthed a stapler from underneath a pile of brown envelopes, and punched a staple into the upper left hand corner.

"Okay, okay, not a problem" he assured. "We'll just adjust the timetable."

Although he did not look up, he heard what sounded like a quick rush of air come from Patrice, sort of a snorted laugh.

"Daddy," she said, "I'm gonna have, keep, and raise this baby. That means me staying home. I don't want to be up in some Canadian roadhouse playing music."

"Without a father?" asked Wendell, his voice a low murmur.

"It looks that way," said Patrice, "but if Dominic were to come back—"

"I'd never let him in my house," interrupted June, sending Patrice a piercing look.

"I don't think he's coming back, Momma," said Patrice, maintaining her composure as she had throughout this entire kitchen interchange. "But if he did, he'd have some rights for visitation."

"I hope you'd never let him touch your child if you thought he was on drugs," asked June, her nostrils in full flare.

"Like I said," repeated Patrice, "I don't think Dominic's ever coming back."

In an effort to offset the tornado that was building momentum in his mind, Wendell began arranging pens into neat little rows, stacking pads, and stapling other loose sheets of paper together.

June lifted a Xerox of the band photo.

"What's this for?" she asked.

"Some of the agents wanted to see a picture of the band," answered Wendell.

"But we don't look like this anymore," countered June with a shake of the head.

Wendell took the print from her hand and stared at it.

"This has always been my favorite picture. All of us together," he said softly, his voice little more than a whisper.

"But it doesn't represent who we are anymore," said June.

Wendell looked across the table at his wife. In his eyes she saw a profound sadness that came close to moving her to tears.

Wendell drew a deep breath, composing himself.

"I'll tell ya, 'Treece," Wendell said with a smile, his look still averted, "after a few months of changing diapers, you might feel different. Playing out might come as a welcome break to being a mommy."

If this interchange had been between his oldest and himself, by now Chantelle and Wendell would be at a volume that would be almost intolerable, with June stepping in to referee, hopefully to separate the two.

But Patrice delivered her words with a quiet conviction.

"No, I'm all done playing in the band. I want to stay home and take care of my baby full time."

She rose from her chair, looked down at her father and placed her small hand on his shoulder.

"I'm sorry, Daddy."

                    *   *   *   *

Patrice had known for quite some time that she was pregnant, having administered a home pregnancy test a short while after her period was late. She had chosen not to tell Dominic during the winter as he seemed so preoccupied with being broke, and appeared to be going through some sort of withdrawal syndrome from not being able to perform in public. The irony was that when the occasion had arisen for him to once more stand on a stage and play his guitar, he had blown it.

Fearing that she would start to show, Patrice took to wearing Wendell's oversize sweatshirts, claiming that they were warm, made her feel close to her dad, and besides, she defended when questioned by other family members, she wasn't going to be modeling in a fashion show anytime soon. Underneath the long, roomy sweatshirts, she could go through the day in relative comfort with the top button of her jeans undone and the zipper fully down.

Her intermittent episodes of morning sickness were never suspect as Patrice was always known for having a very sensitive stomach. If Robert, June, or Dominic heard retching sounds coming from the bathroom when occupied by Patrice, they simply figured, as past history had taught them, that some item of food had disagreed with her.

Only once, nearing the end of his stay at the Charbonneaus, as he ran his hands over her naked belly and breasts in their beginning moments of foreplay did Dominic comment on what he perceived as a slight swell to Patrice's abdomen.

"You feel good," he had whispered in her ear, "but you feel a little...fuller."

"Just a little baby fat," Patrice had said, wondering if he might inquire as to what exactly she meant by that.

"Winter," he had commented. "All this inactivity, stuck in the house."

On the day of their ill-fated *Pic-Kwic Market* gig, Patrice had chosen her black sweater and skirt outfit not because of a desire for the predictable response of sparking Dominic's sexual interest in her, but rather the skirt possessed an elastic waistband and she wore the sweater out, rather than tucked in.

Coming home in the van, as the nightmare of Dominic's relapse continued to unfold, she had told him she was with child, even pulling up her sweater to show him how the waistband strained at her midsection.

His eyes had widened, even wider than what the drug had made them. He had then shook his head and remarked, "If it's true, and I'm not sure it is, I really can't deal with that right now."

In the days following Dominic's departure, Patrice had remained emotionally raw, spending most of her time in her room, sleeping and crying, coming downstairs at odd hours to pick at crackers and lunch meats and take sips of tap water from coffee mugs. On Wednesday, feeling very much alone, she had tearfully disclosed her condition to her mother. June had hugged her daughter, whispered something in her ear about a faint intuition of knowing, and assured Patrice that whatever she decided in regards to the pregnancy, she would support her.

It was from an appointment with an OB/GYN that the two Charbonneau women were returning when they had come upon the new and improved Wendell, colored, bronzed, and whitened...and fired with the enthusiasm for yet another can't-miss scheme for the success of his all important family band.

That night, June and Wendell shared an extended state of insomnia, as they lay in bed, holding hands, and staring up at the ceiling.

"You wouldn't look at her today," said June.

"No, it was more that I just couldn't," admitted Wendell.

"You're ashamed of her," chided June.

Wendell exhaled long and slow before he spoke again.

"No, it's not really that." He paused. "Hard to explain."

"I'll help," she offered.

Wendell slipped his hand out of hers, got up on one elbow and looked out the bedroom window into a moonless, starless night.

"I couldn't look at her because *I* was embarrassed. She's my little girl and the thought of her having, having..."

"Sex?" interjected June.

"Yeah," confirmed Wendell.

"Appears to be the only way we women can get pregnant."

"C'mon June," said Wendell gruffly. "Don't turn into a wise-ass on me. I'm tryin' to figure this out, tryin' to get through it."

June then rose up on an elbow and with her free hand turned her husband's face to hers.

"The solution for you, Wendell, is simple, but it's not gonna be easy."

"And what would that be?" he asked.

"That you start thinking of Patrice as a young woman and no longer as a little girl."

Wendell slid back down to a totally prone position.

"I know she's all grown up," he huffed, annoyance ringing in his tone.

June leaned over him.

"You know it here," she said, placing her fingers on his forehead. "You see a lovely young lady with breasts and hips, and a nicely rounded butt like I used to have."

"June, you're startin' to embarrass me," he warned.

June moved her fingers over onto Wendell's chest.

"But you don't accept it *here*...in your heart."

Wendell said nothing, but lay breathing slowly, evenly, June feeling the rise and fall of his chest under her fingertips.

"Simple, but not easy," she repeated.

CHAPTER 13

Chantelle Charbonneau, sitting at her tiny kitchen table in her studio apartment in Austin, eagerly tore open the small padded mailer that had been sent to her by Patrice. She pulled out a cassette tape in a clear plastic case, two sheets of yellow lined paper on which song titles and lyrics were written in red pencil, and a four page letter in blue ink on white parchment stationery which read:

April 30th
Hey there Sissy-Wissy!

How are things down there (bum, bum, bum, bum) "deep in the heart of Texas"? Is it true that "all your 'exs' live in Texas"? Maybe mine does. Keep an eye out for him, will ya? (Just kidding)

The doctor says my pregnancy is coming along just fine. I had an ultrasound the other day and the technician asked me if I wanted to know the sex of my baby, but I said no. It's really cool, Chantelle, I got a Polaroid picture of her, or him, and you can the outline of the head and everything!

Got a real hot scoop for ya. Guess who got a job? (You're not gonna believe this) MOM! Really. She's working at the IGA as a cashier. She looks so cute in that little red smock they have them wear, even bought herself several new pairs of jeans and some new sneakers. She pulls her hair back into a long ponytail for work...which I think looks so much better than when she wears her hair loose (I'd never tell her, but I've always thought that style makes her look a little witchy)

Robert misses her when she's at the store, but every few days she's been bringing home a paint set for him. I think that's helping him get used to the fact that she's not home all day with him anymore.

Speaking of Robert, he still insists on wearing that stupid helmet whenever he leaves the house, even just to go down the driveway to get the mail. I guess we've all kind of accepted the fact that he's gonna do what he's gonna do.

But Daddy is having trouble accepting some things around here. He doesn't like Momma working at all! She told him she got the job because the doctor bills for my pregnancy were starting to pile up.(Although she told me she was also real tired of just hanging around the house all day) Well now I think that wounded his ego a bit because he's been grumbling about how "no wife of mine is gonna be a check-out girl." I think he's pissed that she never talked to him first, she just went out and did it.

I think he's accepted me being pregnant, but now he's threatening to beat the crap out of Dominic for what he "did" to me, if he ever comes back (I don't think he will...come back that is). Chantelle, it's not like Dominic raped me, like they say "it takes two to tango." We should have been more careful about birth control, that's the long and short of it, simple as that.

Daddy hasn't really said too much of anything about me quitting the band. Maybe he's okay with it, or maybe he's just waiting for another idea to come into his head. Who knows.

So, since I'm out of the music business (not that I'm sure I was ever really in it) enclosed you'll find four songs that I wrote. There's also a cassette with me singing lead (don't laugh too hard) and Dominic playing guitar and providing harmony.

I want you to have them. It's also good for me that you have the only copy of a cassette with Dominic's voice on it. I think if I held onto it I'd just be inclined to listen to it and cry. Even though he's a drug addict and he bailed on me, I still really miss him.

Well that's about it for now. In spite of all the stuff that's been going on here, I think we're doing okay. Hope that you are too.

I miss you lots.

Love,
Patrice

Chantelle wiped a tear from her eye, checked her watch, lit a cigarette, and scanned quickly over the words to Patrice's songs, not really having the time to linger over her sister's compositions. She had a schedule to keep and the boys in her band wouldn't like it if she were late for rehearsal.

Mornings she'd rise early, about seven or so, fix herself a light breakfast, shower, dress, and be at her work station; a small coffee table in the living room that held paper, pencils, and a cheap tape recorder, by 7:45 at the latest. Her Martin six string was always within reach and, with the exception of two short coffee breaks, she'd work steadily until about 1:00pm.

Chantelle would then eat a sandwich or a salad and then settle back for a couple of hours of soap operas before heading out to band practice.

Unbeknownst to her manager Jack Conroy, soon after moving to Austin Chantelle had found a bass player and a drummer, having pulled their card from the bulletin board at a local music store. They were looking for a lead singer with originals, she was looking for a rhythm section. After a few practice sessions all three agreed that it was a good mesh and sealed a verbal commitment to play as a band.

Chantelle had made it clear, however, that she was looking for back-up. She would be the undisputed leader, and the trio would be called, "The Chantelle Charbonneau Band." She had met with no resistance from the other two, her bandmates being shy Austin-bred boys who stood a bit in awe of her.

Conroy probably wouldn't have approved. His directive to Chantelle had been to write new material and then they would talk about procuring back-up musicians. He would have chosen her sidemen, hand-picked referrals from his contacts in Austin, but only after he had determined that what Chantelle had written was quality material, good enough to showcase. As far as he knew, Chantelle was living a cloistered existence, sequestered in her air conditioned apartment, scribbling out chorus and verse twenty four/seven.

But Monday through Friday, at 4:00pm, after the oppressive Austin heat had begun to subside, Chantelle would take a bus to the drummer's duplex where they'd work up her originals in his airless garage until 8:00, at which time they'd crack open a few beers, maybe order out for pizza or Chinese, relax, and talk about things other than the music. By nine, she'd take a bus back home, watch a little TV, and be in bed by 11:00pm at the latest.

To date, she had written five new songs. After completion of the first three, wanting to show Jack Conroy that she was indeed producing, she mailed him copies of the lyric sheets and a cassette of the tunes, voice and acoustic guitar, that she had recorded in her living room. About a week later, via two day priority mail, she had received an envelope bearing the Music City Management return address. Inside, were the lyric sheets. Across two of the sheets Conroy had drawn two diagonal slashes and written "scrap." On the third, at the top he had penned "Not bad, but needs polishing."

*   *   *   *

In her letter to Chantelle, Patrice had speculated that, in regards to the future of The Charbonneau Family Band, perhaps her father was waiting for another idea to come into his head. Little did Patrice know that the idea was already there.

Wendell planned on playing a waiting game. He was convinced that after the novelty of her newborn wore off, Patrice would just be itching to get back in front of an audience. And he was sure June would be more than willing to take over the childcare while he, Patrice, and

Robert embarked on their new venture in Canada.

He was betting that by mid-November Patrice would be ready to restart her musical career. He told the booking agents he had contacted in Montreal that, due to a family member's illness, his band would not be ready to perform until close to the holiday season. The agents in turn had assured Wendell that Christmas and New Year's would hold plenty of work, assuming that his family band from Chazy could indeed produce a quality show.

Secretly, Wendell had slipped several old cassettes, live recordings with Chantelle singing many of the leads when she was still with the band, along with the outdated family band pictures into brown envelopes and sent them to four different agents in the Montreal area. By the time they were actually playing Canada, Wendell figured, Patrice would be handling at least some of the lead vocal duties, so he was betting, hoping, no one would suspect that he had substituted one daughter for the other.

While he waited for Patrice's pregnancy to come to full term, he'd keep his mouth shut, rebuild his finances through the septic business, and set about making his tour bus road-ready.

After returning home from the fateful Nashville trip, he'd parked the bus down in back of his barn-home, wrestling with the wheel a bit before he finally got it nestled underneath a stand of maple trees. There it had sat, undisturbed, now for almost four years.

On a sunny Saturday morning, the first week-end in June, he headed out to the bus, Robert trailing, having announced to his family at breakfast that he wanted to fix the vehicle up, using the ruse of resale as a reason for his efforts. June was pleased as punch, having viewed the old crate as an eyesore and a tangible reminder of the loss of her daughter. The sooner Wendell could fix it up, the sooner it would be off the property.

"You go help your father," June had instructed Robert.

"Do I have to?" Robert had whined.

"Yes."

Always vigilant to the possibility of danger outside the house, Robert had strapped on his helmet and dutifully followed his father out to the former prisoner transport.

The underbrush, mainly grass and weeds, had grown thick, bestowing the bus with a bright green skirt. With weed whips and hedge clippers, the two Charbonneau men spent the better part of an hour cutting and clipping. At one point in the trimming, Robert inadvertently banged his plastic-encased head into the side of the bus. Both he and his father then heard a sudden scramble of scratching noises, like the sound of mice running in the walls.

When Wendell was clearing foliage away from the right rear tire, he noticed that corrosion had eaten a whole about the size of his fist into the wheel well. With his fingers he poked at the flaking rust, and made a mental note to pick up a fiberglas repair kit the next time he visited the hardware store, confident he could do his own body work.

Other than that one hole, the homemade RV looked intact. Wendell wrenched open the side door, and, after telling Robert to stay outside, knowing that the hole plus the scratching noises could mean that a small animal, or a family of animals, had taken up residence in the vehicle, he tentatively made his way up the steps and into his old tour bus.

It stunk of mildew and must, and the first thought that came to mind was that he'd probably have to replace the mattresses. Upon inspection of the shower, toilet, and kitchen cabinets, he found plenty of dust and cobwebs, but no living creatures. Deciding that the bus was indeed empty, and wanting to see if she'd start, Wendell slipped behind the wheel, dropped his weight down full into the cushion, and thrust his hand underneath the seat in search of the keys he'd left there upon returning from Nashville.

It was then that a large gray squirrel dug its claws and sank its incisors deep into Wendell's wrist.

"Jesus Christ!" bellowed Wendell, yanking his injured limb out from underneath the seat as his attacker scurried out the open door.

"Dad?" yelled Robert from outside the bus.

"Be right out, Son," cried Wendell, as he watched blood stream from the dig marks and puncture wound.

"What happened?" asked a wide-eyed Robert, as his father stepped from the bus, his wrist running red.

"You didn't see it?"

"See what?" asked Robert.

"That goddamn squirrel that took a chomp outta me."

"A squirrel bit you?"

"Thought my arm was breakfast, little son of a bitch," cursed Wendell.

"You shoulda worn my helmet."

"That wouldn't have helped, Robert."

Robert drew closer to inspect the injury.

"You better go to the doctor," said Robert, his eyes even wider now.

"Not goin' to any doctor."

"You're gonna get sick," said Robert, "you're gonna get rabies."

"I am not," said his father emphatically, although the possibility had crossed his mind as soon as the rodent had broken Wendell's skin. "Now go up to the house and get me some peroxide, gauze, and tape. And if your mother asks what you're doin', tell her I cut myself on…on a sharp piece of metal. Understand? If she knows it was an animal, she'll insist I go to a doctor."

"Metal, sharp piece of metal," repeated Robert, closing his eyes and attempting to commit the lie to short term memory.

"Now get goin'. Christ, I'm bleedin' like a stuck pig."

Robert turned and took off in a dead run. Ten minutes later he was back with several gauze pads, a roll of adhesive tape, and a bottle of rubbing alcohol.

"Did you see your mother?"

"No," said Robert. "I think she was watching TV. I went into the bathroom, took a pee, and got your stuff."

"You wash your hands?"

"Yeah."

Wendell then realized what was in the plastic bottle.

"Rubbing alcohol? Robert, I told you peroxide. This shit's gonna burn."

"Sorry," said Robert, his helmeted head drooping bit.

"Ahh, it'll work," he said, twisting off the cap and quickly dumping a liberal amount on his wounded arm. Immediately, his face contorted into a mask of pain.

"There," declared Wendell, his face still in a full wince. "That killed any germs that little bugger may have given me."

But as the weeks passed, Wendell wasn't totally convinced that the squirrel hadn't given him something, as he fell victim to occasional night sweats, a fleeting fatigue that couldn't be overcome no matter how much coffee he drank or how many hours he slept, and a transitory loss of his usual appetite.

Reluctant to tell his wife that he may have been infected, he blamed the sweats, the tiredness and the come-and-go anorexia on the summer heat. June was concerned, but bought his reasons, just as she had bought his story that he had cut himself on a errant strip of sharp metal on the bus.

But as the hot summer months dragged on, Wendell's anxieties about his physical condition continued. When he was convinced his throat was closing up, he was tempted to pay a visit to the Chazy public library to read up on rabies. But knowing that he wouldn't be able to find the books on his own, he was unwilling to ask the librarians for help, believing that they could be the town gossips if they so desired, not unlike the clerks at video stores who rented out those pornographic tapes.

By the end of August, with the advent of cooler weather, Wendell started to feel somewhat better. Then, on August 30th, when Patrice gave birth to a seven pound, one ounce baby boy, his attention, as well as the rest of his family's, went into the joy of welcoming, and adjusting to, a new member of the Charbonneau clan.

She named him Lowell. Lowell Wendell Charbonneau.

*   *   *   *

The song that Jack Conroy had mailed back to Chantelle with the comment that it "needs polishing" was a tune she had entitled *Day sin at the Days Inn*, a composition inspired by her afternoon tryst with the Nashville roofer. After submitting it to Conroy a second time, with some lyric changes and an increase in tempo, Jack kept the cassette but sent back the lyric sheet with the word "keeper" written at the top.

Her back-up duo also liked the song, although she had come to believe that her Austin rhythm section was usually short on objectivity if she brought in a new number to work up dressed in cut-offs and a tank top that was made to be worn without a bra.

Over the months of June and July, seven more songs came back from Conroy with the approval mark of "keeper" scripted at the top. She needed a total of ten songs, roughly enough to fill about a half hour, before Conroy would set up a showcase.

Although she thought it sweet that her sister had given her four songs, Chantelle wasn't overly impressed with any of them. But feeling somewhat tapped out creatively, and anxious to fill her quota, Chantelle put her own vocal spin on two of the numbers, recorded them on audiotape and paper, and sent them to Jack.

Both came back with marks of approval, no editing, re-writes, or polishing requested. It was mid-July; she now had her required ten originals.

Jack Conroy flew into Austin a few days later with the intention of setting up a number of solo gigs for Chantelle. He wanted her to begin to build at least a small following, a fan base who could be there when Conroy arranged for record company execs to catch her act.

But Chantelle was way ahead of him. By early June, Chantelle and her boys had begun booking themselves in a number of lesser-known clubs in Austin, offering a selection of both covers and originals. The band had been well received, and a small pocket of loyal fans was already starting to follow the group from club to club.

Soon after his arrival, after she'd poured Conroy an large iced tea in her small kitchen, Chantelle called a taxi, and, refusing to tell Jack where she was taking him, had the cabbie drive the two of them to the drummer's duplex.

It wasn't the Austin heat that caused Jack's face to turn bright red when Chantelle strapped on her electric, stepped up to the microphone, and tore into a song, her mystery drummer and bassist, to Conroy anyway, playing happily behind her. But by the third number Jack had begun to cool off, a smile coming to his lips, as what he heard impressed him, the sound that the tight little trio was putting out being of the utmost quality and precision.

But later, over drinks and dinner, Conroy cut Chantelle the proverbial new bunghole.

"You're goddamn lucky, lady, that I haven't dropped you," he said, following his words with a sip of his gin and tonic. "I told you to wait, that when the time was ready, when *I* determined the time was ready, we'd talk about back-up musicians."

Chantelle slowly swirled butter onto a roll.

"But you got to admit, Jack," she defended, "those boys are good players."

"That's not the point, you didn't listen to what I said, you didn't follow my direction," countered Jack, his voice rising in volume, attracting the attention of at least one of the other diners. "If you want me to manage your career, you've got to follow through with what I tell you."

"Now you're starting to sound like my father," snapped Chantelle.

"And maybe that's the problem, here," said Jack, looking her straight in the eye. "I'm not your father, so stop playing the rebellious, know-it-all teenage daughter."

Chantelle blinked twice, processing his words. With a shrug and a raise of an eyebrow she said, "Maybe there's some truth to that, Jack. I'll...I'll watch it."

She then took a small nibble of her roll and followed it with a swallow of white wine. Conversation momentarily suspended, Jack took a long pull from his cocktail.

"So when do I showcase?" she then asked him.

Conroy swallowed, snorted, and shook his head slowly.

"You don't quit, kid, do ya?" he said good-naturedly. "You never give up, never quit pushin.'"

This time it was Chantelle who stared straight into Conroy's eyes.

"No, never, can't afford to," she said. "I told you a long time ago, Jack, I traded my family for this chance."

CHAPTER 14

Wendell Charbonneau leaned over the bright blue stroller that held his first and only grandchild and touched the edge of a huge, oblong fried confection to the infant's lips.

"Little Lowell want some of Grampy's fried dough, a little pizza fritta?" he asked.

"Daddy, get that away from him," ordered Patrice, reaching out and gently guiding her father's arm away from the child's mouth. "He's too little for that, besides that thing is loaded with grease."

Wendell, who was really only offering the boy some of the sugar that was sprinkled on the edge, lifted the dough to his own mouth and took a mammoth bite. In between chews, he explained, "What you don't understand, 'Treece, is that grease is good for some people. For me, it's like putting high test in the tank."

June, who was resting at a picnic table along with Robert, in helmet, and anxious new mom Patrice, then spoke.

"Well, are you about ready to cruise there, Mr. High Test?" she asked, looking at her husband.

"Yep," he answered, and then looked down at his grandson. "Kids love I-tie food, when he's a little older he's gonna beg for this stuff."

Patrice frowned and pursed her lips.

"What I want to know, Wen, is how come you always manage to buy a piece that's bigger than your head?" asked June.

For that, Wendell had no answer, but kept munching as his family rose from the table.

It was a gorgeous Sunday afternoon, the 1st of October, and the Charbonneaus were at the Plattsburgh Fairgrounds, enjoying a few leisurely hours at an arts and crafts show.

The midway was lined on both sides with an eclectic array of vendors who hawked tie-dye shirts and skirts, silver jewelry, leather belts and bracelets, handmade wooden toys, bonsai trees, balloons, macramé plant holders, crocheted toilet roll covers, velvet Elvises, Christs, and Kennedys, and comical black bears chainsawed from chunks of pine, as well as the usual purveyors of food and drink. As the Charbonneaus walked up the strip, Patrice pushing the stroller, Robert staying close to her side, Wendell and June followed, staying about 15 feet behind.

"When is he gonna lose the helmet?" Wen whispered in June's ear.

"When he's ready," responded his wife coolly.

"Yeah, right," said Wendell, unconvinced. He then polished off the last of his fried dough, brushed the sugar from his hands, and called up to his boy.

"Robert?"

"Yeah," replied his son, who looked back at his parents, but never broke step.

"You need that helmet?" asked Wendell.

"Yep, might fall again," he said, and faced forward once again.

"I give up," muttered Wendell, and cast his eyes in the direction of one of the food stands. June turned her attention to the craft show's program.

"Oh, look," she said, pointing at the back of the pamphlet, "The Wakefields are playing at the gazebo. I always liked them." She glanced down at her watch. "They're scheduled to go on in about twenty minutes. Let's go see them."

"Mmm. Tommy and his tub o'lard wife Tammy," mumbled Wendell.

"Stop it," said June. "She's a nice person, can't help that weight problem."

"All right," said Wendell, " but I want to get a cotton candy first.

Should I pick up a half dozen for Tammy?"

June shot him a look of disgust.

"Kids," she called up ahead.

Both of her children turned to face her simultaneously.

"You head on up to the gazebo," she instructed. "Your father and I will meet you there in a few minutes."

Following their mother's directive, the two kept walking. After a while, Patrice turned to her brother.

"You enjoying yourself, Robert?" she asked.

"Yeah."

"You gonna buy anything?"

"Not sure. Not sure what I want."

Just then, a voice called out behind them.

"Patrice?"

She turned. It was Norman Lipschutz, Jr. of Norman's Electronics Sales & Repair, all eyeglasses and blond hair, coming towards her in a slow jog.

"Hi Norman," she said, coming to a halt.

"Hi," he returned, slowing to a walk. "How've you been?"

"Busy," she answered, nodding at her stroller.

Norman dropped to a squat.

"A boy?" he asked.

She nodded.

Norman spent the next few moments talking softly to the infant, gently stroking the baby's cheek with his finger, lightly brushing the boy's wispy hair from his forehead.

Norman's mannerisms, his kindness, his genuine attention paid to her little son did not go unnoticed by Patrice.

"He looks a lot like you, Patrice," remarked Norman.

"Well that seems only fair because his father's long gone," she returned, an edge to her voice.

"Oh…" said Norman.

A long moment passed as Patrice searched his face for a reaction, but he betrayed only an awkwardness, removing his glasses and pulling a clean white handkerchief from the back pocket of his khakis.

"You really should stop by the shop. We've expanded," said Norman, as he began cleaning the thick lenses of his eyewear. "Landlord knocked down a wall so now we've got the old shop plus the space next door."

Patrice suddenly become aware of Robert, and the fact that she had yet to introduce him.

"I'm sorry, Norman," she said, placing her hand on his forearm. "This is my brother Robert."

Norman leaned forward, peered deep into the football helmet, and extended his hand.

"Nice to meet you, Robert."

Robert nodded, shook Norman's hand, but said nothing. Patrice stood by quietly and watched the interchange, her vision focused primarily on Norman.

"Norman, I never knew you had such pretty blue eyes," she remarked, as the two men unclasped hands. "You ought to think about getting contacts."

Norman Lipschutz, Jr. lowered his head as a full blush flooded into his face, the compliment having caught him completely off-guard.

"Oh, gee, th-thanks," stammered Norman, "I, uh…why don't you stop by the shop when you get a chance?"

"Maybe I'll do that," said Patrice.

"And bring your…um, what's the little guy's name?" asked Norman.

"Lowell."

"Lowell…I like that."

Norman looked down at the glasses in his hand, the lenses now sparkling clean, but chose not to return them to his face.

"I came with my mom and dad, so I better get back to them," said Norman. "Come visit me, the store...really," he added.

"Yeah," said Patrice quietly with a nod, while holding him in a soft gaze.

Norman then took off in his slow jog in the direction of the picnic area. Patrice and Robert resumed walking towards the gazebo.

"Seems like a nice guy," remarked Robert.

"He is," confirmed Patrice.

"Probably not a shirker."

"No, Robert, probably not."

By this time, the sound of guitars being strummed, drums taking single hits, and the well-worn boom of "test, test," coming from the PA speakers could be heard. Soon, Patrice and Robert were at the gazebo, watching the Wakefields and band making their last minute preparations before show time.

Patrice, Robert, and little Lowell were in a crowd of about thirty five, but when Tammy Wakefield looked out into the audience she spotted Patrice immediately and gave her a wink and a wave. Patrice smiled back. Tammy then tapped her husband Tommy on the arm, he turned to face her, and she pointed at Patrice. Tommy then came forth with a slow wave in a wide arc that, if he had spoken, could only have been followed with the greeting "howdy."

The Wakefields kicked off their set with the Eagles' *Lyin' Eyes*, a song selected to feature their harmonies, but for Patrice instantly triggered thoughts of long-gone Dominic Spinosa. But today, it was more of memories without feelings; some anger, resentment, but the sense of loss and longing seemed to be dissipating.

"Wish you were up there?" spoke a voice directly into her ear over the din of the band.

She startled and turned.

"Oh, Daddy, you scared me."

"Well, do you?" Wendell pressed, then taking a bite from a fluffy mass of pink cotton candy.

"I don't know, Dad. Maybe. I don't want to talk about it right now. Let's just enjoy the Wakefield's music."

I'll take a maybe, thought Wendell, letting a thin strip of the spun sugar melt on his tongue. Maybe is very good. Maybe is closer to yes than it is to no. And when maybe became yes, Wendell would be ready.

The bus was ready, Wendell having cleaned out the squirrel's nest, replaced the bedding, checked all the appliances, and replaced the engine's spark plugs as well as changing the oil and filter. When June had questioned the amount of time and money he was pouring into the old conveyance, Wendell had convinced her that his efforts would pay off in a higher asking price for resale. Having surrendered the license plates when the bus had come back from Nashville, Wendell had recently obtained insurance, registered the vehicle once again, and mounted new plates on the make-shift RV, explaining to June that no prospective buyer would think of offering dollar one without first taking it out on the open road for a test ride.

Still, June thought it strange that she had yet to see a *For Sale* sign sitting anywhere on the bus or a listing for the used vehicle in the newspaper classifieds.

When she had questioned Wendell about this, his answer had been a simple one.

"Still not quite ready."

But the jobs in Canada were ready and waiting, one of the booking agents having secured them a string of engagements throughout the holiday season in and around the Montreal area. Some of the jobs, if at large hotels, included sleeping rooms for the band. Otherwise, Wendell would probably have to find a cheap hotel for him and his kids to stay, as the bus was not equipped with adequate heaters.

But Wendell had been cleaning a lot of septic tanks, hiding some of his income from June (and the IRS) in case costs in Canada outpaced what he would earn. He didn't care. He didn't care if he lost a bundle on this whole Canadian tour, just as long as he got his family band rolling again. Get them out there, get them seen.

Patrice wanted to make it appear as though she was immersed in the Tommy and Tammy show, so she kept her eyes focused directly on the gazebo, hoping to ward off any future questions from her father regarding her return to the world of country music.

As the Wakefield's first song was coming to a close, Patrice felt a tap on her shoulder. She turned, and as she suspected, it was her dad again.

"No pressure, but have you been practicing any of those new songs you'd written before I went to jail?"

"No, can't say that I have," she shouted over the applause that had begun for the Wakefields.

Not good, thought Wendell. Still time to get into a studio to record a solid little demo tape, originals only, but if she hadn't been practicing, that left only his three mediocre numbers. He had wanted a tape just in case any Canadian record execs might be in attendance at one of their performances. Still time to cut a tape, but the clock was ticking.

The applause was dying, Tommy Wakefield was thanking the crowd, remarking on the beautiful fall colors, and encouraging people to visit and support their local artists and artisans.

"Even if you never go back to performing, it might be a good idea to put your songs on tape, studio tape, professional, in case Lowell ever wanted to hear what his momma sounded like when she was a musician," said Wendell.

"Daddy, please? I'm not interested in doing that right now," implored Patrice, wishing he'd back off.

"I'd like to call your attention," began Tommy Wakefield over the PA, "to the fact that among us today are some local legends in the field of upstate New York country music. Wendell, June, Patrice, and Robert Charbonneau – The Charbonneau Family Band." He nodded at the Charbonneaus. "Would you folks make yourself known to those very few who might not know you."

Wendell raised his hand, turned left, then right as an applause started to go up. June smiled and waved demurely. Patrice, gripping the handles of the stroller, nodded and forced a tight grin. Robert, arms at his sides, stood as still as a cigar store Indian.

As the applause continued, Wendell then turned and whispered into Patrice's ear.

"You can't tell me you don't miss that."

With many eyes on her, Patrice forced a second smile. Moments later, the clapping faded, and Tommy spoke again from the gazebo.

"You should also know that Wendell and June are the proud parents of Miss Chantelle Charbonneau – a real up and comer on the Nashville scene."

Throughout the crowd, many reacted with "ooohs" and "wows", along with a sporadic handclap or two.

"Say, how's she doin', Wen?" asked Tommy.

"Fine," answered Wendell in a reedy voice, as he was holding his breath, Tommy's first mention of Chantelle having caused him to suck a large volume of air.

"Good to hear," said Tommy, his wife Tammy nodding her agreement. "She's one talented little lady. And speaking of talented ladies, if you don't already know her, this is my wife Tammy Wakefield and she'll be singing our next song."

As the crowd came forth with a polite applause, Tommy stepped away from his wife and bowed deeply. She returned a nod, as her girth, and the salmon pink jumpsuit she was wearing would not permit a bow.

Tammy turned and told her drummer to watch the tempo, then turned back to the crowd and launched into a rendition of *The Bottle Let Me Down*.

"You can relax now," said June to Wendell. "Breathe."

The air came out of Wendell like a deflating balloon.

"You looked like you were going to explode," said June.

Wendell looked up at Tammy Wakefield whose stomach expanded and tested the integrity of her jumpsuit each time she drew a belly-breath for a high note.

"No more so than Tammy," observed Wendell.

He began to laugh at his own joke and June shook her head and turned her attention back up to the gazebo. His laugh then triggered a short coughing jag which quickly spattered the remains of his cotton candy with tiny flecks of blood before he could get his hand up to cover his mouth.

He stared in horror at the peppering of bright red droplets against a background of pink.

"Daddy?" asked Patrice in a trembling voice, as a dazed Wendell brought blood from the corner of his mouth onto the side of his hand.

CHAPTER 15

"Mr. Charbonneau, you have lung cancer."

In fear and confusion, the Charbonneaus had left the fairgrounds in a blinding rush, Wendell holding on tightly to the paper cone which held the blood-flecked cotton candy, somehow believing that the doctors might need it for diagnostic purposes.

In the ride to the Champlain Valley Medical Center, Wendell had sat in the passenger seat while June drove. Upon their arrival, Patrice suggested that she take Robert to McDonald's for a cold drink, in that he'd been whimpering ever since they'd all loaded into the station wagon and headed for the hospital. A crying boy in a football helmet wouldn't help matters if Wendell had to wait for an extended period of time in the emergency room.

June had agreed, telling Patrice to return in about an hour. As the Charbonneau kids drove off, and June escorted her husband towards the emergency room door, it was then that Wendell had made his confession.

"I got bit by a squirrel."

"What?"

"Back in June," he said. "I told you I cut myself on some metal, but it was a squirrel. Little bastard's infected my lungs somehow. Or maybe..."

"Maybe what, Wen?" asked June.

"Rabies."

At the admissions desk, the female clerk had asked Wendell for an insurance card, and June responding that they had no medical coverage. The clerk had then slid a form and a pen across the counter stating, "Read this and sign it. It basically says you agree to assume financial responsibility for any and all charges incurred."

After a quick glance at the form, Wendell had signed it and slid it and the ballpoint back to the woman. The clerk had then asked the nature of their visit to the emergency room.

"Animal bite," Wendell had blurted.

"My husband coughed up blood," said June. "He thinks it may be related to an animal bite."

"Have a seat," the clerk had instructed, pointing with her pen to a row of green molded plastic chairs.

Business in the emergency room had been light on that Sunday in October. Wendell, still holding his cotton candy, had looked around to see who else was seeking medical treatment on a day that had started out so routinely.

To his left, he spied a stoic young boy he guessed to be about thirteen, dressed in a football uniform, gingerly holding his left arm. He was flanked by a baseball-capped man and a pinch-faced woman who would storm up to the admissions desk every few minutes to complain about the wait time. On Wendell's right was a teary-eyed blonde woman in her twenties, wearing bicycle shorts, white cotton anklets, a blue warm-up jacket, and a right knee puffed way beyond its normal size. She was accompanied by another young blonde who held a pair of in-line skates and passed tissues to the injured woman on an as-needed basis.

In the hallway was an ancient man who had been brought in by ambulance and placed on a gurney. He was emaciated, his skin jaundiced, and he held a clear plastic bag full of prescription vials on his stomach as he lay with eyes closed. Wendell found himself focusing on the color of the old man's skin and had resolved, right then and there, to stop using his self-tanner.

After about twenty minutes, Wendell had seen his name go up on one of those plastic boards that uses erasable magic markers. He remarked to June that she might want to sneak over and put a slash over the dell in his name so the doctor wouldn't have a problem with accenting the correct syllable. June had simply stared straight ahead and shaken her head 'no'.

While he waited, Wendell had continued to taste blood, so from time to time, he'd wandered up to the water fountain and taken several long drinks. But eventually, the water and the anxiety had caused an urgent bladder and when his name was finally called, about forty five minutes after entering the hospital, he was in the men's room relieving himself.

June had stood and informed the young female Pakistani physician that her husband was in the bathroom. When he had exited moments later, he was still holding the paper cone of cotton candy.

"Are you about done with that?" the dark-haired, bespectacled doctor had asked him, extending an open hand.

"I coughed blood on it. I thought you might need it for tests," Wendell had explained, relinquishing the treat.

"No," said the physician, taking the now crumpled cone and summarily tossing it into a nearby trash can.

A half hour later June had walked out into the parking lot and found their wagon parked in a spot not far from the door.

After buying Robert a Coke, Patrice had had the good sense to also stop at a toy store in Plattsburgh and let him buy a paint-by-number set. When June had approached the car and peeked in, she saw Robert in the back seat, head down, totally immersed in his project, his brush stroking a dark brown into one of the sections marked with the number 5.

Patrice had appeared moments later, having pushed her baby's stroller slowly around the perimeter of the parking lot at least a half dozen times. By the time he and his mom had arrived back at the car, Lowell was fast asleep, his little chin resting on his chest.

"They're keeping him for tests," was all June had told Patrice.

Wendell was first taken for a chest X-ray, where upon reading the film, and seeing a mass, the radiologist had immediately suspected cancer. Next he was subjected to a cat scat guided needle biopsy, the tissue then having come back from the lab with the determination that it was a cancer of the oat cell variety. Lastly, he went for a cat scan of the head and abdomen, where two small masses were seen in the brain, evidence that the cancer had metastasized.

Now, on the 5th of October, at 9:00am sharp, Wendell and June sat in the office of the one of hospital's oncologists, a Dr. Harvey Gershon.

"And the type of cancer you have, Mr. Charbonneau," continued Dr. Gershon, "is a particularly virulent type."

"I never went to college, Doc," said Wendell, "what does that mean?"

"Oat cell, the type that you have is...not good. You also have two small tumors in the brain."

Deep inside Wendell, a voice began screaming.

"How could he get lung cancer?" asked June, her reaction to the news having triggered a profound anger. "He's never smoked."

Doctor Gershon looked into Wendell's eyes.

"What type of work do you do, Mr. Charbonneau?"

"I clean septic tanks."

The doctor screwed up his mouth and scowled.

"Ever been around asbestos – install ceilings in schools, work in the building trades of any sort," asked Gershon.

"Nope," said Wendell.

"Ever work for an extended period of time in an environment where there was a lot of cigarette smoke? Work as a waiter, a bartender?"

"I've been playing music in barrooms ever since I was a teenager," admitted Wendell.

"Well, there's probably your answer right there," said Gershon. "Your exposure to the cigarette smoke while you were playing music."

Wendell exhaled through his mouth and lowered his head. A

moment later he looked up again, turned to June, and gazing into her eyes, gave her a look that transcended time and place.

"I've always wanted exposure…but I guess I'd never figured on that kind," he said, his mouth forming into a tragic little grin.

In a heartbeat, June felt the bitter sting of tears. She quickly dug into her purse, extracted a wad of tissues, and began dabbing at her eyes.

"Now let's talk about what we can do about this situation," said Gershon, deliberately trying to implant the sound of hope into his voice. "I'd like to start you on a course of treatment; radiation to the lung and head, then chemotherapy – once a week for four to six weeks."

"So…we can cure this?" asked Wendell.

"With your particular case," began Gershon carefully, "I'd believe we should think in terms of extending, prolonging your life."

With that, Dr. Gershon glanced at his watch and asked, "Any other questions?"

Wendell and June, who both had at least a thousand, shook their heads.

"All right then, for now, go home and get some rest, Mr. Charbonneau," instructed the doctor.

All three rose from their chairs and began heading for the door, Gershon leading. Not far from the threshold he suddenly stopped and turned, raising an index finger into the air, a quizzical look on his face.

"You looked familiar to me the minute you came into my office. The Levine Bar Mitzvah! I think it was your band that played," said Gershon. He broke into a wide smile. "Very interesting version of Havah Nagilah. Very…original."

"Yeah, original," said Wendell, managing to muster a weak smile.

*   *   *   *

Chantelle Charbonneau, Mercury Records' newest recording artist, a little tipsy from her celebratory champagne, lay sprawled on the sofa bed in her Austin apartment, holding out her flute to Jack Conroy who reluctantly poured her another glass.

"Keep it flowing, Jack, keep it flowing," instructed Chantelle, her face red, her smile wide from the alcohol.

"Slow down, kid," warned Conroy, "I don't want you cutting the rest of your songs with a hang-over."

"Oh relax, Jack," said Chantelle with a dismissive wave of her hand. "I got two days to sober up."

And that she did, as she wasn't due back into the recording studio, to begin cutting her entire first album, until Saturday, October 7th.

In early September Conroy had showcased her at the *Broken Spoke* in Austin. The place had held more than a few loyal Chantelle Charbonneau fans, and at the end of her set the Mercury Record executives Conroy had brought in offered her a two song demo deal. They would front the money for the pair of songs to be recorded, after which they had the right of first refusal. If the execs weren't happy with the sound of her on tape, she would be free to shop the demo around to other record companies.

That night at the table at the *Broken Spoke*, one of the execs circled two songs on Chantelle's set list and strongly suggested that these be her choices for the demo. His selections had been: *Day sin at the Days Inn* and one of the songs Patrice had bequeathed to her sister, *Take a Chance*.

Conroy booked studio time at Bismeaux in Austin, the establishment having a fine reputation, as they had recorded such country music luminaries as Reba, Vince Gill, Clint Black, and Merle Haggard, to name a few.

After her songs were cut, with seasoned studio musicians rather than her fresh-faced back-up boys, and sweetened with extra instrumentation and singers who sang harmony like angels, Chantelle waited an anxious two weeks during which she doubled her cigarette intake and lived mostly on Diet Coke and Ramen noodles.

But there would be no first or any refusal from Mercury Records as the contract came through with an offer of a complete album, somewhere between ten and thirteen songs total. A Mercury Records artist and repertoire person came attached with the contract, and if Chantelle needed any extra material, some would be bought for her.

Although the exact roster of songs that would make it to the record was still up in the air, there was a definite lock on one of the selections. *Day sin at the Days Inn* would be released as the single.

June had wanted to wait until Wendell had been diagnosed before she called Chantelle. When Wendell had been in the hospital for tests, she could have called her daughter in Austin, but decided that, if Wendell's illness was not all that serious, maybe something that would respond to rest and antibiotics, there was no sense in worrying the girl. Now, with the devastating news of cancer, June desperately wanted to phone Chantelle to let her know of her father's condition.

But now, that would be no easy feat, as Wendell would be at home for an indefinite period as he rested and readied himself for the onset of his treatment.

But after Conroy left her apartment, the bottle of champagne now empty, with her signed recording contract firmly in hand, it was Chantelle who placed a call, believing that at two o'clock on a Thursday afternoon her father would be off somewhere pulling the waste from some homeowner's overloaded tank.

June was in the kitchen and Wendell was dozing in his recliner when the phone rang.

"Hello?"

"Momma, I'm signed!" said Chantelle.

"Oh, Honey, that's wonderful," replied June, cupping her hand around the receiver, trying to contain the sound of her voice...and her enthusiasm.

"Yep, Jack negotiated it all out."

Suddenly, from the extension phone that lived on an end table next to the recliner, Wendell's voice came booming through.

"That snake may have closed the deal, but it was me who got you where you are today!"

"Wen, please get off the phone," pleaded June from the kitchen.

"No, he's right, Momma," said Chantelle, her voice sharpening. "If he didn't throw me out of the family, I wouldn't have stuck it out so long, put up with all the bullshit it took to finally get me signed."

"That's right, lady," growled Wendell, "and you can think about the family you betrayed when you're out spending all that blood money."

"Wen, please?" pleaded June, her voice beginning to break.

"You're just a daughter gone bad, happens in the best of families," said Wendell and slammed the phone down.

"Chantelle," said June, "there's something I need to tell...Chantelle? Chantelle?" But all June heard was the loud buzz of the dial tone. She then dropped into a chair, as tears began to brim, realizing that she'd probably lose them both.

Robert, who'd heard the sound of the phone being slammed back into its cradle, came down the stairs and into the living room, where Wendell remained resting in his recliner.

"Who called?" he asked.

"Telemarketer," lied Wendell. "Come here my boy, my only son, my faithful, loyal, non-betraying child... and bring the TV guide with you."

Robert grabbed the guide from a nearby end table and went to his father, handed it to him, then plopped down at his father's feet. Wendell began thumbing through the small booklet.

"Gotta be something good on TNN," mumbled Wendell, as

Robert dug deep into his front pants pocket, producing a retractable tape measure. He then pulled out the tip and extended the metal tape several feet onto the living room carpet.

Wendell, oblivious, sat turning pages.

"Dad?" said Robert.

"Mmmm?"

"How much longer?"

"How much longer what, Son?" asked Wendell, still immersed in the schedule.

"How much longer on *here*?" asked Robert insistently.

Wendell then placed the TV guide on his knee and looked down at his son. Seeing the tape, and catching the meaning of his boy's question took his breath away.

Robert quickly yanked the tape out to the 72 inch mark, the place where his father had originally predicted his life span, and pointed his finger on the short black line.

"Here?" Robert asked. "You gonna live to here?"

Ever so slowly, Wendell leaned down and planted his thumb on the 61 inch mark.

"No...maybe more like here," said Wendell in a whisper.

Robert stared hard at where his father had placed his thumb and then, without warning, flung his arms around his father's ankles, hugging them tightly. Wendell responded by rubbing Robert's back, feeling the silent sobs begin to wrack his thin frame.

"It's okay, old pal. It's okay," soothed Wendell.

*   *   *   *

Unable to concentrate on any of the magazines in the waiting room at the Champlain Valley Medical Center, June simply sat, arms folded across her chest, and stared off into space.

"June?" a female voice summoned.

She looked up. It was Tammy and Tommy Wakefield.

June quickly rose to her feet whereupon Tammy put her in a bear hug. Upon her release, Tommy extended one very long hand and June shook it, after which he stepped back and let his wife run the opening interchange.

"How you holdin' up, Dolly?" asked Tammy.

"Fine."

"And Wen?" asked Tammy.

June nodded at a large wooden door.

"He's still in taking his treatment."

"Yes, your daughter Patrice told us we'd find you here," said Tammy. She turned to her husband and pinched her nostrils once, then released them. "Don't cha just hate the smell of hospitals, Tommy?"

Tommy nodded, then pointed in the direction of June, directing his wife to stay on track.

"We wanted to come to talk to you right away," said Tammy, back on course.

"About what?" asked June.

"It's a small town, June," interjected Tommy Wakefield in a low voice. "Neighbors talk."

"We know Wen don't have any health insurance," blurted Tammy.

"It's okay," replied June, trying to appear calm. "The hospital put us on a payment plan...we'll pay it off over time."

"Maybe so," said Tommy "but we know he hasn't been working."

"But I've got my job at the IGA," said June.

"Maybe so, but once you get behind the eight ball, that financial eight ball," warned Tommy.

"Cut to the chase, Tommy," Tammy snapped.

Tommy drew a deep breath and began.

"June, we want to have a little fund-raiser for you folks…in the form of a tribute to Wendell."

June lowered her head, smiled, and fought a quivering lower lip.

"Aw, you don't have to do that," said June.

"No, we don't have to," said Tammy, "but we want to. Over the years, Wen, you, and the kids have brought a lot of entertainment to the people here in the north country. In a small way, we'd like to try and take care of one of our own."

June swallowed hard as a long moment passed.

"Yeah, okay. I think that would be nice…real nice. It'd mean the world to him," June finally agreed. She reached out and grasped one of Tammy's hands, then one of Tommy's. "Thanks. Thanks so much."

CHAPTER 16

On a crisp Friday afternoon, November 10th, the day before his tribute was to be held at the Chazy VFW hall, Wendell sat bundled in blankets on a chaise lounge in his back yard, looking out on his barren maples, a few remaining fallen leaves blowing helter-skelter on the ground, from time to time his eyes coming to rest on his newly renovated tour-bus, a vehicle which he had recently termed, "the bus to nowhere." He felt the brace of the autumn wind on his face, and upon hearing the rushing of the Vly, imagined that at this time of year it would be "colder than a frog's ass in a forty foot well."

June was inside, in the kitchen, heating some sweet cider in a saucepan on the stove for him. Robert was either up in his room or in front of the TV, although it was hard to know for certain, as the television often stayed on most of the day providing a background of music and voices. And Patrice was out with Lowell, the two of them having gone into town around noon to meet Norman Lipschutz, Jr. for lunch.

Patrice had recently followed up on Norman's suggestion that she visit his newly-enlarged electronics shop. When she had arrived it was apparent he had followed up on her suggestion to be fitted for contact lenses. June had agreed to watch Lowell while Patrice went to see Norman, giving her a three hour window of time. After taking the grand tour of the store, Norman Jr. asked his father if he'd mind the shop while he and Patrice took a short walk. With a twinkle in his eye, that had made Norman Jr. blush, the elder Lipschutz had agreed, telling his son to take as much time as he wanted.

The two had stopped at Stewart's for a take-out coffee before heading towards the town park for a stroll. It was a weekday and they pretty much had the park to themselves. When they tired, or rather when Norman became somewhat winded, Patrice being in better shape than he due to her miles of stroller pushing, they stopped to rest at one of the stone benches. It was there that Patrice poured out her heart about her father's medical situation.

Norman offered no advice, quick fixes, or false promises; he had simply laid his arm over her shoulders and listened. Simply listened.

For today's meeting, Patrice had fixed a picnic lunch – ham sandwiches, potato chips, soft drinks, and cupcakes for dessert, that she and Norman would eat at the back of the store, as baby Lowell was fighting a cold and Patrice feared the little boy might get chilled outside in the brisk air. Norman Sr., once again, agreed to watch the counter while his son spent time with this girl who seemed to be bringing a happiness into his life.

This time Patrice had decided to bring Lowell, being of the mind that if something were to develop with Norman he best realize that she and her baby came as a pair.

When she was preparing to leave, June asked her, "Does this little lunch qualify as a date with Norman?"

Patrice gave her mother a sly smile.

"Yes, I suppose it does."

When Wendell's cider was hot, June poured it into a mug that contained a stick of cinnamon and headed outside. Through the window of the back door, she could see that the wind was starting to pick up so she detoured to the hall closet and pulled a black woolen watchman's cap from the top shelf.

After she handed Wendell his drink, she tugged the knit cap onto his head.

"Thanks," said Wendell, and took a tentative sip of his cider. "Good, mmm, very good."

Although there was a second chair set up next to Wendell, June chose to stand, and moments later ambled down towards the trees and the bus. When there was a lull in the wind, she bent down and picked up a maple leaf.

While most of the leaves were way past peak in regards to autumn color, all curled and brown, this particular one still held a golden hue with a shock of bright red running through the center.

June came back to the chairs, sat down, and handed the leaf to Wendell.

"Pretty," said Wendell.

"I remember," began June, "winning an art contest in grade school because I had collected a spray of the most colorful and the most interesting autumn leaves. Teacher awarded me a big blue ribbon–*First Prize*. I hung the leaves and the ribbon up on the wall in my room. By winter the leaves had all shrunk and withered, actually crumbled right off the wall...but I still have that ribbon."

Wendell carefully handed the maple leaf back to her and lowered his head.

"I've never won nuthin' in my life, only failures," he said, "And the thing I wanted most..."

"It's okay, Wen. It's okay that you were never a big Nashville star," assured June. "God knows you gave it your best shot. Just wasn't meant to be."

Wendell raised his head, and looked out, managing to catch sight of the fast running waters of the Vly.

"I just wanted to keep the family all together," he said, his voice cracking. "To protect you and the kids – forever."

June turned to face him.

"What?" she asked, her brow furrowing in disbelief.

"Being on stage together," Wendell began to elaborate, "all of us, the whole family, like it was when the kids were little. I dreamed we'd be travelin' around the country in a big shiny Silver Eagle. We'd always be together."

"That's why you wanted to hit the big time, be discovered, be famous?" asked June incredulously.

"*Us*...I wanted all of us to be famous, touring together, so we'd never have to be apart," he explained, his eyes now brimming with tears.

June went to him and cradled his head.

"Oh Honey, it just don't work that way," said June. "It's crazy— you raise your kids, pack 'em full of the stuff they need so that, so that...someday they'll be strong enough to leave you."

Wendell blinked away his tears.

"I've failed," he grumbled.

June then turned his face upward so she could look straight into his eyes.

"Wendell Louis Charbonneau," she said sternly," you claim your life as a triumph, you hear me? We raised some good kids, decent kids, all *three* of them. They got good hearts, good souls, but when it's time for them to leave, you gotta let go. You gotta let them sing their own songs in this world."

Wendell's face remained a dark cloud.

"Been nuthin' but a septic cleaner...Old Shitman Charbonneau."

"Nothing to be ashamed of, Wen, nothing at all," said June. "When people needed you, you were there. You were a respectable, reliable businessman. You hold your head up high on that one too, mister."

Something she said must have gotten through to him as he brightened a bit and a smile tugged at the corners of his mouth.

"I suppose I was as important as one of them bowel doctors," he said shyly. "What do you call them?"

"A proctologist?"

"Yeah, a proctologist," he repeated.

"How's that?" asked June.

"When peoples' pipes got clogged, I unclogged 'em."

"There ya' go," said June.

"When they couldn't go, I came."

"You got that right," affirmed June with a smile.

The two then shared a soft chuckle, as the wind began to pick up even more.

"Dr. Charbonneau," joked June, "it's getting a little chilly out here. I think it's time we move you indoors."

"Okay."

June gently let go of his head and took his hand in an attempt to assist him out of his chair. Instead, with one quick tug he pulled her down on top of him, then kissed her on the mouth.

When the kiss had ended, he asked her," Are you gonna be okay after I…"

"Okay? No," she breathed. "Will I keep going? Yeah."

She traced her finger lightly alongside the outline of his jaw.

"Besides," she added, "In some cases kids don't leave home." She drew a slow breath. "I think I'll always have Robert."

                    *   *   *   *

Nailed to the whitewashed signboard in front of the Chazy Veterans of Foreign Wars Hall was a poster which read:

Today - 1 - 3pm
- A Tribute To A Living Legend In North Country Music -
~Mr. Wendell Charbonneau~
Music - Beer - Soda - Buffet
Minimum Family Donation - $25

Inside the hall, the one hundred seventy five plus metal folding chairs had been set up theater-style, all facing towards the risers at the back of the building which would serve as a stage for the Wakefield band. Attendees would funnel through the front door, where volunteers would take donations and coats. Off to the right in the main part of the hall were the buffet tables, kegs of beer on ice, and tubs of canned soda.

Donations of goods and services had been plentiful. As Wendell was a vet, the hall rental fee had been waived. The IGA had provided all the coldcuts, rolls, vegetables and dip, potato and macaroni salads, as well as the beverages and several trays of baked lasagna. The ladies auxiliary from the Chazy Fire Department had baked cookies, cakes, and pies and brought in two huge coffee urns from the firehouse. Veterans had volunteered to take the cash donations at the door, check coats, and pour the draft beer.

There was an aisle down the middle of folding chairs, and off to the left, the front row was reserved for the Charbonneaus.

Around 1:20pm, with a rather pale, thinner Wendell leading, the Charbonneaus entered the hall. The Wakefields, already on stage and halfway through a Travis Tritt tune, abruptly ended their song and broke into a rendition of *For He's the Jolly Good Fellow*, with the crowd soon joining in.

For the occasion, Wendell was wearing a brand new white cowboy hat his hunting buddy from Plattsburgh, Henry Wagner, had delivered upon hearing of his illness, brown cowboy boots, and his old light blue polyester suit, which now bagged in the butt and hung loose off his shoulders. Along with the self-tanner, the hair dye and tooth whitener had all been dispensed with. His wife June wore new jeans, an immaculate white blouse, cowboy boots, and her hair pulled back in a pony-tail with a silver and faux turquoise barrette. Having lost her weight after the pregnancy, Patrice was clad in her favorite black sweater and skirt outfit, with the black boots with red tooling. Close by her side was

Norman Lipschutz, Jr., the only non-Charbonneau member of the group, who wore khakis, Docksiders, and a starched white oxford with a burgundy knit tie. In his arms he held an adorable Lowell Charbonneau, who, for his Grandpa's gala, was swaddled in a tiny pair of blue corduroy overalls.

Trailing slightly behind the rest, wearing a white shirt with a plaid clip-on tie, jeans, sneakers, and his football helmet, was Robert.

Wendell shook hands, smiled, and nodded acknowledgment to his well-wishers. Ordinarily, if he had been feeling well, he would have made a beeline for the beer and food, but this afternoon he had no appetite to speak of, and after his welcoming song had ended, he stood in the middle of the hall, appearing a little lost.

Tommy Wakefield was quick to notice his befuddlement.

"Down here," instructed Tommy over the microphone, pointing at the first row. "Guest of honor and family sit right down here."

Although one cardboard sign on the end chair of the row read "Charbonneau Family Seating", the fourth chair in wore a sign on its seat that warned, "Do Not Sit". As the family filed into the first row, Patrice took the chair to the left of the off-limits seat, and Robert the right.

His children appeared unfazed by the chair, but Wendell caught June's eye, scowled and nodded at the empty seat. June simply shrugged.

"If we can have you all start to migrate over here and find a chair," asked Tommy Wakefield of those grazing at the buffet table or who remained scattered throughout the hall, "we can start this afternoon's festivities."

The people complied, many bringing plates of food with them to their seats.

For the next half hour Wendell was roasted by an array of individuals, most of whom were in some way connected with the local music scene. One club owner told the story of the time Wendell spend most of the night humming his way through songs, as he kept forgetting the words. A bartender remembered a night when Wendell's amp started smoking, his kids frantically pointing at the piece of equipment, but Wen kept singing and playing until the back burst into flames. A local musician on the same playbill with Wendell at a country music jamboree recalled that the living legend had showed up for the gig still wearing his dirty work coveralls and encrusted rubber boots, explaining that he hadn't had time to change. Luckily, the musician told the VFW crowd, the stage was a pretty far distance from the audience and, mercifully, Wendell performed upwind of them.

The last speaker at the impromptu roast stepped up from the front row. It was Patrice and although she held notes in her hands, she was able to recount her story by heart.

It had been a few years ago and the Charbonneaus were booked at a roadhouse in Saranac just shortly before Christmas. Due to heavy snow and a freezing rain, several times en route to the job, they'd almost slid off the road. When they did arrive, naturally the turn-out for their performance was poor, the weather having kept most of the patrons at home. But there were a handful of people, plus the owner, his bartender, a cook, and a waitress.

The Charbonneaus set up and began to play, and for a while all seemed festive – colored lights twinkling on a Christmas tree, a fire roaring in the hearth, the music, the food, and the drink warming hearts and bellies, allowing all inside to temporarily forget about the blizzard that had begun to rage outside.

But around midnight, the club lost electricity, and the building was instantly plunged into darkness except for the fire that crackled and danced in the fireplace. A patron who had tried to leave a few minutes earlier, came back inside and announced that the roads were impassable, he himself having been able to drive no further than several hundred yards from the club.

Wendell had then spoken privately with the owner, came off the stage and assured everyone that they were safe, that they had enough firewood, food, and blankets to make it through the night. He had everyone circle up around the fireplace, as the owner passed out blankets, free drinks, and snacks. Strumming his unamplified electric guitar, Wendell then began to sing every Christmas song he had ever learned, until eventually, like little children, they all drifted peacefully off to sleep.

When the group awoke in the morning, the storm was over, but the fire was still burning, having been fed through the night by Wendell and the owner. Outside, the county plows had come by, clearing a path for their cars and trucks.

"That night," said Patrice, "when I went to sleep hearing the soothing sound of my Daddy's voice in song, I just knew everything would be all right come morning."

So she ended, biting her lip to keep from crying, as an applause echoed throughout the VFW Hall.

"Weren't those stories great?" asked Tommy from the stage, eliciting another round of applause. He waited until it subsided, then looked down at the man of the hour. "Surprised you, didn't we, Wen?"

Wendell smiled and nodded.

"Well, we're not done yet," purred Tammy into her microphone.

"That's right," said Tommy, cleared his throat, and paused. "Now a certain member of the Charbonneau Family Band, an integral part of their sound, has been missing for quite a while now." He paused again for dramatic effect. "And I think it's time we bring that member out." Tommy then trained a look down at Norman Lipschutz, Jr. "Norm, would you do us the honors?"

Norm passed baby Lowell to Patrice, leapt to his feet and, in his inimitable slow jog, soon disappeared into a side room.

Wendell's emotions ran from fear to hope and finally settled on anger. He leaned over and whispered to June.

"What the hell's goin' on?"

"I don't know, Wen, I honestly don't know what they have planned," she answered.

Wendell began to pant as Tommy Wakefield turned around and spoke to his drummer.

"A drumroll, please," he requested.

The drummer dug into a tight roll on his floor tom-tom.

From the side room burst Norman, holding Rhythm Ace the drum machine high over his head, a long extension cord snaking behind, the box blasting out a double time rumba.

"Ladies and gents," said Tommy, "please give a big round of applause to the Charbonneau's former drummer – Mr. Rhythm Ace!"

The Charbonneaus began to laugh out loud, Wendell even slapping his thigh, while the crowd clapped.

The sound coming forth from the machine scared little Lowell, the baby's lower lip starting to quiver. Norman was quick to lower the volume.

"I thought that hunka junk had long since been pitched on top of a scrap heap," said Wendell to Norman.

"No, I just kept surfin' the 'net until I found the right web site that had parts," said Norman.

"Oh," returned Wendell, not really sure what Patrice's new boyfriend had just explained to him.

"Folks, we're gonna take a short break," said Tommy into his mic, "but please stick around, more to come."

As the Wakefields and band were exiting the stage, Wendell turned and quickly whispered to June, "Tammy's probably hungry."

"She's worked her ass off, chubby as it may be, to make this event happen for you," June shot back.

A sense of shame centered itself in the pit of Wendell's stomach. He looked his wife straight in the eye.

"You're right, I've talked badly about her," he admitted. "She deserves better."

Wendell then turned around in his seat and noticed that the hall was near capacity.

"Be right back," he said to June, "gotta take a leak." As he rose to his feet, he became slightly disoriented and had to grab for the back of the chair.

"You all right?" asked June.

"Little dizzy, got up too fast," said Wendell.

As June watched him walk to the men's room, shaking well-wishers hands as they were extended to him, to her eye he appeared to be listing a bit to the left.

Tommy Wakefield stood next to the beer keg, sipping from a blue 12 ounce plastic cup. Tammy soon joined him, her plate loaded high with vegetables and dip.

"How you think it's goin'?" asked Tammy, biting into a red radish smothered with a dressing that resembled white latex paint.

"Very well, very well," answered Tommy, slowly and lowly. Looking out over the crowd, he then brought his cup up to his lips and took a mouthful of beer, which he quickly took down his throat in one gulp.

"Jumpin' Jesus, Tam!" exclaimed Tommy, his eyes popped. "Look who just walked through the door."

"Never," said Tammy, "never in a million years..."

Handing a worn shearling jacket to the man in the coat check room was a concave Joe Rapant. Next to him, slipping her arms out of a long brown woolen coat was his equally broken-looking wife Martha.

Wendell was just coming out of the bathroom when Joe caught sight of him. He turned, said something to Martha, then strode directly up to Wendell.

"Wen," Joe asked, "can I have a word with you...man-to-man?"

"Sure," replied Wendell.

Joe pointed to an empty corner. Soon, the two were out of earshot of the rest of the crowd.

"How you doin'?" asked Rapant.

"Good days and bad days. Fact is I'm still with cancer."

"That's rough," said Rapant. From his shirt pocket he took a small white envelope. "I'm here to tell you how sorry I am for what Sonny did to your boy. That business with the whore and the beatin' with the ball bat. No way to treat a young man with Robert's problems. Course that don't excuse what you did to my club, understand, but Sonny had no right."

Wendell stood, processing Joe's words, his face then growing quizzical.

"Ball bat?" asked Wendell.

"Sonny beat Robert with a plastic bat to get back at you for dumpin' the sewage. Told your boy to tell folks he'd taken a header off his bicycle. I overheard him one afternoon braggin' about it to one of his asshole friends."

Wendell looked over and saw Robert sitting in his chair, feeding himself a piece of cake underneath the face mask of his football helmet. As this new information sunk in, Wendell felt his jaws begin to clench and a lump rise in his throat as he thought of the pain his boy had endured...silently and alone, never sharing the secret with his family.

At the same time, he understood, well, more like he stopped deluding himself, that he could ever really protect his wife and kids from all the bad things in the world.

Joe extended the white envelope to Wendell.

"I want you to have this," said Joe Rapant

"What is it?"

"Half of what I got for selling the land my bar was on," said Rapant. "The other half I gave to Sonny's wife Millie...for her and my grandson Claude."

"What about you and Martha?" asked Wendell.

"We're okay, got my pension," assured Rapant.

"You sure?"

"I want you to have it...please," insisted Rapant.

Wendell then accepted the envelope.

"Thanks, Joe," he said, and shook the man's hand.

"He wasn't all bad, Wen," Joe began to plead. "Just had a mean streak, an angry side. I blame myself sometimes...maybe I was too hard on him when he was a kid. I just wish that when he was alive he had appreciated the important things...how much his mom and I loved him, how much his wife and son loved him. That's what really matters in life, Wen."

Wendell nodded slowly.

"And when I realize he's gone, my own flesh and blood, gone, really gone, gone forever, never gonna see him again, it hurts, hurts deep, right here," said Joe, closing his right fist and placing it over his heart.

Tommy Wakefield's voice suddenly came booming over the PA.

"Can we get the guest of honor to come up here on stage?" asked Tommy. "Grace us with a song?"

A chorus of hoots, claps, whistles and words of encouragement came from the crowd.

Wen then took Joe's hand off his chest, waited until the fist relaxed, and shook Rapant's hand one more time. Then he headed for the stage.

The Wakefields welcomed Wendell onto the stage, Tommy shaking his hand, Tammy rubbing his arm, then stepped off and took seats in the front row, Tammy easing down into Wendell's chair, and Tommy, removing Rhythm Ace from the chair formerly marked "Do Not Sit."

Wendell strapped on Tommy's Telecaster and nodded to the bass

player and drummer, the Wakefields having left them on stage for
Wendell's accompaniment.

"First of all," said Wendell into the microphone, "let me thank
all of you for coming this afternoon. It surely touches this old man's
heart."

He tested an E string on the guitar.

"And secondly, let me say I got a whole lotta gratitude for these
two who organized this shindig," he said, nodding at the Wakefields, the
audience then responding to his statement.

Wendell waited until the applause subsided, then looked directly
into Tammy Wakefield's eyes.

"I think it was Willie Nelson who once sang that angels appear
in the strangest of places."

Tammy turned a little pinker, grinned and winked up at him.

At that moment, the last guest of the afternoon opened the front
door. As she slipped out of her full length black leather coat, revealing a
red satin Nudie knock-off, the coat room attendant whispered to her,
"I'm sorry, Miss, there's no smoking in here."

Chantelle Charbonneau took the cigarette from her mouth, let it
fall to the floor and crushed it out with the silver-tipped toe of her
cowboy boot.

No one, other than the coat check attendant had seen her enter, as
all eyes in the hall were front and center, focused on her father. The bass
player was fiddling with a dial on his amp, and the drummer could never
see past the wall of cymbals he positioned in front of himself.

Wendell, too, had yet to notice her, as he had turned sideways to
the audience and was discussing song possibilities with the drummer.

Chantelle took a stance, arms crossed, face set in stone and
watched the old man up on the stage.

When Wendell finally turned back to face the audience he saw
her immediately, but did not betray his recognition, only blinking once,

wetting his lips, and turning back to the drummer.

"Scratch *Your Cheatin' Heart*," said Wendell. "*Eighteen Yellow Roses*...you know it?"

"Yeah," said the drummer.

The bass player had overheard Wendell's request.

"Me too, no problem, Wen," assured the bassist.

Wendell then turned back to the audience and smiled.

"Sorry for the delay, thanks for not firing me."

The crowd laughed politely.

He strummed a couple of chords, then spoke again.

"It's been a while since I've sung, so be kind, be forgiving."

He then began the opening chords for *Eighteen Yellow Roses*, a song that was a hit for Bobby Darin in the 1960s.

As he wove his way through the gentle ballad, his voice steady, his tempo even and sure, Chantelle stood watching, her jaw set, not moving a muscle.

After a few minutes, the song was drawing to an end, the final words sung,

"'Cause Eighteen Yellow Roses will wilt and die one day. But a father's love will never fade away. Will never fade away."

He looked directly at Chantelle and repeated the last two lines.

"But a father's love will never fade away... Will never fade away."

Wendell then turned to the bass player and whispered, "Just me." The bassist gave a quick nod to the drummer and the two ceased playing.

Now alone, with just his voice and the lightest of strumming on his guitar, Wendell repeated, "But a father's love will never fade away...Will never fade away."

An audience member in the last row heard the sharp scuff of a boot on the wooden floor.

"But a father's love will never fade away...," his voice now was barely a whisper...

"Will never fade away..."

"Daddy!" she cried, and within seconds she was racing towards him down the aisle, all tears and flashing red. Wendell, tears bursting forth, quickly unstrapped his guitar and waited for his elder daughter with open arms.

"I've missed you so much," she whispered in his ear, once safely in his arms.

"Me too, sweetheart, me too."

The crowd, having witnessed this private drama, had reacted with silence, at the most coming forth with a nervous cough or clearing of the throat. Tommy Wakefield then hopped up on stage.

"They're all here folks," he shouted into the microphone. "It's a homecoming!"

The audience responded with thunderous applause.

Chantelle kissed her father on the cheek, gave him one last hug for now, turned, and leapt off the riser to greet her family.

It was all kisses and hugs and tears, a handshake for Norman whom she really didn't know, but then she stopped short when she came to Robert, who sat in his metal folding chair with his hands in his lap.

With one fluid movement, she unsnapped the strap from his helmet and lifted it off his head.

"No hats!" she proclaimed.

Robert stood up beaming, as free as the butterfly that had just escaped its cocoon.

"Charbonneau Family Band," beckoned Tommy from the bandstand, "Could you, would you, please come up here and join your husband, your father for a song or two?"

Again whistles, handclaps, and words of encouragement from the audience.

As his family rose and headed for the stage, Wendell again

began to feel woozy. And then, perhaps from the tumors that were still in his brain, perhaps from all the stress and chemicals he'd endured during his treatment, he was given a gift of a transitory hallucination that allowed him to see his family as young again; his girls in pigtails and bright summer dresses, Robert in a striped T-shirt, rolled at the cuff jeans, his two front teeth missing, and June, his bride, her face smooth again, all age and worry lines having disappeared, her hair returned to a raven black.

And that day, that afternoon, if only for the seven minutes that it took the family band to perform two Buck Owens' tunes, Wendell Charbonneau had his family back, just the way he wanted…together, forever.

EPILOGUE

It had been Robert who had tipped Chantelle off in regards to her father's illness.

In the days and weeks that had followed the incident of her dad calling her a "daughter gone bad", and slamming the phone down, Chantelle had more or less lived in the studio, never really home for any length of time, totally immersed in the process of recording songs for her debut album. When her mother had tried to call her, from the home phone and various phone booths in and around Chazy, it simply rang on through, Chantelle never having invested in an answering machine upon her move to Texas.

Patrice had a crack at contacting her sister with the news, but, she too, never got through. On a rare occasion when Chantelle was in her apartment, coincidentally Patrice tried to place a call from Norman's store, but was seized with the same amnesia for remembering a phone number that had afflicted her on that cold night when Dominic's van had slid off the Adirondack Northway en route to rendezvous with Chantelle in Lake Placid.

The Thursday before Wendell's tribute, Chantelle, assuming that her father was well and out working, called the house around ten in the morning. June was at the hospital with Wen, Patrice was helping out at Norman's electronics store, which left Robert as the only Charbonneau at home.

Robert had blubbered a teary, confusing mix of information, telling his oldest sister that their dad was real sick and probably wouldn't live to be sixty one inches, while in the same breath announcing that he was going to win an award at the VFW on Saturday afternoon.

It was the "real sick" part of Robert's monologue that hooked Chantelle, and sensing an immediacy factor, had chanced a flight home to investigate.

Robert never told anyone that Chantelle had called...of course no one ever asked him.

Within the year, Mercury Records released Chantelle's album with *Day sin at the Days Inn* as a single. Soon after it began receiving airplay, it came under a cloud of controversy as the hotel mentioned in the song threatened to sue, claiming that the tune gave the impression that the chain plied its trade in renting rooms for the expressed purpose of illicit sexual liaisons.

Day sin never made it out of the mid nineties in the top one hundred, but the second single released, *Take a Chance*, the song given to Chantelle by her sister Patrice, spent six weeks in the top ten of the country music charts.

Although Chantelle went back to Austin to continue to build a strong following, within a year she was touring again...still as an opening act. After a short break, splitting her time between Austin and Chazy, when *Take a Chance* hit, she went back on the road, this time as a headliner.

In early January, Robert was hired as a bag boy at the IGA. Most of the time management placed him at his mother's register, having noticed that he seemed disgruntled when paired with another cashier, and having a propensity to place eggs and other breakables at the bottom of the bag when not working in tandem with his mom.

June helped him open a savings account, insisting that he put much of his earnings away, although she did allow him to keep a little money out of his check for candy, gum, snack cakes and pies, and paint-by-number sets.

In late February, Wendell's oncologist advised June to contact the people at community hospice. A bed was set up in the Charbonneau living room, and on an overcast morning in early June, Wendell, with his family near, quietly and peacefully slipped away.

That afternoon Patrice loaded baby Lowell into his car seat and strapped him into the back seat of her father's old station wagon. She then placed a cold six pack, a six pack of Coca Cola, on the transmission hump. Before getting behind the wheel of the car she reached up and, smiling, gently ran her fingers over the sign on the roof which read, "*Ask Me How Western Auto Ruined My Motor.*" She then buckled herself into the driver's seat, dropped it into gear, and headed out for a drive.

As she drove, she thought about the conversations she'd had with her dad in his final weeks, and how, deep in her heart of hearts, she believed he'd come to honor his life, as he'd realized that all the years he'd spent waiting to be discovered, the truth was he'd already been found.

Eighteen Yellow Roses

Words and music by Bobby Darin

Eighteen Yellow Roses came today
Eighteen Yellow Roses in a pretty bouquet
When the boy came to the door,
Didn't know what to say,
But Eighteen Yellow Roses came today

I opened up the card to see what it said
I couldn't believe my eyes when I had read
"Though you belong to another,
I love you anyway"
Yes Eighteen Yellow Roses came today

I never doubted your love for a minute
I always thought that you would be true
But now this box and the flowers in it,
I guess there's nothin' left for me to do
But ask the boy that's done this thing
And find out if he plans to buy you a ring

'Cause Eighteen Yellow Roses will wilt and die one day.
But a father's love will never fade away
Will never fade away

Printed in the United States
5091